# But Speechless Death

# But Speechless Death

By David Eldon

First published in 2024

Illustration by J Yarbrough

Book cover design by BespokeBookCovers

A catalogue record for this book is available from the British Library

ISBN: 9781068676703

www.davideldonauthor.com

Acknowledgements

To Rob Beddington, James Burley, Sarah Burley and Phil and Marina Tavener for their help and encouragement

"What is thy sentence then but speechless death,
Which robs my tongue from breathing native breath?
Then thus I turn me from my country's light.
To dwell in solemn shades of endless night."

*William Shakespeare – Richard II*

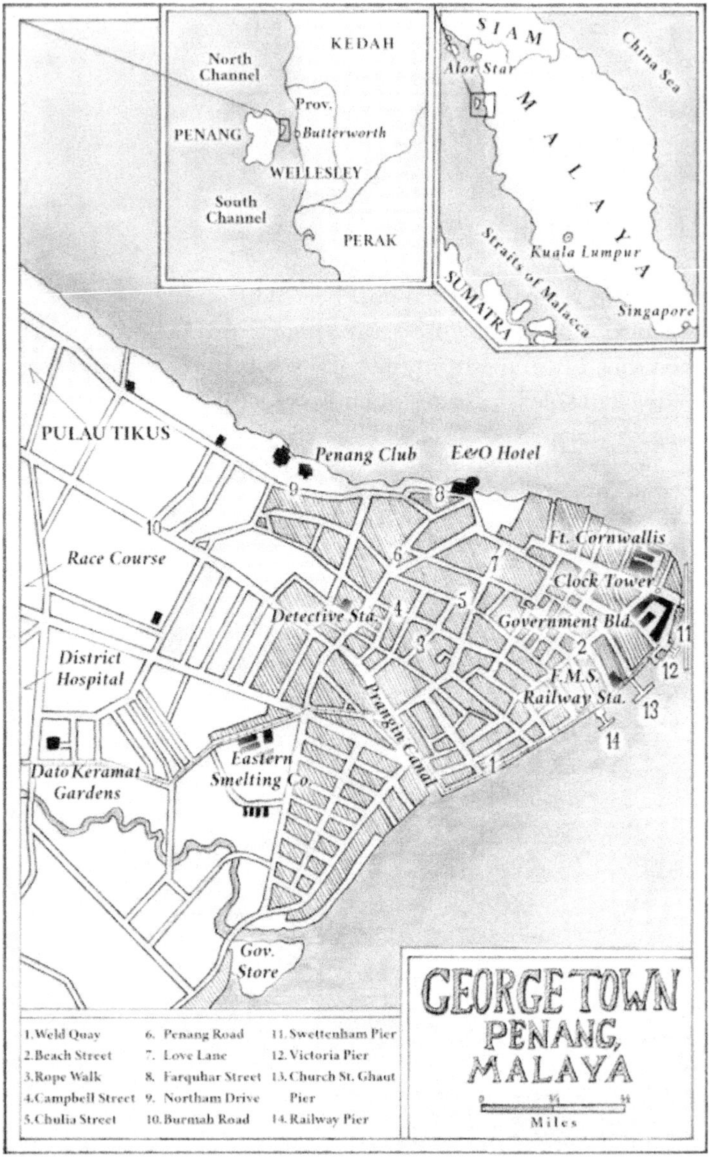
KEDAH
North Channel
Prov.
PENANG
Butterworth
WELLESLEY
South Channel
PERAK
SIAM
China Sea
Alor Star
MALAYA
Straits of Malacca
Kuala Lumpur
SUMATRA
Singapore
PULAU TIKUS
Penang Club
E&O Hotel
Ft. Cornwallis
Race Course
Clock Tower
Detective Sta.
Government Bld.
District Hospital
F.M.S. Railway Sta.
Prangin Canal
Eastern Smelting Co.
Dato Keramat Gardens
Gov. Store
GEORGE TOWN
PENANG, MALAYA
Miles
1. Weld Quay
2. Beach Street
3. Rope Walk
4. Campbell Street
5. Chulia Street
6. Penang Road
7. Love Lane
8. Farquhar Street
9. Northam Drive
10. Burmah Road
11. Swettenham Pier
12. Victoria Pier
13. Church St. Ghaut Pier
14. Railway Pier

# One

*George Town, Penang, 1927*

With two loud blasts of the horn, the constable at the wheel of the police Studebaker cleared a startled path in the crowds that surrounded the car. "Sorry, sir," he said over his shoulder, as they jolted back and forth across the old tramlines. "It is the Chulia Street night market."

In the back seat, Inspector Philip Batchelor of the Straits Settlements Police leant closer to the open window, oblivious to angry glares from those forced to leap clear. At close to midnight, they did not care to see a white man in their midst. The night market was theirs, for the Chinese, Malay and Indian inhabitants of George Town, not for the *angmohs*, who should be long gone – back in their comfortable bungalows and mansions out in the western reaches of the town.

Fifty yards ahead, the pall of smoke from dozens of charcoal burners hung above the roadside stalls, where, despite the late hour, the hungry customers slowing the Studebaker's progress were still flocking to the most popular hawkers. As the car drew closer, the heady aromas of frying meats and bubbling spicy noodle soups stung Inspector Batchelor's eyes and drew a sniff of appreciation from his Malay driver.

"Where to, Inspector?" the constable asked, as he turned the wheel to enter a narrow side street.

"Drive slowly and look out for the sergeant from Carnavon Street Station. He should be waiting for us."

George Town, the capital of Penang, was the only sizeable town on the island. Though an important trading hub, the town itself was small enough that, a mere fifteen months into his posting, Inspector Batchelor had already built a mental picture of most streets within its boundaries: from the quayside with its trading houses and tin-roofed godowns, via the colourful temples and shops of Little India, to Chinatown with its multitude of workshops and at night its brothels and gambling dens. But Love Lane, where darkness lay ahead as the street lights from Chulia Street receded behind them, was new to him.

"I see him, sir," the driver exclaimed, as the headlights picked out a man ahead. "Constable only – no sergeant." The car rolled to a halt, and Batchelor climbed out. He eased his clammy uniform shirt away from the small of his back, for even at night there was no escaping the oppressive humidity, donned his uniform cap, and with swagger stick tucked tight under one damp armpit paused to take in his immediate surroundings.

From the night market, now fifty yards away, he could still hear the echoing clangs of steel spoons on iron cooking pots and the hubbub of the excited customers. But beside the Studebaker, once its engine died out, all was silent except for the scrape of shoe soles on tiles as the constable waiting on the walkway stood to attention.

"Welcome Inspector, sir," he announced, throwing a half-hearted salute that drew a reproving frown from Batchelor. He was standing by an open door into a shophouse, under one of the procession of supporting arches along the walkway.

Despite the gloom, Batchelor recognised Love Lane as a street typical of the old town, though more dilapidated than most. Narrow terraced shophouses on both sides were fronted by their ubiquitous five-foot ways: street-length walkways, a statutory five feet wide, below the projecting upper floors of the houses. They provided shelter from sudden violent rainstorms and shade from fierce tropical sun. Though in Love Lane, unlike most of George Town, they were not fronting stores or workshops, nor blocked every few yards by baskets, or sacks or crates of goods. Here, they fronted residential houses and the only obstacles to progress he could make out were clusters of potted plants and abandoned items of furniture.

"Where is your sergeant?" he asked the constable, who replied with a reluctant motion of his head to indicate the open door beside him.

Batchelor grimaced at the patchwork of cracked tiles at the constable's feet, and the blackening mould, peeling paint and crumbling plasterwork on the arches supporting the floor above. Steeling himself for the squalor he anticipated finding inside, he pointed his swagger stick towards the open door. "Lead the way, Constable."

He stepped onto the stone slab forming a bridge over the deep storm drain that ran parallel with the five-foot way, his nose crinkling at the putrid smell rising from below his feet. Along with the constant heat, this rank cocktail of stagnant water, rotting food and human waste was another aspect of life in Penang to which he was unconvinced he would ever acclimatise.

The constable led the way into a long gloomy corridor, where several doors, from which anxious faces peeped out, then shrank away as they passed, opened to a series of cramped rooms on either side. They are no better than rabbit hutches, Batchelor thought. Windowless and stinking. And, not for the first time, he wondered at the accuracy of the report that had brought him here.

"What's the name of this place?" Batchelor asked the constable.

"It has no name, sir. Lodging house only. You must ask the caretaker. Indian man, sir."

Batchelor cursed under his breath. The caretaker being Indian was a bloody nuisance. The smattering of Malay he had crammed at the college in Kuala Lumpur on the mainland was enough to be understood by the police constables, and he had since picked up some Hokkien Chinese dialect, but the many Indian languages spoken in Penang remained an unsolvable mystery.

"No lights here," warned the constable. They had reached the foot of the staircase, up which they warily climbed.

On the first floor, an identical corridor ran front-to-back, where a door marked its end, outside which a bearded Sikh police sergeant stood guard. His salute on Batchelor's approach was altogether crisper than his subordinate's. "Sergeant Datta, sir," he said, and opened the door to the room beyond.

The smell hit Batchelor first. The unmistakeable sweet fug of opium. In an instant, it whisked his mind back to his first week on duty in Penang – to a raid on an illegal opium den, when, in front of the men, the superintendent had laughed out loud at his perplexed reaction to the then unfamiliar and overpowering scent.

Pausing at the threshold, he shook his head clear of the embarrassing recollection, and surveyed the room. It was lit by a single bare overhead bulb. Along both side walls, bookshelves were stacked high with dozens of English language titles. A desk, and behind it, a small bedframe wrapped in a mosquito net suspended from a hook, were squeezed into the space between them. On the desk was a typewriter, a notebook, a stack of papers held down by a paperweight and an empty whisky bottle tipped on its side, from where its sticky contents had dripped onto more papers strewn across the floor. But these were not Batchelor's first observations. It was the figure slumped on the chair behind the desk that caught his immediate attention – the head lolling unnaturally backwards, out of which sightless eyes scoured the ceiling.

Stepping over the papers on the floor, Batchelor edged around the desk. "It's a white man, all right," he muttered to himself. He had half-hoped the report was correct. Any murder presented a chance to impress his superiors, and that of a white man doubly so. But now, faced with the brutal reality of the corpse, he was reminded of the superintendent's oft-expressed distrust of any case where a white man was killed by a local.

"Hope and pray you never get one," he had said. "They cause a hell of a stink, right up to the Resident Councillor."

Drawing closer to the body, Batchelor gave an involuntary start. Despite his youth and relative inexperience, this was not the first corpse he had encountered, nor the first murder victim.

Perhaps it was the stark overhead bulb that made the sight so monstrous, cruelly exposing the livid ligature marks sunk deep into the man's neck. The victim's mouth was open, his lips grotesquely twisted. It made Batchelor think of an old painting he had seen in a visit to a Manchester art gallery, in which dozens of figures with outstretched arms and tortured faces were crying out from the pits of hell, in voices that would never be heard.

Batchelor wanted to tilt the head forward, to hide the vivid, red welts from view. But that would have to wait for the surgeon's arrival.

He turned to the sergeant. "You were right to send for us. Have you learned the name of the victim?"

"The caretaker called him Tuan Davies," Datta replied.

Batchelor snorted. Tuan indeed. There was nothing lordly about this poor bloody wretch. An opium addict living and now dying in penury among the natives.

"He was a letter writer," Sergeant Datta added.

Batchelor nodded. It explained the typewriter and the papers. He picked up the top sheet on the undisturbed stack. It was a completed typewritten letter addressed to the municipal council and purporting to be from a Chinese man with an address on Magazine Road.

Returning it to the top of the pile, he bent to retrieve the mess of papers from the floor.

"When did you get here?" he asked the sergeant.

"Eleven o'clock, Inspector."

"And when did they find the body?"

"I must ask the caretaker."

"I will question him," he told the sergeant. "But I'll need your help." He felt a pang of relief at having Sergeant Datta at hand. "Hang on, what's this."

While talking, he had been roughly shuffling the retrieved stack of papers into a new pile. About to place them on the desk, he noticed a small card fall from the stack.

He picked it up. A calling card from the Eastern and Oriental Hotel. The distinctive and colourful design hard to mistake for anyone who had spent any time in Penang. It was on almost everything connected with the hotel – the luggage tags, the letterheads, the dinner and dance invitations. Its centrepiece was a scarlet circle surrounding a palm tree on a beach against a vivid orange sunset, with the words "E&O Hotel" in white lettering on a bright scarlet diagonal across the middle, and "Penang" in black against the lower portion of the sky.

Batchelor turned the card over to read the back. 'P Jorgensen – Undermanager'. With a glint of quiet satisfaction in his eye, he turned to the sergeant.

"Change of plan," he said. "Leave your constable to guard the door while you go downstairs to question the caretaker. Ask him when Jorgensen from the E&O was here – let me know the answer straight away."

Though he tried to fight the urge, knowing it was unseemly in front of the sergeant, Batchelor's face had gradually widened into a mirthless grin. Jorgensen from the E&O. That sanctimonious bastard. Here was the long overdue chance to pull him down a peg or two.

Sergeant Datta nodded and left the room. Left alone with the body, Batchelor fought the instinct to stare at the terrible wounds around the neck. Instead, he began to thumb through both piles of papers. They were almost all letters, mostly typewritten. All to various public bodies and written on behalf of dozens of different people with native names: Chinese, Indian, Malay, and others he did not recognise. He was searching for any further mention of the Eastern and Oriental Hotel, or P Jorgensen, Undermanager, but found nothing.

Footsteps in the corridor outside signalled the return of the sergeant, who pulled open the door left ajar on his departure.

"The Tuan had visitors," he announced.

"Was Jorgensen among them?" Batchelor asked impatiently.

"Yes, sir. Mr Jorgensen did visit."

"When?"

"The caretaker was not sure, sir."

Batchelor nodded, deep in thought. Then nodded again as he reached a decision.

"You'll have to question the caretaker and his family alone, Sergeant." He showed Datta the calling card. "I need to follow up on this as a matter of urgency. The surgeon should be here soon to take care of the body and then I'll review the witnesses' statements in the morning."

With a resolute nod, Batchelor left the sergeant in his wake and clattered down the stairs. Poor lighting be damned. This was too good an opportunity to pass up. And to think that tomorrow he could tell Superintendent Cave he had brought his friend Jorgensen in for questioning. The look on the superintendent's face should be something to behold. Sometimes life had a way of dealing a good hand.

# Two

*Earlier that week*

On a typically hot sultry morning, the island of Penang lay alongside the Malayan peninsular coast like a giant beached whale, its spine of jungle-clad hills sloping steeply down through spice plantations to the coconut groves and rice paddies of the narrow coastal plains. Fishing villages, teetering on the edge of mangrove swamps, peeped out over the vivid blue channel towards the remote jungles of the mainland.

And in the channel, shoals of small dark boats, like parasite fish, nibbled around larger vessels. These were tongkangs, small single-masted lighters ferrying cargo from moored steamers to the quayside of George Town – the bustling port on the north-east corner of the island where shipments of tin, opium, rubber and spices sustained the British colony, bringing wealth to the merchants – and immigrant labourers by the thousand – to George Town's teeming streets.

On the quayside, hundreds of loin-clothed stevedores sweated and cursed, and dozens of bullock carts hauled crates and bales to the godowns for storage. Meanwhile, a block inland, the bankers and insurance agents of Beach Street contemplated their ledgers.

Commerce ruled George Town, from the plush shipping offices on the quayside, to the villagers selling scrawny chickens at the wet market. And administering it all, were the tropical-suited colonial officials: locking their desks, replacing caps on their fountain pens and calling for their drivers – because today was

Wednesday, the day of the weekly curry tiffin lunch and orchestral concert at the Eastern and Oriental Hotel.

To an island institution like the E&O, as it was known to anyone of consequence east of the Suez Canal, the maintenance of the highest standards was paramount. Which was why John Broomes, the assistant manager, was in such a state of high agitation.

Though in his late forties, Broomes appeared a good ten years older, like many of his compatriots who had spent their adult lives in the east. He was saggy-jowled, with thinning grey hair and a complexion sallowed by the incessant heat of the tropics. He had come to Penang from Singapore three years earlier, eager for a change of scene after the sudden loss of his wife to a final devastating bout of malaria. Friends of his, and there were many, despite his often testy nature, considered him trapped in a kind of limbo, wearied by the east but troubled greater still by the alternative – a return to an England he no longer knew and where nobody knew him.

His agitation further provoked on receiving news from his secretary that Jorgensen was not on the premises, Broomes slapped both hands down on to the desktop behind which he sat.

"Well, he damn well should be!" he barked. "Why can't he take his tiffin here like a civilised man?"

The secretary, Lim Guan Chee, or Michael, as he preferred to be known, was the well-educated third son of one of Penang's notable Chinese merchants. He was a dapper, well-mannered young man in wire-rimmed spectacles, with near-perfect English.

"Shall I send out for him, Mr Broomes?" he asked.

"Do so and tell him it's damned important he comes at once."

Michael hurried at once to the hotel's grand lobby, marble-tiled and hung with extravagant chandeliers and whirring electric ceiling fans. It hummed with the excited chatter of the parties of European businessmen and their wives arriving for the tiffin lunch and concert, an unmissable fixture in their social diary. Spying one of the Tamil lift boys across the lobby, he beckoned him with a discreet but urgent gesture, then watched while the boy, barefoot below the lift boys' uniform; a long white *kurta* shirt, a cream waistcoat and white half-length pyjama, threaded his way carefully through the throng.

"Dipi," said Michael. "Find Mr Jorgensen and tell him Mr Broomes needs him. Most important and most urgent."

Delighted to be selected for such a task, Dipi gave a wide beam of acknowledgement, before scuttling away through the main doors. There, he slipped past the doormen saluting guests as they arrived; the men removing their solar topees and the women furling their parasols as they escaped the searing midday sun under the shelter of the hotel's canopy.

Dipi skipped between the sleek motor cars pulling up outside the gate on Farquhar Street, the soles of his feet hardened to the scorch of the road surface. Heading inland, away from the seafront hotel, he ran swiftly past the mission church and skirted several green mansion lawns.

He knew just where to go. Reaching the jostling commercial streets, he weaved between bicycles, rickshaws, and carts, ignoring the scolds of their drivers, and past rows of colourful shophouse fronts. At the rear of Chowrasta Market, he stopped to catch his breath and briefly join a small crowd enjoying the spectacle of a motor truck driver haranguing a bullock cart that blocked the narrow side street. Unmoved by the torrent of vicious Hokkien curses, the old cart driver leant against a side wheel and watched his boy lug crates of metal fixings one at a time across the storm drain and through the door of a hardware shop.

Dipi moved on, soon reaching his destination – a corner *kopitiam*, the type of coffee shop found on dozens of street corners in George Town. From the hawkers' stalls, wedged into gaps between the building's supporting pillars, fat spat on charcoal burners and steam hissed from hotplates.

Outside the *kopitiam*, the five-foot way that curved round the corner was clogged by an overspill of chairs and tables from the packed interior. At every seat, sheltered from the glaring sun by the projecting first floor above their heads, diners hunched over bowls of soup and noodles.

Dipi squeezed through the queue at the hawker's stall selling Char Kuay Teow noodles and stood by a pillar just inside the *kopitiam*. Against the far wall, hemmed in by more diminutive neighbours at a table in the corner, he spotted Jorgensen's broad back.

"Mister Mac, Mister Mac," he called out.

Jorgensen felt the insistent tugging on his sleeve at the same moment he heard the piping tones chanting his name.

"Careful, I'll spill the damn soup," he growled. There was little need to turn round to identify the source of the interruption. Even above the cacophony of the hotplates and the noise of the busy street outside, he recognised Dipi's voice. Setting the spoon and chopsticks against the rim of his bowl, he twisted on the bench seat to face the boy.

"So sorry," said Dipi, startled by Jorgensen's frown but resolute nevertheless in obeying his instructions. "Mister John says you must come. Most important and most urgent."

He pronounced the last words with great emphasis, succeeded by a look of relief at accomplishing his task.

"Mr John doesn't appreciate the importance of eating regularly and well," said Jorgensen. "If he did, then maybe his temper would improve."

His brow furrowed in concentration, the boy nodded, as if hearing pearls of wisdom to be forever treasured.

"You come?" he asked.

"What is so important and so urgent?"

Dipi's response was the familiar sideways wobble of the head when presented with an awkward question that he could not answer but did not wish to admit so.

"Tell him I'll be along," said Jorgensen, receiving a wide smile of gratitude in return, before Dipi darted out of the *kopitiam*, ducking his head under the arms of a deliveryman hefting a sack of rice on his shoulder.

Jorgensen chuckled as the boy vanished into the crowds. It had been a mistake to tell him where he was taking lunch. The trouble was, Dipi was so keen to improve his English that Jorgensen had fallen into the habit of short conversations whenever he passed the lift. Today he had revealed he was going to queue for old Khoo's Prawn Mee noodle soup, having not tasted it for several weeks.

Watched with curiosity by the fellow diners wedged alongside him on the narrow benches either side of the table, Jorgensen turned back to his unfinished bowl. Speaking in Hokkien, the most common dialect of the Penang Chinese, he murmured an apology for the interruption, and resumed eating.

Whenever Europeans voiced astonishment at Jorgensen's enjoyment of local eateries, his response was never entirely truthful. He would praise the bold flavours of the food to be found there, the spiciness, the sourness, the sweetness, and the wide variety. He would though, be careful to avoid mentioning how it awakened memories of his distant childhood on the Malayan mainland.

There, deep in the interior, he had lived until the age of seven. His father was a burly red-haired Canadian timber man, hired to establish sawmills in the jungle, and his mother, the mixed-race daughter of the land agent. Those few short years before her sudden death, after which his father retreated with him in grief to the icy winds of New Brunswick, left him with precious memories of cooking and eating in the bungalow's compound, the laughter of his mother's Malay aunts, and fainter with each passing year, the imprint of his mother's face.

Now, thirty years on, he was back in Malaya. It was never planned – he had drifted there, flotsam on post-war currents. A mortar blast in 1917 on the Vimy Ridge ended his fighting part in the war and post-convalescence he returned to Canada to command a training battalion. After the armistice, and with his father too now dead, New Brunswick no longer felt like home, so he crossed the Atlantic again, this time on a passenger liner rather than a troop carrier. In Liverpool he talked his way into a junior officer's role on board a freighter and shipped south to the Mediterranean. Then through the Suez Canal, working tramp steamers ever more eastwards, until one day in Singapore he handed in his papers.

His home was Penang now, though it bore little similarity to the sleepy rural Malay peninsula he half-remembered. George Town, Penang, was a vibrant, loud, often confusing outpost of the British Empire, where dirt and squalor sat cheek-by-jowl with thrusting enterprise and industry. But away from the open drains and the city's streets, and deeper into the green luxuriance of Penang Island there were smells that transported him once more back to the village of his childhood: fragrant hibiscus blooms, the carpets of tiny golden petals shed daily by Angsana trees, and the tempting aromas of curry leaves and spices.

In looks, and in his western clothes, Jorgensen passed for a European, as George Town's inhabitants labelled all white men; irrespective of whether they were North American, like him, or even Australian or South African. He was broad and strong like his father, though not as tall, but had his mother's dark hair and a hint of her more delicate features and caramel skin. In Canada, in the New Brunswick 26th Battalion, his fellow officers assumed he had indigenous ancestors. It was not uncommon – many a McKenzie and McAvity had Micmac tribal lineage.

Here in Penang, the mere fact of his Canadian nationality established him in most eyes as a European. It suited him not to correct that assumed status. To be considered as a European opened many more doors than were available to mixed-race Eurasians. And in his job – it was always handy when doors were willingly opened.

As soon as he took his last slurp of broth from the bottom of the bowl, old Aunty Khoo arrived to collect his dish, while in the instant he rose from the bench, another diner shuffled into the vacant space, his own overflowing bowl of soup in hand.

Jorgensen folded the broad kerchief he had used as a makeshift napkin and re-pocketed it, rolled his shirtsleeves back down to the wrist, donned his panama hat and slung his white linen jacket over his shoulder. With his appearance closer to the respectable image expected at the E&O, he headed north towards the seafront.

***

Outside the main doors of the E&O, Vikat, the Sikh head doorman, resplendent in a brass-buttoned khaki uniform and dark-blue turban, stood to attention at the top of the steps and saluted as Jorgensen approached. Below his tunic – let out at the waist for a considerable stomach – were knee-length breeches, from which bare feet with toes like sausages protruded.

"Mr John is in his office, Major Mac sir," said Vikat, with a grin. Being a step ahead of the undermanager never failed to delight him.

Entering the lobby, Jorgensen paused to take in the scene. Nothing seemed amiss that might explain the urgent summons. The migration of patrons and guests towards aperitifs in the bar and lounge was well under way, though several latecomers still gathered in clusters just inside the entrance doors.

It was fifteen minutes since Dipi had delivered his message, and Jorgensen was keen to dodge any chance of Mrs Justice Sproule or one of her bridge partners waylaying him to debate the credentials of their new driver. Just one of a hatful of reasons why Jorgensen preferred to avoid the curry tiffin lunch altogether. Judging that the coast was clear, he waved briefly to the reception office clerks in their immaculate white suits as he breezed through the lobby towards the managers' offices.

Broomes' office, connected by an anteroom to that of the hotel's manager, Robinson, was along a short corridor leading off the lobby. Waiting at his desk in the anteroom was the secretary, Michael, who greeted Jorgensen with a studiously polite nod and a knowing half-smile.

"What's the hullabaloo?" Jorgensen asked.

"Mr Broomes will explain," Michael replied while tapping his perfectly knotted silk tie as a hint to Jorgensen, who quickly tightened his own knot, before knocking on the door to Broomes' office and, without waiting for a response, entering.

In common with most of the accommodation in the E&O, the office's dark teak-lined walls mirrored its heavy teak furnishings.

Through the open window, wooden floorboards of a narrow verandah overlooked a path running between two buildings and strips of mown grass. It led to the stables and staff sleeping quarters and was closed to guests at its seaward end by a gate in a low wooden fence. Though the office had no direct view of the sea, a distinction afforded only to guest rooms and the office of the hotel's owner, there was the merest suggestion of its breeze through the window, which aided by the ceiling fan clanking overhead brought some relief from the stifling heat.

Broomes, who for the last thirty minutes had been drumming his fingers on the desk's leather inlay and silently cursing Jorgensen's name, glanced up with a mix of irritation and relief.

"You've been a bloody long time," he snapped, the folds of loose skin around his neck quivering in indignation.

"I came as soon as I could," Jorgensen replied evenly.

Broomes' response was a grunt of displeasure. He had spent the period since sending for Jorgensen in impatient anticipation of his arrival, while conscious that this wish was highly uncharacteristic. On a normal day, when things were running smoothly, Broomes entertained little desire to see much of his undermanager. Despite decades of experience in managing hotels, of dealing with a kaleidoscope of porters, housekeepers, clerks and waiters speaking a dozen different languages, he all too often found himself discomfited in Jorgensen's presence.

He remembered when soon after taking up the assistant manager's post at the E&O, Robinson the hotel's manager took him to one side.

"A piece of advice, Broomes," Robinson had said. "It's best not to ask too many questions about Jorgensen."

"Why not?" Broomes had asked in all innocence.

"Arshak took him on last year. Returned from a trip to Singapore with Jorgensen in tow and announced him as the new undermanager."

Arshak Sarkies was the owner of the Eastern and Oriental Hotel. A member of the Armenian family whose hotel businesses extended across the Indies. Having followed his three older siblings east and after a spell at the Strand Hotel in Rangoon, Burma, Arshak eventually arrived in Penang to take over the E&O. Now almost sixty, he was the only brother still alive.

"But what does Jorgensen do?" Broomes had asked.

"Oh, he oversees several routine tasks, though his primary role is more difficult to describe."

"I don't quite follow." Broomes remembered the feeling of bafflement.

"Jorgensen is fiercely loyal to Arshak, and by extension the hotel and its guests. And … how should I best put it? He deals with certain problems that arise from time to time."

"Such as?"

"This is the East, Broomes, I don't have to tell you that. All you need know is that Arshak has absolute trust in the fellow. I'd advise you to leave Jorgensen to his own devices and remember he's there when you need him."

As he studied the undermanager now, Broomes' frown was prompted as much by those recollections as with the problems at hand. And with Robinson laid low with another bout of malaria, it fell to him to handle the situation.

"One of our more prominent guests was robbed last night," he told Jorgensen. "Though why he has only just reported it, I'm damned if I know."

"Who?"

"Arthur Cromford, Hilton Morley's secretary. The robbery wasn't here at the hotel, thank heavens. It apparently took place elsewhere."

"Have you informed the police?"

"Morley insisted I shouldn't. Instead, he asked to see you in his suite."

Jorgensen began to understand why Broomes was so agitated. Hilton Morley, the famous English novelist, was one of the more eminent recent guests at the E&O. He and his secretary had disembarked from the P&O steamer via Bombay just days earlier, along with the mail from London. Excitement levels were always high in Penang on mail day. The E&O ran a popular ball to celebrate its arrival, and throughout Penang newsstands hoisted the Union Jack to announce that the London papers, albeit a month old, were now available.

Reporters from Penang's own newspapers; the Straits Echo, the Star and the Gazette, all desperate for an interview with the famous visitor, had hovered around the hotel ever since Morley's arrival, like flies around rotting fruit. And as the news spread, more of the European community found reasons to visit the E&O for dinner or lunch, hoping for a glimpse of the man of the moment.

"Why does he want me?" Jorgensen asked. As one of the hotel's greeting party at Swettenham Pier, Jorgensen had been introduced to the author on his arrival, but since then had not engaged in any conversation lasting beyond the usual pleasantries. Certainly nothing to explain the request to see him now.

"Why indeed." Broomes said, making no effort to hide the disapproval in his voice.

"Okay, I'll go straight up there. Does Arshak know?"

Broomes grimaced. Another reason for his anxiety. Both Morley and Cromford were recent dinner guests of Sarkies and his wife, and Broomes was dreading the owner's reaction on hearing about the robbery.

# Three

To reach Morley's suite in the Victory Annexe, Jorgensen took the path alongside the seafront lawn. There, a sprinkling of patrons braved the midday heat to enjoy a pre-lunch tipple, cooled just enough by the gentle breeze off the sea and the shade afforded by the giant Angsana trees that straddled the lawn. To his left, glimpses of lowering clouds above the green heights of Penang Hill were visible in the gaps between the white hotel buildings that faced the sea. The recent run of dry days was soon to end.

He passed under the gleaming white minarets marking the corners of the substantial annexe and continued to its far entrance, below two more domed towers above. After speaking briefly to the annexe doorman, he strode up the marble staircase to the upper floor.

A strikingly tall bareheaded Chinese manservant opened the door to Morley's suite. Seeing Jorgensen, he hesitated, then bowed. Jorgensen was sure he had seen him before – but not at the E&O.

"Jorgensen. To see Mr Morley."

He was ushered through the small vestibule and onward to a sitting area furnished with a pair of sofas and two rattan armchairs. The jalousies to the balcony beyond were closed, and they diffused the sunlight into a warm glow that owed its tone to the varnished wood of the slats. Lying prone on one sofa was Arthur Cromford, a slimly built man with a youthful, unlined face topped by a shock of golden curls. He was clad in silk pyjamas wrapped around with a silk dressing-gown and was clutching a compress to his high-domed forehead.

Seeing him laid low now, Jorgensen recalled seeing the secretary in more zestful health on mail day – the day of his and Morley's arrival, when in the bar after the ball, Cromford had climbed up onto a table, jacket abandoned on a nearby chair, collar undone, and face shining with perspiration, to conduct a captivated audience of young men and women in an exuberant rendition of 'Blue Skies'.

"Ah Jorgensen," said Hilton Morley, rising from his chair at Cromford's side. "Good of you to come." A tall spare middle-aged man, with brilliantined thinning hair, Morley cut an unremarkable figure, though his patrician manners and cultivated air of superiority were tailor-made, like his expensive suits, for the role of famous author.

With a theatrical groan, Cromford struggled to a sitting position on the sofa.

"Do take care, Arthur," said Morley, resting a solicitous hand on the younger man's shoulder.

Even in the half-light, lurid bruising above Cromford's left eye was visible. Jorgensen stepped forward. "May I?" He bent to inspect the injury. A ribbon of dried blood caked a small welt above the eyebrow. Painful no doubt, though not serious enough to require stitching.

"Who cleaned him up?"

"Ah Cheng," Morley replied. "And then we felt a doctor wasn't required. I hope we did the right thing."

"It doesn't look too bad. No need for bandages or stitches, though I recommend Dr Burtt has a look. I'll send for him after I leave."

Jorgensen turned to look at the manservant who bowed in acknowledgement of his role. He was barely into his twenties, thought Jorgensen, far too young for the Ah epithet,

Reminded of Ah Cheng's presence, Morley waved the servant from the room. "Do find out where the hell our lunch has got to."

"I understand Mr Cromford was robbed," said Jorgensen once Ah Cheng had left the suite.

From the sofa Cromford gave a derisory laugh.

"You must forgive Arthur's manners, He's in a degree of pain," said Morley.

"I've got a fucking awful headache, Hilton," snapped Cromford, covering his eyes with one hand.

"Will you join us for luncheon when it arrives, Mr Jorgensen?" said Morley, studiously ignoring his secretary's flash of temper. "I'm afraid that due to Arthur's incapacity it's more of a late breakfast."

"No thanks, I'm fine."

With another moan, Cromford staggered to his feet. "I apologise for my outburst, Jorgensen. Let me get you a drink at least. God knows I could do with one. Whisky Stengah?"

"Arthur, allow me," said Morley.

"Don't be ridiculous, Hilton. You know you can't mix a good drink."

"Not for me, thanks," said Jorgensen, as Cromford stepped gingerly towards a side table, on which a clutch of spirit bottles and a soda-syphon surrounded an ice bucket. While he fixed the drink, a business punctuated with muttered imprecations, Morley ushered Jorgensen towards the rattan armchairs by the balcony doors.

"You sent for me," said Jorgensen once they were seated.

Uncertain how to respond, Morley's eyes turned in appeal towards Cromford at the drinks table.

"This is your idea Hilton," was Cromford's response, before knocking back a slug of his scotch and soda, then returning cautiously to the edge of the sofa. "It's you who believes Jorgensen can help us. Although I'm damned if I know how."

"We're led to believe that despite your rather vague job title, you're the hotel detective, Mr Jorgensen," said Morley. "Or the house peeper, as your colourful American cousins are wont to call it."

"You've been misinformed, but I'll see what I can do to help."

"Arthur was indeed robbed last night," said Morley. "His pocketbook and a small diary kept with it were both stolen."

"I'm sorry to hear it. Though it sounds like a matter for the police."

"Well, that's the kernel of our problem. Police involvement may cause us some difficulties."

"Are you discreet Jorgensen?" asked Cromford, after downing another mouthful of his drink. "Hilton seems to think so, although, as far as I can tell, that judgement rests solely on stories he's heard about you not bragging about your war record."

"I'm Canadian, Mr Cromford," Jorgensen replied. "We don't tend to brag."

"What choice do we have Arthur?" said Morley. "We must put our trust in Jorgensen."

"I suppose you're right – as always," said Cromford with a resigned shrug, then flopped back down on to the sofa.

With a sigh, Morley picked up a manila envelope from the low table at his side. "Please read this," he said to Jorgensen. "It arrived an hour ago."

Jorgensen took the envelope and read the typewritten address – to Mr Arthur Cromford c/o the E&O Hotel. From inside it, he slid a single folded sheet of typewritten paper.

*Dear Mr Cromford,*

*If you wish to avoid the contents of your diary becoming public knowledge, then you must raise ten thousand Straits Dollars by tonight to secure its return. I will send a further note this evening, with details of the time and place for the handover. Any failure on your part to bring the money will lead to immediate publication of the diary.*

Jorgensen whistled softly. Ten thousand Straits Dollars was a hell of a lot of money. More than many men would expect to see in a lifetime. Although he was careful not to show any signs of it, a familiar tremor of anticipation ran through his body. "Let's start with the robbery," he said. "You'd better tell me what happened, Mr Cromford."

Cromford glanced at Morley before he replied, receiving a nod of encouragement in return. "Here goes then," he said. "After dinner in the dining room last night I persuaded Hilton to accompany me to a club. Some of the young fellows from Goldie's Bar led the way. I daresay you know them."

In George Town, going on to a club late at night held an altogether different connotation to that understood in London, Paris, or New York. In George Town, it meant a visit to a gambling house, an opium den, a brothel, or a seedy drinking parlour. Jorgensen had not noticed any scent of opium in the room, and neither man's eyes, though in Cromford's case red-veined, were glazed over in that tell-tale sign of an opium smoker.

"Given who accompanied you – am I right in thinking that the club was in fact a brothel?"

The bluntness of Jorgensen's question led Cromford to once again exchange glances with Morley, before he gave a cursory nod, as if accepting that their need for help trumped any remaining expectation of delicacy.

"The robbery took place immediately after I left the club," he continued. "Two thugs jumped me within a few yards of the door. While I was on the ground they searched through my pockets and took my pocketbook and diary." He touched the bruise on his head and winced.

"Were you alone, or with Mr Morley or others?"

"By that time, I was alone."

"I'd left beforehand," Morley volunteered. "Our man waited outside, and he hailed a rickshaw for me."

"Your man? The fellow who let me in?"

"Yes, Ah Cheng. He took me back to the hotel."

"At what time?"

"Two-thirty perhaps. Maybe later."

"And how about you Mr Cromford. When did you leave?"

"I couldn't say for sure. Late, but not quite morning. You must know the drill, Jorgensen."

"After the robbery, how did you return to the hotel?"

"A pair of coolie chaps found me on the street, groggy as hell, but it appears I made known where we're staying, and they got me back here somehow. To be frank, I remember very little about how."

"After the doorman sent word, Ah Cheng brought Arthur up to the suite," said Morley. "We cleaned him up as best we could, then let him sleep."

"What was the name of the establishment?"

"We expected you to ask that," said Morley. "But I'm embarrassed to admit we've no idea, or even how to find it."

"Tommy Essenden took us there, and we just tagged along," said Cromford. "Both nights. Do you know Tommy?"

Yes, Jorgensen knew Tommy Essenden. If a party was happening, it was a safe bet that Tommy Essenden's houseboy was brushing down his dinner jacket in preparation.

"Both nights, you say?" Jorgensen asked. "So, you visited more than once?"

"I'm sorry if I didn't make that clear. I'm still feeling a little fuzzy," said Cromford. "Last night was Hilton's first visit, however."

Jorgensen thought for a moment. There was no delaying the inevitable question. "If you don't want the police involved," he asked. "Then what do you plan to do?"

Morley grimaced. "I've been thinking long and hard about this, and I don't believe we have any choice in the matter. You see, we simply cannot allow the diary's contents to be published. It's not just our own personal reputations that are at stake." He shook his head firmly. "No, we have no choice – we must pay up. By my estimate it's around twelve hundred pounds sterling. Now by good fortune, I've amassed some wealth over the years. In fact, in the hotel safe there are several drafts to a bank in Singapore, which taken together exceed the sum demanded, but the difficulty is raising the cash by this evening."

"If you're decided, then there's somebody I know who could lend you the money."

Morley's look was beseeching. "Do you really think that's possible?"

"There'll be a question of collateral."

"But of course." Morley puffed out his cheeks in relief. "There are the bank drafts – would they suffice?"

"They should do."

"Then we place our fate in your hands, Mr Jorgensen."

"You must realise that even if I help you to raise the money, there's no guarantee you'll recover the diary." Jorgensen tossed the letter onto the table. "It's never a good idea to trust a blackmailer."

"The letter is written by an Englishman though, wouldn't you say?" said Morley.

"He's unlikely to be any more honourable than the characters in your stories – and they're usually Englishmen."

"You're right, of course. I concede the point."

"Can you give me a description of the diary's appearance? I want to be sure I'm picking up the genuine article."

"Do you mean you intend to go in place of Arthur?" asked Morley.

"I couldn't let him take the risk. There's no knowing what he'd be walking into."

"This is more than we dared to ask for," said Morley. "You have our heartfelt gratitude."

Jorgensen grunted. He had heard that kind of platitude many a time and seen how the kind of people who uttered it soon acted as if his help was their right.

Cromford stumbled through the description Jorgensen needed; a pocket-sized diary, in a navy-blue leather cover embossed with a gold AFC monogram. The pages inside were half-completed, and, on the inside cover, Cromford had copied out a favourite quotation.

*But words are things, and a small drop of ink,*
*Falling like dew, upon a thought, produces*
*That which makes thousands, perhaps millions, think;*

"Byron," said Jorgensen, unembarrassed at the satisfaction he took from Morley's startlement. Not all Canadians were barbarians.

"If you succeed in recovering the diary," said Cromford. "I must beg you not to read its contents."

"I won't need to. You've given me sufficient detail to identify it."

"We must trust Jorgensen, Arthur," said Morley, then turned to Jorgensen. "I don't suppose you have any idea who sent the letter?"

"Of course, he hasn't," said Cromford. "Oh God, what a fucking mess."

"If it was the diary the robbers were after, we must presume somebody told them about it," Jorgensen replied. "Did your valet see it? The one calling himself Ah Cheng?"

"Is it possible he saw the diary, Arthur?" Morley asked.

"I can't say for certain," Cromford replied. "I may have left it in my jacket. But, even if he did, he'd never have understood the code."

"It's written in code?" asked Jorgensen in surprise.

Cromford looked shamefaced. "A very simple one. And only on certain pages."

"Would anybody else in Penang have known about it?"

Cromford glanced nervously at Morley before replying. "I'm sorry, Hilton," he began. "After dinner the other day, I dropped the damn thing without realising. It must have happened when I was in the bar."

"For God's sake, Arthur," Morley snapped. "There are times you're so fucking cavalier."

"Which night was this?" Jorgensen asked.

"Monday."

"How did you discover you'd dropped it?" Jorgensen was trying to picture the group in the bar that night. There were the usual members of the younger crowd – the ones whose over-exuberant behaviour sometimes upset other patrons and guests, leaving Jorgensen to rap a few knuckles in the aftermath.

Essenden was among them, he recalled, along with his friends Ginger McHugh and Dickie Chelmsall.

"A girl handed it to me, just as we were all leaving. Dilys somebody. A friend of Tommy Essenden's."

"Phyllis Smith. Petite, dark-haired?"

"Yes her. A pretty thing."

Noises from the vestibule signalled Ah Cheng's return, with two of the hotel's white clad waiters in tow, bearing silver trays laden with toast and fried eggs, and dishes of sliced fresh fruit.

"I'll go and raise the money you need," said Jorgensen, rising from the chair. "First, I must ask your man a few questions."

"Go ahead," said Morley.

"I won't disturb your lunch. I'll speak to Ah Cheng outside."

Jorgensen waited in the corridor as the two waiters exited and made for the service stairs. A moment later, Ah Cheng appeared in the doorway and approached Jorgensen, his eyes downcast in the deference expected of servants to white men.

"You are known as Ah Cheng?" Jorgensen asked.

"Yes."

"You're young for such a name. How did you come by it?" The servant's name had bothered Jorgensen since he had first heard Morley use it. The informal prefix Ah was a mark of respect or familiarity among families or friends and was usually bestowed upon their elders. Men like Ah Soon and Ah Ming, both long serving employees of the E&O.

"I am Ah Cheng since a small child," the valet replied, his eyes flashing briefly in anger before resuming their studied gaze of Jorgensen's feet. "The Uncle and Aunty who raised me called me Ah Cheng because I was solemn and quiet, like a grandfather."

It was a clever answer, though Jorgensen was unsure if he believed it. "You worked up at Choo Fat Yee's mansion, didn't you?" he asked. It was the waiters carrying in the trays that triggered his memory. In the garden of *Towkay* Choo's grand mansion on Northam Road, he had seen Ah Cheng serving drinks to guests, and, because of his height and build, standing out from his fellow servants then as he stood out now.

Ah Cheng nodded in acknowledgement, accepting that there was little point in claiming otherwise. Jorgensen had been one of a handful of white guests at the function, and Ah Cheng too had recognised him the instant he had opened the door to Morley's suite.

"Why did you quit Choo's house?" Jorgensen asked.

Ah Cheng shook his head as if to deny any nefarious implications. "Not for a bad reason. Mr Choo was a kind employer. He gave me good references."

"So why?"

"I wish to see more of the world." He raised his eyes, fixing Jorgensen with a frank gaze.

"And you plan on doing that by travelling with Mr Morley. How did you become Mr Morley's manservant?"

"Through Yap Lin agency. Mr Cromford wired ahead looking for a valet for their travels."

Jorgensen nodded. It was likely that the hotel had set up the arrangement. Guest requests for temporary servants for the duration of their stay were not uncommon, and he knew several instances where valets had stayed on for the guests' onward travels. Still, he made a mental note to check Ah Cheng's story with Michael, and whether there really was a glowing reference from *Towkay* Choo.

"Tell me about last night," Jorgensen asked. Through the open window at the end of the corridor, he heard the first rumbles of thunder from up on the ridge. Fifteen, twenty minutes away by his reckoning.

Ah Cheng too cocked an ear to the sound.

"Last night," repeated Jorgensen. "Mr Morley gave me permission to ask you about it, so don't hold anything back. Where did Mr Morley and Mr Cromford go?"

"To Campbell Street."

Jorgensen had guessed as much. When Cromford admitted visiting a brothel, it was likely to be in the area around Campbell Street, a grid of streets that many Europeans referred to as Chinatown. In daylight hours the area was a commercial hub, where customers visited the watchmakers, goldsmiths and other merchants in shophouse ground floors. But at night the brothels, opium and gambling dens above and behind these shops catered for the island's overwhelmingly male population.

"Which house?"

"I do not know the name."

"Can you take me there?" Jorgensen asked.

Ah Cheng bowed his head in agreement. "I remember where."

"I'll come back for you at two o'clock."

# Four

There were three department stores in George Town where wealthy European residents preferred to shop. Each of them had its devoted adherents, on the lookout for items to bolster their standing in the community or better advertise their western sensibilities: English porcelain, Italian glassware, American gadgets. Pritchard and Co on Union Street was popular, and old India hands favoured the three-storied branch of Whiteaway Laidlaw, founded in Calcutta and with outposts in Singapore and Penang.

The third of these stores, occupying the ground floor of the splendid Kongsoon House building on Beach Street, was a lesser rival for those *mems* hungry for the latest cloth designs from London – Lock & Co, the "people's store".

Aping its grander competitors up the street, Lock & Co required its doormen to wear a uniform – in its case, a silk sarong, worn with a colourful silk shirt and topped with a dark felt *songkot* hat, as befitted their Malay wearers – unlike the military style tunics, shorts and turbans worn by their Sikh counterparts at Whiteaway Laidlaw.

One of Lock & Co's perennially cheerful doormen held open the store's side door onto Church Street. With a practised smile, he bowed his head to the two white women sweeping past him. Trailing behind them was a Chinese store assistant, whose chin pressed down on a tower of brown paper-wrapped parcels carried in his outstretched arms.

The leading woman stopped dead on the covered walkway. She was tall and spreading into plumpness, with pale skin and fair hair, marking her out as the mother of the slender, pink-faced young woman in her footsteps.

"Where is that man?" she declared in irritation.

Her daughter, Anne Prescott, who had paused to thank the doorman and to check that the assistant had made it safely onto the walkway beside them, moved to her side. "What is it mother?"

"The driver. Where is he? I distinctly told him twelve-thirty."

Anne regarded the busy scene in front of her. On the walkways, pedestrians of all backgrounds bustled hither and thither. Among the shoppers were bowler-hatted Chinese men and a few Europeans, the men sporting white linen suits and wide solar topees, while the women sheltered beneath parasols in their long skirts. Maintaining a respectful distance from their colonial rulers were scores of porters and messengers from the banks and trading houses: barefoot Indians and Malays in loose-fitting sarongs. On Beach Street, among a sea of rickshaws, bicycles, and slow-moving bullock carts, were limousines, driven by uniformed Malay chauffeurs. Carrying their white passengers in the rear, they competed for the remaining space with the sports saloons and roadsters of keen young Chinese businessmen.

"Here he comes, mother," said Anne, on spotting the slow progress of the family's dark blue Nash Six automobile. "I imagine he's had to circle round. It is awfully clogged up today."

"If you say so, Anne dear," replied an unconvinced Mrs Prescott.

Anne turned to the doorman as the Nash turned the corner into Church Street. "Here is our car."

With a quick nod of understanding, the doorman stepped out into the road, waving the Nash into a position directly in front of where the women and the assistant waited on the walkway. Below them, a pair of granite slabs bridged the deep storm drain, paving the way to the car's doors.

"I'll be getting along then, mother," said Anne.

Mrs Prescott turned a peeved expression upon her daughter. "We mustn't keep your father and Magnus waiting at the E&O. You know how much they look forward to the curry tiffin."

"I only agreed to accompany you because I wanted to pop into the bookshop. Or have you forgotten?"

"Yes, dear. But it all took longer than I expected."

"All the more reason for me to hurry. Now don't fret, I won't keep father waiting." She gently caught the shop assistant by the elbow and guided him to where the Prescott's Malay driver held open the car's rear door. "Hurry now, mother. You're obstructing the highway."

With a suppressed giggle, Anne turned her back on the group and rounded the corner on foot into Beach Street, heading north towards the Queen Victoria clock tower. The bookseller, GH Kiat, was situated towards the street's top end, opposite the west wing of the imposing government offices, but Anne had no intention of going on that far. As soon as she was out of her mother's sight, she approached a group of rickshaw pullers huddled in the shade around the next street corner.

"Take me to Love Lane, via Chulia Street," she said, wanting to avoid crossing paths with her mother in the Nash as it made its way to the E&O.

"Long way round, miss," said the first puller to respond, a snaggle-toothed old Chinese man in a vest and ragged shorts.

"I don't mind that," she replied blithely, climbing up the step onto the raised seat behind the puller's position. "That's the way I want to go."

Shrugging in indifference to the peculiarities of white women, the wiry puller hoisted the arms of the rickshaw and starting at a walk soon accelerated into a trot, his bare feet pattering rhythmically on the tarmacadam road surface. As his passenger had requested, the rickshaw ran south on Beach Street, before turning right into Chulia Street at the fire station and leaving the banks, trading agents and importers' offices behind. On their right a Muslim shrine and a Hindu temple guarded the edge of the streets of Little India. Ahead, the shophouses crowding both sides of the street overflowed with endeavour. Dirty industry, in the form of glassmakers, engineering workshops and tinsmiths nestled between tailors, shoe merchants and haberdashers. Baskets of goods jammed the five-foot ways, where they fought for space with craftsmen perched on low stools and customers picking their careful way among the chaos.

"Stop here, please," Anne called out soon after the turning into Love Lane. She climbed down and paid the fare, waiting until the puller hauled the rickshaw round in a U-turn.

She had arrived at a singularly unimpressive lodging house, one of several in the street. Pausing uncertainly at the door, which was wedged wide open, Anne looked down the length of the dark corridor.

Behind her, she heard the padding of feet on the tiles of the walkway, and turned to see an Indian boy, skinny, with a dark mop of hair and earnest brown eyes that gazed up at her.

"Oh, it's you, Suri," said Anne. "Is Mr Davies in his room?" she asked.

"Yes, missie. I will tell him you are here."

He disappeared swiftly along the corridor, while Anne waited at the doorway. After a minute or two she made out the return of his slim figure, silhouetted against a patch of light from the open kitchen at the rear of the lodging house.

Suri stopped just short of the door and beckoned her into the corridor. "Follow me, missie."

An aroma of spices and frying onions hung in the air. From the kitchen, Suri's parents earned extra money by cooking for some of the residents. She had encountered a few of the lodgers on previous visits; Indians, Eurasians and Chinese, with one family of six crowded into a small room on the first floor.

Suri led her upstairs and to the door of the room at the rear end of the corridor. There he left her, and Anne waited until the sound of his footsteps down the staircase had receded. She pushed open the door and stepped inside the room.

The wan face that looked up from the desk inside belonged to a young man, not yet past thirty, though only those who knew his history took him for so. Strangers on the other hand, on seeing the man's puffy pock-marked features, and the dark rings around his rheumy eyes, might understandably assume they were addressing someone on the cusp of an unhealthy middle-age. This was Frank Davies, the sole white resident of the lodging house.

"Hello Anne," he said, with a sad smile. In front of him was a typewriter, in which a half-finished letter curled over the top of the roller. To one side, an eight-ounce weight, long separated from the scales to which it once belonged, held down a sheaf of completed letters, though as there was no fan in the room and only a faint passage of air through the closed shutters, there was little reason to justify its deployment. On the other side was a foolscap-sized notebook, full of neat handwritten notes, held open with a smaller weight.

"You see I've been busy this morning," he said.

"Anything interesting among them?" Anne asked. She stood before the desk as there was only the one chair, occupied by Davies, and the grubby bedsheets on the bed behind him held no attraction.

"Not terribly," he replied. "I had a visit from a chap whose street is plagued by rats. The municipality are dragging their feet, so I've agreed to write a separate letter for each of his neighbours. The trick is to give all of them a note of individuality."

"And are you successful?"

"It hardly matters. It's more for a kind of professional pride that I'm attempting it."

Anne smiled, as brightly as she could. She was pleased to see him so engrossed, and though the cloying sweetness of opium still permeated the room, she felt and hoped it was stale, from old clothing, and not from a visit last night to an opium den.

"I wasn't expecting you today," Davies said. "Otherwise, I'd have arranged for food or drink. If you like, I can send the boy out for tea."

"There's no need, Frank," she said. "I can only stay for a moment. Mother and I are joining father and Magnus at the E&O for lunch."

"How splendid," said Davies. "Do give my respects to your father."

"Don't be an ass, Frank. I came to see if you were still going ahead with that business."

"It's already happening," he replied.

"It'll be all right. Frank. This time it will be. If you only do as they say – I'm sure of it."

Davies's sorrowful smile, which had briefly disappeared while he spoke about the letters to the municipality, returned as he cast his bloodshot eyes upon Anne. "Why do you keep coming here?" he asked.

"You know why. I can't bear to see you like this."

"Don't come then," Davies snapped, and turned his face away.

"That's not what I meant, and you know it, so there's no need to be cruel." Though she wanted to snap back, Anne spoke with gentleness. "I want to help you get back on your feet. You must understand that."

"Is that all?"

"We've been over this a hundred times, Frank. And the first step is to pay off your debts."

"It's a damned dirty job though. I've slept badly thinking about it."

"I realise that Frank, but we've discussed it and there's no other way."

"I suppose you're right. You usually are."

Anne moved closer to Davies's chair and placed a soft hand on his shoulder, causing him to look up in surprise. The nearness of her, the scent of her soap and her favourite perfume brought a tear to his eye, which he wiped roughly away with the back of his hand.

# Five

On the five-foot way almost opposite Davies's lodging-house, a stocky white man with mottled skin and a bristly walrus-like moustache that hid his entire upper lip and most of the lower, pulled a notebook from his pocket. While he was by no means god-fearing, he nevertheless raised his eyes to the glowering sky above and mouthed brief thanks to the almighty.

Seeing the girl leave the lodging-house at the very moment of his own arrival was a slice of luck he knew he scarcely deserved. He had hurried like the devil to get to Love Lane, fretting during the eternity of the rickshaw's journey along Chulia Street that he was on the point of failing before he had started. Every fifty yards he had checked his pocket watch, each time hearing in his head the stern warning he was given that morning. 'You'd damn well better be in position by eleven o'clock – and not a minute later'.

For once, the almighty was on his side. Though the stroke of good fortune forced him to dismount clumsily from the high rickshaw seat, then duck behind its tall wheels to avoid being noticed by the girl. Fumbling in his pocket for the ten-cent fare, he had watched her over the top of the puller's bald head, off which a steady stream of sweat trickled, for the stocky white man represented a heavy load to pull.

Not that he expected her to recognise him, though he had spotted her immediately: Miss Anne Prescott – recently returned from a nursing college in England.

He had watched her pause in uncertainty on the walkway, before briskly walk up the lane towards Chulia Street, then disappear round the corner.

Now, secure in his hiding place, behind a tattered rattan screen shielding the walkway opposite the lodging house from the fierce midday sun, he found himself thinking how much she had changed, and hoping she would not turn out like all those other English women who passed him on the street without so much as a sideways glance. After school or university in England, even the decent ones returned to Malaya as fully-fledged snobs.

Licking the tip of a pencil, he thought for a moment and wrote 'arrived at Love Lane 11 o'clock' in his notebook, then, further down the page, 'Miss Anne left the house at 12 thirty'. But what was he to say about the arrival he had failed to witness? Another lick of the pencil and he added in between the two entries, 'Miss Anne arrived at 12'.

He drew a pack of cheroots from the same pocket in which he replaced the notebook, sliding one free, tearing off the band and letting it fall to the walkway's tiles at his feet, where it joined a collection of other torn bands and ground out cheroot stubs. Striking a match on the brick archway against which he leant, he was soon cloaked in a cloud of smoke, a habit developed to keep mosquitos at bay during the evenings, and now a way of passing the long hours of boredom.

Despite the part-shade offered by the rattan screen, the walkway was hot, and sweat soon spread across his shirt. The notion of staying put all day held no appeal, especially with the gathering dark skies threatening the deluge to come. Fewer than a hundred yards away around the corner was the Victoria pub. He gave a grunt of quiet satisfaction at a good morning's work and, with a tuneless whistle that a generous listener might recognise as 'It's a long way to Tipperary', set off in search of a cold glass of beer.

# Six

From the Victory Annexe, Jorgensen made his way across the seafront lawn under the same ominous sky, pregnant with the thunderstorm to follow, that had rolled down from the peaks of Penang Hill to George Town's outer reaches. At the first distant crashes of thunder, patrons had retreated indoors to the curry tiffin lunch, leaving in their wake two white-jacketed waiters who scurried to clear deserted tables of linen cloths and empty glasses.

Back in the managers' offices to report on his findings, Jorgensen found Michael busy at his desk in the anteroom.

"I need your help," he said.

"At your service, Mr Paul. But Mr Broomes requires you on another urgent matter."

"It'll only take a moment," Jorgensen replied. "Morley's valet. Did you arrange his appointment?"

"Ah Cheng? Yes. Mr Broomes asked me to handle it. I contacted the Yap Lin agency and Ah Cheng fitted the bill."

"Were his references good?"

"Impeccable. He worked for Choo Fat Yee at one time."

"So, he told me. Isn't *Towkay* Choo a friend of your father's?"

"I believe so. Is that relevant?"

Jorgensen noted the prickliness in Michael's response. He had learned that the subject of the wealthy Chinese merchants and their friends and allies was tricky to navigate. Business and family relationships among the substantial Chinese community in Penang were complex and intertwined: the tycoons often serving as directors of companies owned by their fiercest competitors.

Family interests, and shifting alliances through their children's marriages, played their part and layered above were centuries' old clan loyalties made manifest in Penang in the different clan houses.

"Ah Cheng told me he left Choo because he wanted to travel," said Jorgensen, wisely choosing to sidestep Michael's question. "Does that ring true to you?"

"Something along those lines. Not everybody considers Penang the apex of their ambition."

"You came back though. After university."

Michael permitted himself a brief smile. "Loyalty to family is important." His eyes turned towards Broomes' closed door. "He is most anxious to see you again. Another problem has apparently arisen that requires your expertise."

It was Jorgensen's turn to smile. Michael's careful enunciation of the word expertise was dripping with meaning, though how to interpret it would likely depend on the nature of Broomes' problem. He nodded, then strode over to knock on Broomes' door, entering through it to find the assistant manager out of his chair and pacing irritably up and down the office.

"I'd hoped to see you back before now," Broomes affixed Jorgensen with a resentful glare.

"It was a delicate matter, but I'm dealing with it."

"Can I expect to see the police marching in during the curry tiffin lunch?"

"There'll be no need," Jorgensen said, having decided that adopting a reassuring tone and keeping Broomes in the dark over the particulars was the pragmatic way to proceed. "Now, Michael said there's another issue on your hands?"

"Damn right there is," said Broomes mournfully. "It's been reported that a guest has an unwelcome visitor in his room. You'll have to get rid of her."

Jorgensen glanced at his wristwatch. Apart from his memories, and the former military rank that often proved useful, the watch was the only remaining link he had to the war. With surprisingly light scuffs at the sides, several replacement straps and a new glass face bought in Singapore, it still told near perfect time. Just gone a quarter to one. "She's still there now?" he asked with a note of incredulity.

"As far as I know. But if you don't get to it, the damn woman will walk out right through a crowded lobby in full view of our patrons."

"Who reported it?"

"Housekeeping made several attempts throughout the morning to clean the room, but the guest rebuffed them every time. On the last occasion, a maid caught a glimpse of a woman inside the room."

"You're being coy, Broomes," said Jorgensen. "Do I assume she's a prostitute?"

"How the devil would I know? According to the maid, the woman was a young Eurasian. Whatever she is, we cannot permit the scandal that'll ensue if she's seen leaving via the lobby."

"Who's the guest?"

"Fellow called Durrant in room twenty-three. Arrived yesterday."

"Upstairs, in the old wing," said Jorgensen. "I see your problem. She'll come right down the main staircase."

"That's what I'm trying to impress upon you. And, in case it had escaped your attention – the hotel is full of our most eminent patrons."

"I'll see to it."

"And the Durrant fellow."

"I know what to do."

Leaving Broomes to resume his fretful pacing, Jorgensen strode through the anteroom and along the short corridor to the lobby, where there were still enough patrons around to justify Broomes' fear of embarrassment. He waved over the nearest porter, David, a dark-skinned Tamil, with severely parted hair and shrewd eyes that rarely missed a trick. Wearing a white shirt, monogrammed cream waistcoat, and white knee-length pyjamas, David, in common with Dipi the lift boy, and all the other porters, was barefoot.

It was no coincidence that David was the first porter Jorgensen spotted. An observant and ambitious young man, one of the first things David noticed after joining the E&O's staff, was the respect with which Jorgensen was treated by Arshak Sarkies. Since then, whenever the undermanager appeared in the lobby, David conjured a way to stay in his line of sight.

Summoned now, he rushed to Jorgensen's side as quickly as his training to remain unobtrusive would allow.

"How may I help?" he asked.

"Follow me," Jorgensen replied. "You're needed to escort an unwelcome visitor from the hotel, without her passing through the lobby."

"No problem, Mr Paul. Room twenty-three?"

Jorgensen raised an eyebrow, though why he should still be surprised at how fast news travelled through the E&O, he knew not. Eyes down, to avoid catching the attention of any of the patrons, he led the way to the foot of the grand staircase and bounded up the two flights to the floor above.

"Take her out down the staff staircase," he said over his shoulder to David as they climbed. "And onto the street from the stable entrance."

"Certainly, Mr Paul. Nobody will see her."

The many buildings that comprised the Eastern and Oriental Hotel stood on a narrow tract of land between Farquhar Street and the shoreline of the North Bay, alongside which the hotel's lawn extended for nine-hundred feet – the longest hotel seafront in the world, according to Arshak Sarkies' proud and oft-repeated boast.

Room twenty-three was one of the smallest and oldest rooms in the hotel, and one of the few without a balcony overlooking the sea. The old wing, part-cobbled together from the E&O's original building and a neighbouring row of shorefront bungalows into one impressive white-painted façade, no longer contained the hotel's better rooms. For the last few years, these were to be found in the newer Victory Annexe.

Jorgensen and David followed the twisting path of the first-floor corridor, up and down half-flights of stairs and around corners, almost to its far end. At the door to room twenty-three, two voices, one male and hectoring, the other female and submissive, could be heard from inside.

Jorgensen rapped hard on the door. "Hotel management," he called out.

The door was wrenched open by a man wearing a white tropical linen suit, who with a mocking curl to his lip, looked Jorgensen up and down. His eyebrows, black as tar, jutted over a broken nose that turned as many corners from its bridge to the tip as the corridor along which Jorgensen and David had travelled. A thick neck tipped his head forward in an intimidating posture.

"What the hell do you want?" he growled. His accent was unmistakeably Australian. Not the well-bred timbres of wealthy landowners heard on occasions in the E&O's dining room, but the coarser tones encountered at the quayside, and with which Jorgensen was equally familiar.

"Mr Durrant, I'm Jorgensen, the undermanager."

"What of it?"

"May I come in?" Without waiting for a reply, Jorgensen pushed past Durrant into the room.

It was decorated in the E&O's house style, with teak panelling on the walls to match the bedframe, chest of drawers and wardrobe. The mosquito net hanging above the bed was pushed to one end, exposing unmade bedclothes below. A young woman stood at its foot. She was Eurasian, as Broomes had suggested; dark-haired, with a delicate oval face. Her short green silk dress helped Jorgensen identify her as one of the dance hostesses from the Strand Hotel. Wide-eyed, she stared at Jorgensen, who smiled reassuringly in return.

"I'm afraid this lady needs to leave," said Jorgensen, turning to face Durrant, who had angrily followed him into the centre of the room.

"I will go," said the young woman. She snatched up a small purse from a sideboard.

"Stay there," Durrant barked. He stepped between her and Jorgensen, blocking her way with his broad back, his forehead pushed close to Jorgensen's. "You set yourself up pretty high and mighty, don't you?" His low voice, barely above a whisper, was weighted with menace.

"I'm doing my job, Mr Durrant. The lady needs to leave. Our porter will escort her from the hotel."

"That blackie's going nowhere near her," said Durrant, on seeing David take hesitant steps into the room, and then to the woman. "You stay where you are."

"It's all right," she replied. "I will leave." She tried to slip past, but Durrant grabbed her arm. "Hey," she cried out as his fingers dug into her flesh.

"I said no," said Durrant. "You stay here until I say you can leave."

"You'd better let go of the young lady's arm," said Jorgensen. "You're hurting her."

"And you're the bloke to make me, are you?" Durrant sneered.

"I'm no pampered Englishman, Durrant," Jorgensen replied in an even tone. "I'm a Canadian backwoodsman and I'll take great pleasure in throwing you out, if that's the way you want it."

For a moment, the two men stood immobile, their faces inches apart. Jorgensen could see the tendons tightening in Durrant's bull neck and feel his breathing quicken as he clenched the two heavy fists at his side. Without backing away, Jorgensen shifted his weight, ready to dodge a swinging fist. But suddenly – the stand-off ended. Instead of boiling over, Durrant gave a derisive snort and turned his head away. Behind the rage in the man's eyes, Jorgensen had seen the rapid calculations running through his mind. It was not fear that led Durrant to give ground but some other factor that trumped his natural desire to fight.

"Go on, get lost," Durrant said contemptuously to the woman.

"Go with David," said Jorgensen to the woman. "He'll lead you out of the hotel. And next time don't forget the rules. Out of here before the bell rings at six in the morning."

"Yes. Do as the undermanager orders," said Durrant scathingly.

With a last fearful look at both men, the woman hurried from the room, Jorgensen catching a whiff of stale perfume and alcohol as she brushed past him.

"This way, miss," said David and ushered her along the corridor.

"I'll send another porter up for your baggage in fifteen minutes," said Jorgensen, turning back to Durrant. "And we can help you find an alternative place to stay. You're no longer welcome at the E&O."

"I don't need your poxy help. I'll go to the Australia Hotel. They know me there."

"As you like. I'll see you at the reception desk."

Durrant's glare was still charged with hostility. "I won't forget this."

"Sure."

"Get out then." Durrant waved Jorgensen towards the door with a mocking courtesy.

"Fifteen minutes," said Jorgensen as he left the room. He was annoyed he had allowed the problem to flare up. The warning signs from the churlish way Durrant had spoken to Goldie and the other bar staff the night before should have been plain enough. If he had done his job properly and instructed the porters and doormen to keep a sharp eye out, the girl would have been ejected before sunrise. Long before most guests descended for breakfast.

# Seven

In the E&O's expansive dining room, the Wednesday curry tiffin lunch bowled along, as considerable a success as ever. From one corner, the hotel's small house orchestra provided a jaunty but muted accompaniment to the army of white-jacketed Chinese waiters carrying aloft enormous silver platters laden with steaming bowls of rice, curries, fried and roast meats. All to be ceremoniously distributed across the two dozen tables.

Every seat at every table was occupied, and the high-ceilinged room rang with the buzz of conversation pitched above the music. The twice-weekly frequency of the occasion, on Saturdays and Wednesdays, failing to diminish its popularity with its devoted patrons. Administrators of the Malayan Civil Service and their families mingled with those of rubber and tin traders, of planters visiting from their estates, of bankers and insurance agents, of engineers, of police superintendents, of department store managers, of railway and harbour officials. And mostly, though not exclusively, the attendees were white and of British origin. Most of the men were clad in white duck trousers and white linen jackets, the ubiquitous uniform of these self-proclaimed colonial masters, though here and there the younger among them sported shades of blue, grey, and brown. Relative youth also determined women's dress, where traces of pre-war Edwardian severity lingered in older matriarchs' long skirts while American and French fashions for looser straight fitting dresses just below knee length, were flaunted by the younger wives.

Dotted around the tables, a handful of Eurasian citizens could be seen enjoying their access to these spoils of privilege. Serving in prominent roles such as assistant harbour master or municipal architect, they had been granted a tacit acceptance among the Europeans.

And for reasons not unconnected with the potential for mutual profit, the odd Chinese businessman sat as a guest of a British trading house. Among them was Choo Fat Yee, the former employer of Ah Cheng, and honoured luncheon guest of Lawrence Prescott.

Choo was a wealthy and successful entrepreneur. What was known in Penang as a *towkay*. A Chinese business tycoon with a web of commercial interests – in rubber, tin mining, shipping, and a dozen other areas. He had inherited the family business from his father, at one time a key member of Penang's opium syndicates, before the British seized control of the trade. Part-educated in England, Choo exhibited an ease in both his business and social interactions with Europeans. Whereas some of his Chinese business rivals were warier of the European trading houses, having suffered in recent years from their aggressive growth founded on access to the City of London's ready capital, Choo's instincts were to stay close to the British. Never to trust them completely, but to invite them to social occasions at his mansion, where in side rooms he would willingly negotiate new business arrangements.

His hosts at the curry tiffin lunch were the Prescott family. Their trading house – simply known as Prescott's, one of the longest-established and most respected in Malaya, was based in George Town, with subsidiary offices in Singapore and on the mainland. Its current proprietor, Lawrence Prescott, the son of the founder, was of a similar age to Choo, but there the resemblance ended. Where Choo was a compact figure, dark-haired and urbane in a grey business suit, Lawrence Prescott, wearing white ducks, was large and florid, both in complexion and speech. He was not a heavy drinker, merely a powerful man used to speak his mind to an audience accustomed to acquiescing to his every view. However, in the case of Choo Fat Yee, Prescott tempered his declarations in the interests of the deal for tobacco export he hoped to conclude that month.

Also at the table were Prescott's wife, Mary, and daughter Anne, his son Magnus and daughter-in-law Gwendoline. They all knew the form. Entertaining a prospective partner of Papa's at a curry tiffin lunch was an important family duty. And as befitted members of a family engaged in business in Penang since the 1880s, they exhibited no open prejudice towards the island's Malay, Chinese and Indian inhabitants, unlike many of their compatriots, more recently arrived from Britain and Europe after the Great War. Their business would have faltered long ago if they had – for Chinese traders had established such strong footholds in traded commodities that to ignore them was foolish. That said, the openness of the Prescotts rarely extended to invitations to their place of residence. Dining with Penang's natives in public at functions such as the curry tiffin lunch was as far as they extended the hand of friendship.

Magnus was especially solicitous. He was a more youthful version of his father, slimmer in appearance, with less ruddiness of the cheeks and dark hair yet to fully retreat across his scalp. He liked to believe his approach to business was more nuanced and less autocratic than his father. And by their mutual agreement, more suited to courting Choo Fat Yee. So, at the table, Magnus and Choo discussed the upcoming arrival of a touring Shakespeare company, the recent newspaper interviews with Hilton Morley and the first appearance on the island of a Bentley motor car, bought by one of Choo's fellow *towkays*. Anything but the imminent tobacco contract. To Magnus's mind, this was a topic better addressed at Prescott's office on Beach Street the following morning.

Across the table, Lawrence Prescott, who had been following the conversation, turned to face his daughter Anne at his side, temporarily resting his knife and fork on the half-finished plate in front of him. From the corner of her eye, Anne noticed the slow deliberation of the act and braced herself for the inevitable inquisition.

"Your mother tells me your tardiness was because you went in search of a book," said Prescott. He had noticed she had arrived without a parcel.

She turned to him and smiled spiritedly. "Oh yes, Papa. But they didn't have what I wanted in stock. It was rather disappointing."

"In that case, why were you so late getting here? It's damned discourteous."

Anne gathered grains of fluffy white rice on her fork and dipped them into a rich beef curry. "I was browsing," she said, popping the mouthful in.

Prescott glanced over at Choo and Magnus. They were still engrossed in conversation and paying little heed to him and Anne. "What the devil do you mean?" he hissed.

"I was trying to find an alternative book. But I couldn't make my mind up. And then I realised the time and rushed here."

"Is the bookshop the only place you visited?" Prescott asked.

Anne turned to face her father; her expression guileless. "But of course."

Prescott's eyes narrowed, conscious she was mocking him, but he felt his wife's restraining hand on his arm.

"Darling," she murmured. "Don't forget our guest."

He looked up to see that both Choo and Magnus were watching him.

"Mr Choo has some interesting news to share with us," said Magnus.

Prescott took a deep breath. Now was not the time to pursue the matter with his daughter any further. He forced a cheery smile. "Really? Do tell us, Mr Choo."

Choo's eyes flitted knowingly between Prescott and Anne before he nodded. "Gladly. I was telling Mr Magnus that I sit on the board of the Chinese Methodist Hospital and of the hospital's plans to build a new children's ward."

"A splendid notion," said Prescott.

"Most gracious of you to say so. I can tell you the board will commission an architect in the next week or so. I'm hoping we can persuade Mr Boutcher."

"An excellent idea," interjected Magnus. "Wasn't Boutcher the architect for your place on Northam Road, Mr Choo?"

"He was."

"It all sounds terribly exciting, Mr Choo," said Anne. "At Guy's Hospital in London where I trained, there was a separate children's hospital next door. And I know the nurses at St Ermin's were adamant that separation from the adult wards aided the children's convalescence."

"Perhaps you should join the staff when the ward is finished, Miss Prescott," said Choo.

Anne laughed. "I'm sure you can do better than hiring an inexperienced newly trained nurse, Mr Choo."

"Everybody must start somewhere, Miss Prescott. As I told my youngest son when I sent him to Sumatra," said Choo with a smile.

"And how is your son doing, Mr Choo?" asked Mary Prescott. "You must send him our regards." She had been listening intently, waiting for an opportune moment to join the conversation. Her contribution was expected at some point and though she had no recollection of ever having met Choo's son or even knowing he had one, it felt as good a time as any.

Magnus's wife Gwendoline, who had met Choo's son at the last Penang Turf Club meeting, was not however expected to volunteer much on this occasion. So, she contented herself with smiling warmly at Choo's response – though in common with her mother-in-law, she struggled to make out every word of it. Choo's spoken English, its eloquence honed at Cambridge University, was nevertheless delivered with a strong enough accent to confuse those, such as Gwendoline and Mary, who were unused to hearing it on a regular basis.

"Thriving, thank you, Mrs Prescott," said Choo. "But I believe your son wishes to defer any talk of tobacco plantations until tomorrow."

“Hardly,” said Magnus in protest. “But do continue, Mr Choo, with what you were telling me. I believe the Chinese Methodist Hospital seeks extra funding for the children’s ward?” He glanced meaningfully at his father as he asked the question.

“That is correct.” Choo’s eyes met Prescott’s across the table. “We are close to raising enough and as I was telling Mr Magnus – the board would welcome one or two new benefactors to lift us to the summit.”

Prescott noted the almost imperceptible nod from Magnus that accompanied Choo’s words. He straightened in his seat and looked around the table. “Well, Mr Choo,” he said. “I do hope you’d be prepared to accept a donation from our family. We’d consider it an honour.”

Choo bowed his head to Prescott and again to Mary. “That is most generous of you Mr Prescott. I look forward to informing the board of this kind gesture.”

“Not at all, Choo. Glad to help such a worthy cause.”

“And thank you again for the invitation to this lunch,” Choo added. “If my ancestors could see me now – tucking into so many plates of delicious curry, I believe they would be astonished. But of course, here in Penang, we absorb the influences of so many cultures that even us Chinese can appreciate spicy food from India. And in turn the Indians and Malay people crave our noodles.” He laughed and Magnus was the first to join with him, followed by all, even Mary, who had eaten noodles once and swore never to repeat the ghastly experience.

“Quite so,” said Prescott. He gestured around the large dining room at the mass of people working their determined way through similar tables piled high with silver tureens and porcelain bowls. “And the British share that enthusiasm.”

The rest of the lunch passed away amid idle talk. Choo made his apologies and left shortly before the phalanx of waiters returned to clear the table at its end. As with all his actions during the lunch, it was well judged. By allowing Prescott and Magnus a few moments to bask in the success of their efforts to cultivate his favour, he ensured it was done under the benign influence of the gin pahits and the several glasses of wine they had already knocked back.

Magnus's good cheer, however, evaporated the moment he found himself alone with his sister, Anne, as after the lunch, they waited under the arcade near the hotel's entrance for their driver. Not quite alone, for Gwendoline stood mute at their side. Lawrence Prescott and Mary dawdled behind in the lobby, engaged in conversation with Albert Essenden, the chairman of the Peninsular Bank, their main lender.

Around them under the arcade, sheltering from the storm that had broken during the lunch, other families and groups gathered for the same purpose – the more diligent men ready to return to their offices for an hour or so, others to be driven home to their mansions and bungalows, there to rest and perhaps doze under a fan on a covered verandah.

"Did that go as well as you hoped, Magnus?" Anne asked her brother, more by way of conversation then any sincere interest in the matter.

"No thanks to you," Magnus replied with a sudden glare. "What the fuck were you playing at, irritating father in that manner?"

"It's none of your business, Magnus."

"The hell it isn't. If it affects Prescott and Co, then it is my business."

"Oh, come off it, Magnus. You're acting as if you're already the proprietor."

"I'm a director of Prescott and Co, as you well know, and I've been busting a gut for weeks on this contract with Choo. It'll be a big boost to the company, and you shouldn't be distracting father at such a pivotal moment."

Anne cast a scornful look at her brother. "Do you realise how ridiculous you appear at times?"

Magnus moved in close to his sister so that he would not be overheard, though the hammering of the rain on the steps up to the arcade rendered that precaution unnecessary. "Now see here,

Anne," he said menacingly. "I'm going to put a stop to your games."

"Here come mother and father," interjected Gwendoline in bright tones. "At last, we can leave."

At the gate, the family's Nash Six automobile splashed to a halt, and Anne, Magnus and Gwendoline joined Lawrence and Mary Prescott in a dash from the pillared arcade. Safely on board, they drove first to the Prescott building on Beach Street, to drop off Lawrence and Magnus. Then the car crawled through the crowded streets of Little India and Chinatown while Anne sat alongside her mother in silence, staring straight ahead until they passed along Chulia Street and the opening into Love Lane. There, turning her head for one brief second, she caught sight of the sorry looking lodging house with its peeling paint and cracked tiles.

# Eight

After making sure that Durrant's departure from the E&O went without further incident, Jorgensen walked through the lobby to Goldie's Bar. The bar, an elegant teak-lined room, was an institution in Penang, with, on most days, a glorious view through its open doors across the tile-floored verandah to the lawn and the azure hues of the Andaman Sea beyond. Today though, the dark outlines of ships moored in the North Channel were slowly engulfed by the advancing inky mass of cloud. On the verandah, a gathering of patrons, drinks in hand, leant on the balustrade and savoured the brief respite to the heat that the storm afforded.

Goldie, after whom the bar was named, was a mainstay at the E&O. As much a part of the building's fabric as the domed minarets on the Victory Annexe; more so perhaps because he had been there fifteen years longer. A Hainanese Chinese man, now as bald as his long-time boss, Arshak Sarkies, he remained as vigorous as any of the younger men who assisted him.

With a sixth sense borne of years of experience, he was somehow in position to meet Jorgensen at one end of the long bar counter.

"Drink to celebrate the rain, Mr Mac?" he said, flashing a smile in which the two gold teeth that originated his nickname glittered in the electric light of the overhead chandeliers.

"Not this time." Jorgensen looked around. There were several patrons within earshot. A handful sat on stools at the bar and others at nearby tables, where white-jacketed waiters buzzed around collecting orders. He lowered his voice. "Do you know the guest Mr Morley?"

"Famous man, yes I know."

"And his secretary, Mr Cromford?"

Goldie grinned again. "Everybody know him, lah. He comes in every night."

"Who was with them last night, after dinner?"

"Is about the robbery?"

"Yes. It's about the damn robbery." Jorgensen had long ago given up trying to work out how the E&O's staff knew of events before he did.

Goldie furrowed his brow in concentration. "Mr Morley and Mr Cromford had drinks on the lawn before dinner. But, after dinner – I did not see them."

"So, they weren't in here during that row between Tommy Essenden and Miss Phyllis that I heard about?"

"So loud a racket, Mr Mac. But they were not here."

"Now tell me about Essenden's group. Who were the last ones here, right before they left for the night?"

Goldie's frown returned. "Only one, two, three people maybe. Mr Tommy, Mr Gordon there, I think. I ask the staffs, Mr Mac, see if they remember already."

"Thanks Goldie. Send for me when they do."

***

At the far end of the bar, Rowland Burgon, a slender bespectacled man with wispy sandy hair and a long thin nose, watched Jorgensen leave.

Mopping beads of sweat from his forehead with a capacious handkerchief, he wondered how many weeks it would take before he could begin to abide the intense tropical heat. He had hoped for some relief after those three days spent in each of Singapore and Kuala Lumpur and the long clammy hours on the trains crawling up the Malay peninsula but was finding Penang just as intolerable. The bar provided the coolest environment he could find. Though several swigs from a tall glass of whisky and ice, the temporary drop in temperature afforded by the overhead storm, and the faint wafts of air produced by a nearby ceiling fan, were still inadequate relief after a morning spent walking between lawyers' offices on Beach Street.

He used the dampened handkerchief to wipe clean his rounded spectacles, drained the last of his drink and signalled for another. Following that, he intended to return to his room, where his wife had retired straight after a lunch where neither had eaten much. Their experience of food in the east matched their struggles with the climate. They had watched in fascination as diners on nearby tables in the hotel's dining room devoured huge plates of rice and curries, while for their part a few mouthfuls precipitated hot flushes.

"Whisky Stengah, sir," said Goldie, giving Burgon his characteristic grin as he placed the fresh drink on the bar top.

"Good man," said Burgon. "By the way, who is that fellow you were just talking to? I imagine he's the hotel manager?"

"Mr Jorgensen. Undermanager only."

"Undermanager. I see."

Burgon sipped thoughtfully from the tall glass in front of him, glancing at his reflection in the mirrors on the back wall of the bar and wondering idly what business of Hilton Morley's led an undermanager to urgent muttered conversations. Behind him he noted with distaste that the bar was filling up with diners vacating the dining room after the curry tiffin lunch, who, conscious of the hammering rain, were intent on loud conversations. He signalled to a barman, not Goldie this time but one of his underlings, for a chit to sign, drained the second glass and left as soon as he was able.

His room was in the old wing, not the Victory annexe, so he climbed the stairs from the lobby, pausing at the half-landing to gaze through the windows at the storm. Although he had witnessed two similar cloudbursts already, during their brief and unprofitable sojourn in Kuala Lumpur, there remained novelty and a degree of awe in seeing nature's rage at first hand. An interest shared by his wife, Winifred Burgon, who having not heard him enter their room a few moments later, was stood on the balcony rails watching the lightning forks over the sea and shivering at the proximity of the roaring thunder.

"Isn't it inspiring?" she said, lips apart and eyes shining with delight as Burgon appeared at her elbow. Younger than her husband by five years, Winifred Burgon was just past thirty, dark-haired, softening to plumpness with the pink rounded cheeks of a Victorian child's doll. She wore a light cotton dress, having changed after lunch, and evidently deciding that observing the storm was worth the deferral of an afternoon nap.

Burgon folded an arm around her waist, feeling small folds of flesh, unconstrained by the corset she had recently removed, squeeze between his fingers. "I ran across an interesting fellow downstairs," he said.

"Really, darling. Who was that?" Winifred continued to gaze out to sea as another bolt of lightning crackled in the distance, followed immediately by crashing rolls of thunder.

"An undermanager at the hotel by the name of Jorgensen."

Winifred turned to face her husband. "And why would you think a hotel undermanager was interesting? He doesn't strike me as the type of person to whom you'd normally pay attention."

"You might think differently if you'd seen him eject Durrant from the hotel. He's a resourceful looking chap, quite unlike a typical hotel manager. I was trying to overhear a conversation he was holding with the barman and though I didn't catch everything, I gained the impression he's the type who overcomes difficulties."

"He ejected Mr Durrant?"

"I watched from the edge of the lobby, so Durrant didn't see me, but it was all surprisingly civilised."

"I'm glad of it. It was awkward, thinking one would run into Mr Durrant around every corner. And do you think this undermanager, Jorgensen, could be of use to us?"

"It's worth considering. The fellow spoke with the Chinese barman almost as if talking to an equal and quite unlike what we've come to expect from other Englishmen out here."

"You must point him out when you next see him."

"I will – and then my darling, perhaps you can arrange a chance meeting with Mr Jorgensen."

# Nine

Though Ah Cheng led Jorgensen to Campbell Street, it was not to the stretch he expected. There was a geographical hierarchy to the brothel area in George Town, descending from the more exclusive establishments on Campbell Street, frequented by Europeans and richer merchant Chinese, through the dozens of brothels on Cintra Street and Rope Walk, to the seediest houses on Kuala Kangsar Lane for the poorest rickshaw pullers and casual labourers.

Here, almost opposite the Carnavon Street wet market, they were at the very edge of that whole territory.

The building Ah Cheng pointed to, on what was, after the storm had passed, once again the sunny side of the street, was one of four near identical houses in a terrace. Three-storey, with full-length louvred and decorative corniced arched windows on the first projecting floor, and, jutting out from the top floor – the unusual feature, for a shophouse, of a balcony. To either side were commercial premises, a cloth merchant to the left and a tailor's shop to the right. Banners in Chinese script proclaiming their trades hung from archway pillars and Chinese and English language signs above the doors named the proprietors.

"How sure are you?" asked Jorgensen.

"This is the place," Ah Cheng replied, unintimidated by Jorgensen's sharpness. "I remember the blue door. I waited across the street." He pointed to the open-sided market building behind them, closed now for the day. "I sat on the steps to wait."

"Did you see anybody suspicious hanging about, waiting for Mr Cromford?"

"I would tell if I did. Many people passed by the house, some entered, but nobody waiting outside. The robbers must have come later. Someone told them to come later."

Jorgensen gave Ah Cheng a sharp look. It was exactly what he had been thinking, and wondered if Ah Cheng's suggestion was an attempt to deflect any suspicion away from himself.

"Thanks for showing me. You should get back to the hotel now to look after your masters."

"You try to find the thief; I wish to stay and help you."

Jorgensen looked Ah Cheng up and down. Not knowing what he could be walking into, it was tempting to have an ally close at hand – especially someone as physically imposing as Ah Cheng. But, on the other hand, it was more than possible that the valet was involved in the theft – perhaps as the person who discovered the diary's secrets.

"No. You get going."

He watched Ah Cheng walk reluctantly away, then stepped over the storm drain on to the clay-tiled walkway in front of the house. Shutters behind the barred windows either side of the blue door were closed tight. He rapped a knuckle on a wooden door panel, waited and rapped again. Silence from inside. He rapped again, this time hearing footsteps inside on a wooden floor, before the door was opened by a heavyset Chinese man straining the four jacket buttons of his dark suit and wearing a lurid patterned tie around his thick neck. The man eyed Jorgensen sourly.

"We are closed."

"I am Jorgensen, from the E&O. Please tell the proprietor I am here on important business." Jorgensen removed his panama hat as if expecting immediate admission.

"Let Mr Jorgensen enter," said a woman's voice from behind the doorman. Obeying the command, he stepped aside and wordlessly held open the door for Jorgensen to walk through into the hall. It was more in keeping with a traditional Penang home than a brothel. The decor was unmistakably Straits Peranakan, that amalgam of peoples created by the intermarriages of early Chinese settlers with Malay women and found throughout the three Straits Settlements. An ornate wrought iron screen, its patterns heightened with gilt, separated the hall from the rooms beyond. Two rows of carved wooden chairs faced each other across the room, forming a wide corridor in the centre of which stood a petite woman. She wore a brocade jacket with a high neckline pinned by a brooch, looking for all the world as if she was the wife of a nineteenth century Peranakan merchant. She made a delicate bow of greeting and took Jorgensen's hat. Behind her, a younger woman and what looked like the twin brother of the first doorman guarded the openings at each side of the screen.

"It is pleasant to meet you, Mr Jorgensen," the woman said in clear English. "My name is Madam Cho. Shall we go through?"

Jorgensen followed the click of her mules to a second hall the far side of the decorative screen, where the house began to bear closer resemblance to a brothel. There was a bar, several divans and a piano, but at this early hour no pianist nor a bevy of girls in clinging silk dresses.

Jorgensen followed Madam Cho through a further door, opening into the cool of a courtyard area below an open air well in the roof. Built to ventilate the inner reaches of these long, narrow shophouses, these were a traditional feature of Straits architecture. Below the airwell, water filled a square, tiled pond fringed with verdant pot plants. To one side, a wide wooden staircase led up to internal terraces overlooking the pond.

They passed the foot of the staircase, knocked, and entered through yet another door.

"This is Mr Jorgensen from the E&O," Madam Cho said to a dark-haired man, elegant in a well-cut charcoal pin-striped suit paired with a red bow tie, who rose from a seat at a small table. His darker skin colour and deep-set eyes hinted at Peranakan descent, and perhaps explained the décor of a house passed down through several generations.

"Welcome to the house of Xyiu Tang. I am Norman Yao, the proprietor."

He offered his hand, well-groomed and soft. "Will you join me in a drink?"

"If that's lime juice," Jorgensen replied, indicating an iced jug on a sideboard.

Madam Cho poured two glasses from the jug for Jorgensen and Yao, then took a seat close to, but not at, the table. Her fixed smile had gone, and she sat with hands on her lap, watching Jorgensen intently.

"What can we do for you Mr Jorgensen?" asked Yao.

"A guest from the E&O visited your establishment last night. A young man, who was attacked and robbed in the street outside. His pocketbook was stolen."

Yao nodded gravely. "Yes, I was informed of this by my doorman. A most regrettable incident."

"That it was."

"I presume you suspect that the house is responsible for the attack. I assure you it was not. Theft is not the work of this house. We have a well-deserved reputation for discretion to uphold."

Yao's response was so smooth, Jorgensen suspected it was not the first time he had trotted it out.

"I'd like to talk to the doorman," said Jorgensen.

"That can be arranged."

After a deferential look to Yao, Madam Cho spoke next, as if by preconceived arrangement. "The young man in question was very drunk."

"We tell you this, so it is clear we do not obstruct." Yao added.

"He was perhaps more than drunk," said Madam Cho.

Jorgensen frowned. "Was he smoking opium?"

"Opium is prohibited in the house of Xyiu Tang. Your gentleman brought cocaine. It did not come from the house."

"Cocaine?" This was news to Jorgensen. It was rare to come across cocaine users on the island – not when opium was so easy to procure. Where the hell did Cromford lay his hands on cocaine in Penang?

"Who was with him when he took the cocaine?" Jorgensen asked.

Madam Cho and Norman Yao exchanged brief glances.

"I'm not here to report you to the authorities," Jorgensen said. "I'm interested only in finding out who robbed my guest. Was he with one of your girls? Can I talk to her, to see what she knows?"

At a sign from Yao, Madam Cho disappeared through yet another door deeper into the building. Jorgensen heard an exchange and then, a moment later, she returned.

"They will be with us shortly. From the private stairs at the rear of the house."

"They?" said Jorgensen.

"Yes. There are three boys."

Boys. For the second time in a matter of moments, Jorgensen was surprised. Not at Cromford's predilections, more because he had formed the wrong assumptions about the house of Xyiu Tang.

"They are a speciality of our house," Yao explained. "Unknown to all but a few of our clients."

A knock on the same door preceded the entry of three young Javanese men, each wearing white linen shirts and colourful patterned sarongs. Their wide brown eyes stared at him from over the shoulder of Madam Cho.

"How old are these boys?" Jorgensen asked.

"All are sixteen," Yao replied.

"They don't look it." Young Javanese men, with characteristically smooth skin and delicate features, appeared younger than their European counterparts – but to Jorgensen's eye, these three looked no older than thirteen or fourteen.

The brothel owner shrugged. His indifference to such questions could not have been plainer. "What do you wish to ask them?"

"The man here last night, was he alone, or with others?"

"I regret I cannot permit them to answer that question," said Madam Cho. "We must preserve our other guests' privacy."

"I didn't ask for their names."

"He was with friends," said Yao. "You perhaps know who."

"Did they leave together?"

"No, Mr Arthur was the last to leave." Madam Cho again. "His friends left some time before him."

"Including Tommy Essenden?"

"One hour before," said the boy who had entered first, drawing a sharp glance from Madam Cho. Jorgensen had noticed him following the conversation as if he understood every word.

"Why didn't they leave together?" Jorgensen directed his question at the boys, who sniggered between themselves until quietened by Madam Cho's reproachful look.

"We could not wake Mr Arthur," said the first boy. "Not for long time."

"And then?"

"Then he go." The boy waved his hand from side to side as if imitating the unsteady departure of Arthur Cromford, setting off another round of giggles from all three, before another of Madam Cho's sharp glances caused their grins to vanish.

"Do you have any more questions?" Madam Cho asked Jorgensen.

"Has Mr Tommy visited the boys before?"

The forced smile back on her face, Madam Cho bowed her head in apology. "I cannot tell you."

Behind her back, the most forward of the three boys gave Jorgensen a wink and the smallest of nods, unseen by either Madam Cho or Yao, which Jorgensen took as confirmation that Mr Tommy was well known to them.

"You must go now," said Madam Cho to the boys, clapping her hands to shoo them from the room, and they filed out obediently, leaving an aroma of floral scent and musk in their wake.

"Could these boys have seen the pocketbook before it was stolen?" Jorgensen asked.

Norman Yao assumed a pained expression. "I have already explained this crime is not the work of the house of Xyiu Tang."

"But are you sure of all your people?"

Yao's smile was complacent. "None would dare. The consequences to anyone caught would be severe."

Jorgensen was sure Yao meant every word, but that did not preclude one enterprising employee taking a chance if well enough recompensed. For it to be targeted, someone must have seen the diary, and understood the nature of its contents.

"We understand the victim and his companion are staying for several weeks," said Yao. "We hope that, despite this regrettable incident, they will visit again. Do you wish to speak to the doorman now?"

The inference was clear. They had opened their establishment to Jorgensen to remove any taint of association with the robbery. Now they wanted him off the premises.

At the front door, Jorgensen stopped and looked the doorman over. Yao had explained he was a new arrival to Penang, who spoke Cantonese and limited Hokkien.

"Your boss says you witnessed the robbery last night," Jorgensen said in Cantonese. "Tell me what happened."

"Did not see. It was too dark. But I heard shouting and then feet running."

"Which direction?"

The doorman pointed towards Penang Road.

"Did you see anybody hanging around before?"

The doorman gave a sullen shake of the head.

"Did you go to help the man who was attacked?"

"It is not my job. Other men helped him."

In ordinary circumstances Jorgensen would tip a doorman for information, but as this fellow had abandoned Cromford to his fate without a second thought, he didn't deserve a damn cent.

# Ten

When Jorgensen suggested to Hilton Morley that he knew someone who could raise the money at short notice, he had only one man in mind. The only person in Penang likely to help, and with the means to do so at short notice. And that was Arshak Sarkies, the owner of the E&O.

Part of Sarkies' routine when in Penang was to spend the late afternoons with his wife, and those daughters who still shared his home, in the family's private rooms in the old wing of the E&O. It was a ritual observed most days, before his inevitable later gravitation down to the public rooms, where he carried out his responsibilities as the hotel's owner and figurehead; dinner with prominent guests, drinks with the Penang social set, and on ball nights, to indulge his greatest passion – dancing. This he performed with a gauche enthusiasm, mopping the sweat from his head with a giant handkerchief and entertaining guests with his famous party trick – waltzing with a glass of whisky stengah balanced on his bald pate.

Ping Pong, Sarkies' faithful Chinese servant of thirty years' service, opened the door to Jorgensen's knock. He left Jorgensen waiting in the hallway, while, with the bouncy walk from which his nickname originated, he hurried off to announce the visit.

While he waited amid the paintings and sculptures occupying every spare inch of the marble-tiled hallway, Jorgensen wondered at Arshak Sarkies' fascination with the aristocratic English and their country houses. In the sitting room, where he was eventually ushered by Ping Pong, the décor was richer still; a sumptuous mix of Persian and classical influences, all in sympathy with the architectural medley of the E&O's buildings.

Sarkies and his wife Mary sat on a Chesterfield sofa, both with reading matter in their hands. For Mary, an olive-skinned woman whose fiftieth birthday celebrations were due within months, a Hilton Morley novel; for Sarkies, a copy of The Times, brought in by the P&O boat and flung upon a cushion as he sprang up to greet Jorgensen. He was a small man, brimming with energy despite the corpulence that had crept upon him in his sixth decade. His shiny, domed head was seemingly held in place by the formidable moustaches blanketing his lower face. Above these, two keen eyes fixed upon Jorgensen. Mary, shy and as reserved as her husband was outgoing, greeted Jorgensen with a mournful smile that recognised the unexpected visit was unlikely to bring any good news.

"Jorgensen, it is good to see you," said Sarkies, gripping the younger man's arm. "You don't visit often enough. Isn't that so Mary?"

Without waiting for his wife to respond, he guided Jorgensen to an armchair. "Sit, sit. We will have a drink with you. Ping Pong – fetch lemon water for our guest."

"Now Jorgensen, old fellow," he continued, patting the undermanager on the shoulder before resuming his own seat. "On the telephone you intimated your call is in relation to Mr Hilton Morley. You remember him, Mary – the charming man we dined with earlier this week. A famous author too. Entirely the calibre of guest we should encourage."

"Yes, Arshak," she replied. "See here." She showed him the book on her lap.

Sarkies tipped back his head and roared with laughter. "Of course, you are reading his novel." He turned to Jorgensen. "It honours us that such a man as Mr Hilton Morley is our guest at the E&O. Many important guests have stayed with us. Do you remember the film stars, Mary? Douglas Fairbanks and Mary Pickford – they were the biggest news in Penang, no, in all Asia."

Jorgensen, having heard the story countless times, hoped to avoid a repeat, and thankfully Sarkies' tone soon became serious. "But I fear you have worrying news," he said, scrutinising Jorgensen with a sudden intensity.

Jorgensen had thought long and hard about how much of Morley and Cromford's predicament he should reveal to Sarkies. In his employer's generosity he had confidence, having witnessed it frequently, but of his sympathy towards homosexuals, Jorgensen was less certain. While as outward looking and enterprising as the Sarkies brothers' myriad hotel ventures testified, Arshak was also close to sixty years old, and the son of an Armenian family steeped in tradition.

So, Jorgensen settled on a version that was true insofar as it went. He told Sarkies about the blackmail letter and the robbery, but omitted mention of the brothel, and hinted the retrieval of the stolen diary would prevent a scandal.

Arshak Sarkies listened in rapt attention, perched on the edge of the Chesterfield, his bald head bobbing at the more salient points of the narrative, his concentration disturbed only by Ping Pong's return with a tray of drinks. When Jorgensen had finished, Sarkies exhaled theatrically and rose to his feet, completing several agitated circuits of the sitting room while he recounted what he had heard.

"I am ashamed of all that has passed," he declared. "Ashamed for the E&O, that these gentlemen guests should be so cruelly mistreated." Turning to his wife he said, "My darling, I must talk to Jorgensen alone."

"If you are prepared to listen to Mr Jorgensen's guidance, I will leave you to discuss the matter," she replied, and with a pointed look at Jorgensen, gracefully left the room.

"It is for the best," said Sarkies to Jorgensen as soon as they were alone. "There is more to this incident. Now Mary has gone you must reveal what you hold back."

"The robbery occurred outside a brothel in Campbell Street."

"And this stolen diary? What is it that threatens such scandal?"

"I've promised discretion," said Jorgensen, hoping not to offend Sarkies by his reluctance to say more.

"I have met Mr Cromford," said Sarkies meaningfully. "Therefore, I will pry no further. Given their circumstances, I assume you did not inform the police?"

"I didn't see how I could."

Sarkies banged the palm of a hand on the top of the sofa cushion. "You must get to the bottom of it, Jorgensen. Pry out this damn blackmailer."

"You know I'll try."

"For now, though, it will be my honour to help our esteemed guests. Let us repair to my office and I will issue you with a letter and cheque payable to cash at the Peninsular Bank."

Arshak Sarkies was as good as his word. He sat at his magnificent walnut desk, his elbows resting on the green leather inlay. The desk was English made, shipped out to the Strand Hotel in Rangoon, from where it followed him to Penang and his ornately decorated corner office with a commanding view of the seafront.

"A letter to the bank authorising the withdrawal, and of course the cheque." Sarkies sealed them in an envelope and handed it to Jorgensen. "Sayfudin will drive you in my car, and by telephone I will request that the bank provide a guard for the return journey."

In return, Jorgensen presented Sarkies with the bank draft he had asked Morley to reclaim from the hotel's safe. Reaching for reading glasses, Sarkies scanned it quickly, muttering to himself as he did so. When he had finished, he placed the document in a lockable drawer in his desk. "Satisfactory, as I expected. Mr Morley is a true English gentleman. We must introduce him to the British Adviser for Kedah. You have seen him at the hotel this week. I trust?"

"Maurice Hill? Yes, I saw him yesterday."

"I had the pleasure to attend lunch with the Resident Councillor today, where Mr and Mrs Hill were also guests. I gained the impression they wished to meet Mr Morley. If you see the chance, will you introduce them?" Sarkies' eyes twinkled with mischief as he spoke, knowing full well that Jorgensen hated any involvement in those stiff English formalities.

"Sure."

Once he had locked the drawer and pocketed the key, Sarkies glanced up at Jorgensen as if surprised to see him still standing in front of the desk. "Is there something else you wished to discuss?"

"It's possible one of the hotel's patrons may be mixed up in this blackmail attempt."

A dark cloud crossed Sarkies' brow, erasing all trace of his previous smile. "A patron? Who?"

"I'm not at all certain – but the diary was seen by one or more of them here at the hotel."

"Are you suggesting that one of our patrons is a blackmailer?"

"Maybe."

Sarkies sigh betrayed his deep sense of disappointment. He prided himself on not just owning the premier hotel in Penang, if not in all the East Indies, but also attracting the very best of Penang's society to its balls, its concerts, and its dining room. And hearing that among their number was a blackmailer, felt like the cruellest of betrayals.

"You will find him, Jorgensen," he said. "You must."

# Eleven

At the Peninsular Bank, a three-storey stone building that would not have looked out of place in London's Threadneedle Street, the manager, Greig, received Jorgensen in the cool of the high-ceilinged banking hall. A grey-haired Scotsman, a veteran of the east and a prominent figure in the local European community, Greig eyed Jorgensen with ill-concealed disapproval. Warned of the arrangement by Sarkies' phone call, he conveyed his opinion of it through the set of his mouth rather than spoken word. Irregular as it was, the transaction nevertheless fell within the bank's rules, and Greig felt reluctantly obliged to proceed.

"If you'd be kind enough to wait, Jorgensen," said Greig. "Mr Bell will show you the way when we're ready."

Greig marched off, leaving Jorgensen in the company of the senior clerk; a Eurasian of small stature whose half-smile as he watched his employer's departure caught both Jorgensen's eye and sympathy.

"I guess he doesn't like to part with the bank's cash," said Jorgensen.

"He is unsettled, sir," said Bell. "It is the second such occasion this afternoon. Will you come this way?"

"Is he worried there's going to be a run on the bank?" Jorgensen asked, as they left the hall to enter an anteroom, where an array of low rattan chairs awaited them. Two more doors led from the anteroom deeper into the bank's interior.

"Mr Greig is a cautious man," said Bell. "It is unusual to see such large sums of cash withdrawn ad hoc."

"Who was the other client making a big withdrawal?"

Bell smiled at Jorgensen's question, his eyes twinkling. "That I cannot say, sir. If I may, I will sit here with you. It should not be for long."

They waited for five minutes, during which Jorgensen fended off Bell's enquiries into whether Mr Hilton Morley, the E&O's famous guest, was as witty as the newspapers claimed. Then, through one of the onward doors, Magnus Prescott appeared, clutching a shiny tan leather document case under one arm. Startled on seeing Jorgensen, Prescott paused uncertainly in the doorway, causing a Chinese bank clerk who was following close behind, to nearly bump into him.

"Good afternoon, Mr Prescott," said Jorgensen.

"Good afternoon," Prescott replied, frowning as he attempted to recall Jorgensen's name.

"Jorgensen, from the E&O."

"Oh yes, of course." Prescott's face showed some unease over the unexpected encounter. "If you'll excuse me." He passed through the anteroom, leaving the Chinese clerk on his heels hurrying ahead to open the door to the main banking hall. After Prescott had left them, Jorgensen winked at Bell. "The other client, I suppose?"

Bell smiled and rose to his feet. "Let us proceed to Mr Greig's office."

There, under Greig's icy gaze, Bell counted out the cash onto a gleaming polished wood tabletop – glossy enough that the white surround to the ten-dollar notes reflected from its surface. With a glance of amusement at Greig's stern expression, Jorgensen carefully stacked each bundle, held together by Peninsular Bank branded money-wraps, into an attaché case borrowed for the purpose from Sarkies. He snapped the case shut, signed the receipts, and was then introduced to a hefty, turbaned, and bearded Sikh security guard. Together, they left Greig's office, traversed the banking hall and descended the steps into Sarkies' waiting Buick.

On returning to the E&O, Sayfudin, Sarkies' driver, pulled up outside the main door. Vikat, somewhat distracted by the crisp white uniform and navy blue socks of Jorgensen's companion, for once forgot to salute. With the Sikh bank guard in tow, Jorgensen headed straight for the reception desk, through a door at its rear and into the small office behind. A clerk opened the tall safe where guests' valuables were housed. Finding a space between rows of jewellery boxes, pouches, and document folders fastened with ribbon, the clerk placed the case inside.

"I suppose you've got a chit," Jorgensen said to the guard.

"Yes, sir." Back at the reception desk, he produced a document which Jorgensen approved with a press of the hotel's rubber ink stamp and his signature. Chop and sign, it was known as in Malaya. A seemingly unavoidable practice, without which, no progress was made in any sphere of operations. It was little wonder that the Penang commercial directory listed dozens of rubber stamp manufacturers.

The bank guard saluted and departed through the main doors, where, once again, Vikat could not help but stare as he passed.

# Twelve

After Jorgensen watched the bank guard leave, he turned to face Richard Hong, the chief desk clerk at the E&O. A man whose broad moon face was enlivened by a natural uplift at the corners of his mouth, an expression that helpfully conveyed a look of sincere delight in his dealings with guests, irrespective of any private thoughts he might be entertaining.

"You've got news then?" Jorgensen said.

"Yes, Mr Paul. I spoke to the clerk who received the message. It was hand delivered as you thought. The messenger was a young Indian boy. Very poorly dressed in rags but spoke English."

"Would the clerk recognise him again?"

"Yes, Mr Paul. Also, Vikat remembers him too. The boy ran off after delivering the message – towards the Esplanade."

"Good. Have him stay on for the evening shift, I will see he is properly recompensed. Mr Cromford is expecting another message this evening and I'll want to know the moment the boy arrives."

Jorgensen glanced at the clock above the reception desk. There was plenty of time to prepare and to allow for a last patrol around the main accommodation rooms. He was halfway across the lobby towards the main staircase, when he found his path blocked by a woman in a white blouse with a lilac bow at the neck, cream skirt and a straw cloche like hat that framed a round and delicate face.

"I do apologise for accosting you in this way but are you Mr Jorgensen?" she said. Her voice was bright, and her eyes sparkled with an amused devilment.

Jorgensen recognised her as a guest at the hotel. He had noticed her twice since her arrival the day before. Once with her husband enjoying pre-dinner drinks on the seafront lawn and again that morning at breakfast in the dining room.

"I am," he replied.

"Mrs Winifred Burgon." She held out a soft white hand for him to take. "My husband, Mr Rowland Burgon, promised to introduce me to you, but as he's elsewhere dealing with business matters, I decided in a moment of impetuosity to take the plunge without him. I hope you don't object to my forwardness."

"I'm afraid I don't recollect speaking to your husband."

"Oh dear," she replied, her mouth turned down at the corners in a comical gesture. "You are offended by my behaviour. And I hadn't taken you for one of those stuffed shirts."

Her eyes held more than a hint of mockery and her full-lipped mouth twitched into a half-smile.

"How may I help you, Mrs Burgon?"

"Ah, you see straight through me. I had little notion my need for assistance was so transparent."

"I've got an instinct for when a guest requires help."

"Is there somewhere more private?" she asked, looking around the lobby.

Jorgensen followed her gaze. As was often the case in the afternoon following the curry tiffin lunch, no chairs in the lobby were free that were not within earshot of other patrons. Over by the porter's desk he saw David and beckoned him across.

"At your service, Mr Paul," said David, after bowing his head to Winifred Burgon. His eager smile was wider than normal. Thrilled at playing a part in the eviction of the Australian guest just hours earlier, he was keen to take any new chance to impress.

"We need two seats in relative privacy," said Jorgensen. "Check if there's space in the lounge and ensure the waiters reserve it."

With another quick bow to Winifred Burgon, David hurried off on his errand.

"How long are you and Mr Burgon staying with us?" Jorgensen asked.

"It rather depends," she replied.

"I see. And have you enjoyed your stay so far?"

Winifred Burgon laughed, matching dimples forming in each of her doll-like cheeks. "I suspect small talk with guests isn't really your thing, Mr Jorgensen."

With relief, Jorgensen saw David emerge from the corner of the lobby and make his unobtrusive way over to them.

"If you please, madam," David said to Winifred Burgon, "I will take you to your table."

The spacious teak-panelled lounge was next to the bar, with an identical view through its flung open doors of first, the tile-floored verandah, then the seafront lawn. Rattan chairs, made comfortable with cushions upholstered in white cotton, were arranged around low tables. Most were occupied by groups of European ladies who had chosen to stay on after the lunch. Several of whom turned to cast an inquisitive eye at the clothes worn by the unknown white woman who followed Jorgensen into the room.

David led them to one of only two free tables, in the corner furthest from the open doors to the lawns. By the time they were seated, David had retreated with another bow and smile, to be replaced by a white-jacketed Chinese waiter who hovered nearby.

"Will you have a drink with me, Mr Jorgensen?" Winifred Burgon asked.

"Thank you. Just a lemon water."

"I believe I should follow your lead. I'd prefer not to be seen as one of those women who pickles herself with gin from luncheon onwards."

"How may I help you, Mrs Burgon?" asked Jorgensen, when the waiter had left them alone.

She looked down at her lap and smoothed away a few imaginary creases among the pleats of her skirt. "It's a little difficult to know where to begin. I hope you won't think I've gained your attention on false pretences but I'm afraid my problem has little connection with the hotel. It's a delicate matter that has brought my husband and I all the way here from London."

"I see."

She lifted her head to look directly at Jorgensen. Her hazel eyes open wide in appeal. "It's rather a complicated story. Would you object to hearing it?"

"Please go ahead."

"Seven years ago, a business partner of my husband disappeared. He was on his way to Australia in connection with some new opportunities for the practice. You see, my husband is a solicitor with a very well respected firm in London. But Leslie never arrived. The last letter we received was posted in Aden, after he passed through the Suez Canal. In it, he announced a rather shocking intention to change his plans and disembark from the ship elsewhere."

The waiter returned, bearing a salver from which two tall glasses of iced lemon water were placed on the table. With a look of gratitude to both Jorgensen and the waiter, Winifred took a delicate sip and screwed up her face at the taste.

"It is awfully sharp," she said.

Jorgensen nodded and took a longer sip from his own drink. "And you're here in search of him?" he asked.

"I see I was right to approach you. You're as sharp as this drink."

"Why now, if he disappeared several years ago?"

"Last year, the senior partner died, and much to the consternation of the remaining partners, it was discovered that he had chosen to leave his share of the firm to Leslie. I'm sorry, I'm getting this all in a muddle. I should have made it clear that Leslie was his son and we had all been led to believe that because of Leslie's disappearance he had been disinherited."

"I see."

"But as nobody knew where he could be found, my husband was asked by the other partners if he would undertake the search. And here we are in Penang."

"Why do you believe this Leslie is in Penang?"

"I'm doing it again," Winifred giggled coquettishly. "I should have told you Leslie's full name – it's Leslie Brougham Worrilow. Though we believe he has since changed his name. It was discovered through correspondence with the P&O line that Leslie disembarked in Singapore, not Bombay or Colombo, as we had always assumed. Our search led on to Kuala Lumpur, then here to Penang. Of course, I realise Leslie may not have stayed on in Malaya. After all, it was seven years ago."

"And you want my help in trying to locate him?"

"Rowland heard of your reputation for assisting guests in difficulty, and though our situation may not fall into that category, we do hope you'll take pity on our predicament."

"If you suspect he changed his name, how were you able to track him?"

"In Singapore, and after he arrived in Kuala Lumpur, he was still Leslie Worrilow. A manager at the Majestic Hotel in Kuala Lumpur remembered him enquiring about hotels in Penang. Apparently, they had a lengthy discussion about the island, and he distinctly remembered Leslie's confidence in his prospects."

"What makes you believe he changed his name?"

"For some reason he confided his intention to the manager at the Majestic. To break with the past, and turn over a new leaf, he'd apparently said."

"He may have changed his mind."

"Rowland has been making enquiries after Leslie with various legal firms, but with no success. Can you help us?"

While Winifred had been telling the story, Jorgensen had pondered what his answer was going to be. He suspected that the true motivation for her and her husband's trip in pursuit of the long-lost Leslie Worrilow was financial, rather than altruistic. That in some way her husband's own share in the firm depended upon their search.

"There's another matter that's taking up most of my time at the moment," he said. "But I can make a few enquiries once I'm free."

"Oh, that's marvellous, Mr Jorgensen. I didn't dare believe you'd be willing to help."

"Tell me more about Leslie Worrilow. How old will he be now?"

"I'm ashamed to say that I don't know the answer to that question. He was awfully young to be made partner. I suspect he can't be much more than thirty."

"Why do you think he disappeared?" Jorgensen asked.

"Leslie once confided to me that he had a very difficult relationship with his father. I don't believe he ever really wanted to join the family firm. He always seemed to me to be something of a dreamer."

"Do you have a photograph of him? If I've seen him in Penang, I might remember where and when."

"Oh yes, my husband Rowland has the photographs. When he returns, I'll ask him to find you and show you a copy. Leslie was a quite handsome young man. I'm sure you'd remember him if you'd seen him."

"I may not be around much today. Ask your husband to leave it at the front desk," Jorgensen drained his glass. "I've got to go, I'm afraid. Thank you for the drink. I'll be in touch if I find anything out."

Winifred Burgon reached across the table to clutch Jorgensen's hand. "I can't tell you how grateful I am. It will mean so much to my husband."

# Thirteen

The promised second letter from the blackmailer arrived just after seven o'clock that evening, as twilight crept over the seafront lawn of the E&O, where waiters, laden with trays of gin pahits and whisky stengahs, hastened between tables crowded with the usual sunset drinks mix of hotel guests and regular patrons.

Among them, Hilton Morley and Arthur Cromford sat with the British Adviser for Kedah State, Maurice Hill. They smiled politely as the Resident's wife expounded at length upon her belief that society in Singapore was superior to Penang.

Back inside the hotel, Jorgensen sat in an easy chair in the centre of the lobby, facing the main doors and at an angle to the reception desk. He was wearing clothes that were rarely seen in the E&O – a dark suit, navy-blue tieless American style work shirt and a soft dark blue fedora hat. Clothes that were drawing several curious looks, and, from one or two of the more hidebound patrons, the odd offended stare.

Not that Jorgensen cared. He was dressed for a specific purpose and would be on the move as soon as the letter reached him. He saw its arrival – brought on foot, by an Indian boy, no more than twelve years old and barefoot in ragged half-length trousers and a grubby shirt. He watched as the boy, half-terrified with fear, begged entry from the doorman, then with downcast eyes approached the reception desk.

The reception clerk took the proffered envelope and leant across the counter to hear the boy's faltering voice, making sure he caught Jorgensen's eye to give a brief but unmistakeable nod.

Then, on the pretext of not understanding if the sender expected a response, he held the boy in stilted conversation for as long as he could.

That was Jorgensen's cue to send his own signal to Dipi, the lift boy, who was stationed by the porter's desk on the opposite side of the lobby. Like a gun dog awaiting a command, Dipi's gaze had been fixed upon Jorgensen. He grinned in acknowledgement, then slipped through the main doors, through the gateway, past the congregation of gossiping chauffeurs, and across to the far side of Farquhar Street. There, under trees, he waited for the reception clerk to release the messenger. Dipi's heart was racing. Never had the hotel entrusted him with such an important task.

The reception clerk snapped his fingers for a porter to carry the message on to its recipient. Needing no second invitation, the young Indian messenger boy slipped quietly away through the main doors.

On the lawn, a rustle at Cromford's elbow, followed by the polite cough of a junior porter, drew his attention to a silver salver on which lay a manila envelope, the same size and shape as the one received earlier that day.

Striving to control the tremble in his fingers, Cromford reached out to grasp the envelope, then passed it straight to Morley. With an apology to their companions for the interruption, Morley extracted and read the typewritten letter, before replacing it in the envelope and handing it back to the porter. "Take this to Mr Jorgensen in the lobby."

Then, as if nothing of import had occurred, he resumed the conversation with the Hills. "Do tell us more about the Tanglin Club."

When the envelope reached Jorgensen, he slid the letter from it.

*Dear Mr Cromford*

*Bring the agreed sum to 56 Muntri Street at eight this evening. It is imperative you come alone. I trust you appreciate the grave consequences of not so doing.*

Jorgensen checked his wristwatch. It was seven-fifteen. By seven-thirty the last of the fading sunset glow would give way to darkness. Muntri Street was fewer than ten minutes on foot. Whoever the blackmailer was; he was no fool. Careful to leave little time for an advance arrival, and the rendezvous itself was cleverly chosen.

Jorgensen knew Muntri Street well. A peaceful, narrow lane, unlit at night, with few commercial premises, and none in its middle stretch. It ran west to east, parallel with Chulia Street, lined on both sides with traditional old houses. These were longer and grander than most shophouses, indicative of the fact that wealthy Chinese *towkays* once lived there before their escalating fortunes led them to build noble mansions further west on Northam Road or Burmah Road. Among the Chinese, Muntri Street was infamous as a road where the *towkays* had installed kept mistresses, secreted behind shutters in separate houses across the street from their own residences.

Jorgensen tried to picture the street as it would appear in darkness. As best he could recall, Number 56 was in the middle stretch, one of a terrace with elaborate facades, chosen no doubt because it was unoccupied. Come the evening, neighbours' doors would be locked, and shutters closed, rendering it an ideal spot for an ambush with little chance of the victim escaping. His hunch strengthened that the blackmailer intended to set a trap, he pocketed the note, and set off for the stable block.

Inside the stables, just a few old stalls at one end of the block were still dedicated to stabling horses, for when Penang's more notable European families maintained old traditions and rode into the E&O for Sunday tiffin. Otherwise, the building was almost entirely given over to the storage and maintenance of the hotel's motor cars and bicycles, and it was a chief mechanic and not a head groomsman who was in charge. This was Abdul, a lean figure who appeared from a small office at the rear to greet Jorgensen. He was a Bengali Muslim, lighter skinned than most Indians in Penang, the majority of whom were Tamils, from the south.

Tinges of grey at the temples and a creased, weatherworn face betrayed an age at odds with a conspicuous strength and vitality.

"Zamir is ready, Mr Mac," he said. "Will I come too?"

"No need."

As if on cue, Zamir too appeared. Younger than the other Malay drivers and first to volunteer for the task, he had left behind his E&O uniform tunic and hat at Jorgensen's request. "We go?" he asked, and, seeing Jorgensen's nod, ran around the bonnet of the dark-green Bullnose Morris which was parked just inside the double-doors, grinning in anticipation as Jorgensen climbed into the front passenger seat.

The drive to the western end of Muntri Street took less than two minutes. At the turning, Jorgensen leant forward in his seat. "Slow and steady, and don't stop if anyone jumps out," he said.

They first passed the small Thean Hou Buddhist temple on their right, where lit by lanterns hanging from the gates, a pair of worshippers were entering. No more than thirty yards further on, a shape broke away from the dark block of houses to wander into the street, before quickly retreating to the five-foot way. As the Morris passed the spot, Jorgensen glimpsed two figures in the shadows. The first, picked out briefly by the car's headlights, was a man in a wide straw-hat, who stared closely at the car as it crawled by. Behind him, a second larger figure loomed over the smaller man's shoulders.

There was little doubt in Jorgensen's mind. His suspicions were correct, and these two were the western end of the reception committee for Cromford, ready to jump him if he came on foot from the hotel.

As they neared the terrace of houses on their left that included number 56, Jorgensen pulled the brim of his hat lower over his eyes, wanting to see, but not be seen in return. Sure enough, in the darkness of the walkway outside the house, there was a second team of two men. One hulking figure wearing a white cotton skull cap, and the second in a dark suit, both making inadequate attempts to evade the glare of the Morris's headlights.

Beyond them, they passed two more groups on the walkways, but these were poor, homeless Indian families bedding down for the night – a familiar sight across much of George Town. Then, when the Morris had almost reached the far end of Muntri Street, Jorgensen looked right, where he knew there was an alley running alongside the open drain that led south to Chulia Street. He suspected that a third back-up group was lurking within it, but this time, they were better hidden. At the eastern end, the junction with Love Lane, his hunch of an ambush confirmed, and recognising that the odds were stacked against him, he ordered Zamir to return to the hotel.

***

"I followed him all the way Mr Mac," said Dipi breathlessly, emerging from the arcade near the E&O's entrance, where he had waited for Jorgensen to return.

"Where did the boy go?"

"Love Lane, sir. Very near."

"You've done well, Dipi."

"I can show you the house." The boy's chest was bursting with pride at Jorgensen's praise.

"We'll walk," said Jorgensen.

Dipi led Jorgensen along the same route the Indian boy messenger had taken earlier; east on well-lit Farquhar Street, between the two Catholic schools and then a right turn into Love Lane before the Church of the Assumption. Past the end of the church, Love Lane narrowed and darkened.

Jorgensen halted there and spoke in a low voice to Dipi. "When we reach the place, I want you to point it out, but talk quietly. Then head straight back to the hotel."

"I understand."

They walked on in silence, passing the entrance to the eastern end of Muntri Street, where Jorgensen glanced along its length, wondering whether any of the ambushers were still in position, waiting for their prey to show.

Up ahead, light bleeding from the junction with busy Chulia Street enabled Jorgensen to begin to pick out the fronts of individual shophouses in the terraces that now lined both sides of the street.

Dipi paused and nudged Jorgensen. "There," he whispered, pointing to a house on their left. Even in the faint light, Jorgensen could see it was a ramshackle affair, with half of its paintwork peeled off amid blackened mould stains.

"The one with the open door?"

Dipi nodded.

"I see it. Go back to the hotel."

"I can stay."

Jorgensen gently took hold of Dipi's shoulders and turned him around. "Go now."

Although reluctant to leave, the quiet command in Jorgensen's voice brooked no argument. Dipi padded away, while casting looks of regret over his shoulder.

Directly across the street from the house that Dipi had pointed out, Jorgensen noticed one of the shophouses was dark, not a crack of light emanating from any of its closed shutters. Hanging from its projecting upper floor was a half-unfurled rattan blind, meant to provide extra shade to the walkway below during the day. He slipped quickly onto the walkway behind the blind, and by moving close to an archway pillar was able to see through the gap between it and the frayed edge of the blind.

He heard muffled chatter filtering through the first-floor shutters of the house opposite, Hokkien Chinese as far as he could tell, then watched as a young Indian entered through the open door. There was no sign outside, but the mix of residents led him to assume it was a lodging house.

Oblivious to his presence behind the blind, a handful of people filed up Love Lane, returning home after eating at the hawker stalls on Chulia Street.

Jorgensen waited patiently, watching the open door, until, almost an hour later, a gang of Chinese men turned the corner into Love Lane from Chulia Street, calling to each other as they swaggered down the street. Two bigger men on the flanks, solid in cut-down trousers and cotton caps. Two others in the centre, one, wearing a dark suit, gesturing as if he was in charge. They stopped in front of the lodging house, while behind them Jorgensen shifted out of sight behind the blind. Their leader, whose angular frame Jorgensen recognised as one of the men waiting outside the house on Muntri Street, barked an order, and galvanised, they all piled through the open lodging house door, the two big men leading the way.

Sure now that Dipi had identified the right place, Jorgensen waited to see what would happen next. Moments later, the gang emerged in boisterous triumph with a dishevelled white man sandwiched in their midst, gripped tight on each arm by the two big cotton-capped bruisers. They hustled him back up Love Lane, with the leader to the fore, and out onto the hurry-scurry of Chulia Street.

Jorgensen delayed for a few moments, then followed, twenty paces behind. The gang marched the man through the crowds approaching Chulia Street's night market stalls. An electric trolleybus whirred and clanked into view, heading inland from the quayside, bisecting the market stalls, the mass parting to make way. Nobody paid the gang any attention, not even the off-duty British soldiers and sailors in front of the Hong Kong Bar. The white man in the gang's midst remained docile, his head down, his feet struggling to keep pace with his abductors.

Threading his way through the throng, Jorgensen saw the group ahead turn south into Rope Walk. Away from Chulia Street's crowds, he dropped back a few more paces in case they checked behind – though such was their blithe confidence they did not bother about such demonstrations of caution. They crossed Campbell Street, into the continuation of Rope Walk and, within thirty yards, disappeared into a building on the left. Like most of George Town's side streets, Rope Walk was lined with shophouses, but there any comparison to the relative quiet of Muntri Street or Love Lane ended. By day, Rope Walk was alive with the clamour of workshops and traders. By night, its shophouses were shuttering, and the din, almost as loud as during the day, came instead from barkers from the many brothels, loudly exhorting passers-by to favour their house.

Jorgensen stopped outside the building. A modest sign, written in both English and in Chinese characters, hung from its projecting first floor – Lam Copra Export Company. Inside a brightly lit office on the ground floor, half-screened by blinds, were two men at desks, one using an abacus, the other bent over a ledger. There was no sign of the gang, or of the white man they had dragged from Love Lane.

Shrugging off a particularly persistent barker, Jorgensen retraced his steps all the way back to the lodging house on Love Lane. Sitting on the walkway outside it, cross-legged on the chipped tiles, and part-illuminated by shards of light creeping through shutter slats in the ground floor window, were three male Indians, eating rice and curry from folded banana leaves. The youngest of them was the skinny boy who had delivered the message to the E&O.

"I saw you at the E&O," Jorgensen said, startling the group with his sudden appearance out of the gloom. He pointed at the boy with his thumb. To use a forefinger to point was considered offensive across much of Asia. The boy, like his companions, stared at this stranger in undisguised apprehension.

"I have a message for the Tuan who sent you," Jorgensen added.

The three exchanged uncertain glances. As it was unclear whether they had understood him or were just acting dumb, Jorgensen joined them on the walkway, smiling to reassure the group he was no threat. "Tuan," he said, indicating the house.

"Not here," said the boy, replying in English.

Jorgensen moved towards the door. "Show me his room."

The boy rose, submissive in the face of the white man, and led Jorgensen through the open door into a long corridor, passing doors on each side to narrow lodgers' rooms before reaching a staircase. At its foot, Jorgensen glanced through an opening into the shared kitchen at the rear of the building. Under a bare electric bulb, a tiny Indian couple were sitting at a small table and eating the same curry and rice as the group on the walkway.

"Bringing a message for the Tuan," he called out to them.

Jorgensen followed the boy up the staircase, where at the top he was directed to an open door at the rear end of another long corridor. The boy stood to one side to allow Jorgensen to pass. Framed in the doorway, Jorgensen paused, his nostrils picking up the scent of opium amid the fustiness of stale sweat and grime.

The far end of the room was a chaotic mess. Clothes spilled out of a low cupboard and on the bed a half-eaten meal had slid off a tin plate onto rumpled stained bedsheets. But the ordered stacks of paper on a desk just inside the door and the neatly arranged bookshelves lining both sides of the room told a different story.

"Who lives here?" Jorgensen turned to ask the boy.

"Tuan."

"Which Tuan?"

"Tuan Davies."

Jorgensen took a step into the room to stand over the desk. A black American made Underwood typewriter sat in the middle, out of which curled a sheet of paper. He removed a half-pound weight holding a stack of papers down and lifted a handful free – they were all letters, some typewritten, others handwritten in uncluttered script. He flicked through them – letters to the municipal council, the police court, the water authority, the health and sanitation board, landlords and banks. The names at the foot of the letters were all different, and from several nationalities. A smaller neighbouring stack of yellowing calling cards proclaimed FL Davies to be in the business of correspondence and translation.

A cheap card bound notebook on the desk proved to be full of carefully handwritten notes. Against each entry that matched a completed letter, Davies had cross-referenced the date and address of the recipient. Though, unsurprisingly, there was no record of two typed letters sent to Arthur Cromford at the E&O.

"Did you see the men come for Tuan Davies?" he asked the boy, who stood silently in the doorway behind him.

The boy nodded but kept his eyes fixed on the floor, not daring to catch Jorgensen's eye.

"They'll return him soon," said Jorgensen. "When they leave, you must tell Tuan Davies that Jorgensen from the E&O was here. But only tell him when he's alone. Do you understand?"

"Yes, Tuan."

"Good." Jorgensen fished a twenty-cent coin out of a pocket and offered it to the boy who, dumbstruck at its value, was at first too cowed to accept. Jorgensen tossed it up the air, and the boy snatched it with alacrity.

Back out in the darkness of Love Lane, Jorgensen checked the luminescent dials on his wristwatch. It was eleven-fifteen. By his estimation, the gang who had frog-marched Davies off to Rope Walk were likely to return at any minute.

He paused for a moment, lost in thought, while the boy rejoined his companions on the walkway. If his hunch was correct, the blackmailers' original plan was to rob Cromford at the meeting point. It had failed, and, from the way they treated Davies, it seemed they suspected him of involvement in that failure. But if they wanted to try again, as he was sure they would, the gang would need Davies to write another letter to Cromford.

Jorgensen headed north, walking up Love Lane in the direction of the junction with Farquhar Street. Once he was out of sight of the lodging house, he ducked onto the covered walkway on the left, finding another house in darkness where he could blend into the shadows. If he was right in his assumptions, all he needed to do was lie in wait and intercept the new letter en-route to the E&O.

***

Thirty minutes passed before the boy from the lodging house appeared, trotting down the lane clutching a new envelope.

"I'll take that," said Jorgensen, stepping into the street. Unfazed at Jorgensen's sudden appearance, as if he had been expecting it, the boy meekly handed over the letter.

"Let's see what it says, shall we?" said Jorgensen.

With a gesture to the boy to follow him, he walked to the very end of Love Lane, where the electric streetlamps of Farquhar Street were among the few still switched on at this late hour.

*Dear Mr Cromford,*

*Perhaps you do not care whether your diary is published. You should know that several bidders are expressing interest and will publish in London.*

*Because of your reckless behaviour, the price for the return of the diary is now fifteen thousand Straits Dollars. I shall write tomorrow with a new handover location.*

*Next time, please do not attempt any tricks.*

Jorgensen pocketed the letter. "What's your name?" he asked the boy.

"Suri."

"Well Suri, I think it's time to go back and talk to Tuan Davies," he said.

"Cannot," said the boy.

"Why not? Isn't he alone?"

Suri shook his head. "Not that. He will be angry."

"Let's not worry about that."

# Fourteen

Jorgensen and Suri found Davies on the bed, propped up on two filthy pillows with a bottle of scotch and a half-empty glass clasped in his hands.

"Who the hell are you?" he said as Jorgensen walked through the door. His eyes were blood-red holes in a pallid face and his voice was thickening with drink. "What have you done, boy?" he shouted on seeing Suri standing behind Jorgensen. He staggered to his feet, the glass tipping its contents onto the bedsheet, and leant forward unsteadily against the edge of the desk.

"I'm Jorgensen, from the E&O." He let the words sink in, seeing the effect of hearing the hotel's name in Davies's eyes. "You go now," he said, turning to Suri. "I'll speak to Tuan Davies alone."

Caught between Davies's wrath and the steel in Jorgensen's eyes, the boy needed no second bidding, retreating hurriedly downstairs to the kitchen.

Jorgensen took the letter from his pocket. "I saved time by intercepting your boy. It's not his fault so don't blame him. Why don't you sit here at your desk? Then we can talk."

Davies glared at Jorgensen for a moment or two, then fell sideways onto the chair with a resigned slump.

"I read your card," said Jorgensen. "Translation and correspondence."

"What of it?" said Davies, a sudden passion easing his speech. "I'm good at it and respected. I don't suppose you've any notion of the help the ordinary people here need with the government. They can't all read and write and without someone like me on their side, they'd get nowhere."

"I get it," said Jorgensen. "You're a modern-day Samaritan."

"What would you know?" Davies shot Jorgensen a challenging look. "In your ivory tower in your precious hotel. You don't give a shit for the rest of society."

"Have a cigarette," said Jorgensen. He flicked open his case. With shaking hands, Davies reached out and fumbled a cigarette free. Jorgensen struck a match and Davies took a deep drag.

"Thanks," he said, bringing the cigarette back to his lips for a second long draw of its smoke. "Now you know about the letter, what are you going to do? Hand me over to the police?"

"Look Davies, I'll give it to you straight. I saw the gang come in here and haul you off, and I followed you to Rope Walk. My guess is they've got something on you. You're an opium addict. Maybe you owe them money and now you're forced into doing their bidding. Am I close?"

Davies grimaced and hung his head. Too ashamed to reply.

"Blackmail is a serious crime, and the punishment is severe," said Jorgensen. "But I guess you realise that."

"What do you want? Why are you torturing me like this?"

"I think I can help you – if you help me in return. Tell me everything you know about whoever runs things at Lam Copra Export Company, and I won't go to the police."

"They'll kill me if I talk. You don't know what they're capable of."

Jorgensen felt pity for the devastated shell of a man slumped on the chair. He knew the toll taken by opium addiction, and how decency and self-respect were soon lost, even in people of formerly good character. "They led me to their address – not you," he said. "So, there's no need for them to know you've helped in any way. And they're going to get paid so won't have any reason to come looking for revenge."

"And you'll keep the police out of it?"

"Cromford is a guest of the hotel, and he wants to pay off the blackmailer. My job is to protect his interests, and that doesn't include bringing in the police." Jorgensen placed a hand on Davies's shoulder. "Look, Davies. This gang can't be trusted. They chose a rendezvous point where it would be easy for them to rob me of the cash without returning the diary, and I'm sure they'll try again. I want to be a step ahead of them next time, so let's start with what they have on you."

"Oh God," said Davies, burying his head in his hands. "You're right about how I got caught up in this. I owe money to George Lam."

"I can smell the opium on your clothes. Is that why you're in debt to Lam?"

"I suppose you think that's pathetic."

"I know it's not easy. How much do you owe?"

"Three hundred dollars. I've been trying to repay it for months but I'm getting nowhere. He knows I'm a letter writer and I've written several on his behalf, but I can't get the debt down that way alone – it's not enough. That's why when this business came up, I felt I had no choice."

"Does George Lam own the opium den or is he a moneylender you borrowed from?"

"He owns both dens I visit."

"Where?"

"One is on Kimberley Street and the other on Rope Walk."

"Handy for his office," said Jorgensen. "What else is he into, besides his legitimate trading company and these opium dens?"

"He's always boasting about the money he makes off gamblers. Especially the *angmohs*. I don't know who he despises the most. The gamblers who lose or opium smokers like me."

"I look forward to meeting him. He sounds like a real gentleman."

Davies, who for most of the conversation had sat, chin sunk in his chest, looking down at the scuffed and scratched desk surface, suddenly raised his head and looked into Jorgensen's eyes. "He's a cruel, callous and dangerous bastard," he said. "I've seen what he can do to his enemies. He terrifies me."

"Was it you who came up with the scheme to steal the diary?"

Davies looked in horror at Jorgensen. "How could you think that? I know I've sunk low but I'd never…" He buried his head in his hands again, seeing in Jorgensen's eyes that his part in the blackmail was no better than originating the scheme.

"Who did?" asked Jorgensen.

"I don't know. It was a white man, that's all I can tell you. Lam enjoyed telling me it was an *angmoh*. And he told me what to look for in the diary. It was in some childish code that took an instant to untangle," Davies gave a bitter laugh. "Even for a confused mind like mine. Whoever told Lam about it knew there was a code."

"So, you know the secrets our guest wants to keep?"

"I do, but I don't care a jot about them. They're not as shameful as the things I've done." He gave a hollow laugh.

"Tell me more about George Lam and his gang. Was it Lam who came to fetch you?"

"It was Kei Hin. He's another malevolent sadist." Davies ran a hand across his stomach and winced. "He beat me earlier. He didn't have to. I'd have gone with them without protest."

"Any others in the gang I should watch out for?"

"I don't know, I just don't know. It's all so bewildering."

"Nearly done, now, Davies. How many of them did you see at the office?"

Tears welled up in the corner of Davies's eyes and he rubbed them roughly with the back of his hand. "Five or six I suppose. And then the clerks on the ground floor. What do you intend to do?"

"Cromford wants to pay up so that's what I'll do. And now I know the lay of the land I should avoid any more ambushes. In the meantime, you'd better lock your door. I promise you, you'll come to no harm."

# Fifteen

At night, the beating heart of George Town shifted inland from the wharf-side to the geometric grid of streets marking the centre of the Chinese quarter. Even after midnight, the brothel barkers on Rope Walk were still at full cry hustling for business from the steady stream of customers not yet staunched by a need to sleep.

Having first detoured back to the E&O to retrieve the attaché case, Jorgensen now stood outside the door to the Lam Copra Export Company, feeling a restless prickle in his chest and arms. He was familiar enough with the sensations. They were the same he had experienced years earlier in the trenches – in those last few minutes before the whistle sounded for an attack. Chest drumming, arms tingling, senses heightened. He had felt the very essence of life, at the very moment it might end.

Was he rushing into action now to try and recapture that visceral feeling? He shook his head clear – it was not the time for sudden bouts of introspection.

After checking for the reassuring ridges of the pistol grip under his jacket, he pushed open the unlocked door and strode into the now darkened office – where the desks lay abandoned for the night and dust hoods covered the typewriters. A closed connecting door led deeper into the building, from where he heard muffled voices. He opened it softly and moved through into the hallway beyond, towards the foot of a staircase. The voices were coming from above, a little indistinct, as if from behind another closed door off the landing. He mounted the staircase, flinching at the creak of the worn wooden treads. Halfway up, he froze, as a door on the landing opened, and two figures were framed against the light – the two cotton-capped thugs last seen hauling Davies up the street. At the head of the staircase, they halted in shock on seeing Jorgensen below them.

"Hey, cannot!" the first cotton-cap exclaimed.

"I'm here to see Mr Lam," said Jorgensen, continuing upwards.

"You must go back. Now." The first cotton-cap's threatening tone was bolstered by the jut of his chin and the squaring of hefty shoulders.

"Tell Mr Lam I'm from the E&O. He'll want to see me." Jorgensen lifted the attaché case. "He's expecting this."

"Who is out there?" called a voice from inside the lit room. A voice used to command.

The second cotton-cap on the landing hurried back to explain, returning seconds later to the head of the stairs, from where he beckoned Jorgensen. "Come."

The first cotton-cap blocking the way stepped aside, though his hostile glare stayed fixed on Jorgensen as he made his way onto the wooden landing floor and through the open doorway.

It was the boss's office, overlooking Rope Walk, and furnished with mission-style wooden chairs scattered around a table by the window, and facing the doorway an ostentatious leather-topped desk. Seated behind it, and shrouded in a haze of cigarette smoke, was a balding middle-aged man whose patterned silk shirt stretched taut over a bulging stomach. Through beady eyes in a round face, he coolly surveyed Jorgensen, an arrogant curl to his full lips.

Jorgensen halted a yard into the room, facing the desk, while the two burly cotton-capped men brushed past him to take up positions flanking their boss.

Slouched on one of the mission chairs was a fourth figure, a younger man Jorgensen recognised as the earlier expedition's leader, and assumed must be Kei Hin. Darker skinned than his boss, he sported a thin moustache, in the style of a Hollywood film star, that he no doubt imagined complemented his sharp cheekbones. He shot Jorgensen a scornful sideways glance before resuming the careful filing of his fingernails.

"You must be Lam," said Jorgensen to the man behind the desk.

"And you must be lost, eh?" Lam laughed at his own wisecrack, turning to the slouching man to check he had understood the joke.

"I'm Jorgensen from the E&O."

"What are you? Bag carrier for the boss?"

"I'm here for Mr Cromford."

From the mission chairs, Kei Hin called out to Jorgensen. "You bring the money?"

Jorgensen lifted the attaché case. "It's half the amount you originally demanded. You'll get the rest once I've returned the diary to its owner."

"That is not the agreement," said Lam.

"The terms changed once you set your ambush for Cromford. I saw your men hiding along Muntri Street. You intended to rob him and keep the diary. These are the new terms."

Jorgensen wished he felt as confident as he sounded. It was four to one in the confines of the room, and there was every chance that more of Lam's men might spring from elsewhere in the building. All that he had on his side, apart from the pistol under his jacket, was his promise of the additional money to come and the hope they would view him as European, with the protection that status often gave – even from Penang's gangsters.

Lam signalled to the younger man. "Take the case."

"The diary first," said Jorgensen, and in one swift movement slipped the pistol from its holster and pointed it at Kei Hin, stopping him dead in his tracks. "Those are my terms."

The bodyguards either side of the desk twitched and moved forward a step but stopped at a sharp command from Lam.

"You don't trust me, hotel man?"

"Not for a moment. Tell your men to sit down over there with Ronald Colman, and we'll talk business."

It took Lam to spit out another command before the two cotton-caps and a sullen Kei Hin retreated to the table by the window. From the edges of their chairs, as if poised to leap up at any moment, they glared at Jorgensen with undisguised loathing.

Jorgensen turned to level the pistol at Lam and backed up a pace to the open door. He had noticed when entering that the key was still in the lock.

"What do you do for the E&O, hotel man?" asked Lam, his eyes flicking from Jorgensen to the gun and across to his henchmen in a manner that belied his newly placatory tone.

"I help look after the guests. Let's get on with it. Where's the diary?"

"Here in the drawer," said Lam.

"Take it out slowly and don't be tempted to try anything," said Jorgensen, watching Kei Hin and the bodyguards out of the corner of his eye. If Lam concealed a weapon in his desk, and they knew it, this might be when they rushed him.

But all Lam brought out was the diary, which he held up for Jorgensen to view. It matched Cromford's description, a pocket-sized book with a gold monogram on a navy-blue cover. Jorgensen placed the attaché case on the floor, swapped the gun to his left hand, advanced to the desk to take the diary from Lam's outstretched hand, then backed up again all the way to the door, until he felt its handle digging into his side. He glanced down at the diary, the gold monogram on the top corner of the cover read AGC. He flipped it open. The Byron quotation, written in a flowing hand, was on the inside cover, just as Cromford had described.

"Do you know, Mr Hotel Man, I made a big mistake," said Lam. "This was worth more than ten thousand dollars. Why do you protect a man like this?"

"He's a guest at the E&O."

"Yet he is not honourable." Lam sounded almost indignant.

Jorgensen, keeping an ear cocked for the sounds of anybody mounting the stairs behind him, felt his patience wearing thin.

"That's rich coming from a blackmailer."

Lam chuckled. "It's trade, Mr Jorgensen. Trade, pure and simple, and everything has a price."

Jorgensen slipped the diary into an inside jacket breast pocket, then switching the same hand to behind his back, deftly palmed the key from the door lock. "I'll return tomorrow with the rest of the money."

"How did you find me?" Lam asked.

"I followed your hot-tempered man," Jorgensen nodded towards Kei Hin. "He led me straight here."

From somewhere downstairs, Jorgensen heard a commotion, footsteps on the tiles, muttering, and then a loud thump. The sudden alertness in their eyes showed that Lam and Kei Hin had heard it too. He had to move fast. He shoved the case with his foot, skidding it across the floorboards and under the desk. Lam bent forward to retrieve it, his head dipping below the desktop. With the gun's barrel swivelled to point at Lam's gang, Jorgensen stepped backwards through the door, swinging it shut behind him. Desperate not to fumble, he inserted the key at the first attempt and the lock clicked into place, just as the door handle was twisted from the inside.

Jorgensen ran down the stairs. Behind him, fists banged at the door amid frustrated yells. At the foot of the staircase, he turned the corner, and in the gloom almost tripped over a prone body on the corridor floor. Ahead of him, in the office and silhouetted against the building's front windows, stood a lumpy figure with two odd-shaped heads.

"Come quick," said a head. As Jorgensen neared, he saw that the strange shape was made up of two men, the one in front wearing a straw hat and gripped in position by a metal jemmy held tight against his throat by the taller man behind.

"We go now," said the taller man.

It was Ah Cheng, Morley's valet, who was holding the jemmy. He released his grip, and, with a violent shove, sent straw-hat sprawling across the office floor. Jorgensen was first through the front door, across the walkway and onto Rope Walk, the pistol slipped back into its holster. Ah Cheng followed, a pace behind, the jemmy held loosely at his side. On the street, it was at last quietening down, with fewer men still milling about, and the barkers' shouts were more muted. Even brothel keepers and their customers needed a few hours' sleep.

At the crossroads with Campbell Street, Jorgensen turned to see if anybody was following. Straw-hat had appeared on the walkway outside the building and was watching them.

"This way," said Jorgensen, crossing Campbell Street and continuing along Rope Walk – the most direct route back to the E&O. They half-ran, half-walked up the street, turning occasionally to check on pursuers. If he could, Jorgensen would have run all the way, but he knew that his leg, in which shards of shrapnel still remained, would not allow him to sustain the pace.

At the next junction with Chulia Street, they looked back again, this time seeing four men in pursuit. Jorgensen paused, weighing up the options. The fastest route back to the E&O was down Love Lane, past Davies's lodging house, but the gang would catch them somewhere along its secluded and dark length. Unless, that is, he handed the diary to Ah Cheng and entrusted him to sprint back to the hotel ahead of any pursuers. Or should they stand and fight? Lam was sending the gang to take back the diary by force, but they had seen his pistol and he had not missed how nervous it made them. In Penang, scores were settled with knives and clubs, not guns. Jorgensen hoped that confronted with it again, their hearts would not be in the fight.

On Chulia Street, the trolleybuses had ceased running and the night market stalls were long gone. All that was left in their wake was the scratching of rats and dogs among discarded meat bones, and on the walkways more of those occasional huddled shapes of the homeless bedded down for the night. But light still shone out of one building – the Hong Kong Bar.

"Follow me," he said to Ah Cheng.

In the Hong Kong Bar – a long, narrow converted shophouse, a Chinese waiter stacking chairs onto tables scowled at Jorgensen's entrance, while at the bar, a small knot of off-duty British soldiers were attempting to wheedle the barman into refilling their glasses one last time.

"Stay here by the door and keep an eye out," said Jorgensen to Ah Cheng. He walked past the disgruntled waiter. One of the soldiers, two stripes on his uniform denoting the rank of corporal, noticed his approach and nudged his companions before making a half-hearted attempt to stand up straight.

"Let me get you fellows a round," said Jorgensen.

The barman eyed him in helpless resignation. "We're closing, Major Mac."

"One more drink, Yeoh," said Jorgensen. "Then I'm sure these fellows will go home."

Yeoh sighed heavily. "For you Major Mac, can."

"Major, is it?" slurred a burly red-headed man with three stripes on his arm. "Officer present," he called out suddenly, alarming his drinking companions. "Look to it lads."

"No longer a serving officer, sergeant," said Jorgensen. "What are you all having?"

"Bottles of Tiger all round, eh?" said the sergeant. "Thanks to the major. Once a soldier, always a soldier. Isn't that right sir?" He leant forward and placed a large hand on Jorgensen's shoulder as the two young privates making up the rest of the group, bemused by Jorgensen's sudden appearance, tried to follow what was happening.

"Which regiment were you with Major?" the sergeant asked.

"26th New Brunswick's."

On the counter, five opened bottles of chilled beer appeared, one finding its way into Jorgensen's hand. He tipped it back, savouring the cold hit at the back of his throat. His first beer for almost two years, but now was not a time for lemon water.

"A Canuck?" asked the corporal.

"Ferocious fighters – the Canucks," said the sergeant. "You were in the worst of it."

"It was a lifetime ago," said Jorgensen.

"But we don't forget, do we, sir?" said the sergeant. "These young lads here don't know the half of it. Think it's all square-bashing and calming the natives. Here's to your health, Major."

All took long swigs except for one private, whose eyes were glassy and unfocused, and who looked at his fresh bottle as if wondering what he was expected to do with it.

"How about you fellows?" said Jorgensen. "What's your regiment?"

"First Battalion, Royal Warwicks," said the sergeant, sticking out his chest and standing at attention, or as close to it as he could manage.

"Royal Warwicks. You were at Vimy," said Jorgensen.

"The regiment was, Major, although I was beating off the flies in Mesopotamia. But we left a lot of our fellows behind at Vimy. I messed with a good few of them."

"Here's to the fallen," said Jorgensen, raising his glass.

Over by the door, Ah Cheng was waving to catch Jorgensen's eye. Lam's men had followed them and were now grouped in a huddle across the street from the bar.

The corporal piped up. "What's up with him?" he said, pointing to Ah Cheng. "Is he with you?"

This was the opportunity Jorgensen had banked on. "He is. There's a gang of bushwhackers outside looking to rob us. I came in hoping to throw them off, but I guess they've worked out we're inside."

"Bloody villains," said the sergeant and spat on the tiled floor. "Let us at the bastards and we'll send them on their way, Major."

By the counter, the private who had been turning steadily paler, slumped against the bar, prevented from falling only by his mate grabbing his arm.

"Steady on young 'un," said the sergeant lurching forward to help haul the youngster back upright.

"Tell you what, Sergeant," said Jorgensen. "You're not all at fighting strength and I think there's a better way you can help. Do you know the E&O Hotel?"

"I do," the corporal said eagerly, "it's that grand place overlooking the sea. You know, sarge. Where the officers have their do's."

"I work at the E&O," said Jorgensen. "If you fellows could escort me and my man back to the hotel in safety, I'll see you get a ride in the hotel's motor car back to your barracks. I don't expect the gang outside will try again if they see I'm with British soldiers."

"What make of motor car is it, Major?" asked the corporal.

"There's a Morris, a Standard or a Buick."

"Pick the Buick, sarge," said the corporal.

"You're on then, Major," said the sergeant. "And I'd like to see them villains try anything with the Warwicks."

Jorgensen turned to the barman. "Yeoh, here's five dollars for these gentlemen when they're next off duty. You won't forget them now, will you?"

Yeoh nodded and smiled wryly. "No, Major Mac. I cannot forget them."

"Right lads," said the sergeant. "Escort duty, attention."

What followed was far from straight off the parade ground, given that one private needed supporting by a second, but they rolled onto the street as one loose body, Jorgensen in their midst and Ah Cheng and his jemmy at the rear.

"To your right, Sergeant," said Jorgensen. In the faint light from the open door of the Hong Kong Bar, he saw the gang's faces. In front, Kei Hin glowered, but made no move. They had measured the change in the odds, and, when Jorgensen reached the corner of Love Lane, and looked back, he saw they had melted away into the night.

With frequent halts for the soldiers to urinate in an alley or for the drunk private to vomit, the journey to the E&O was long and tortuous. A few paces behind, Ah Cheng watched with growing bemusement.

"Now that's a handy weapon," said the sergeant, dropping back and pointing at the jemmy. "I bet you've bashed a few heads with that."

"One only tonight," replied Ah Cheng, receiving a heavy clap on the shoulder in return.

At the E&O, Maniv, the night doorman, had heard the men's rowdy approach over the course of several minutes, and was mightily relieved, if a little baffled, to see the familiar figure of Jorgensen at the group's head. He helped herd the soldiers round to the stables, away from the guest rooms, and sent a night porter in to wake Abdul.

Bewildered at seeing the four British soldiers outside the entrance to his workshop, Abdul turned beseechingly to Jorgensen. "Major Mac, what is happening?"

"Is this the Buick?" the corporal asked, stepping through the open door to run a hand along the car's long, polished bonnet. "Beautiful machine, isn't it? Do you drive it mate?" he asked Abdul enviously.

"Why don't you climb aboard Corporal," said Jorgensen. Turning to Abdul he added. "These fellows helped me out of a jam. I promised them a lift back to the barracks – in the Buick."

"Is this to do with the robbery?" Abdul asked.

"In a way."

"I will do it."

After pushing the two stumbling privates up into the Buick's rear seat, the sergeant stood to attention, and, with a conspiratorial grin, saluted Jorgensen "It's a grand place this," he said, gesturing towards the hotel buildings. "Grand indeed."

The Buick's engine sparked into life and its deep growl shattered the stillness of the night. Abdul nosed it out of the open stables' door and through the gate onto Farquhar Street. Jorgensen gave a farewell wave to the soldiers, then turned to Ah Cheng.

"I owe you my thanks," he said. He looked down at the jemmy, still held loosely at Ah Cheng's side. "How come you've got that?"

"I took it from there," he said, indicating the workshop in the stables.

On the walk back from the Hong Kong Bar, Jorgensen had looked back several times at Ah Cheng, pondering the many questions he wanted to ask.

"Why did you help me?" he asked now.

"Honour," said Ah Cheng. "My masters were robbed."

# Sixteen

Early the following morning, Jorgensen walked across the seafront lawn at the E&O to the sea wall, where he lit a cigarette and watched as the sun began its slow ascent over the Kedah hills on the mainland. While he smoked, a handful of guests loomed up out of the dark on their early morning constitutionals. A few he recognised; rubber planters and district officers for whom the habits of many years in the tropics proved difficult to shake off while on leave. Rise early to get the bulk of the day's work done before lunch and earn a deserved break from the sweltering afternoon heat. Among the pre-breakfast strollers was, after Hilton Morley, the most eminent current guest of the hotel – Maurice Hill, the British Adviser to the Sultan of Kedah State. Already dressed as if for an audience with the Sultan, the Adviser wore pristine white ducks and his wife a new dress, shawl and hat, no doubt bought from Whiteaway Laidlaw during their stay in George Town.

"Good morning, sir," said Jorgensen as they approached.

"Hello Jorgensen," the Adviser replied, and looking across the narrow strand of beach added, "And a fine morning it is too. I believe you've met Mrs Hill before."

Jorgensen inclined his head in the briefest of bows, though obvious enough to earn the gratification of the Adviser's wife. "How was your dinner with Mr Morley last night?" he asked her.

"It was perfectly delightful, thank you Mr Jorgensen," replied Mrs Hill. "He's a most fascinating man. And charmingly, both he and Mr Cromford have accepted our invitation to join us at the residence. I rather believe that Mr Morley is enthralled at the prospect of an introduction to the Sultan."

"When do you travel?"

"They've sent word they can go up with us today. We're taking the railway ferry across to Butterworth this afternoon and then the train up to Alor Star. Mr Morley is looking upon it as an adventure."

"I wish you a pleasant journey."

Moving on to the dining room Jorgensen sought the head waiter, a bull-necked, bullet-headed Chinese man known to all and sundry as Hindenburg due to his uncanny resemblance to the German chancellor.

"Will you be taking breakfast with us this morning, Mr Paul?" he asked Jorgensen.

"I'm afraid not."

Hindenburg winced, as if personally affronted by Jorgensen's rejection of the suggestion, though it must have come as no surprise, given that the same question and response occurred several times a week.

"Have you sent breakfast up to Mr Morley's suite yet?" Jorgensen asked.

"Yes, Mr Paul. They are leaving today so requested an earlier time."

"So, I hear."

On his way to the Victory Annexe, Jorgensen once again crossed the seafront lawn, where the low sun cast long shadows from the Angsana trees across the grass, and beneath their branches, men with besoms were sweeping up the overnight carpet of golden leaves.

This time, the door to Hilton Morley's suite was opened by a new servant Jorgensen did not recognise – a compact Chinese man of around forty with sinewy hands who took Jorgensen's hat and gestured for him to enter.

In the sitting room, half-eaten breakfast items: fruit, eggs, fried fish and coffee, were spread across three low tables.

Morley appeared at the door to his bedroom, and, abandoning his usual reserved manner, rushed to shake Jorgensen warmly by the hand. "Good God man, you succeeded. I can't begin to express how relieved I was when I read your note this morning."

From a breast pocket, Jorgensen produced the diary and handed it to Morley. "Here it is."

Hearing voices in the sitting room, Cromford wandered through from his bedroom.

"Arthur, Mr Jorgensen has brought your diary." Morley held it for Cromford to take, watching with a benevolent expression as the secretary's eyes opened wide in delight before he grabbed the diary and quickly skimmed through the pages.

"It's intact," said Jorgensen. "I checked."

"Without reading it, I hope?"

"Other than the inside cover to be sure it was your diary, no." Jorgensen held Cromford in a steady gaze, angered by the insinuation. "But others did," he added.

"What do you mean, others?"

"You can forget about them. Without the diary itself, whatever they think they know is worthless. My advice to you would be to either keep it locked away or destroy it."

"I hope you appreciate we didn't meet their demand to save our own reputations," said Cromford, chastened by the reproof in Jorgensen's tone. "Those were thoroughly trashed, long ago. We did it to protect others."

"Sure."

"I'm sorry, Jorgensen" said Cromford. "I'm putting on a poor show of thanking you. It's just I'm so awfully fucking relieved. We both are."

Cromford offered his hand and Jorgensen shook it, its manicured softness causing him to imagine the outcome if Cromford had gone to the rendezvous in Muntri Street instead of him.

"You should know it wasn't me alone who retrieved the diary," he said. "Ah Cheng, your valet, came to my aid."

Both Morley and Cromford looked at Jorgensen in astonishment.

"The valet?" said Morley. "That's rather awkward. All we knew was that he went missing last night without informing us. When he reappeared this morning, I informed him he would not be accompanying us on our trip."

"The damn fellow should have said something," said Cromford. "What were we supposed to believe? We thought he must have been mixed up in the robbery – as you yourself suggested."

"He put himself in danger to help you. Are you being fair to him?" Jorgensen asked.

"Perhaps not," Cromford replied. "But it can't be helped. As you'll have observed, we've taken on a replacement. He's already completed the packing and we'll be away shortly."

"If I may, Arthur," said Morley. He had seen the tightening of Jorgensen's mouth and the glint of anger in his eyes "Now that we know the circumstances, that changes things." He spoke in his most charming manner, as if smoothing over an accidental breach of etiquette. "Your Mr Broomes found us a new valet for the trip, and I suspect it's too late to change the arrangements now, but on our return, we'll do the decent thing and take Ah Cheng back. I don't suppose the hotel could put him up while we're gone?"

"I'm sure that'll be fine," Jorgensen replied, conscious of what he owed Ah Cheng. Though inwardly he was seething at the ease with which Morley and Cromford moved on from their plight of the previous day. No sooner had they heard the diary was retrieved, they were readily taking advantage of Maurice Hill's invitation. "I understand you're off to Kedah?" he said, resetting his face into a more amiable expression.

"Yes. The British Adviser invited us last night. As soon as we read your note, and realised we were free to go, we couldn't possibly refuse. I think I told you I was desirous to see the peninsula states."

The desire to puncture their new-found complacency was too hard for Jorgensen to resist. "You might wish you were taking Ah Cheng along after all," he said. "There may be fresh attempts to steal back that diary, in Alor Star maybe. These criminals have connections right across the peninsula."

Enjoying the look of alarm on their faces, Jorgensen left the suite, heading down the stairs of the Victory Annexe for the covered walkway to the main building.

# Seventeen

"Tell me everything, Jorgensen," said Arshak Sarkies, ushering the undermanager to a chair in his office. He was flushed with excitement from a successful telephone call held that morning with an investor from Singapore. The plans for the new east wing of the E&O were gathering pace and the investor's support was both timely and welcome.

"Sit, sit, Jorgensen, you must tell all." Sarkies could barely keep still long enough for Jorgensen to focus on him, such was his nervous energy. He moved to the upholstered leather chair behind his desk, but instead of sitting, walked instead to the window, and gazed out across the seafront lawn.

"I got the diary back last night," said Jorgensen, twisting in his chair to look around at Sarkies. "There was a little difficulty."

"A difficulty, you say. I realise you are fond of understatement, my dear Jorgensen, so I hesitate to imagine the circumstances."

"It was settled."

"And will you not vouchsafe how?"

Jorgensen shrugged.

Sarkies chuckled. "I suppose you think it is best I do not know the details, such as the Chinese boy who assisted you?"

Jorgensen smiled ruefully. He should have known the news of last night's return to the hotel would have already reached Sarkies' door. It probably arrived with Ping Pong's delivery of morning tea and a copy of the Straits Times.

"A young fellow, by the name of Ah Cheng. Mr Morley's valet," he said.

Sarkies walked to his chair and rested his hands on its back, facing Jorgensen across the desk. "Now this Ah Cheng. Would you say he is resourceful?"

"Yes."

"I am pleased we were able to provide Mr Morley with such a fine valet. Perhaps, when his employer returns to Europe, we will take Ah Cheng on. You need a resourceful chap to help you. I will appoint him as your driver."

"I doubt he can drive a motor car, Arshak. And I don't know if I trust him. I've not got to the bottom yet of how George Lam knew about the diary."

"He came to your aid, just as once you came to mine. Have you not forgotten?"

"His past is too much of a mystery."

"I think he is a fine fellow," said Arshak.

"Have you met him?"

"Earlier this morning. I have an instinct about him, Jorgensen. As I did about you."

# Eighteen

In the lobby of the E&O, Rowland and Winifred Burgon sat on rattan chairs close to the main doors, their eyes trained to the gateway to Farquhar Street beyond. They were both in travelling clothes, to withstand the anticipated dust and grime of hours on a ferry and then the train. Burgon, in a grey flannel suit and a panama hat with a grey band, held a briefcase on his lap, while Winifred, in a brown skirt suit with a cloche-shaped straw hat, clutched a large handbag and yellow parasol.

As Jorgensen strolled through the lobby, he spotted them and headed their way. Halfway there, he was surprised to see Winifred, who had happened to glance round in his direction, immediately turn away and urgently whisper something in her husband's ear.

There was a porter hovering nearby, guarding their luggage and with half an eye on the main doors. He bowed his head as Jorgensen approached.

"I guess you're leaving us," said Jorgensen to the Burgons.

Winifred looked up in feigned surprise on hearing Jorgensen's voice. "Ah, Mr Jorgensen. Good morning. I'm so pleased we've run into you as it saves the trouble of putting pen to paper. You see, we've received information that Leslie is on the mainland. And we're off now to the railway building to collect our tickets."

"That's good news. Where are you travelling to?"

Burgon drew a pocket diary from his jacket. "You'll have to forgive me if I pronounce the name incorrectly." He thumbed through the diary until alighting at the page he sought. "A district in Kedah state called Padang Terap. We're taking the train today up to Alor Star, and we'll journey onward from there tomorrow to..." he rechecked the diary page, "… a small town called Kuala Nerang."

"I know of it. Up near the border with Siam."

Winifred tipped her head to one side and favoured Jorgensen with a pensive expression. "As you can imagine, Mr Jorgensen, the news is beyond our most cherished hopes." She leant forwards and extended a hand to grasp her husband's. "I just hope we find Leslie healthy and prosperous. I've heard such tales of how debilitating life can be in the jungle."

"He'll be fine, my dear, you wait and see," said Burgon reassuringly, receiving a grateful smile in return.

"What's he doing in Padang Terap?" asked Jorgensen.

"We're not entirely sure," said Burgon. "He was seen at the club in Alor Star and known to be returning to this Kuala Nerang outpost. I'm told there are European-owned rubber plantations in the vicinity, so our assumption is he's an estate manager."

"That makes sense. Other than rubber planters, there are few Europeans that far north. How did you discover his location?"

"Through assiduous enquiry at the law firms," said Burgon. "And a healthy helping of good fortune."

"It helps that Rowland is such a well-respected solicitor," said Winifred. "It's opened so many doors for us."

"I guess you'll no longer be needing my help," said Jorgensen.

"That's why I intended to drop you a line," replied Burgon. "We have followed more than one false trail, and it remains possible that this journey shall again be fruitless, though we are optimistic. I know Winifred persuaded you to assist our endeavours and you were kind enough to agree. Therefore, I have arranged for our solicitors to provide you with a photograph of Leslie."

"I hope it's not needed, but I'll be glad to take a look at it. You'll have company on your journey. Other hotel guests are catching the same train – one being the British Adviser for Kedah, Maurice Hill. If you're stuck, he'll be able to point you towards the District Officer for Kuala Nerang."

"Thank you for telling us, Mr Jorgensen, though I don't expect it'll be necessary. Ah, this must be our motor taxi." Burgon turned to look through the glass doors as the porter received a signal from Vikat on the door. "Yes, well many thanks once again."

Burgon extended his hand and Jorgensen took it, before bowing his head to Winifred Burgon.

"Good luck," he said.

# Nineteen

Michael Lim, diligent as ever, was at his post in the anteroom between the hotel managers' offices, attending to yet another sheath of papers, when Jorgensen walked in. The assistant manager, Broomes, was visiting the still housebound Robinson at his home, and was not expected back until midday.

"Good morning, Mr Paul," said Michael, rising to greet Jorgensen with his usual elegant courtesy.

"Good morning, Michael. I must have a talk with you."

"A talk? How agreeable. Please take a seat."

Jorgensen lit a cigarette and settled back in the proffered chair, one of two reserved for visitors waiting to see Robinson or Broomes.

"Your father, Lim Yeok Sun is a member of the Lim Kongsi Association board, isn't he?" Jorgensen asked.

"You are correct. It has been his honour for many years to serve on the board."

The Lim Kongsi Association owned and managed the Lim Kongsi complex in George Town: the temple, the properties around it and a myriad of other economic interests. The board, of which Michael's father was one of several prominent local businessmen acting as members, represented Lim clan members in both Penang and on the mainland.

Jorgensen had learned that to better understand how Chinese civil and commercial life worked in Penang, you had to first understand the role of the many Kongsis. These various Kongsi associations, sometimes linked to specific clans, carried out many good works. They sponsored Chinese schools and provided charity to clan members fallen on hard times. Though little was ever straightforward in Penang, and association board members had many fingers in many pies, some of them stemming from the outlawed secret societies for which the Kongsis were the legal and respectable successors.

"I imagine your father enjoys considerable influence with clan members," he said.

"My father is held in high esteem."

"I've run into a little trouble with a fellow called Lam. That's a Lim clan name, isn't it?"

"Many Lam are clan members, though not all are welcome at the Kongsi. It is a Hokkien association. Your troublesome Mr Lam might be of Hakka or Teochew ancestry."

"This fellow runs a copra export company on Rope Walk. It might well be a legitimate business, but it's also a front for criminal activity."

"I do not believe I know of him."

"You may recall I withdrew a large sum of money yesterday from the Peninsular Bank," said Jorgensen.

"I witnessed its arrival at the hotel."

"That was a loan from Arshak Sarkies to a guest."

"I see."

"It was to pay off a blackmail attempt from Mr Lam, copra exporter of Rope Walk."

"Goodness me, Mr Paul," said Michael, after a pause. "You must have considered taking the matter to the police."

Jorgensen blew out a few rings of smoke and watched them drift across the room. "I volunteered to settle with Mr Lam on the guest's behalf and found him dangerous and unpredictable. His men twice attempted to rob me."

"That's quite extraordinary, Mr Paul."

"That it is, Michael."

"Why are you telling me all this?"

"I must go back to resolve outstanding matters with Mr Lam. To be frank – the sooner the better."

At that point Michael understood Jorgensen's intention. "You cannot be suggesting my father should involve himself in such an enterprise?"

"I'm hoping he might propose a course of action. Perhaps by asking one of your brothers to intervene."

"I cannot take such a matter to my father," Michael replied. "It is not my place."

Jorgensen rose from his chair. "You'd be doing the E&O a great favour. Blackmail's a dirty business. It doesn't reflect well on the hotel, on the Lim clan or on George Town. Your father might agree that it should be stamped on, hard."

"Very well, I will speak to him on the matter."

"Thanks Michael. I'll be around the hotel."

# Twenty

In the middle of the afternoon, Ah Cheng left the oppressive confines of the drivers' dormitory above the stables, to descend the short flight of wooden steps to the comparatively cooler workshop below.

Earlier that morning, when still employed by Hilton Morley, Ah Cheng had woken before sunrise, stirred by the coughs and splutters of servants along the length of the first-floor corridor of the Victory Annexe, as they gathered up their bedding mats to begin preparations for the day ahead. Only a few hours earlier, after the soldiers from the Hong Kong Bar were driven back to barracks by Abdul, Ah Cheng had picked his way past the sleeping bodies to find his own spot outside the door to Morley's suite.

He had no objection to the sleeping arrangements. As a valet – they were expected. A necessary duty if he was to fulfil his ambition of travelling overseas. An ambition first fostered when he served as a houseboy at the mansion of Choo Fat Yee. It was Min Yoo, Choo's head boy, who had suggested it. "You speak good English," he said to Ah Cheng. "Work as a valet to a rich white traveller – and you will see many places: Singapore, Batavia, Hong Kong, Manila, Shanghai."

Having himself once worked as a valet for European men, Min Yoo had impressed upon Ah Cheng the most important lesson – that his primary duty was to care for his employer, no matter what he thought of him.

So, Ah Cheng had ignored the gossip of the other servants in the hotel, vying to outdo each other with tales of the fussiness of white people, and their complaints if the water for the Shanghai Jar was too cool or too warm. Though that was not a problem in the Victory Annexe, where the private bathrooms featured an English long bath with hot and cold running water. Not for his master the need to stand in a Shanghai Jar and pour water over himself from a jug.

Ah Cheng had seen an English long bath once before, at the mansion of Choo Fat Yee, where Min Yoo had twisted the taps and steam rose from the gathering pool of water, and he had laughed out loud at the wonder of it.

"Must not be too hot," Min Yoo told him. "If your arm turns red when you sink it – water is too hot. Your new masters will blame you." Min Yoo fiddled with the taps until he was satisfied and instructed Ah Cheng to immerse his arm into the water. "*Angmohs* like to turn pink, not red as their hair. You see."

It was a lesson well learnt, and when he first ran a bath for his new employer at the E&O, he made sure an ashtray was at hand for cigarettes, and a dry space for the book Morley was reading. His master had reappeared half an hour later, nodding in satisfaction. "First class," he had said.

At the foot of the stables' staircase, Ah Cheng checked his thoughts. There was no point in dwelling on what might have been. He remained stuck in George Town, while the new valet accompanied Morley and Cromford on their journey to Kedah state. That Morley had promised that on their return, Ah Cheng would be restored to his role, was little consolation for missing his first opportunity to leave Penang, and nor was the straw mattress he had been temporarily given in the drivers' dormitory.

He wandered out through the main stable doors. Across the courtyard by the service gate, two men stood below the cloudlike fronds of a towering Casuarina tree: Jorgensen, with a canvas satchel slung over his shoulder, and Michael Lim, dark-suited, blinking in the brilliant sun and sporting a straw boater.

"Ah Cheng!" Jorgensen called, beckoning him over. "How is the dormitory?"

"Good. Thank you," Ah Cheng replied, though with little enthusiasm.

"Last night, you told me you helped me as a matter of honour."

Ah Cheng bowed his head in acknowledgment, while Jorgensen regarded him thoughtfully. Maybe now was a good opportunity to test Arshak's judgement of the valet's worth.

"Mr Lim and I are just going to visit that same office in Rope Walk," he said. "To conclude last night's unfinished business." As he spoke, he watched the change in the young man's demeanour – from discontent to sudden bright-eyed interest.

"You want my help?" Ah Cheng asked.

"That's what I was thinking."

***

A short while later, the hotel's Buick sedan, which, with Arshak Sarkies' agreement, Jorgensen had commandeered for his expedition, stood ready with five passengers on board.

Abdul insisted on driving, and while not entirely abreast of the expedition's purpose, he had gained some idea when Ah Cheng requested to borrow a jemmy. He responded by retreating into the workshop and returning with it, together with a large steel wrench, wrapped in a clean cloth, which he placed between him and Zamir on the front bench seat. With hands and face washed and his normal greasy overalls replaced by an E&O driver's uniform, he gunned the throaty six-cylinder engine to ease the Buick out of the stables' entrance.

Within a few short minutes they were in Rope Walk, and outside the office of the Lam Copra Export Company, where the clang of hammers from the street's many workshops rang loud in the narrow street.

In the back seat, Jorgensen turned to face Michael. "Are you ready?"

Michael blinked rapidly, his heart racing. The journey had been too brief to properly prepare himself. "Who should I thank most? You or my father?"

"You'll be dandy," said Jorgensen. He climbed out and walked round the bonnet, stepping over the drain and onto the five-foot way in front of the office.

"Zamir, you must stay and watch the motor car," said Abdul, lifting the cloth-wrapped wrench, and feeling its pleasing weight in his hand. "When we come out you will drive." Then, with Michael and Ah Cheng, he joined Jorgensen on the walkway.

Jorgensen led the way through the front door, pointedly ignored by the two clerks in the front office feigning absorption in their work. Behind them, Kei Hin, Lam's capricious lieutenant, sneered in contempt on spotting the weapons carried by Ah Cheng and Abdul,

"You are punctual," he said. "Follow me, please."

In single file they made their way to the upper floor, passing the same cotton-capped man guarding the head of the stairs whom Jorgensen had encountered the night before. The door to Lam's office was open. There, Kei Hin stepped aside, and with a mocking bow, waved Jorgensen and Michael through, but held out an arm to stop Ah Cheng and Abdul following. "You will wait here."

"The door stays open," Ah Cheng replied.

"Cousin, if you insist, it shall be done." Kei Hin replied, looking Ah Cheng up and down dismissively.

Inside the office, Lam, wearing another hand-stitched brightly coloured silk shirt, sat at his desk facing the door. Alongside him stood one of his bodyguards. This time, the second stayed on the landing with Ah Cheng and Abdul.

"You are welcome gentlemen," said Lam, gesturing expansively at the two chairs placed before the desk.

"We're fine standing," Jorgensen replied. "We won't be long."

"As you wish." Lam's beady eyes glittered as he took in the satchel. "Will you throw the money at me again, hotel man?"

"This is Lim Guan Chee," said Jorgensen, indicating Michael. "Son of Lim Yeok Sun. You will know of him."

Lam turned to look at Michael with interest. "It is an honour to receive the son of Lim Yeok Sun. I am George Lam Wu Fu, the proprietor of Lam Copra Export Company."

Michael took a deep breath, inclining his head in a small respectful bow. "I have a message from my father." His voice shaky but clear. "It is a simple one, which he hopes you will not misinterpret."

"Go on," said Lam, leaning forward intently.

"My father wishes you to know that Mr Jorgensen has his full support in the matter we are here to conclude. You may consider Mr Jorgensen as his representative."

Lam looked cagily from Michael to Jorgensen and back again. "That is his wish?"

"It is," replied Michael.

"Very well." Lam turned to Jorgensen. "Proceed." There was none of the anger in Lam's manner that Jorgensen had anticipated.

"Before we finish our business, Mr Lam," said Jorgensen. "Please tell me who put you on to the diary?"

Lam's laugh was disdainful. "You Europeans. You are all the same. You think you are better than us Chinese. It was an *angmoh*." With a smug relish he emphasised the Hokkien pejorative term for a white man. "But I believe you knew that already."

"Will you tell me who?"

"It is of no matter. Come," said Lam. He beckoned Jorgensen closer. "Show me the bag."

"One more thing before we conclude our business," said Jorgensen. "I saw how your men treated the letter writer. If he comes to any further harm at your hands, you will have me to answer to. Is that clear?"

"You are the representative of Lim Yeok Sun. Is this his wish?"

"It's mine alone – but I mean every word of it."

Lam pulled a face, pretending to be intimidated by Jorgensen's threat, before adopting an irritated expression, as if tired of these distractions, "I have no interest in the letter writer. Come, bring the bag."

Jorgensen approached the desk and opened the satchel, spreading the sides wide.

Lam's head snapped back. "It is empty."

"That's right," said Jorgensen.

"You promised to bring the money,"

"And last night, after I left you, you set your gang to steal the diary back," said Jorgensen. "That was the second time you tried a double-cross. And for that you forfeit the balance." He dropped the satchel onto Lam's desk. Behind him he heard a growl of anger from Kei Hin.

"Stop," barked Lam, and lifted a pudgy hand. "Wait. I am speaking with our visitors." He fixed Kei Hin with a glare. "You will sit."

Kei Hin stalked across to the mission chairs by the window, where he sat with a bristling reluctance, eyes blazing in rage.

"This decision is known and agreed by Lim Yeok Sun," said Jorgensen.

"That is so," added Michael. Faintly, but loud enough for Lam to register.

Lam turned towards Michael, forcing an ingratiating smile. "Some days the returns in business do not always match our hopes."

"That is true," Michael replied. "But I believe my father will be grateful for your understanding,"

Lam nodded, as if in recognition of the favour. "I am honoured to receive the son of Lim Yeok Sun."

With a touch on Michael's arm, Jorgensen encouraged him to step back from Lam's desk and retreat through the open door. Watching from the landing, Ah Cheng and Abdul let them pass, lingering for a few moments more to keep an eye on Lam's men inside the office. Satisfied there was to be no immediate violent reaction, they too descended the stairs,

They walked through the front office and out into the dazzling heat of the street, where Zamir stood ready. He opened the Buick's rear door on their approach. Jorgensen and Michael climbed in.

"You did well," Jorgensen said to Michael.

The secretary removed his spectacles and, with trembling fingers, wiped them with a cloth. "And you went there alone last night?"

“Not quite alone,” said Jorgensen, opening his jacket to show the pistol in its shoulder holster.

# Twenty-One

*The morning after the discovery of Davies's body*

Few of Jorgensen's acquaintance knew where he lived, and he preferred it that way. Most assumed he occupied rooms at the Eastern and Oriental Hotel, or in one of the nearby grace and favour bungalows, where the hotel's two English managers made their homes.

To discover that, instead, he owned a narrow shophouse in George Town, with Chinese and Indian families as neighbours, would have raised more than a few eyebrows among the E&O's patrons. The house was a third of the way down the short length of Datuk Koyah Road, named after a famous Malabari faith healer whose shrine stood nearby. Businesses operated in half of the street's shophouses, the rest, like Jorgensen's, were residential.

At six o'clock, an hour before sunrise, Jorgensen turned into the street, hearing from its far end, the familiar, raucous hooping call of a lone Asian Koel. There, from within the dense foliage of a Terap tree, and animated by the promise of daylight, it cried out for a mate, as it had done every morning for the last few weeks.

In one hand, Jorgensen held the handle of a tin tiffin pot, inside which nestled the breakfast he had picked up from a nearby roti canai hawker: two fluffy roti breads and a separate pot of spicy lentil dhal. In the other, he carried a flask of hot, sweet teh tarik.

He noticed the headlights first, from a car parked outside his house, then, as he grew nearer, he saw the welcoming committee on the walkway.

Alongside Inspector Batchelor, haughty in his peaked cap, was a Malay constable in a black *songkot* hat, and the two Chinese bakers from the next-door shophouse, drawn onto the walkway by the unexpected presence of the police car. Together, the group watched Jorgensen's casual progress down the street.

"Good morning, Inspector, I take it this isn't a social call," said Jorgensen as he stepped up onto the walkway.

"Where have you come from?" Batchelor asked, the hostility in his tone obvious to even the two non-English speaking bakers.

"Fetching breakfast," Jorgensen replied, lifting the tiffin pot as evidence.

"Now look here, Major," said Batchelor. There was a distinctive trace of a Lancashire accent in his speech, hard as he tried to disguise it. And more than the hint of a sneer when pronouncing the word 'Major.' "You weren't at home last night – so I want to know where you were."

"Why?"

"Just answer my question," Batchelor snapped.

"Not until I know why you're asking it."

"We've been searching for you since midnight, at which time we placed a constable at the end of your road. So, where were you?"

"You're still not telling me why you want to know."

"It's always this way with you, isn't it? Acting as if you're above the law. How about this then, since you're not going to cooperate; we'll take a trip to the detective station and see if we can knock that smug look off your face."

"I'm not going anywhere until after my breakfast," said Jorgensen. There was something about Inspector Batchelor that never failed to needle him.

Incensed, Batchelor stepped forward and knocked the tiffin pot from Jorgensen's hand, sending it skittering along the walkway. "I couldn't give a fuck about your breakfast," he barked. "Now get in the car."

"You'd better have a good reason for doing that," said Jorgensen, a cold fury running through his veins.

"How does murder sound to you?"

Jorgensen's anger vanished in a heartbeat. "Who was murdered?" he asked. It must be somebody he knew – the only possible explanation for Batchelor's questions. The faces of lovers, friends and colleagues flashed through his mind.

"We'll discuss all that at the detective station," said Batchelor. "Now, get in the car."

"It was Frank Davies, wasn't it?" That gallery of faces running through Jorgensen's mind had stopped suddenly and ominously at that of Davies's haunted features as he had watched Jorgensen leave his room at the lodging house.

With a grim but triumphant smile creeping across his face, Batchelor gestured to the constable to open the rear door of the car.

Jorgensen handed the flask of teh tarik to the two bakers, who had nervously retreated a few yards from the angry exchange. He stepped down from the walkway and into the waiting car. 'I'll see you come to no harm' he had promised Davies.

***

On the ground floor of the detective station on Penang Road, the door to the cell opened and Jorgensen looked up from the bare wooden bench, where he had sat in isolation for the best part of an hour, to see the bearded face of Sergeant Singh. Throughout that period, though he had not moved from the bench, he had felt a resurgence of the tingling across his chest and arms that he last experienced before retrieving the diary from George Lam's gang. A heightened sensitivity to events. A restlessness that he knew could only be quelled by action.

"Is that what I think it is?" he said.

"Teh tarik, sir," the sergeant replied. "From a hawker at Chowrasta Market." He handed a tin mug to Jorgensen who took several grateful sips of the hot, sweet liquid, while he watched patiently.

"You are to come with me," Sergeant Singh said, once Jorgensen finished the drink, then led the way down the narrow corridor outside the cell, unlocked the door at its end and escorted Jorgensen up a staircase to a small office on the first floor.

"Are you sticking to your story?" Batchelor asked, without looking up from a notebook on his desk.

"I've nothing more to add," Jorgensen replied. Through the open window behind Batchelor's head, he could see the first-floor windows of shophouses, shuttered against the bright morning sun. His watch was taken from him on arrival at the detective station, but from the angle of the shadows on the roofs opposite, he estimated it was now around nine o'clock.

"You could make it much easier for yourself, you know," said Batchelor, lifting his pink-tinged face to level an expressionless stare at Jorgensen.

"I'd like to ring the hotel. Tell them where I am."

"There'll be plenty of time for that. For now, though, I need to hear the truth. No more of your cock and bull nonsense. Now sit."

Sergeant Singh brought a plain wooden chair from the side of the room and placed it in front of Batchelor's desk for Jorgensen.

"Where were you between ten o'clock and midnight last night?" Batchelor asked.

"With a friend."

"As you keep saying. But as you won't tell us which friend, I'm finding it difficult to believe you."

"I can't help that."

"And so might a jury, Major Jorgensen. Have you considered that possibility?"

"I didn't kill Frank Davies, so it's irrelevant."

"Having no alibi is hardly irrelevant in a murder trial. Because that's where you're going to end up. In the dock in front of the Chief Justice. And I doubt all the times you've taken his hat at the E&O and shown him to the dining room are going to help you one tiny jot."

"Are you going to charge me?"

"All in good time, Major," Batchelor's grin was mocking. "Now, let's re-examine your story about a letter." He consulted his notebook. "You claim you went to see Davies about a letter he'd written to one of the hotel's guests."

"Yes."

"But you won't divulge which guest, or what the letter was about?"

"As I told you – the guest in question left yesterday afternoon. It's irrelevant."

"There's that word again. Irrelevant. I do so appreciate the way you're teaching me my fucking job." Batchelor's glare across the desk was full of contempt. "I'll tell you what's relevant. Your calling card was found in Davies's room. I know you visited him before he was killed. You have no alibi, and you knew about his murder before I told you. That makes you look as guilty as hell, and any jury would agree. But I'd like to know why you did it, Jorgensen. Did the poor bastard owe you money? Did he owe money to the E&O? I know you'll do anything for your precious fucking hotel."

"I didn't kill Frank Davies. You're wasting your time."

"Oh, that's right. You claim it was some mysterious Chinese moneylender Davies owed money to. A man whose name you can't remember. Unfortunately, that's not going to wash, Major Jorgensen. A Chinese moneylender." Batchelor almost spat with disgust. "It's not even original."

Jorgensen sat in silence, deliberating the wisdom of his decision not to reveal George Lam's name. He was far from convinced it was the right one, especially as he considered Lam, or more likely, his lieutenant, Kei Hin, as prime suspects in the killing of Frank Davies. Their blackmail scheme had only part delivered, and they were more than capable of taking revenge for its failure. But if he gave Lam's name to Batchelor, it risked exposing the scandal of which Hilton Morley and Arthur Cromford were so afraid, and his own part in paying over the blackmail demand.

Behind him the door opened. Sergeant Singh stepped aside to salute the newcomer and Jorgensen turned to see a second officer, Superintendent Bob Cave, in the same uniform as Batchelor – cap, khaki shirt, and short breeches, complete with engraved brass buttons and a black leather belt with the police force's badge prominent on the buckle. In one hand, Cave held a silver topped swagger stick, the end of which he tapped thoughtfully on his calf while surveying the scene that met his eyes.

Superintendent Cave was of medium height with a neat sandy moustache, a look that said much for his contempt of the prevailing fashion for clean-shaven faces. The moustache had first appeared after Cave's wartime promotion to Captain in the 2nd Glosters, and he was damned if it was coming off now.

"I've just had Inspector Mottram on the telephone from Carnavon Street," he said to Batchelor, ignoring the presence of Jorgensen between them. "He was wondering what to do with the witness statements taken by his sergeant."

"Sir?" Batchelor replied.

"They relate to the murder in Love Lane. Taken by Sergeant Datta at your request."

"Of course. I'll send over for them now."

Cave drew a pack of cigarettes from the breast pocket of his tunic and, ignoring Batchelor's sharp intake of breath, offered one and a light to Jorgensen, before taking and lighting his own. At the desk, Batchelor gritted his teeth and tried not to growl in annoyance.

Cave turned to address Singh. "Sergeant, please take Mr Jorgensen from the room. I wish to consult with the Inspector. Wait in the corridor outside until I call for you."

The sergeant saluted and escorted Jorgensen through the door.

"If I was you, Inspector," said Cave to Batchelor as soon as the door closed behind the sergeant. "I'd go over in person to the Carnavon Street station. According to Inspector Mottram, the residents of the lodging house have named a man who, only yesterday, threatened the victim's life. An Arab trader from Acheen Street by the name of Bin Hakim. All to do with a dispute over money for a letter the victim had written. I should imagine you'll want to bring him in for questioning."

"I'm already questioning a suspect, sir."

"Jorgensen?"

"He's being highly uncooperative and has no alibi for the time of the murder. He was not at home and refuses to say where he spent the night."

"I should imagine he thinks it's none of your business."

"This is a murder inquiry, sir," Batchelor protested.

"And you consider him a suspect?"

"He called on Davies over the weekend and refuses to explain why, beyond some hard to swallow nonsense about a letter written to one of the guests at the E&O – who, incidentally, Jorgensen refuses to name."

"According to Sergeant Datta, several other people called on the victim too," said Cave. "I want you to get over to Carnavon Street, collect those witness statements, and then get this Arab trader into custody in double time."

"But what about Jorgensen? His entire attitude is suspicious," said Batchelor, sensing that he was about to lose his catch. "He's up to something – something that's connected to the murder, I'm sure of it."

"I know you don't care for him, Inspector, but there are more obvious paths to follow. If this is indeed the murder of a white man by a native, then we need to bring the killer to justice, and quickly. Before the Resident Councillor walks in to ask what the hell we're playing at." Cave moved towards the door. "You'll have to let Jorgensen go, but let's have another word with him first."

He opened the door to call Singh and Jorgensen back into the office.

From behind the desk, Batchelor watched his superior in barely suppressed anger. Angriest of all with himself, for believing for even a moment that Superintendent Cave would not hesitate to favour an old friend.

"Can nobody vouch for you for last night?" Cave asked Jorgensen as he re-entered the office.

"It'd be awkward."

"I see," Cave said. "And you'd rather rot in our cells than reveal her name?"

"I hoped it wouldn't be for too long."

"Just what the hell were you doing at that lodging house?" Cave asked. "Even for you, Davies sounds a rum choice for an acquaintance."

"I called there about a letter Davies sent to a guest at the E&O."

"So the Inspector tells me. To whom was this letter sent?"

"I can't tell you, Superintendent," said Jorgensen, looking Cave straight in the eye. "It's a confidential matter relating to the hotel and unconnected to Davies's death. If I thought it was relevant, I'd tell you. Besides, the guest in question left the island yesterday morning."

"Leaving you to do the dirty work," interjected Batchelor.

"That's quite a jump, Inspector," said Cave smoothly, seeing the flash of anger in Jorgensen's eyes. "We both know that Jorgensen has sometimes overstepped the line in his mission to protect the E&O's guests – but his strangling someone to death on their behalf is perhaps unlikely."

"What about his refusal to name the guest?" Batchelor asked.

"On this point I rather sympathise with the Inspector," Cave said to Jorgensen. "It's up to the police to decide what's relevant – not anybody else. This is a murder case, not some bedroom carry on at the E&O that you need to hush up."

"Here I stay, then," said Jorgensen.

"That won't be necessary," said Cave. "For now, you can maintain your guest's confidentiality. We've more important matters to attend to. We received information about a man who threatened Frank Davies yesterday, and we intend to bring him in this morning. So, you're free to go. But understand this – if I discovered you were withholding vital information, I'd arrest you at the drop of a hat. I'd even take pleasure at doing so in the lobby of your cherished hotel. Luckily for you, however, we have our man and I've no wish to complicate the case."

"Who is it?" Jorgensen asked, unabashed by Cave's speech, assuming it was delivered to placate the clearly resentful Batchelor.

"It's a police matter, Jorgensen. Now bugger off before I change my mind."

# Twenty-Two

It was a ten-minute walk from the detective station to the E&O, but Jorgensen made it in half the time, trotting at a brisk rickshaw puller's pace, and arriving at the stable block with beads of sweat running down his neck.

Inside, under electric lights hanging from a wooden beam, he found Abdul and Ah Cheng looking under the bonnet of the Morris Bullnose.

"Something's come up," said Jorgensen. "I need Ah Cheng to come with me." He retreated through the door and across the yard to the shade of the Casuarina tree.

After a bemused exchange of glances with Abdul, Ah Cheng hurried after him.

"The police came to see me this morning," Jorgensen said when Ah Cheng caught up. "Tuan Davies, the man I asked you to call on yesterday evening – he's dead. The police say he was strangled."

"When?" asked Ah Cheng.

"Sometime between ten and twelve. What did you see when you went back to Love Lane last night?"

"As you asked me. I went in the evening."

"What time?"

"As it came dark. I did not see Tuan Davies, but the boy from the house brought in food for him from the night market."

"Food for Davies?"

"Yes. Roast duck noodles. The boy told me it was for the Tuan, so I let him eat and did not bother him."

"Did you see Kei Hin or any of Lam's men?"

Ah Cheng shook his head, then added "Do you think Kei Hin killed the Tuan?"

Jorgensen considered his reply for a moment. Throughout the walk back from the police station his thoughts had bounced about without settling on any one idea. He had been blaming himself for sending Ah Cheng to check on Davies the previous night when he should have gone instead. But what would he have done differently if there was no sign of any of Lam's men?

"I thought we'd frightened Lam's gang off," he said. "But I may have made a mistake in not paying up the entire blackmail demand." As he spoke, he knew his words rang hollow. That choice had led to a man's death. It was so much more than a mistake.

"What will you do?" Ah Cheng asked.

It was a good question. He felt pulled in different ways. Part of him was suffocated by guilt. That the blame for Davies's death lay with him and his longing for action. That in confronting George Lam, he had left Davies vulnerable to retribution. But at the same time, that thirst to act, the restlessness he felt in the police cell was impossible to ignore. He needed to do something.

"I'll start by talking to the boy, Suri. I must know whatever he and others at the lodging house told the police. Now, Ah Cheng. When I spoke to the police, I told them nothing of the diary. And you must do the same."

"Will the police question me?"

"Depends what Suri told them. If they do – don't mention the blackmail letter and the pay-off. You must say you called on Davies at my request – to check on his wellbeing."

"I understand."

Jorgensen studied Ah Cheng. The young man's brow was furrowed in concentration, as he in return contemplated Jorgensen's face – waiting to hear what was expected of him. Though Jorgensen's first instinct was to act alone, perhaps it was time to further test Arshak Sarkies conviction that Ah Cheng would prove a useful ally.

"I'd like you to go now to Love Lane. Come straight back as soon as the police leave."

Ah Cheng nodded and then took a deep breath. "Boss, I must tell you about the fat man."

"What fat man?"

"A fat white man with a thick moustache. Yesterday, I saw him watching the house from the walkway across the street."

A similar spot from where Jorgensen himself had watched Davies's lodging house. Who the hell else was doing the same thing, he wondered, and why?

"When the police have gone, show me the place."

# Twenty-Three

An hour later, Ah Cheng returned to the E&O, waiting to one side of the steps up to the main entrance, while a porter ran inside to fetch Jorgensen.

"Two policemen left the house," Ah Cheng said, as soon as Jorgensen joined him. "One white one and one Malay. One more waited by the motor car. All gone already."

"Did they take anybody with them when they left?"

"No."

"Okay, let's get going."

A brisk ten-minute walk brought them to the Chulia Street end of Love Lane, where Ah Cheng pointed to the same suspended rattan screen, across the street from the lodging house, behind which Jorgensen had hidden two days earlier. On the walkway behind it, Jorgensen's eye was caught by glints of light off a reflective material at his feet. Crouching down, he scooped up a small handful of tobacco ash studded with cigar stubs and ripped cigar bands, bright with gold-coloured Chinese characters. He sifted the ash through his fingers, leaving in the palm of his hand half a dozen inch long stubs and a similar number of the coloured bands.

"Cheroots," he said to Ah Cheng. "Compressed at the ends like they were squeezed into a holder."

"The fat man smoked these," said Ah Cheng. "I saw him."

Jorgensen scraped the toe of his shoe through the remaining pile of ash on the walkway. There were twice as many stubs still on the floor as in his hand. Several hours' worth. He picked out three of the bands from his open palm and let the rest float to the ground, together with the stubs, then brushed the ash free from his fingers and palms.

"Do you recognise these?" he asked Ah Cheng, showing him the bands.

"No boss. I do not smoke."

"Do they identify the maker?"

Ah Cheng picked a band from Jorgensen's hand and flattened it out on his own palm. "They are Hokkien characters," he said. "Te-Pat brand. Number Eight cheroots."

Jorgensen took the band back from Ah Cheng, pocketing it with the two others. "If they're Hokkien, then there's a good chance they're made here in Penang."

They stepped off the walkway and crossed Love Lane to the lodging house, where Jorgensen walked through the open door into the gloomy central corridor, Ah Cheng following. At its far end, three figures in the kitchen huddled together in murmured discussion. By the time he reached them they had heard his approach and fallen into silence. Three wary pairs of eyes turned towards him: Suri and the couple Jorgensen assumed were the boy's mother and father.

The kitchen was typical of many older shophouses. In its centre, a square, granite-bottomed sink stood below an airwell open to the roof and, at the rear, a doorless opening led to a tiny walled-in courtyard. On a charcoal burner, a curry bubbled away in a blackened steel pot, filling the space with the pungent aromas of garlic, shrimp paste and spices.

"Good morning," said Jorgensen pressing his hands together in the namaste greeting. Both he and Ah Cheng towered over the diminutive couple, no taller and no heavier than their skinny young son.

"Welcome," said Suri's father, responding with the same formal gesture.

"I am sorry for the sadness in this house," said Jorgensen. "My name is Jorgensen from the E&O Hotel and I wish to speak with Suri."

Suri's parents exchanged glances before his father spoke in halting English. "Suri is good boy. He has done nothing wrong."

"I know," said Jorgensen. "I am here to help find who killed Tuan Davies." He looked directly at Suri. "Show me his room and we will talk there."

Suri's father gave a nod of assent, and the boy collected a key from a hook on the wall. He led the way from the kitchen to the staircase and up to the door of Davies's room, which he unlocked, holding it open for Jorgensen and Ah Cheng to enter.

Jorgensen was surprised at how unchanged the room was from his last visit. It was impossible to picture it as the scene of a brutal killing. The shelves, crammed with books, were untouched. The bed roughly made, and the typewriter still sat in the middle of the desk. All that was different was the empty whisky bottle now tipped on its side, and the stacks of papers either side of the typewriter. One, neatly cornered and even, the other spread untidily.

He placed a hand on Suri's shoulder as the boy entered the room alongside them. "Was Tuan Davies a good friend to you?"

Suri looked into Jorgensen's eyes, as if to check for sincerity in the question. Seemingly satisfied, he nodded. "He was teaching me how to read in English." He gestured towards the bookshelves. "He let me choose books to read. I have one on my bedding. Must I return it?"

"No, you keep it. What is it?"

"*Kidnapped,* by Robert Louis Stevenson."

"A good choice. Was it you who found Tuan Davies?"

Suri gave a glum nod. "On his chair, sir. At first, I thought he was drunk..." Suri's voice tailed off into a whisper and he seemed on the verge of breaking into tears, but he gulped hard, fighting to restore his powers of speech, "...but his head was fallen to one side. I went to make him comfortable and saw his eyes were open, and his mouth gaping, like he was trying to cry out."

Jorgensen squeezed the boy's shoulder in reassurance. "I'm sorry you had to see it. You're too young to witness death."

"I have seen death before, sir."

Jorgensen grunted in acknowledgement. He should have realised. Though Penang's residents had not endured the horrors of the Great War, like he and his comrades, many of them had fought every single day before and since to avoid starvation and disease. Even a young boy like Suri would not have been spared the grim sight of bodies found in the alleys and on the walkways during the last typhoid fever epidemic.

"Was the rest of the room like this?" he asked.

"No, sir. There were many papers spilt across the floor. The policeman replaced them on the table."

"What time was it you found him?"

"I do not know exactly. There is no clock in the house. The policeman asked me and became angry when I could not say."

"Why did you come up here?" Jorgensen asked.

"I brought hot tea. Every night I brought the Tuan hot tea from the night market stall. I take a tin mug from the kitchen to the hawker."

"Was the night market closing down when you went?"

"Some hawkers were still open."

That put it somewhere between eleven and midnight, Jorgensen calculated. The customary time for the night market to shut down, though one or two stalls ran on longer if no officials from the municipality were around to prevent them.

"And when did you last see Tuan Davies alive?"

Suri pointed with his thumb to Ah Cheng, who was watching from the doorway. "When he saw me. I took food to the Tuan – also from the night market."

"How about after that – to clear up maybe?"

"No, sir. I cleared up straight after. Tuan Davies asked me to stay while he ate. He wanted to talk to me about my book."

"Now Suri, the police told me a man threatened the Tuan. Who told them about this man? Was it you?"

"It was my cousin Kadhir. You have seen Kadhir, sir."

"Was he with you on the walkway?"

Suri nodded. "Kadhir spoke to the policeman. He told him about the merchant Bin Hakim. He heard the shouting with the Tuan and saw the merchant leave."

"When was this?"

"Yesterday morning."

"That was several hours before the Tuan was killed."

"Yes, sir. Bin Hakim has caused much trouble. Once, many weeks ago, he swore to kill the Tuan. I heard this happen, and my father too."

"Why was Bin Hakim so angry with the Tuan?"

"I do not know. He came many times to the house and more shouting like yesterday until the Tuan told him to leave."

"Where does Bin Hakim live?"

"Kadhir told the policeman he saw him once in Acheen Street. Tuan has business with many men from there. They come for letters to be written. But only Bin Hakim is angry."

"Now Suri, do you know Kei Hin?"

The boy nodded, a glimpse of fear behind his eyes.

"Kei Hin visited the Tuan in this last week," said Jorgensen. "I saw him. Did you or Kadhir tell the police about this?"

Suri stared wordlessly at the floor; his mouth stretched in a pained grimace.

"I understand. You're reluctant to speak against him. But I know he came here with other gang members. You must tell me if Kei Hin or his men came again after you took Tuan Davies his meal?"

Suri raised his eyes to meet Jorgensen's. "No, sir. I did not see him."

"Are you sure? Were you here the whole evening?"

"I was not. But my family know of Kei Hin, and they did not see him."

"Now tell me, did Tuan Davies receive any other visitors?"

"The policeman asked the same question. I told him a white man came in the morning."

"A white man. Do you know who? Did the Tuan say his name?"

"I do not know his name. He came once before – two days ago."

"Can you describe him?"

Suri looked Jorgensen up and down. "Less tall than you. Same dark-coloured hair."

"Older or younger than me?"

"I do not know. His clothes were clean, not like the Tuan. He brought a letter for the Tuan and threw me ten cents for taking him to the room, though he did not stay for many minutes."

"Did the Tuan seem worried about this man?"

Suri shook his head. "No, I don't think so."

"So, apart from Bin Hakim, Ah Cheng here and the unknown white man, did the Tuan have any other visitors over the last few days?"

Suri thought hard for a moment. "You know of Kei Hin," he said. "Also, two men from Malay Street to speak about letters. These men had been many times before. A Chinese man and woman too, wanting the Tuan's help. All of this I told to the policeman."

"Thank you, Suri. You've been a great help. Now, I'd like to look through these papers. I'll call in at the kitchen when I'm leaving."

"Yes, sir." Suri left the room after a last lingering look around it, then silently descended the stairs.

"Damnit," said Jorgensen to Ah Cheng. "I forgot to ask if he'd ever seen that fat fellow with the moustache across the street. Go downstairs and ask if anyone saw him."

As soon as Ah Cheng left, Jorgensen began to leaf through the papers in the disturbed pile, scanning the contents and reorganising as he went. Most were letters, typewritten on the black Underwood typewriter and ready to be sent. Jorgensen guessed they were scooped from the floor by the police and heaped onto the desk with no attempt at order, leaving longer letters, comprising multiple sheets, dispersed haphazardly among the pile.

Underneath the last of the papers was Davies's notebook. Jorgensen opened it and found the most recent entries towards the back. They showed commissions from some of the people Suri had mentioned – a Malay from Acheen Street and a Chinese husband and wife from Hutton Lane. Davies had scrupulously noted down points the client wanted to cover, and to whom letters were to be addressed. Columns to the right of each listing were drawn to allow room for dates to be entered, to show when letters were sent, and replies received. Halfway down the third to most recent page, he found Bin Hakim's name against an entry relating to a letter to the municipal council, about his licence to operate as a moneylender.

A search around the rest of the room yielded nothing of surprise until he started to feel behind the musty books, damaged over time by the humidity, that lined the shelves. Most were pushed tight against the wall but, on the highest shelf, reachable by standing on the desk chair on which Davies had met his end, Jorgensen's fingernails tapped against tin. He pulled out the books in front to reveal a floral patterned box, lying on its side. As he slid and tilted it free, an object rattled inside. Climbing down from the chair, he placed the box on the desk and unclipped the lid. Inside, there were just two items – a piece of folded card and a small wooden ring case. He popped the case open, revealing a solitary diamond ring, with the tiniest of stones set in a plain gold band. Then, he unfolded the card, which held within it a lock of blonde hair.

Jorgensen contemplated his findings. The tin box was oversized for just the two items, and he wondered what else it once contained. Perhaps letters or photographs that might have provided a clue as to the identity of the blonde-haired woman whose lock of hair Davies had so discreetly kept.

He climbed back up onto the chair and returned the box and its contents to its hiding place behind the books. Before leaving the room, he paused and looked around it once more, picturing Davies in the chair, as he had last seen him. "I'm sorry," he said out loud. "I hadn't meant for this to happen – but I promise you, your killer won't get away with it."

Suri had left the key in the door, so Jorgensen turned it to lock the room, before descending to the kitchen, where he handed it to Suri's father, then walked along the long corridor, past the doors of the four ground-floor lodgings. Watched over by Ah Cheng, Suri was squatting on the walkway, digging his fingers into a bowl of rice and curry. Jorgensen crouched down beside him.

"Among all Tuan Davies's visitors, was there ever a white woman, with fair hair?" he asked.

Suri shook his head. "No, sir. No woman."

"Are you sure?"

"Yes, sir. No women came to see the Tuan."

"And is that what you told Inspector Batchelor?"

"He did not ask."

"Okay then. Ask your family, your cousin Kadhir. If anybody remembers a woman visiting – come and tell me at the hotel."

# Twenty-Four

According to the 1927 edition of the Chinese Commercial Directory of the Straits Settlements, a copy of which Jorgensen found in the E&O's library on the first floor above the bar, there were seven Chinese run tobacco merchants in George Town. The majority sited along the southern end of Beach Street or on Penang Road, two areas where Chinese businesses predominated. Maybe a dozen more, run by Indian and Malay merchants, were dotted around the town, but Jorgensen figured that, as the cheroot bands he found in Love Lane featured Chinese characters, it made sense to start with the Chinese establishments.

"I can help you," Ah Cheng had said to Jorgensen, who considered the request for several long seconds, then copied out the details of all seven on a single sheet of E&O stationery.

To aid Ah Cheng in his quest, he was outfitted in clothes that bore some resemblance to an E&O driver's uniform, though his too small dark green tunic perforce remained unbuttoned, and his trousers, borrowed from a clerk's white linen outfit, stopped several inches above his ankles. He was used to uniforms – he had worn one at the house of Choo Fat Yee - but donning the tunic with the E&O crest sewn onto the breast gave him an unexpected feeling of belonging that he had never experienced at Choo's. And, combined with a card case holding a stack of Jorgensen's business cards, he soon found that it opened doors that would otherwise remain closed.

One of which was Sin Eee Trading – a business that occupied the ground floor of a two-storey Chinese shophouse towards the bottom, southerly end of busy Beach Street, three-quarters of a mile and a world away from the European bank buildings at the top end. Its neighbours either side were a rattan furniture workshop, whose half-finished products littered the walkway, and a rope and hardware merchant.

Entering from the bustling street, it took a moment for Ah Cheng's eyes to grow accustomed to the gloom. He stood just inside the door, gradually becoming aware of the high shelves stacked with blocks of tobacco wrapped in waxed paper, tins of tobacco and cartons of cigarette packs. He screwed up his nose at the shop's bitter and woody odours.

"Hot day," called out a voice from behind a counter at the far end. Ah Cheng moved closer to see a thin-faced Chinese man balanced on a high stool. "You come to collect an order?" the man asked.

"No, uncle," Ah Cheng replied. "I come from the E&O to ask a question."

"E&O Hotel. We are honoured."

For what was the sixth time already that day, Ah Cheng fished in his tunic pocket and pulled out the torn cheroot band given to him by Jorgensen. He placed it on the wooden counter in front of the proprietor and, next to it, he laid one of Jorgensen's cards.

"This band here," he said. "Number Eight. Who sells this?"

The proprietor slid open a drawer below the counter and extracted a rusty handled magnifying glass. Bending close over the band he scrutinised it through the lens.

"Our Number Eight Cheroots," he said. "You want to buy?"

"I regret, uncle, that is not why I am here. I look for a white man who buys these cheroots."

The proprietor frowned. "Here is a wholesale merchant. Your one must buy Number Eight Cheroots elsewhere."

"From one of your customers?" said Ah Cheng.

The proprietor nodded, then picked up Jorgensen's card to examine it. "E&O," he muttered, glancing shrewdly at Ah Cheng.

"Uncle," said Ah Cheng. "If you sell good cigars, I will tell my boss to buy from you."

"Mr Jorgensen, huh?"

"Tell me where to look and he will buy cigars from you."

"Okay, can." The proprietor turned towards an open door behind him that led into a second storage area and yelled for his son to come running. "You wait," he said to Ah Cheng. "I will give you the list. Not many buy Number Eight Cheroots. Good quality, lah."

For a moment, Ah Cheng allowed himself the hope that tracking down the white man with the broom bristle moustache might even happen that morning, but by the time the proprietor's son had laboriously copied out a list of all their Number Eight Cheroot customers, he realised the size of the task ahead. Twenty names were on it, spread right across George Town.

"Thank you, uncle," he said.

"You don't forget now. Cigars for Mr Jorgensen."

***

Holding the list of customers given to him by the proprietor, half of which were bars and pubs, and the other half newspaper stalls and tobacconists, Ah Cheng plotted a route in his mind. He knew the town as well as any rickshaw puller. Better in some parts. There were stretches of old George Town, in the narrow lanes near the quayside, where he knew the exact number of steps it took from a street corner to reach a place of safety. A door through which he could escape and hide from pursuers. Though today, wearing a tunic bearing the name of the Eastern and Oriental hotel, he would walk with his head held high without any cautionary look back over his shoulders.

As the discarded cheroot bands were found in Love Lane, opposite Davies's lodging house, Ah Cheng's first instinct was to concentrate on the addresses nearby. On the way, he made two fruitless calls at tobacconists along Beach Street but then on Chulia Street, he struck lucky.

The Hong Kong Bar was just around the corner from Love Lane. Ah Cheng remembered it from two nights earlier, when he and Jorgensen had sought refuge from the threat of George Lam's gang. Now, it was early afternoon, and one solitary customer sat in a chair by the open-shuttered window, lost in reverie as he watched the flood of humanity stream past on Chulia Street.

"You came in with Major Mac," said Yeoh, looking up from polishing glasses as Ah Cheng approached the bar counter.

"Cousin, you are right," Ah Cheng replied. "I am Ah Cheng."

"No jemmy today," Yeoh chuckled.

"No need."

"So, why you here?"

"Major Mac asked me to find a man." Ah Cheng had noticed how some people called Jorgensen Major Mac, though he had no idea why, other than the people who did it were on friendly terms. "A white man with a thick moustache – like the bristles of a broom." Ah Cheng raised his hands to his face with knuckles bent below his nostrils and two fingers on each hand drooping down over his lips. "Cover lips like this."

Yeoh's assistant, busy washing glasses at a sink at the far end of the bar, paused in his work to laugh at Ah Cheng's contortions.

"He is a fat man – and smokes cheroots," Ah Cheng continued. "Number Eight Cheroots from Sin Eee. Could be he bought a tin from here."

"I know who you mean," said Yeoh. "A real *Ah Pooi* one. Come in many times this week to drink beer."

"You know his name?"

Yeoh shook his head. "Said he stays in Pulau Tikus."

"Is he big mansion one?" Ah Cheng asked. Pulau Tikus was a village to the north-west of George Town, further along Penang's north shore. Where once it was separated from the main town by acres of coconut groves, in more recent years it had become linked by the new network of wide leafy avenues, home to the newly built mansions and bungalows of the wealthy.

Yeoh snorted in derision and shook his head emphatically. "Shabby clothes and not smell good. Not big mansion one."

"I understand you, cousin," said Ah Cheng.

If the white man lived in the village of Pulau Tikus, he should be easy enough to find, thought Ah Cheng. Around the wet market in the centre there were terraces of smaller houses, many occupied by the Eurasian and Burmese communities. Few white men lived among them.

"If he comes in again, let Major Mac know. Here is his telephone number."

From a tunic pocket, he slid one of Jorgensen's cards from the case and handed it to Yeoh.

"Can," the barman replied, tucking the card into his own tunic jacket, then resumed polishing the row of glasses on the counter.

On the walkway outside the Hong Kong Bar, Ah Cheng ran a finger down the list of Number Eight Cheroot customers. There was only one in Pulau Tikus – a bookseller and tobacconist on Burmah Road, the main street through the village. Two miles from where he stood and quicker on two wheels. He set off for the E&O, hoping Abdul would agree to lend him one of the hotel's bicycles.

# Twenty-Five

Whenever possible, Arshak Sarkies set aside the early afternoon for precious hours with his wife and daughters, and left strict orders not to be interrupted, except for emergencies – or the arrival of an important guest. It was, therefore, a far from ideal time for Jorgensen to be knocking at the door of Sarkies' private family suite, but the news of Davies's murder could not be held back any longer.

From the corridor, Jorgensen could make out the faint notes of a piano and tried to recognise the tune. When Ping Pong swung open the door, the music grew suddenly louder, reverberating in the suite's marble-tiled hallway – it was one of the popular favourites played by the hotel's orchestra leader, F. O'Neill Shaw, in the dining room. Something about a kitten. Kitten on the Keys, that was it.

"Mr Sarkies is busy," said Ping Pong, not bothering to disguise a look of reproof at Jorgensen's untimely appearance.

"It can't wait, Ping Pong," said Jorgensen. "I must speak with him in private – not in the family's hearing."

Ping Pong's frown deepened, but he ushered Jorgensen into the hall and instructed him to wait. Moments later, the rendition of Kitten on the Keys slowed in a hesitancy of wrong notes as Ping Pong delivered his message.

"My dear Jorgensen. I do not believe we have ever seen this much of you." Sarkies bowled into the hallway, beaming from ear to ear, his face so creased that his moustaches almost hid his eyes. Gone were the tailored jacket and pleated trousers he wore for most of the day. In their place were a dark green and red patterned silk sarong and a light cotton tunic – the clothes of a man anticipating a welcome period of relaxation. "You must come and greet the family. Ena is playing such a pretty melody."

"I think we should speak here," said Jorgensen. "There's a problem I need to tell you about."

"It must be a serious matter," Sarkies said. "That much I can tell from your expression."

"It relates to the business with Cromford."

"I understood that was settled."

"The man who wrote the blackmail letter has been murdered."

"Here, in George Town?" The shock wiped all traces of Sarkies' previous good humour from his face.

"He was an Englishman by the name of Frank Davies. As far as I can tell, he was pressured into writing the letter to settle a debt."

"This is terrible." Sarkies' voice rose a pitch and, from further into the rooms, the piano stopped abruptly on hearing it. Noticing the sudden lull, Sarkies ushered Jorgensen closer to the front door, further from the rest of the apartment's occupants, his voice dropping into a murmur. "That there should be blackmail was bad enough, and that it could happen on our peaceful island. And now, far worse – a murder."

"The police suspect a trader from Acheen Street who had previously threatened Davies's life." Jorgensen too, kept his voice low.

"Acheen Street. An Arab trader?"

"Maybe Sumatran. Not somebody I know. For now, the police are searching for him and know nothing of Davies's involvement in the blackmail. When I was questioned this morning after the police found my card in Davies's room, I was forced to admit my visit related to a guest. But I refused to name him. Because they have this trader in their sights, they didn't press me."

Sarkies' sharp eyes scrutinised Jorgensen carefully. "You think differently to the police," he said.

"I can't shake off the feeling it was the blackmailer, George Lam, or his gang, who killed Davies. They were angry they didn't get all the money they'd hoped for. If it was them, I need to find out before the police do, or my involvement in paying off the blackmail demand may come to light."

"Our involvement, dear Jorgensen."

"And there's another reason, Arshak," said Jorgensen. "It was through Davies that I tracked down Lam. I should have protected him better."

"Doubtless you are being too hard on yourself. It is in your nature. What do you require of me?"

"To tell Robinson and Broomes I am working on a private matter on your behalf. They won't like it, but it's the easiest way to prevent their interference."

"I wish I had known earlier. Your absence this morning did not go unnoticed. Nevertheless, you may leave Mr Broomes to me. As for poor Mr Robinson, I am afraid he is still incapacitated."

"Thanks, Arshak. And I'll need the use of a motor car and a driver."

"For today you may use my driver, and car. I have no plans to leave the hotel."

"Thanks, but I've arranged to borrow the hotel's Standard Tourer, though if Broomes asks, it'd be better if you approve it."

"Of course." Edging closer to Jorgensen, Sarkies looked back over his shoulder to the room where his daughter Ena's fingers once again picked out the melody on the piano keys. His voice dropped further still to a hoarse whisper: "What you are proposing could be dangerous. You must take care, Jorgensen."

"I will."

***

In Goldie's Bar, Jorgensen waited until Goldie had finished pouring drinks for an order. By the time the head barman was free to speak, he had noticed the resolute set of Jorgensen's jaw, and refrained from greeting him with his usual grin.

"I came to ask about Tuesday night," said Jorgensen. "You were going to check with your staff for me." Knowing that one of the E&O's patrons was responsible for instigating the blackmail of Cromford was hard to bear. They were the very people that

Arshak Sarkies asked Jorgensen to protect. And worse, that person now bore some responsibility for Davies's death.

"You wanted to know who was last with Mr Tommy. Yes, I remember. The boys told me it was Mr Ginger and Mr Dickie."

"What about the night before? Cromford was in here then. He told me he dropped his diary. Can you remember who was with him?"

"Monday, lah?"

Jorgensen nodded.

"Same people," said Goldie. "Mr Cromford is popular with the young ones. There was Mr Tommy, Mr Ginger, Mr Dickie, Miss Phyllis and her friend. Fair-haired one."

Fair-haired. Jorgensen pictured the lock of hair in the tin box in Davies's room. "Do you mean Miss Anne Prescott?"

"Yes," grinned Goldie. "Miss Anne."

# Twenty-Six

In the village of Pulau Tikus, two miles to the west of the E&O, the shadows from the shophouses lining Burmah Road were beginning to lengthen. A boy from the booksellers led Ah Cheng past the entrance to the wet market, where a yoked bullock stood idle, while on the cart behind it a swarm of flies buzzed around watermelon fragments, stripped sugar cane leaves, fish bones and severed chicken heads – waste from the market ready to be carted off for animal feed.

At the crossroads, the terraces either side of Burmah Road gave way to tall trees, and ahead on the right, they took the first of several short dirt tracks leading to clusters of shacks hidden among the dense green foliage. Ah Cheng bumped the borrowed bicycle across deep ruts until they halted in front of a timber sided building, high on stilts and painted pale green, with a corrugated tin sheet roof.

"Here," said the boy, then turned to scamper away back down the track.

A short flight of steps led up to a square wooden-boarded verandah on the corner of the building. Ah Cheng looked up to see a stout Malay woman, well beyond her youth, but with an unlined face that retained traces of its once youthful prettiness, looking down on him from the balustrade. Her long black hair was tied behind her head, and she wore a colourful patterned long-sleeved *baju kurung,* a knee-length dress worn over an ankle-length skirt.

"I look for Tuan Loddon," said Ah Cheng. It was the name given at the booksellers in Pulau Tikus for the fat Tuan who bought Number Eight Cheroots.

"This is his house," the woman replied. "What do you want with him?"

"I come from Mr Jorgensen of the E&O. My name is Ah Cheng."

"I do not know Mr Jorgensen, nor anything of the E&O. Why does he ask about my husband?"

"May I come up to speak with you? It will be more private if I do."

"There is a stool. Come."

Ah Cheng leant the bicycle against a wooden post supporting the staircase and climbed the few steps. "Are you Tuan Loddon's wife?" he asked.

The woman's heavy-set shoulders shook with mirth. "For twenty years I am married to Loddon, and it is as long since he was called Tuan. My name is Zulla."

On the verandah, stretches of silk in floral patterns lay draped across several wooden stools, and a box of needles and threads lay at Zulla's feet. She cleared one of the stools and invited Ah Cheng to sit.

"You will take lemon tea?"

Zulla disappeared through the flimsy wooden door into the house, returning a few minutes later with a glass, in which a shrunken lime floated in the cloudy tea.

"Thank you," said Ah Cheng, taking a sip of the lukewarm drink. Aware of Zulla's patient expression while she watched him, he was unsure how to proceed.

"Mr Jorgensen needs your husband's help. There is information he wishes to learn."

"Do you not know why? Are you messenger boy only?"

"I know it is important."

"Tell your boss if Loddon has finished work, he will be at the Hong Kong Bar or the Victoria Inn. Where he works today, I cannot say, because I do not know."

Ah Cheng bowed his head in thanks, drained the glass of lemon tea in one go, then bowed again before descending the short staircase to the bicycle. He hoped Jorgensen would be impressed by the news he would bring.

# Twenty-Seven

The Victoria Inn on Chulia Street stood a couple of hundred yards west of the Hong Kong Bar, and like it, was carved out from the ground floor of a traditional narrow shophouse. Inside, a teak bar counter ran along one wall, and a scattering of wooden tables and chairs mimicked the layout of many unassuming English public houses.

The few Englishmen, or their fellow Europeans, who drank in the Victoria Inn were unlikely to be patrons of the E&O, or members of the Penang Club. Too poor for the return fare to Europe, ill fortune or unwise decisions had left them washed up in Penang and struggling to get by. In the Victoria Inn, these castaways mixed with the Chinese and Tamil customers, and were guarded whenever they stumbled across one of their own.

Jorgensen had little trouble in recognising Loddon from Ah Cheng's description. Sat at a small table towards the back, with rounded shoulders hunched over a bottle of beer, he was the sole European in the almost empty interior. In front of him – a cheroot, embedded in its holder, glowed in an ashtray.

"Anchor Beer," said Jorgensen to the Chinese barman. "Cold."

Holding the bottle, Jorgensen approached Loddon's table. "Good afternoon, Mr Loddon," he said. "Can I join you?"

Startled at hearing his name spoken aloud, Loddon eyed Jorgensen with a mixture of bewilderment and suspicion. His walrus moustache, with beer foam clinging to its bristles, was yellowed with tobacco. Tired, beaten eyes peered out from folds in his grey skin, patchy with dark discolorations, as was the once white linen jacket stretched tight around his bulky frame.

"Your wife said I might find you here," said Jorgensen.

"My wife?"

Ignoring Loddon's unwelcoming stare, Jorgensen pulled out a low stool, and, once seated, placed the bottle on the table next to Loddon's glass. "For you," he said.

"I don't know you," said Loddon, his voice a little thickened by an afternoon's drinking. His eyes darted nervously to the door.

"My driver spoke to your wife, at your home. She said you'd probably be here or the Hong Kong Bar. My name's Jorgensen by the way. From the E&O."

"What do you want with me?"

"I'm interested in why you were watching Frank Davies's lodging house in Love Lane."

The sudden look of alarm in Loddon's eyes removed any doubts that Ah Cheng had led Jorgensen to the wrong man. "You were recognised," Jorgensen said, picking up the cheroot from the ashtray, from which a lazy plume of smoke drifted up to be shredded under the ceiling fan. "And you left a pile of these at your feet. Why were you watching the house?"

"You're not from the police," Loddon said. "Why should I talk to you?"

"I guess you heard what happened to Davies."

Loddon made the sign of the cross on his chest. "Poor bugger."

"How did you hear about his death?"

"Same as everybody else," said Loddon surlily. "It's reported in the afternoon edition of the Echo."

"Now let's understand each other, Mr Loddon," said Jorgensen, his voice hardening. "If you don't tell me why you were there, my driver will go and fetch the police. And they might think it strange you were watching the house of a man who was murdered. They might even suspect you had something to do with his death."

Loddon's mouth opened and closed soundlessly, like a fish hauled out of the water to flap helplessly in a net. He was trapped – and he knew it. As the realisation dawned, he tried to buy himself some thinking time by draining his glass and replenishing it from the new bottle.

"I swear I had nothing to do with his death," he said after a long pause. "And I had no idea it was murder, until you told me. The report in the Echo said his death was unexplained. You must believe me."

"Convince me. Why were you watching him?"

"I was told to."

"Who by?"

Loddon's deep sigh of resignation seemed to physically deflate him, as if any remaining strength of purpose had been exhaled into the inn's smoky atmosphere. "I'm not a wealthy man, Mr Jorgensen," he said. "If you'd known me before, you might venture I'd fallen on hard times. And if I give you what you're looking for, I'll end up destitute."

Jorgensen hesitated. Loddon's words were a reminder of Davies's similar plea. He too had appealed to Jorgensen to not pressure him into revealing too much.

"I guess you don't want to jeopardise the little work you do get?"

"Your driver would have told you about my wife. Once it didn't matter so much if a white man married a native woman – especially up-country. These days though, the newcomers from England, the new breed, look down on you."

"I sympathise, but I can't let it go. A man was killed. You'll have to talk to me."

Loddon's head dropped and with the heel of both palms he rubbed his eyes in mute anguish. "I'll never be trusted again if I do," he pleaded. Torn by indecision, he drank greedily from his glass while Jorgensen watched in silence, waiting for him to crack.

"Magnus Prescott asked me to watch the house," Loddon said eventually, the words pried from him as if having a tooth pulled.

"Magnus Prescott. From Prescott and Co?"

Loddon nodded wretchedly, "I was once a visiting agent for Prescott's. They always said they hadn't wanted to let me go, but I'd left them with little choice. Now I help with the occasional task – just enough to keep us from starving."

"What were you supposed to be watching for?"

"I had to report whether Miss Anne ever visited the house – to see Frank Davies."

"Magnus's sister?" Jorgensen asked sharply. It looked like his guess about the lock of hair hidden in the tin box in Davies's room was right – it belonged to Anne Prescott. "Why did Magnus believe she'd be calling on Frank Davies?"

"All he told me was that the family had forbidden her from seeing him. It was to protect her, Magnus said, as she was too young to know what kind of a fellow Davies was."

"And did you ever see her visit? Don't leave anything out, Loddon, I'll find out if you do."

"Twice that I witnessed. On Wednesday, and then again yesterday. I was supposed to let Mr Magnus know immediately."

Suri had claimed Davies was never visited by a woman. Jorgensen wondered why the boy chose to lie when he had been so forthcoming about Davies's other visitors.

"How did you communicate with Magnus?"

"On Wednesday I went to the company's office on Beach Street to see him in person," Loddon replied, his face contorted with anguish as he forced the words out. "And yesterday I called from the telephone in here."

"Did Magnus go to the house in Love Lane after your call?"

"I didn't see him."

"You'd better me telling me the truth."

"What choice have you left me?" asked Loddon plaintively. "I can't afford trouble with the police."

"Did anybody else call on Frank Davies while you were watching the house?"

"People went in and out of there all day. All sorts – Malays, Chinese, Burmese, Indian. But I've no means of knowing if it was Davies they were visiting."

"What about the gangsters who went to see Davies?" Jorgensen asked. "One young swaggering type, backed up by a couple of thugs. You must have seen them?"

"Like I said before, Chinese were always going in and out of the house."

"This group would stand out. They don't bother to hide what they are."

"Maybe I missed them. I need to go and piss now and then, you know."

For the first time since Loddon had reluctantly started answering questions, he seemed suddenly evasive. Though Jorgensen was unsure whether he was lying about not seeing Kei Hin, or trying to hide how easy it was to slink away to the Hong Kong bar or the Victoria Inn instead of watching the lodging house for Magnus Prescott.

"No white men? I was told he had a male visitor yesterday."

Loddon shook his head "Not that I saw."

"Didn't you see me go in the house on Wednesday night?" Jorgensen asked.

"No. I didn't watch that night." Loddon stared into his glass, leaving Jorgensen certain that he was withholding something.

"What time did you stop yesterday?"

"About half past four."

"An Arab trader called to see Davies yesterday morning, and there was a row between them. Did you see or hear any of that?"

"It must have happened before I arrived." Loddon's responses were growing increasingly resentful. Figuring that, for now, he had got all he could from the man, Jorgensen handed over one of his calling cards. "If you remember anything else, contact me at the hotel. And if I discover you've not told me everything, I'll be back."

"Are you going to tell the Prescotts I spoke to you?" There was a note of desperation in Loddon's voice.

Jorgensen shook his head. "I've no reason to. But don't you think you should tell the police why you were there? Davies was killed and if you don't come forward now, and they find out later – they'll be suspicious of your motives."

***

Outside the Victoria Inn, Ah Cheng was waiting for Jorgensen on the five-foot way, while Chulia Street bustled with the movement of people hastening to beat the oncoming rainstorm signalled by the thunderclaps over Penang Hill. Rickshaw and bicycle wheels whirred, hugging close to the storm drains on each side of Chulia Street. Hustling along among them were dozens of pedestrians: Chinese men in loose cotton smocks and trousers, wearing bowler hats or wide-brimmed straw hats; Malays in sarongs; barefoot, shirtless Indian labourers in loincloths, tramping home to wherever their bed lay. And down the middle of Chulia Street, a chauffeur driven motor car cleared an imperious passage.

"It was him, sure enough," said Jorgensen to Ah Cheng. "You did well."

Ah Cheng nodded in satisfaction, conscious of the compliment. "What now, boss?" he asked.

Jorgensen regarded Ah Cheng appraisingly. Maybe Arshak Sarkies was right after all. "Would you be able to follow somebody, without them knowing about it?"

Ah Cheng grinned. "This I know I can do."

"Loddon is holding something back. I'd like you to follow him when he leaves the pub. See where he goes. It could be to an office on Beach Street where a man called Magnus Prescott works, and that would tell us something." Jorgensen checked his watch. "It's a couple of hours until sunset. Stick with him until then, or until he returns home. I'll see you at the E&O later."

"Can."

Jorgensen rummaged in a pocket for some coins and glanced upwards at the darkening sky. "You'll need these for rickshaws. Don't lose sight of him."

Ah Cheng dropped the change into a drawstring cotton purse, which he had pocketed in his borrowed white trousers, while Jorgensen walked up the road to where the E&O's blue Standard Stratford Tourer was parked. Zamir was loosening the straps that secured the furled canvas rooftop from its position behind the rear seat.

"We're going a few yards up to Love Lane," said Jorgensen, checking his watch again. Time was tight, but the plan he had in mind might still work. "You can finish pulling the top over once we're there."

At the lodging house, Suri's mother was chopping vegetables on a stone slab in the rudimentary kitchen at the rear, while her son scrubbed a steel pan in the sink below the airwell. When Jorgensen appeared at their doorway, their apprehensive looks were so similar that it was obvious they were mother and son.

Jorgensen greeted them in Tamil, then spoke to Suri in English. "Ask your mother's permission to come with me to Beach Street for two hours' work. A dollar should cover it. It's to do with Tuan Davies."

A dollar for two hours work was twice as much as Suri's cousin Kadhir would earn for a day's labouring at the docks. Jorgensen watched Suri's mother as she listened to her son's explanation, her wariness slowly giving way to reluctant acquiescence.

"What do you wish me of me?" Suri asked as he followed Jorgensen to the street outside. Zamir had dragged the Standard's top into position, moments before the first raindrops began to drum against its taut canvas.

Jorgensen hesitated. He wanted to ask the boy why he had lied about Anne Prescott's visits to Davies but decided it was best to set that question aside. For now, he needed his willing cooperation.

"The dark-haired man you saw yesterday," said Jorgensen. "The one who gave you ten cents to show him to Tuan Davies's room. I might know who he is – and I want you to tell me if I'm right."

***

Five minutes later, the storm had reached the town. Zamir pulled the car to a halt on Beach Street and Jorgensen and Suri leapt from it, dashing through the fast-forming puddles to the cover of the five-foot way outside the premises of a Chinese rubber merchant.

From the long line of chauffeur-driven cars parked down the middle of the road, it was clear that they had arrived just in time. Any moment now, the chauffeurs' masters would begin their daily migration from office to bungalow, for a wash and change before gin pahits on the verandah.

While along both sides of the street, nose to tail rickshaws took up every available square yard, ready to pick up the clerks and supervisors who could afford a few cents to keep out of the rain. For the rest, it was walking or cycling home, and already a forest of umbrellas was springing up around them.

"We'll watch from here," said Jorgensen to Suri. "If I'm right, then the man I'm expecting will come out from that building and walk to his car somewhere in that queue. There are two front doors. I'll watch both and let you know when I see him." He was pointing to the Prescott Building across the street, partly obscured by a bullock cart, on which the driver was frantically dragging a heavy canvas sheet across a pile of sacks.

The Prescott Building's gloomy, grey stone façade, two-storeyed with arched gothic windows on the first floor, was the width of half a dozen shophouses. At street level, a single archway designed for horse-drawn carriages led under the building to a yard which ran over two hundred yards down to the quayside.

On one side of it were tin-roofed godowns for storage, and on the other two long brick-sided buildings from which smoke and fumes belched forth through a series of low chimneys. These were Prescott's tin smelting facilities. Though a fraction of the size of the competitor's newer Eastern Smelting works further inland, they nevertheless remained the most dependable source of the Prescott family's wealth.

Within a few minutes, and almost catching Jorgensen by surprise, two cars drove out in quick succession from under the central arch. First, a dark blue Nash Six limousine, followed by a smaller two-seater sports car – the stylish lines of a maroon Chrysler Roadster with a grey canvas hood. To Jorgensen's relief, both cars turned right, heading north for the clock tower, to pass directly in front of where he and Suri stood.

"Quick Suri." Jorgensen grabbed the young boy's arm. "He's in one of these two."

The upright Nash Six crawled past first, the roar of its powerful engine nearly drowning out the pounding rain. A uniformed *sais* was at the wheel, while behind him, deep in the rear seat, a solitary passenger removed his hat to reveal grey hair. It was Lawrence Prescott. Close behind was the Roadster, in which instead of a Malay chauffeur, its driver was a younger white man sporting a panama hat – Magnus Prescott.

"This one," said Jorgensen, turning Suri's shoulders to face the Chrysler and urging him to the edge of the walkway. Through the car's open windows – for the cooling rush of air was never undesirable, even at the height of a rainstorm – they had a clear view of Prescott as he stared straight ahead through wildly flapping windscreen wipers.

"Was that the man you saw on Wednesday?" Jorgensen asked as they drew back under the cover of the walkway.

"Sorry, sir. It was not him," Suri said,

"Are you sure? He was wearing a hat."

"So too the man yesterday, sir."

"Damn it," said Jorgensen, the frustration in his voice leaving Suri crestfallen, convinced he had somehow failed.

"It's not your fault," said Jorgensen, noticing the boy's anxious look. "I guessed wrong. Tomorrow we'll try somewhere else – for another dollar. Deal?"

Suri gave a vigorous nod of assent, and quickly pocketed the dollar note that Jorgensen gave him.

Just then, the storm around them reached a crescendo, forcing Jorgensen to raise his voice to be heard. "Before you go," he said, "You must tell me the truth about the woman who called to see Tuan Davies."

Suri frowned in concentration, straining to hear above the driving rain. "No woman, sir," he replied.

"Her name is Anne Prescott. I know about her visits."

Unable to hide his discomfort at being caught in a lie, Suri bent his head.

"I don't blame you for trying to keep her out of this business," said Jorgensen. "I imagine she's been kind to you. But you must tell me about her visits. How often did she call on Tuan Davies?"

The boy lifted his head, his eyes full of concern. "Does Miss Anne know the Tuan is dead?"

"I'm sorry but I don't know. Now tell me, did she often call?" Jorgensen leant in close to Suri's head, so that he could catch every word.

"Many times, sir," Suri replied, nodding sadly. "She brought gifts of ink and paper to Tuan Davies, and sometimes clothes."

"When did she first call?"

"One month ago. She came to the house and asked if Tuan Davies lived there. I showed her to his room as I did with many visitors. I was to knock on the door and shout though the name of the visitor, then wait until the Tuan said enter. Sometimes I would wait for many minutes. When Miss Anne called, the Tuan did not answer my knock, so she went away. But another day, Tuan called for tea for them both."

"How long did she stay on her visits?"

"Some days the Tuan called for tea but others she came for a short time only. To bring gifts for the Tuan. He was always sad when she left."

"You've done well to tell me this, Suri."

"Will you see Miss Anne?"

"I will. You get along home now, and I'll call again tomorrow morning, when we'll try again to find the man who visited the Tuan."

Jorgensen watched as the boy rounded the corner towards the heart of Little India, stepping out from under the walkway into the heavy rain. Suri had lent his trust to Jorgensen – it was there in his eyes when he decided to talk about Anne Prescott. Jorgensen hoped to Christ he merited it.

# Twenty-Eight

While Jorgensen and Suri went to Beach Street, Ah Cheng was following Loddon. He had waited on the walkway opposite the Victoria Inn for his quarry to appear. Here too, the rain fell in torrents, cascading into the storm drains either side of the street, and carrying along with it straw and paper, fragments of wood and torn sacks, empty tin cans and glass bottles.

As the detritus swept past, Ah Cheng smiled to himself. Jorgensen had asked if he could follow a man without him knowing. 'Can,' he had responded.

He had learnt how when still a boy. On George Town's teeming streets, barefoot boys in torn clothes were a common enough sight, and few men gave them a second glance. Old or drunk men, fumbling with their purses; arrogant men, complacent near their strongholds; foreigners off the ships, confused among George Town's labyrinth of narrow lanes. All could easily be followed, waiting for the perfect moment to relieve them of their possessions.

Few of the tricks acquired in his youth were needed to follow Loddon. The Englishman left the Victoria Inn twenty minutes after Jorgensen departed, long enough to down another bottle of beer, before hurrying out onto Chulia Street as if in a sudden rush to get somewhere. He bowled along in a curious gait; head, chest and ample stomach pivoted forward, his short legs chasing the unfurled umbrella before him. Overhead, the trolley-bus wires sizzled and spat in the rain. He crossed the street into Rope Walk, and eventually came to a halt near the office of the Lam Copra Export Company.

For half a minute, Loddon stood marooned in the middle of the street, holding the umbrella over his head with one hand and with the other repeatedly wiping his forehead with a large kerchief taken from a jacket pocket. Oblivious to an approaching rickshaw and the loud grumbles of its puller, he stared at the building while Ah Cheng crept closer along the opposite walkway.

Then, his indecision finally cast aside, perhaps emboldened by the continual strengthening of the storm, Loddon stepped up onto the walkway. From further down the street, Ah Cheng squinted through the wall of rain, to be as certain as possible that the door to Lam's office was the one Loddon entered. He knew this was news that would greatly interest Jorgensen.

Now it was Ah Cheng who hesitated. Though he wanted to stand watch, to see how long Loddon stayed and with whom he might leave, there was the risk of discovery by Lam's gang. Near where he stood, overspills of crates and sacks from several of Rope Walk's traders were stacked on the walkway, and in the gaps between, a knot of people were taking shelter from the storm. Ah Cheng moved to join them, seeking inconspicuousness among the crowd.

Thirty minutes later, with the rain easing, the people around him on the walkway stubbed out their cigarettes and slowly ventured back onto the street. Worrying that he was too close to Lam's office, Ah Cheng retreated thirty yards – to outside the dispensary on the corner of Campbell Street and Rope Walk. From there, peering round the corner, he continued to watch, while the dispensary's staff, paying him no attention, locked and bolted the shutters and left the premises for the day.

Another ten minutes passed before Loddon finally emerged from Lam's office, in the company of Kei Hin. The two men held a brief discussion, then Kei Hin summoned two rickshaws from a group sheltering nearby.

Ah Cheng looked quickly up and down Campbell Street. There was a similar cluster of rickshaws, maybe three or four, huddled together in the direction of Penang Road. He hurried towards them, gambling that Loddon and Kei Hin would come his way, out from Rope Walk and onto Campbell Street.

"Boss," he said to the first puller to acknowledge him, an old man with grey beard tufts on his chin. "I want you to follow another rickshaw. But they must not see me."

The puller considered the odd request. "You pay twelve cents, then extra ten cents," he said. "No, you pay twenty cents extra. Can pay?"

Ah Cheng pulled the cotton purse from his pocket and showed the coins within it. "Must hurry," he said.

Up ahead, the rickshaw carrying Loddon appeared at the junction with Rope Walk. "Here they come. Two rickshaws from Rope Walk."

"If they fast, then double price, ah. I am an old man."

"Do not worry. The first carries a fat man."

The puller hoisted the rickshaw's shafts in readiness. "You are no infant," he grumbled.

Loddon and Kei Hin's rickshaws turned west into Campbell Street, heading directly towards Ah Cheng. He slouched down on the bench seat as the two passed in convoy, while risking a sidelong glance at the second rickshaw. Kei Hin was staring straight ahead and blind to anything but the back of Loddon's rickshaw in front.

"Let's go," said Ah Cheng, but the puller stayed put.

"You want follow in secret, so I wait one," he said, then with a heave began to drag the rickshaw round. By this time, other rickshaws had passed, all with the same dark canvas hoods draped over the back of the seat, obscuring any view of their passengers dodging the rainstorm.

"You catch up," called Ah Cheng.

"Hey, I see them, ah. Leave it to me," the puller replied in irritation.

At the end of Campbell Street was the junction with George Town's widest and busiest street – Penang Road, where the queue of rickshaws ahead all dispersed in different directions. Two turned left, heading south, three right, north towards the seafront and the E&O, and one headed over the crossroads. All forcing their way through the sudden rush-hour congestion. When Ah

Cheng's puller arrived at the crossroads, he turned right without hesitation, jolting across the tram lines. Then, with a stutter and a sudden sprint, he merged into the stream of vehicles heading north.

Stuck behind a trundling motor car, Ah Cheng peered ahead, fearing they had lost Loddon and Kei Hin, but his puller padded on regardless. After another fifty yards they slowed up, and the puller drew to a halt just beyond the junction with Datuk Koyah Road.

"They stop ahead," said the puller. "Can see?"

There they were, two rickshaws at the corner of the next junction, angled in towards the side of the road. From the first, the rotund figure of Loddon was carefully climbing down.

"I see them."

"That fat man cannot walk far, ah," said the puller. "Still twelve cent add twenty cent extra." His sunken cheeks pulled back in a grin that revealed a handful of betel nut-stained teeth.

"Here, you earned it," Ah Cheng dropped the coins into the puller's hand. He stepped down, his eyes fixed on the scene ahead, where Loddon and Kei Hin were entering a building on the corner.

After pausing for a few moments, Ah Cheng walked on to where their two rickshaw pullers were arguing over the division of the fares.

"Boss," said Ah Cheng, approaching them. "The *angmoh*, did he go in there?" he pointed to the entrance door of the corner building – the Australia Hotel.

One of the pullers spat on the ground and nodded, before returning with enthusiasm to the argument.

The Australia Hotel was at the south-west corner of another busy junction on Penang Road – where three other roads converged. Its red-brick pillars supported gracious arches, behind which the five-foot way curved around west into Argyle Road, where the hotel's frontage continued for another eighty feet. On the projecting upper floor, the tall windows were covered in wooden shutters painted in burgundy and green, matching the blinds shading the entrance arch below.

Not wanting to be caught waiting outside, Ah Cheng crossed Penang Road, dodging the traffic to hide in a queue forming under the canopy outside a *nasi kandar* restaurant, where he was soon enveloped in the intoxicating scents of mixed curries.

A few minutes later, Loddon and Kei Hin came out of the hotel together and parted immediately. Kei Hin setting off on foot the way he had come – back down Penang Road, while Loddon crossed Argyle Road to engage another rickshaw from outside the cinema. It was Loddon that Ah Cheng was following, so he waited to see where he was headed, while glancing occasionally the other way to make sure he was not surprised by Kei Hin suddenly turning back.

As soon as Loddon climbed up onto a rickshaw seat, and the puller struggled to get his heavy load underway, Ah Cheng recrossed Penang Road in pursuit. Without Kei Hin to worry about, there was little need for him to hide away under a rickshaw's cover. The skies were clear again, as if the storm was just a trick of the memory, and he was able to follow on foot. At a steady trot, twenty yards behind, Ah Cheng trailed the rickshaw down Argyle Road, heading west out of George Town. On they went, leaving the shophouse terraces behind, passing the Fraser & Neave aerated water factory, before reaching the wider tree-lined avenues of the western suburbs. Loddon was heading home to Pulau Tikus.

Ah Cheng continued in pursuit until Loddon paid off the puller at the entrance to the kampung, where his green painted house was a hundred yards away down the track into the trees. At which point, Ah Cheng turned back. There was much to tell Jorgensen.

# Twenty-Nine

In the back seat of the Standard Tourer, Jorgensen gazed out of the side window as they passed the Esplanade without taking in any of the view, preoccupied as he was by a series of thoughts that refused to fall neatly into place.

It was a quarter past four. By now, he expected the police would have apprehended Bin Hakim, their suspect for Frank Davies's killing. And if Inspector Batchelor had begun the interrogation at the Penang Road Detective Station, he wondered how long it would be before any doubts crept in. Perhaps none would – and Bin Hakim would be charged with Davies's murder. Jorgensen had seen enough of European justice in the colonies to know it was often far from impartial, and if a confession was beaten out of the prisoner, then that might be the end of the matter.

He grimaced in frustration. As the day had worn on, the nature of Davies's murder troubled him more. Death by strangulation, Batchelor had said. And from Suri's description of finding Davies's body slumped in the chair, it suggested a surprise attack, giving him little chance to resist. Which did not match with the little he knew of the police's suspect. Bin Hakim had threatened Davies – more than once, apparently. He had shouted and caused a disturbance. It made no sense that Davies would sit quietly in his chair and wait to be strangled to death by a man known to have a volatile temperament.

The trouble with that argument, Jorgensen realised, was that the same logic ruled out Kei Hin. Davies was terrified of Kei Hin and would not have submitted quietly. Unless Kei Hin had returned with one or more gang members, to subdue him first.

The car passed the Church of the Assumption and Jorgensen glanced up Love Lane, picturing the room at the rear of the lodging house where he had promised to protect Frank Davies. The feeling of guilt that had cast its pall since Batchelor first told him about the murder hung heavier than ever.

Jorgensen pressed his fingers against his temples to try and clear his thoughts. He recognised the element of selfishness in what he was doing – that in determining to find Davies's killer, he was attempting to assuage his own feelings of remorse. Whatever the reason – he was committed now. Looking the other way while the police convicted the wrong man, was not what he had agreed with Arshak Sarkies.

The problem was that he had zero evidence that Davies's killer was anyone other than Bin Hakim. Without that proof, his suspicions about George Lam and Kei Hin were worthless and there could be no question of taking them to the police. Cave, and particularly Batchelor, would laugh in his face. Maybe his setting Ah Cheng to follow Loddon might lead somewhere. But if not – he needed to be pursuing other avenues. Finding some tangible link back to George Lam and Kei Hin.

One avenue to follow was identifying the white man who called on Davies. With Magnus Prescott ruled out, perhaps the mystery man was the *angmoh* who George Lam claimed had told him about Cromford's diary. In which case, the most obvious candidate was Tommy Essenden. Essenden had been in the bar on the night Cromford's diary was dropped, and he was part of the group at the house of Xyiu Tang.

"Here we are, Mr Paul," said Zamir, as they stopped outside the E&O's main gate.

Jorgensen hopped out of the car, returning Vikat's hearty greeting and entered the lobby, quiet by its normal standards. A few guests and patrons were dotted about: a husband and wife leaving the telegraph office, a cluster of new arrivals gathered at the main desk, a man checking luggage at the porter's desk, half a dozen regular patrons in low armchairs drinking tea, and in the background, the gentle sound of the piano, played as ever, by F. O'Neill-Shaw.

On the off chance that Essenden, or McHugh and Chelmsall, the other men who went with Cromford and Morley to the house of Xyiu Tang, were in the hotel, Jorgensen walked in turn to Goldie's Bar, the lounge and out on to the seafront lawn, but drew a blank in every location.

At the porters' desk he asked them to send Michael to his office in ten minutes time, then he detoured towards the corridor leading to the accounts' office. He should just catch the man he wanted before office hours ended.

"Good afternoon, Mr Paul."

A chorus of voices greeted him as he pushed through the door. Three clerks, all Chinese, and their supervisor, Anthony Loke, met him with wary smiles. Visits from Jorgensen, while welcome in principle, often resulted in extra work.

"I'm after an address," Jorgensen said. "For one of our patrons – Mr Lawrence Prescott."

"Mr Prescott, ah," said Loke. "Important man. I'm not aware of any problem with his accounts," he added uncertainly.

The E&O was run on chits. None of the resident guests or the patrons who attended the hotel's regular events; the dinners, luncheons, balls, afternoon teas or orchestral concerts, ever paid for their food or drinks at the time of purchase. Instead, they signed chits. For resident guests, these were settled at the time of departure, while patrons settled theirs at monthly intervals from accounts prepared by the three clerks.

From time to time, Jorgensen was called upon to remonstrate with a patron whose accounts remained persistently unsettled. However, Arshak Sarkies' generosity, and his desire to avoid unpleasantness, caused the likes of Tommy Essenden and others to frequently take advantage, so this intervention was not as often as the hotel's managers would have preferred.

"It's okay. It's nothing to do with the accounts," said Jorgensen.

"It is Hamstead, Mr Paul – on Anson Road."

"And for Mr Magnus Prescott?"

"Ah, that one I do not know by heart. One moment please." Loke rose from his desk and walked over to a tall, narrow wooden filing cabinet, where brass label holders on the drawers showed the alphabetical progression. Inside each draw, dividers separated the records of the E&O's customers. "Here it is." Loke extracted a piece of card. "Merrydown, on Logan Road."

"Are their accounts in good order?"

"Oh yes, Mr Paul. Settled promptly every month."

"Thanks." He was about to leave when another question came to mind. Two of the clerks exchanged knowing glances as they saw him hesitate. "Can one of you bring me a summary of the accounts for three other patrons – Mr Tommy Essenden, Mr Richard Chelmsall and Mr Gordon McHugh. I'm going to my office now; you know where it is."

"It will be a pleasure, Mr Paul," said Loke, with a sidelong glance to the clock on the wall as it passed half past four, their usual end of shift.

Michael was waiting in Jorgensen's office. "You sent for me, Mr Paul," he said. His appearance was as fastidious as ever. A dark pinstriped suit, with a blue and cream patterned pocket square matching a striped tie in the same colours.

Squeezing past, into the confined space, Jorgensen tossed his hat onto the desk, taking the chair behind it and offering Michael the one nearest the door.

"Is there a reason we're crowded in here?" Michael asked. "There's more room in my office."

"There's more room in the hotel safe. Now, this business we thought we'd concluded yesterday. Unfortunately, that's not the case."

"I see, and you don't wish Mr Robinson or Mr Broomes to hear of it?"

"You catch on quick. Arshak does know, however, and he's asked me to get to the bottom of it without any... interference."

Michael nodded. Jorgensen's meaning was clear enough.

"What's happened is pretty damn serious," Jorgensen said. "The man who wrote the blackmail letter was found dead last night, and the police believe he was murdered."

Michael's outward veneer of bland calm vanished in an instant, eyes widening in shock behind his spectacles.

"The letter writer was a man named Frank Davies," Jorgensen continued. "An Englishman down on his luck, who owed money to George Lam. You might remember that when we went to see Lam, I warned him not to harm the letter writer."

"Yes, I remember. Do you believe George Lam is responsible for the man's death?"

"At the moment, the police suspect someone else, an Arab merchant from Acheen Street who threatened Davies over some dispute. By now they'll have arrested him, and I figure that within a day they'll realise they've got the wrong man. For the moment, they know nothing of Davies's involvement in the blackmail of Arthur Cromford and I'm in no hurry to tell them until I know for sure who killed him."

"My father will be disturbed by this news. Your warning to George Lam was given with my father's tacit support."

"It's out of respect to your father, and to you for helping me, that I tell you this now."

"I will go to see him tonight."

"Tell him, that whatever happens, I will keep his name, and your name, from the police. I may not be able to protect my own, or Cromford's, but there's no need to implicate anybody else."

"What will you do?"

"I'm trying to find evidence that points to Lam, or someone from his gang."

"If you do discover George Lam killed this man, then my father would expect to be told. As a mark of his standing within the Lim clan."

Jorgensen gave Michael a sharp look, wondering if he had understood the unspoken implication. Maybe the younger son was closer to his father's dealings than he had hitherto thought.

"Sure," he replied. "But when I find proof, I intend to take it to the police."

"I understand."

"Now, as far as Robinson and Broomes are concerned, I'll be working on a private matter for Arshak. They won't like it, so it's best you act ignorant of the truth if pressed."

A fleeting smile crossed Michael's face. "Is that everything, Mr Paul?" He rose from his seat and gave a stiff nod of farewell before leaving the small room.

Jorgensen lifted the earpiece from the telephone on his desk, grasping the candlestick frame to move the mouthpiece nearer.

"Hello Margaret," he said when he heard the operator's voice. "Please connect me to the house of Mr Lawrence Prescott."

His next move was to speak to Anne Prescott. If his assumptions were correct, then she knew Davies well, and he may have confided in her. But one important question bothered him. Did she know yet about Davies's death?

Prescott's head boy answered the call. "Mr Jorgensen?"

"Yes, I wish to speak to Miss Anne Prescott."

"Please wait."

The houseboy's voice echoed, in what sounded to Jorgensen like a marble tiled hallway. He had never visited Hamstead, only seen glimpses of its ornate pillars, arches and balustrades through the great trees surrounding a lush green lawn. It was built before the great war, in the style of a French chateau, with a conical roofed tower on one corner, rising above a steeply pitched tiled roof. And from what he understood, Prescott had purchased the house from a Chinese tin-mining tycoon, whose own riches led to an even more palatial mansion on Northam Road.

"Mr Jorgensen." It was the head boy again. "Miss Anne cannot come to the telephone. She is unwell. Mr Magnus will speak."

Magnus was the last person Jorgensen wished to talk to, but before he could respond, Magnus's voice came on the line. "Is that the E&O?"

"Yes, Jorgensen here."

"You're one of the managers, aren't you?" Prescott's tone was curt. "What is it you want with my sister?"

"I'm sorry to hear she's ill. It can wait until another time."

"I don't understand what possible business my sister may have with the E&O. I must insist on knowing your purpose."

"If you could let her know I called, I'd appreciate it."

"Not without telling me what it concerns."

Briefly tempted to say Frank Davies's name aloud, to gauge Magnus Prescott's reaction, Jorgensen resisted the impulse. "It's a private matter, I'm afraid."

"Do you realise who you're addressing?" Even across the crackly telephone line, Prescott's surge of anger was unmistakeable. "Sarkies will hear about this. Good day to you."

The line went dead, and Jorgensen replaced the receiver on the hook. Until now, he had never exchanged more than a few dozen words with Magnus Prescott. Enough to form a view that, like many of his privileged background in Penang, Prescott was both arrogant and snobbish. But those far from unusual traits among his kind did not explain the undisguised hostility he had just experienced. Jorgensen wondered what else lay behind it. There was Magnus's obvious desire to protect his sister – the same overly developed protectiveness that led him to employ Loddon to watch over Frank Davies. The question that worried Jorgensen was – how far might Magnus's obsession with protecting her from Davies have led him?

# Thirty

Ah Cheng returned to the E&O shortly before six o'clock. He entered the grounds through the small gate in the wall on Farquhar Street that led to the kitchen, then found the staff path to the offices.

Jorgensen's office was empty, and Ah Cheng hesitated at the doorway, uncertain what to do next. Though Jorgensen had not laid out strict rules, he knew that his wandering into the lobby would not meet with approval. He retreated instead to the stables, to consult with Abdul, and found Jorgensen there before him, leaving through the main double-doors.

Seeing Ah Cheng, Jorgensen led him to the edge of the cobbled yard. "What can you tell me?" he asked.

"Loddon did not see me following. He went from the Victoria Inn to Rope Walk. To the office of Lam."

"Lam?" Jorgensen was incredulous. "Are you sure?"

"Yes, boss. Then Loddon came out with Kei Hin. I followed them to Penang Road. They went into the Australia Hotel. After, Loddon went home to Pulau Tikus."

Jorgensen continued to eye Ah Cheng in disbelief. "I think I underestimated friend Loddon. We need to find out what the hell he's playing at."

***

Within ten minutes, they were heading for Pulau Tikus in the Standard Tourer, with Zamir at the wheel. Forty minutes by rickshaw. Not much more than five by motor car, with the darkening north-eastern slopes of Penang Hill away to their left. They turned inland towards them, driving between the facing gateways of the Thai and Burmese Buddhist temples, whose ornate golden carvings sparkled in the vivid orange glow of approaching sunset.

Ah Cheng directed Zamir onto Burmah Road and through Pulau Tikus. In the village, the earliest of the evening diners were beginning to gather around the coffeeshops.

"Very famous Mee Goreng here," said Zamir. "Bangkok Lane Mee Goreng. Too spicy for you, huh Ah Cheng?" He pointed through the window to the popular corner *kopitiam* as they passed it. Tables crowded the gaps between its walkway pillars, and a young boy carried two plates heaped with noodles and fried squid pieces. "Soon they close," Zamir added unhelpfully.

"Slow now," said Ah Cheng as they left the shophouse rows of Pulau Tikus behind, and trees screened both sides of the road. "Here on the right is the kampung. Turn now."

Peering carefully through the windscreen, Zamir bounced the Standard onto the track leading through the trees, and they jolted down it for sixty yards, passing a jumble of atap and corrugated tin roofed buildings, many modified from traditional kampung houses built up on stilts. Two mongrel dogs, brown and short-haired, shot out from the undergrowth across the car's path.

"This one," said Ah Cheng, and the Standard stopped close to Loddon's green painted wooden house. Zamir switched off the engine and it spluttered to a stop. In its place they heard the noisy chatter and indignant screams of monkeys in the trees and the high-pitched buzz of cicadas all around.

Ah Cheng and Jorgensen climbed out to walk the few paces to the foot of the stairs. Above them, light glowed from behind the mosquito screen door leading off the corner verandah. Leaving Jorgensen below him, Ah Cheng climbed the wooden stairs.

"Hello," he called out. "Here is Ah Cheng from the E&O. I have brought Mr Jorgensen."

The door was pulled open and, in the gathering twilight, Zulla, Loddon's Malay wife, stood silhouetted in the frame against the bare electric light bulb behind her.

"You once more," she said, though without irritation.

"Mr Jorgensen is here to speak to your husband." Ah Cheng stepped aside to point back down the stairs, up which Jorgensen was climbing.

"Good evening," he said to Zulla, with a bow of his head. "It is important I speak with him."

Zulla let the door swing closed behind her wide hips. "You missed him by twenty minutes, but did you not speak with him already?"

"He told you?"

"Loddon tells me little. Only I should not worry. What has he done that you should all come from the E&O by motor car?" Before they could answer, Zulla looked accusingly at Ah Cheng. "You said your boss wanted information from Loddon. Then tell me why he is here again now."

"Ah Cheng told you the truth," said Jorgensen. "And your husband did give me information when we met. Though as he omitted something important, I need to talk to him again. Where is he now?"

"I do not know. He straight away set off again to George Town."

"Is he going to meet somebody?"

"I already say he tells me little. Tell me, Mr Jorgensen – where did you meet him before?"

"At the Victoria Inn."

"I would try there again." There was a catch in her voice, and the glint of a tear in her eye. "You must tell me if Loddon is in trouble," she said.

"I hope he is not," Jorgensen replied. "When I find him, I will try to help."

"We have little money," she said. "I tell Loddon it does not matter." She gestured to the door and timber walls behind her. "We have this house, and always have food. It is enough, though Loddon does not believe me when I tell him so."

"Has he talked about getting hold of more money?"

Zulla shook her head, a wistful smile on her face. "Many years ago, Loddon worked for Prescott's and drove a motor car. An old vehicle that broke down many times. He was proud of it, and ever since, he wanted his own. Yesterday he spoke about the coast road to Batu Ferringhi and the beauty of the beaches. With our own motor car, he said, no more than one hour." She shook her head again as if suddenly making up her mind. "When you see him, tell him I do not want a motor car, or to visit Batu Ferringhi."

***

After dark, the Victoria Inn was busier than on Jorgensen's earlier visit. With its clientele drawn from many of Penang's different races, nobody raised an eyebrow when Ah Cheng entered alongside Jorgensen.

While Ah Cheng checked the rear of the bar, Jorgensen spoke to the barman, who knew Loddon but had not seen him since the afternoon.

It was a similar story at the Hong Kong Bar.

"Tuan Loddon. No, not today," said Yeoh, the head barman. "Yesterday he last come."

"Where now?" Ah Cheng asked Jorgensen. "Australia Hotel?"

Zamir parked the Standard Tourer down the side of the Australia Hotel in Argyle Street and, this time, Ah Cheng remained with him in the car while Jorgensen walked back to the corner entrance doors.

The lobby of the Australia Hotel was a fraction of the size of the E&O's grand equivalent. A handful of rattan chairs and round glass topped tables hugged the windowed wall along the Argyle Street side. Facing the windows was first a staircase, leading to the bedrooms above, and then the reception desk. A few feet on from the desk were double doors, leading to the bar and dining room, through which Jorgensen heard the buzz of voices and the clink of glasses.

Two male clerks at the desk, one Malay and one Chinese, both wearing cream-coloured jackets, with the hotel's name embroidered on the breast, smiled in greeting as Jorgensen approached.

"I'm Jorgensen from the E&O. I'd like to speak with Mr. Bailey."

Bailey was the manager of the hotel. An Australian, as befitted the establishment's name, and a man whom Jorgensen had aided in the past. Though competitors, George Town's hoteliers long ago learnt the value of cooperation in dealing with wayward guests, and, considering himself their de-facto leader, Arshak Sarkies had offered Jorgensen's services to rivals on several occasions.

The Malay clerk, young and watchful, bowed his head deferentially. "I regret Mr Bailey left for the day."

"All right, I'll ask you instead. Did you have two visitors earlier this afternoon? A large white man, shabbily dressed, who came in with a young Chinese man?"

"No sir. I did not see such persons."

"How about you?" Jorgensen turned to the Chinese clerk. "They don't look much like your normal guests, so they'd have stood out."

"I was not on duty this afternoon," the second clerk replied.

"Perhaps chief clerk saw them," the Malay clerk offered. "He was on duty today and left with Mr Bailey."

"Can I see your guest register?"

The clerk visibly blanched at the suggestion and exchanged glances with his colleague before turning back to Jorgensen. "Cannot, sir. It is not permitted."

"Is Mr Bailey on the telephone at home?"

"Yes sir. We have his number for emergencies."

"Please ring him and explain that Jorgensen from the E&O requests to see the guest register. I'm sure he'll consent."

Following another exchange of glances with his colleague, the Malay clerk moved reluctantly towards the telephone stand at the far end of the desk. "Mr Bailey may be at dinner," he warned.

"Tell him it's important."

While the clerk spoke to an operator and waited to be put through, Jorgensen looked around the empty lobby. Two electric ceiling fans whirred overhead, new additions in the last few years, unlike the paintings on the walls – a series of Victorian era renderings of the Penang and Singapore racecourses.

The Malay clerk beckoned Jorgensen. "Mr Bailey for you," he said, passing the receiver and pushing the candlestick stand forward.

"Jorgensen here."

"What are you up to?" said Bailey. "Cookie's dished up a nice piece of fish that's spoiling as we speak."

"Sorry, Bailey. It's important or I wouldn't have insisted. Did your man tell you what I wanted?"

"It wasn't clear."

"I'd like a look at the guest register. Two men came into the Australia this afternoon and I'm trying to find out who they were after."

"Will checking the register help?"

"Maybe."

"Go right ahead."

"Thanks, Bailey. Will you tell your man it's okay?"

"As long as I can return to my dinner."

Jorgensen handed the receiver back and waited while the clerk listened intently to his instructions, before placing the guest register in front of Jorgensen.

There were twenty rooms in the Australia Hotel, a mere fifth of the number in the E&O, and their guest register was correspondingly simpler: a foot-wide leatherbound book, printed in London and as could be found in hundreds of small hotels across the empire.

Jorgensen flipped through the pages to the most recent entries. With little idea of what exactly he was looking for, he ran a finger down the listed surnames. Most were of British or Irish origin, with home addresses listed from across Malaya and some further overseas – from India, England and several from Australia. Against a few of the names, the *SS Balmain,* home port Perth, was noted as their address. And apart from one married couple from Singapore, all were single men.

None of the names were recognisable as connected with Davies, or Morley and Cromford. Or indeed with Essenden, McHugh, Chelmsall or Prescott. Nothing jumped out, so he asked the clerk for paper and a pen and spent two minutes copying down the details and arrival dates of the current guests.

He folded and pocketed the completed list and thanked the clerks for their help. "I'll have a drink before I leave," he said, and walked through the double doors to the bar.

The bar was small but crowded. A dozen guests were either seated at small tables against the side windows, or on tall stools by the bar. A further set of double doors to the dining room beyond swung open as a waiter carried through a tray of drinks.

Jorgensen strolled across to the bar counter. He ordered an F&N lemon water, then leant with his back to the bar casting an eye over the guests. As with his scan of the register, he did not quite know what he was hoping to find. He figured most of the men in the bar were commercial agents. Though none of them were known to him, their breed was familiar enough from the E&O – visiting Penang with their cases of samples and catalogues, to drum up orders for European or North American products.

He finished his drink and walked to the dining room doors. Pushing them open, he ignored the quizzical look from the head boy, and looked around the assembled diners. There was no sign of the officers from the *SS Balmain*. In or out of uniform, merchant seamen were easy enough to spot. He had spent long enough in their company. Instead, it was more of the same clientele as in the bar – commercial agents dining with their fellow agents or perhaps their George Town customers.

If it was one of these anonymous men that Loddon and Kei Hin were seeking, then Jorgensen was damned if he could work out which one.

***

Jorgensen sent Zamir back to the hotel in the Standard Tourer, while he and Ah Cheng walked to a coffeeshop fifty yards further down Penang Road.

"You wish to eat with me?" asked Ah Cheng, puzzled at Jorgensen's suggestion.

"I eat in local places all the time," Jorgensen replied. "Don't worry, I know how to hold chopsticks."

Open from four until midnight, the corner coffeeshop was Cantonese owned. Between its supporting pillars, curving around the building's edge, the hawkers at the mobile stalls were tossing noodles in giant skillets.

"Do you know this place?" Jorgensen asked Ah Cheng, as they edged past the prawn mee stall at the entrance. Inside, at a dozen small round tables squeezed close together, heads bobbed over plates and bowls, and loud chatter was punctuated with snorts of laughter and regular calls to the proprietor and his wife for more drinks. Electric lights cast an orange glow over the haze of smoke from cigarettes and the hawkers' stoves. A few customers eyed Jorgensen with curiosity, but most ignored him. He was a regular, known by sight and no longer worthy of a second glance.

"Ha, Mr Paul!" cried out the proprietor, a sprightly dark-haired man wearing a stained apron over cotton shirt and shorts. "Here, here!" He gestured towards a table where a lone diner sat over a plate of Char Koay Teow noodles. Getting there first, he shooed the bewildered customer to a spare seat at a nearby table and wiped the marble top clean the instant the man's plate was lifted clear.

"Kopi O?" the proprietor asked Jorgensen. Black coffee with sugar was the shop's most popular drink and the first question he asked every customer.

"Kopi Peng," Jorgensen answered. Right now, the chill of an iced coffee with condensed milk was more tempting.

The proprietor tutted in dismay. "Kopi O better, but you never learn. And you?" He jerked his thumb at Ah Cheng. "Kopi O?"

Ah Cheng nodded.

"Two plates Char Koay Teow?" the proprietor asked. "Spicy or not?"

There was a ritual to Jorgensen's exchanges with the proprietor, part of which was the repeated insistence that as a foreigner, Jorgensen could not possibly stomach spicy food.

"I get for you," said the proprietor on seeing Ah Cheng's nod of assent. "Spicy huh?" he said to Jorgensen, wincing at his customer's poor choice. Without moving from their side, he turned to bellow the order to the Char Koay Teow hawker at his stove half a dozen yards away, before retreating to the back of the shop to fetch the drinks.

"I don't know this place," said Ah Cheng.

"It's close to where I live," said Jorgensen, pointing across Penang Road to the opposite corner. "Down there," he said. "In Datuk Koyah Road."

Ah Cheng gave Jorgensen a curious look, unsure whether Jorgensen was teasing him.

Their food was carried to the table by the hawker's assistant: two plates of flat rice noodles with two plump prawns per plate, bean sprouts, sliced sausage, plenty of cockles and spiced with a good spoonful of chilli sambal. In Jorgensen's opinion, it was close to the best Char Koay Teow in George Town. He handed the boy twenty cents. Each of the hawkers paid rent to the proprietor for their stall, but then took all the food proceeds direct, a common arrangement among Penang's coffeeshops. Though it was the proprietor who made money from the drinks. Ten cents in the case of the two cups of coffee in china cups that he soon brought to the table.

When they had finished and dropped their chopsticks onto empty plates, Jorgensen offered Ah Cheng a cigarette, to be met with a shake of the head. Jorgensen lit his own. "I'll return to the E&O now," he said, tossing the spent match into the ashtray. "There's a chance one or two people I should question might show up this evening."

"You want me to look for Tuan Loddon?" asked Ah Cheng.

Jorgensen appraised Ah Cheng through the curl of exhaled smoke. "If you're up for it. Where will you look?"

"Same places we looked before. I will come for you if I find him. Why do you think he and Kei Hin went to that hotel?"

"It's got to be something to do with the lodging house in Love Lane – but I wish I knew what. Maybe Loddon saw someone there who he recognised from the Australia Hotel. As for Kei Hin's involvement, I've no idea."

"I see what I can find, boss."

"I'd prefer it if you don't call me boss," said Jorgensen.

"But what will I call you?" Ah Cheng asked. "You have many different names."

Jorgensen chuckled. "That's true."

"People call you Mr Mac. Why is that?" Ah Cheng asked the question with some trepidation. Though invited to eat by Jorgensen, he remained wary of overstepping the boundaries. After all, Jorgensen was a white man. But his curiosity overcame his caution.

"It's an old nickname. I thought I'd got rid of it when I came to Penang, but it somehow followed me. When I joined the army, everybody in my training platoon had a Scottish name – like McDonald or McKenzie. They thought it was funny to christen me Mac, and it's kind of stuck ever since."

Ah Cheng nodded, though he had no conception of what having a Scottish name meant, never having heard of Scotland. But he felt honoured that Jorgensen had chosen to share that confidence.

Jorgensen fished a fresh pack of cigarettes from his pocket and tossed them to Ah Cheng.

"I don't smoke," said Ah Cheng.

"Not for you – they're to help other people remember."

Ah Cheng grinned in understanding.

"Steer clear of Kei Hin," warned Jorgensen.

"He does not worry me," said Ah Cheng scornfully.

# Thirty-One

On his return to the E&O, Jorgensen went first to the cloakroom, where he gratefully splashed water on his face and neck, drying himself with the towel offered by the attendant, Then, he walked to his office, where he extracted a clean dry shirt from the folded pile in the bottom desk drawer.

From a jacket pocket he took out the folded sheet of the Australia Hotel's embossed notepaper. He spread it onto the desk, running through the names on the list as he shrugged off his jacket and tie, peeled off his shirt and buttoned up the clean replacement.

*Skine, Haigh, McAusland, Griffiths, Samini, Solly, Wentworth, Edmonds, Stubbock, McMaster, Driver, Vickerman, Jewell, Van Esten, Murphy, Corbett, Hilliard, Rorke, Chapman.*

The names were as unfamiliar as the faces he had seen in the Australia Hotel's dining room. Even the last three – the officers from the *SS Balmain*, were unknown to him. But the reason for Kei Hin and Loddon's visit to the Australia Hotel had to lie with one of them – it was the only explanation that made sense.

He lit a cigarette and sat at his desk for a while, hoping that some inspiration would strike. None came, other than a hardening view that the key lay within those names. Tomorrow he would return to the Australia Hotel – and dig deeper. Decision made, he put his jacket and tie back on and left his office, thinking that while he was waiting for ideas to form, he might as well take a patrol of the hotel's grounds.

"There is a telephone call for you, Mr Paul." Gopi, one of the porters, intercepted him the moment he set foot in the lobby. "I was told to find you."

"Who was it?"

"You must ask at the desk."

A message scribbled onto a memorandum pad was waiting at the front desk for him. It was from Anne Prescott.

*I believe you wanted to speak to me this evening. I wish to meet with you in private. Come to the stables at Hamstead at ten-thirty. Anne Prescott.*

***

When George Town spread westwards at the end of the last century, and new mansions were built for tycoons enriched by tin mining and mercantile trade, Anson Road was one of the first avenues to be laid out. Behind imposing stone gateways and screens of palm trees, spacious residences overlooked extensive lawns and well-tendered tropical gardens.

By ten-thirty at night, most of the mansions were lost in the all-enveloping shroud of nightfall, save for the distant flicker of lights from entrance porticoes, and the occasional dimmer glow behind closed shutters and blinds.

A pair of headlights picked out the broad trunks of the Tanjong and Angsana trees lining the street and briefly shone on two Indian men, padding home barefoot from kitchen duties at one of the mansions. At the wheel of the car – the E&O's blue Standard Tourer – was Zamir. Though called out for the third time that day by Jorgensen, the driver did not object to the suddenness of Jorgensen's latest summons. Anything offering more excitement than his normal duties: the regular ferrying of guests to and from the railway building, up to the botanic gardens or, on rare occasions, down the length of the island to the snake temple, was fine by him.

He touched the brakes to glide the car to a halt. In the silence after the engine noise died away, the nearby whoops and cries of monkeys rang loud. At night, troops of macaques, encroaching from the jungled slopes of Penang Hill, marauded happily among the leafy suburbs, as much a feature of the manicured gardens as the snakes and lizards.

"You wait here, Zamir," said Jorgensen. "I'll walk the rest of the way."

They had parked fifty yards from the entrance to Hamstead – the home of the Prescott family. Jorgensen walked along the metalled road surface, his eyes growing accustomed to the dark until he reached the iron gates, left open, as if a vehicle was expected to return before a servant closed them for the night.

Beyond the gates, the driveway curved for thirty yards to an apron below the tall conical tower at the corner of the house. Anne Prescott had specified the stables in her message, and as he drew close, Jorgensen noticed two smaller buildings off to the left, hidden from the road by trees, even in daylight.

There was no sign of a servant stationed below the portico of the main house and his stealthy approach had raised no alarms. He hung left on the driveway, angling towards the outbuildings, searching in the darkness for a sign of Anne Prescott.

"Mr Jorgensen," a male voice hissed. "This way, please."

A man materialised from under the eaves of the first outbuilding and beckoned Jorgensen closer. "Miss Anne is here."

Drawing near, Jorgensen saw the man was dark-skinned and narrow-shouldered, six inches or so shorter than himself. He followed him down the side of the building, past stable doors and the strong scents of hay and manure. At its far end, the man led the way up a flight of external stairs, opening a door at the top into a room above the stable. In the shaft of light from within, Jorgensen saw the man was Malay, around thirty years old, wearing uniform breeches and a blue shirt.

"Please," the man said, holding the door open for Jorgensen to enter.

The living quarters inside were those of live-in servants, cramped, and sparsely furnished, but more comfortable than most such quarters on the island. Meant, Jorgensen presumed, for the man and his wife, a slim Malay woman with dark eyebrows knitted in a disapproving frown, who rose from a wooden chair as Jorgensen entered. Beside her, on another seat pushed close to the first, was Anne Prescott. Even in the faint light of nearby tabletop candles, he realised she had already heard news of Davies's death. Her eyes were red-rimmed and puffy, and her face drawn.

"Miss Prescott," said Jorgensen.

"Thank you, Sarah," said Anne to the woman. "I'll be all right now."

"I will stay," Sarah replied. Her face etched with concern.

"No, I wish to speak with Mr Jorgensen alone. Please wait outside. And Rayyan," she added to the man who waited at the open door. "Keep watch."

With a last look at her employer, Sarah left the room with Rayyan, and shut the door behind her. Jorgensen heard only one set of footsteps descending the staircase, which he presumed were Rayyan's. He figured that Sarah was waiting just outside the door, no doubt listening in.

"Rayyan is our *sais*," Anne said. "And Sarah our *amah*. They've both been with us for many years. Will you sit, Mr Jorgensen?"

He pulled the spare chair forward and faced Anne from a couple of feet away. Her fair hair was tousled as if she had run her hands through it countless times.

Anne lifted her chin. "Why did you wish to speak to me this afternoon?" she asked. "Why did you ring the house?"

"I thought you ought to be told."

"You mean about Frank?"

"Yes. I wasn't sure whether you'd heard."

Anne twisted her head to the side and stared at her reflection in the small window. "Oh, I heard all right. Papa read it in the afternoon edition of the newspaper and thought fit to show me the story when he arrived home. How could he be so callous?"

"I'm sorry you had to find out like that."

Anne turned her gaze back on to Jorgensen. "I left the drawing room and fled to my bedroom. I couldn't face a single one of them – they were all so cruel and heartless."

"Do your family believe you're still in your room now?"

"Mama came up a few times to see how I was. Knocking on the door and calling through it. But I refused to let her in, and when she thought I'd fallen asleep she stopped trying. I suppose they believe I'm still in there, but frankly I've wept enough for tonight." Her jaw was set in a determined manner, as if refusing to countenance any more displays of emotion. "The Echo didn't state the cause of death, Mr Jorgensen, do you know how Frank died?"

"I'm afraid the police believe he was killed."

Her hand flew to cover her mouth, and she stared wide-eyed at Jorgensen. "Killed," she gasped eventually. "My God, why would anybody kill Frank?"

"Tomorrow's newspapers are likely to report an arrest in the case."

"An arrest? Who?"

"A man called Bin Hakim. A merchant from Acheen Street. One of Frank's clients who'd apparently threatened him."

She shook her head slowly, trying to come to terms with what Jorgensen was telling her. "None of his clients would do such a thing. Frank moved heaven and earth to help them, and they respected him enormously for it."

"It's not known why Bin Hakim made the threats."

"I know Frank owed a lot of money," she said. "But he was trying to set that right. Is it possible he owed money to this man?"

"Bin Hakim is a moneylender."

Anne fell silent, wringing her hands on her lap and lost in agonised thoughts. Then she looked up again. "How did you know about me and Frank, Mr Jorgensen?" she asked. "Did he tell you?"

"No," said Jorgensen. "It was a man called Loddon."

Anne's brow creased in confusion. "Loddon," she repeated. "I know that name."

"He once worked for your father's firm."

"I remember him now, old Aubrey Loddon. An odd, rather shambling man. But he left the company years ago. How would he know about Frank?"

"He was watching Frank Davies's house on Love Lane. On the orders of your brother, Magnus." Jorgensen spoke in deliberately matter-of-fact tones, and his stomach lurched when he saw the look of horror spread across Anne's face on hearing her brother's name. She reached forward to grab Jorgensen's wrist with both hands, her fingers digging hard into his flesh.

"He was spying on us?" she asked, her face contorted in misery.

"Yes."

"Oh God. Poor Frank. He never stood a chance." She released her grip and held her head in her hands, while Jorgensen watched uneasily, until she lifted her eyes to meet his. "Why are you here, Mr Jorgensen? It's not just to tell me about Frank's death. It's because of what you discovered about Mr Loddon, isn't it?"

"It is."

"How much do you know? About Frank and me?" she asked.

"Loddon told me your family forbade you from seeing him. But nothing more."

"There's an entire sad history to tell then. Do you want to hear it?"

"Only if you want to tell it."

"I fell in love with Frank after meeting him at the theatrical society." She smiled in sorrow. "I know you saw him recently, but I wish you'd met him back then. He was clever, and passionate about so many things. He was six years older than me, though the age difference didn't seem to matter much. We made plans to marry but somehow my father found out. I pleaded with Frank to consider eloping, but he wouldn't hear of it. He feared I'd ruin my life, living like an outcast with him. So, I gave in to my father's plans and was sent home to a girls' school in Yorkshire. All that kept me sane for two years were the letters I received from Frank, which came via one of my friends so the school would never know. When I finished school, I intended to return immediately to Penang, but Frank wrote to tell me he'd met another girl – and that he was going to marry her. I was heartbroken, so I stayed on in England to study as a nurse in London, but I guess you know that much."

"Frank didn't marry though," said Jorgensen.

She gave another sad smile. "No, he didn't. It was a ruse to stop me from coming back and seeing how low he'd fallen."

"What happened to him?"

"My father is a vindictive man. It wasn't enough for him to separate me and Frank. He had to go further. When we met, Frank was a clerk at James Merry, the solicitors on Church Street. Once I'd left for England my father used his influence to see Frank dismissed, then pressured the firm into writing a damning reference that Frank couldn't possibly use, and he and Magnus spread word to all the law firms that Frank couldn't be trusted. They wanted him banished from Penang, though try as they might they failed. Of course, I didn't find out any of this until much later. Frank never mentioned a word in his letters about the persecution. I knew he'd left James Merry, but he made it seem it was his choice to set up as a letter writer. How stupidly naïve I was."

"Why do you think your family turned against Frank?"

"Before he met me, Frank had a mistress – a Chinese girl. Papa found out, but it's not the whole story. Frank is quite different from my father and my brother…" her voice caught as she realised what she had said. "…was quite different. He loved poetry, and music, and literature and took an interest in politics. I suppose they didn't trust him because of the sort of man he was. One they couldn't understand or control."

"Do you still love him?"

"Not in the way I did. Not after he'd broken my heart. We'd stopped exchanging letters, but for some reason, after I'd qualified, I wrote to him again. His address was always poste restante at the Post Office on Weld Quay, so I had no idea he'd abandoned his digs and was living in such a run-down lodging house. His reply shocked me. Though he didn't confess the whole truth, he admitted an addiction to opium. I imagine he could tell from my letter that I was quite different from the young girl he'd known, and therefore felt able to prepare me for what I'd find on my return."

"Is that when he told you what had happened since you left?"

"He told me the whole sorry tale when I first visited him. I was furious, but he pleaded with me not to confront my father. He was afraid it would only make things worse – that he'd be prevented from continuing his work and be left with nothing."

"Is his work the reason he stayed in George Town?"

"He fell into it by accident. He'd studied some of the languages of Malaya while he was a clerk. Malay, of course, and the Chinese dialects – Hokkien and Cantonese. They came naturally to him somehow, and he learnt Tamil and later scraps of Urdu and Hindi. At first, he wrote letters to help his landlord, then for other traders on the same street. Over time he began to appreciate how valuable his help was to them all."

"He was proud of it when I spoke to him."

"He was," Anne pursed her lips, not in disapproval, more in anxiety. "Was he very drunk when you last saw him?"

"He'd been drinking. He was unhappy."

"Because of the money he owed?"

Jorgensen wondered if she knew the full extent of Davies's debts and his plans to repay them. It would be piling one cruelty on top of another to tell her about his involvement in the blackmail plot. She had suffered enough that day. And part of him baulked at admitting his promise to protect Davies from George Lam and Kei Hin.

"He told me about a debt to a moneylender," he said.

"Do you think that's why he was killed?" she asked.

"I don't know."

"What do you think Mr Jorgensen? That's why you're here, isn't it? You don't believe the man the police arrested is responsible."

"I wish I knew the truth, Miss Prescott."

"Do you believe my brother is responsible for Frank's death?"

The unemotional way she asked the question startled Jorgensen. "In what way?" he asked.

"Directly responsible."

"Do you think he might be?"

"When you told me about Mr Loddon spying on Frank, the idea jumped straight into my head that Magnus was to blame for his death. I knew he hated Frank, but the more I thought of it, I realised it's not possible. Magnus is a bully and a coward, and always has been, but too much of one to risk his own prospects. He'll take over Prescott's from Papa one day..." her words trailed off and she stretched a hand to the corner of the nearby table for support, the colour suddenly draining from her face.

Jorgensen jumped from his chair, bounding over to the door which he wrenched open. "Quick," he said to the startled woman outside. "Miss Prescott is fainting."

Sarah rushed in and wrapped Anne in her embrace. "Miss must go back to the house," she said. "Please fetch Rayyan."

Jorgensen ran down the staircase, finding the driver from the orange glow of a cigarette end in the dark.

He waited at the foot of the stairs while Rayyan went to help his wife. Soon, Anne appeared, and with a hand on Sarah's arm, began a slow descent, followed by Rayyan.

"I'm terribly sorry, Mr Jorgensen," she murmured when she reached the foot of the stairs.

"I will see you again soon," said Jorgensen. He had wanted to tell her about the ring and the lock of hair found on the bookshelves in Davies's room. She deserved to know about them, but it would have to wait.

"Boss, you must go," hissed Rayyan. "Hurry please."

Jorgensen left the grounds of Hamstead as quietly as he had arrived and was at the door of the Standard Tourer before Zamir heard him coming.

# Thirty-Two

Ah Cheng's search for Loddon began at the Victoria Inn, then moved on to the Hong Kong Bar, where off-duty British soldiers spotted him as he entered. But it was a different group from the one led by the red-headed sergeant a few days earlier, and their calls were mocking rather than welcoming.

After the bars on Chulia Street, he next tried the street's few coffeeshops still open into the evening. His height easily allowing him to see over the heads of the hawkers from the five-foot ways. At the night market, he wandered among the busy food stalls, but there were no Europeans among the predominantly Chinese crowd.

As dusk gave way to night, Ah Cheng doubled back down Chulia Street to the Australia Hotel on Penang Road, where he hung around for a fruitless hour on the opposite corner to the hotel, attracting curious looks from the jostling line of Indians and Malays outside the *nasi kandar* restaurant.

With no sign of his quarry and increasingly doubtful that Loddon was likely to return to the Australia Hotel, Ah Cheng decided to go on to Rope Walk.

By this hour, the street's transformation from its daylight economy to its seedier night-time equivalent was well underway. The barkers from the brothels were out in full force, accosting the men in the street who shuffled past. These were the working men of George Town, the labourers, the stevedores, the plantation workers. Mainly Indian or Chinese, many were recent immigrants, alone without families in a new and strange country.

Mindful of Jorgensen's warning to beware of Kei Hin, Ah Cheng walked among the crowds, risking a cautious reconnaissance of Lam's office, where only the two clerks at their desks were visible through the half-open window blinds.

He considered a second tour of the same coffeeshop and pub circuit in search of Loddon, but instead settled into a relatively quiet spot further back on Rope Walk towards Campbell Street. From there, sat with his back against the closed shutter of a tinsmith's workshop, he kept vigilant watch on the office of the Lam Copra Export Company, pausing only to shoo away the occasional brothel barker.

Twenty minutes passed before Ah Cheng saw a small man in a wide straw hat entering Lam's office, reappearing moments later with Kei Hin at his side. With a gesture of impatience, Kei Hin beckoned a third figure from inside the office to join them on the five-foot way. It was Loddon. He had been in Lam's office all along.

Together, Loddon and Straw Hat set off on foot away from Ah Cheng's position, while Kei Hin retreated into the office. Almost immediately, Straw Hat turned left, followed by Loddon, both disappearing into a narrow alley.

Picking his moment, Ah Cheng dashed across the street, dodging between the knots of men who had not yet made up their minds as to which brothel to frequent. He knew the alley. Unlit and narrow, it ran for over a hundred yards at the rear of shophouses on Campbell Street, leading eventually into Claimant Place, between the Campbell Street market hall and the Carnavon Street police station.

Ah Cheng peered around the corner, seeing no further through the sudden darkness than a few yards. The noise from the street behind him drowned out any sound of receding footsteps.

He clenched both fists tight, released them and clenched them again. Taking a deep breath, he strode boldly into the pitch black of the alley. He walked on for a dozen paces, quicker than his eyes could adjust, then stopped dead to listen out for any movement. All he could hear were the shouts and catcalls from Rope Walk behind him, a little muffled now by the tight alley walls. No sound of footsteps ahead, though the alley's far end was still another hundred yards away.

Then, from behind, Ah Cheng heard the creak of a gate. He whirled round to see two wide, dark figures, silhouetted against the light from Rope Walk. His muscles tensed, before a voice called out from behind him.

"Cousin, you forgot your crowbar."

It was Kei Hin. Ah Cheng span round again. He was trapped. Two men blocking off the exit to Rope Walk, and Kei Hin and at least one other closing in from the other direction. He turned back, intending to break through to Rope Walk. Charging forwards, he leapt up and crunched a hard heel into one man's ribs, sending its victim crashing against a wall. He swung a balled fist at the second man, catching only a glancing blow off a dipping shoulder. He swung again, an uppercut into a stomach, hearing the agonised grunt and feeling the man's wounded gasp against his face as he tried to shove him aside.

A blow to the back of his head dropped Ah Cheng to one knee, before a volley of punches and kicks rained down on his back, ribs, and head. He attempted to stagger to his feet, grasping a handful of an assailant's shirt, but a kick swept his legs from under him. He crashed to the ground, shoulder first, pulling the man down with him. More kicks thudded in. The attacker was dragged off him, and he was surrounded. Survival was his only recourse. To curl into a ball, his arms wrapped around his head as the blows kept on coming.

"No red devil with a gun to help you today, cousin." Kei Hin snarled from above.

The last thing Ah Cheng saw was the sole of Kei Hin's shoe as it stamped down into his face.

# Thirty-Three

The next day, Jorgensen woke before sunrise, leaving home to the sound of the call for Fajr prayers from the mosque on Chulia Street. He paused at the front door, half-hoping to find a message pushed underneath. Yesterday, he had pointed out his street to Ah Cheng, and thought him more than capable of finding the right house if necessary.

But there was no note from Ah Cheng. The mat held only his shoes.

A two-minute walk through the still dark side streets took Jorgensen to Argyle Road, where bare electric light bulbs strung under a tree lit up the roti canai hawker's stall. There, pots of chicken curry and lentil dhal steamed over a charcoal fire, and circles of oiled dough for the roti bread puffed up in seconds on the hotplate.

He took a stool at one of the low trestle tables under the spreading branches, calling a greeting to the hawker. Two pre-dawn regulars, Malays on their own way to work, grinned at him over cups of teh tarik. The hawker's young son soon trotted over with Jorgensen's own tea, placing a trimmed banana leaf on the table, to serve as a plate for two roti and a large spoon of dhal. In exchange, Jorgensen took a few cents from his pocket, while enquiring politely about the health of the hawker's family.

The roti was crisp, the dhal spicy and the tea hot and invigorating. Jorgensen ate with his hands, as did all the hawker's customers and, once he had finished, rinsed them clean at the nearby standpipe. Unlike the other customers, however, Jorgensen never lingered over breakfast, a custom that puzzled them more than his being European.

On reaching the E&O, Jorgensen headed straight for the stables, from where Abdul hurried out to meet him.

"Is Ah Cheng here?" Jorgensen asked.

"No, Major Mac. Is why I rush. He did not return last night."

Jorgensen frowned, perturbed by Ah Cheng's absence. In the middle of the night, he had woken, and lying there could not shake off a conviction that he had been somehow hoodwinked. That Ah Cheng had seen an opportunity greater than the one offered by Arshak Sarkies at the E&O, and tempted by it, had thrown in his lot with George Lam or Aubrey Loddon on whatever scheme they were hatching.

But in the freshness of the morning, and fortified by breakfast, those night-time imaginings seemed less plausible. More likely, Jorgensen hoped, Ah Cheng's efforts to locate Loddon had taken up most of the night and he had slept elsewhere in George Town to avoid disturbing the other drivers in the dormitory.

"I'll need Zamir again this morning," he said to Abdul. "Have him ready for eight o'clock.

"The Standard is ready for you and Zamir is at the kitchen."

"I'll check around the hotel first. Let me know if Ah Cheng returns."

In the lobby, a handful of early-rising guests were dotted among the array of chairs, sofas, and potted plants, from where they quietly perused the morning newspapers. Jorgensen stopped at the porter's desk to speak to Rama, the head porter, a straight-backed dark-skinned Tamil of medium height, with greying temples and a thin grey moustache that gave him an air of sophistication suited to the lobby of the E&O.

"I need to borrow a porter's uniform," Jorgensen said. An idea had finally occurred to him about the next step.

Trained never to be fazed by the often peculiar requests coming from the E&O's guests, Rama nevertheless could not help the quizzical look that appeared on his face.

Jorgensen indicated the junior porter who was standing at Rama's side. "One in Gopi's size would do just fine."

"Of course, Mr Paul," said Rama, having recovered his equanimity. "When do you require it?"

"Now. Send it out to the stables. I'll be taking it with me when I leave at eight o'clock." Leaving Rama to issue the necessary orders, Jorgensen set off on his morning patrol of the grounds.

***

Gordon McHugh, known as Ginger, was a redhead of the type unsuited to life outdoors in the tropics. His pale freckled skin turned a dangerous crimson hue when overexposed to sun. And three years of acclimatisation in Penang had not diminished a tendency to heavy perspiration. It was to his credit that McHugh never allowed such shortcomings to prevent his gung-ho participation in outdoor sports: a hulking rugby forward, a bruising cricket batsman, a strong sea swimmer at the Penang Swimming Club. But during the working week he thanked his lucky stars for the electric fan in the harbourmaster's office.

Which was where Jorgensen found him after leaving the E&O. In the marine department on the corner of the first floor of the U-shaped Government Buildings. These stately buff-coloured blocks stood proud on the north-eastern tip of the island. The east wing fronting Weld Quay. The north wing, overlooking the ruins of Fort Cornwallis, the original fortification built by the East India Company when it first took possession of the island. And the west wing, the northern end of Beach Street. At their rear, in the quadrangle between the wings and the separate Chinese Protectorate building, were tall trees and formal flower gardens.

Jorgensen's E&O calling card gained him entry past the guards, and he walked through the vividly coloured gardens, reaching stone steps on the far side to the first-floor colonnaded verandah. The doors to the harbourmaster's office were just around the corner, in the wing overlooking the quayside. Through the second door, wedged open to gather up any trace of the scant breeze, he saw McHugh, alongside three Malay assistants, slaving over reams of cargo manifests.

As befitted the corner offices of the harbourmaster, the windows provided a vista of much of the harbour. At its northern end was Swettenham Pier and the hulking superstructure of the SS Westfalen, a recently arrived liner voyaging from Bremen to Yokohama. Heading south was Victoria Pier where smaller steamers unloaded cargo. And further down, before Church Street and Railway Piers, were the dozens of tongkangs and junks lashed together against the wharf, like a giant pontoon stretching out into the channel.

McHugh glanced up in surprise. "Mr Jorgensen, isn't it?"

"Can I have a word, McHugh?"

"Do you want me to dismiss these fellows?" McHugh spoke in a distinctive Belfast accent.

"Perhaps if you joined me on the verandah?"

"Right enough."

Leaving a careful mark on the open manifest on the desk, McHugh followed Jorgensen out onto the marble tiled floor of the verandah and over to the balustrade away from the door. Shielded from the cacophony of the quayside by the eastern wing, the quadrangle was a relative oasis of calm.

"How can I help you, Jorgensen?" said McHugh.

Jorgensen looked around the verandah to check nobody was close. The nearest person was fifty yards away outside the Land Office wing. "I'll come straight to it," he said. "On Tuesday night, one of our guests was the victim of a robbery, and I'm led to understand that earlier in the evening he was part of a group with you."

"What's this? Who are you talking about?" McHugh bristled with indignation.

"Arthur Cromford."

"Cromford. Who's saying I was there?"

"Keep your voice down, McHugh. I'm not here to embarrass you. Cromford told me you were part of the group."

"Did he? Look here, Jorgensen. Can this not wait until I'm away from the office? I've got my position here to think of."

"Relax, McHugh. I'm not interested in what you do with your evenings away from the E&O. All I want to know is who was in the group on Tuesday and whether you saw anything relating to the robbery."

McHugh looked up and down both wings of the verandah from the corner where the pair stood. All was clear. "All right then, if that's all it is – there were five of us: Tommy, Dickie, me, Cromford and the man who employs him, Morley isn't it?"

"What time did you go home?"

"About two in the morning. I wasn't there long; I'd had a skinful you see."

"Did you leave with any of the others?"

"No, they'd disappeared off away somewhere."

"And did you see anybody suspicious waiting outside the club?"

"I'll tell you for free, gone midnight there's a lot of odd characters around in that part of town. Cromford's valet was there, waiting outside when I left. Looking after their bloody bicycles. Can you believe they took bicycles?"

"Was the valet alone?"

"That he was. Just sat on the walkway outside the shop next door, with the bicycles behind him. I happened to notice because I'd stopped to light a cigarette while I searched for a rickshaw. He's a strange one that valet. Stared right back at me, so he did."

"Was Essenden's presence the cause of the shouting match at the hotel with Phyllis Smith before you left."

"When isn't there uproar with those two? I'll not be telling you anything you don't already know, but Essenden is a swine with women. God knows what they see in him."

"Have they rowed a lot?"

"Well, I don't follow them around, but they'd had another humdinger just recently. One minute all cosy together in the corner laughing at some book and in the next moment she threw the thing at him and burst into tears."

"She threw a book at him?"

"It was only a wee notebook. Pocket sized, like a diary."

"Did you get to read it – to share in the joke?"

"It was their private joke," McHugh snapped back. "What would I care about it?"

A few yards along the verandah, two figures emerged from one of the offices. Deep in conversation, they began walking towards Jorgensen and McHugh.

Conscious of their approach, McHugh dropped his voice to a low murmur. "It's a bad do this, interrogating me at my place of work."

"One more question. Did you know Frank Davies?"

"Who?"

"The man found dead in Love Lane."

McHugh shook his head. "I read about the poor bastard in the Echo, but that's the first I'd ever heard of him. Now, if you're through I'll return to my manifests."

The two officials' echoing steps were close to rounding the corner, so Jorgensen nodded, and McHugh stalked off, two dots of crimson in his cheeks testament to the indignation that was rising within him.

***

Jorgensen's second destination that morning was the landmark Logan Building, home to a miscellany of businesses occupying the cream-coloured brick fronted block on the western side of Beach Street. The shops on the ground floor included a pharmacy, Robinsons Pianos, Dickson's wine merchants, the Pritchard & Co department store and half-a-dozen others. On the two floors above, behind wrought-iron balconies shipped over from an engineering firm in Scotland, were the offices of another dozen businesses, including the Aerated Water Company, David Brown's auctioneers, no less than four solicitors' firms and the share brokers, Cunningham Clark – the employer of Dickie Chelmsall.

Beneath the main building a central arch led to a shaded rear courtyard between the two side wings, where tables and chairs belonged to a small coffeeshop. At one of the tables, sat uncomfortably on low stools, were Jorgensen and Dickie Chelmsall, the only white men in an establishment preferred by the locals – the clerks and messengers who worked in the Logan Buildings. Chelmsall was brown-haired, slim and lithe; a pacy rugby winger and a nimble dancer: two attributes that earned numerous house-party invitations and cemented his position among the social set. Though facing Jorgensen in these unfamiliar surroundings, he felt decidedly ill at ease.

On the table between them were two cups of Penang white coffee – a drink with a distinctive taste, whitened with condensed milk and brewed from coffee beans roasted in margarine. One that had taken Jorgensen several weeks to grow accustomed to, and which Chelmsall now regarded with suspicion, in common with most of his fellow Europeans.

"I'm not in the soup with the hotel, am I?" Chelmsall was asking. "I thought my chits were up to date."

"I doubt that Dickie," said Jorgensen. "None of your crowd pays on time. But that's not why I wanted to speak to you. I have an ulterior motive."

"If you're paying, I'll do my damnedest to meet the obligation."

"I thought it better to speak in private. After the last ball you were with your friends in Goldie's Bar. And with those people who arrived on the P&O – the writer and his secretary."

"Oh Cromford, you mean. He's a gas – a fellow who knows the way to a good time." As Chelmsall spoke, he cast a sidelong glance at a nearby table, where a young Indian boy pulled uneasily at the collar of the E&O porter's uniform tunic. Chelmsall was sure the boy was staring at him, but as the boy arrived with Jorgensen, he could do little about it.

"So, I'm told," said Jorgensen. "Do you remember a diary that Cromford mislaid? It might have been the cause of the row between Essenden and Phyllis."

"Oh that. The one Philly threw into Tommy's face."

"Why did she do that?"

"She was bored because Tommy wouldn't stop reading passages aloud from it."

"Didn't Cromford mind?"

"I don't think he knew. He must have dropped it by accident and Tommy picked it up. We were all pretty pickled and it was just a bit of fun for a few minutes, Though, I must say, some of the passages were rather outré."

"Apart from you, who else heard Tommy read from it?"

Chelmsall took a sip from the coffee, and screwed up his face, both at the taste and the effort of recall. "Ginger, I suppose, and perhaps Anne. Why are you asking. Has Cromford made a complaint?"

"Weren't you with Tommy again in the bar on Tuesday evening?" Jorgensen asked, ignoring the question.

"Yes, I think we popped in there before it closed."

"I was told he went on to a club with Arthur Cromford – and that you and Ginger McHugh accompanied them."

"To a club?" Chelmsall was nonplussed. "Which club?"

"I think you know what I'm driving at, Dickie."

"Good god no. I was a bit tight, so a chap I room with at the mess suggested we cut off home to bed. We dug out the driver and that was it for the night."

"Then it was just Essenden and McHugh who went with Cromford?"

"I suppose so. I say, are you after Tommy's hide?"

"Should I be?"

"Look, I oughtn't to say this, but I'm concerned about him. I remember that when I first arrived in Penang, I was warned off giving Tommy a loan."

Jorgensen grunted a non-committal reply, wondering why Chelmsall was bringing this up now.

"From what I hear," Chelmsall continued. "He's in a worse position than ever. The thing is – he's landed in trouble with gambling debts."

"Has Essenden admitted that to you?"

Chelmsall shook his head. "We're not exactly the best of pals nowadays. I must confess that because of the way he treats Philly, I've little time for him. But this is more than a rumour. Tommy owes a fortune to a gambler in Chinatown."

"Who's the creditor?" Jorgensen asked, trying to sound no more than mildly interested.

"I've no idea of the chap's name, only that he's a Chinaman."

"Thanks for telling me, Dickie. I guess it's something of which I should be aware."

"That's what I thought."

"By the way, I expect you've heard about the man found dead in Love Lane?"

"The Englishman?"

"Frank Davies, yes. Did you know him?"

"I did once run across him." Chelmsall said, the hint of a stammer suddenly appearing in his voice.

"How did you meet him? He wasn't part of the crowd I see you with at the E&O."

"I can't say as I remember. Look, Jorgensen, why all these questions?"

Jorgensen took a sip of coffee and slid a cigarette from his case, offering one to Chelmsall, who declined.

"It's E&O business," he replied, lighting his cigarette with a match struck on the cobbles beneath their feet. "Come on Dickie. There's no need to be slippery."

Chelmsall let out a deep sigh as the realisation sank home that was this the real reason why Jorgensen had asked to meet him, though what the hotel's interest was in Frank Davies, he could not fathom. He supposed he had to surrender himself to the inevitable. It was no good getting on the wrong side of Jorgensen – and by extension, the E&O.

"It was soon after I came to Penang," he said. "Through the church I volunteered at a home for wounded servicemen. Frank Davies was another of the volunteers. I wouldn't claim we ever became firm friends. His ideas were quite different from mine. We both stopped volunteering at the home at around the same time, but for quite different reasons. Did you know he was an opium addict?"

"Yes. Did you keep in touch?"

"For a short while. There were occasions he wanted help and, thanks to my position at Cunningham Clark, I became knowledgeable about property ownership in Penang. He was aware of that and could be quite persuasive once he put his mind to it. But the old man upstairs soon put a stop to it, and after that we lost touch."

"When did you last see him?"

"Several months ago, I should think."

"Okay Dickie, thanks," said Jorgensen. "I guess you'd better get back to your desk." His eyes met those of Suri at the next table, for he was the boy that Jorgensen had persuaded to don the porter's uniform and accompany him on this visit. A slight shake of Suri's head confirmed what Jorgensen had already guessed. Chelmsall was not the man Suri had seen call at Love Lane before Davies's death.

Rising uncertainly from his stool, Chelmsall muttered his farewell, and hurried back under the arch leading to the staircase to his office.

Jorgensen watched him go. Though Chelmsall claimed not to have visited the house of Xyiu Tang on the night Cromford was robbed, there was still the possibility that he was the *angmoh* who had tipped off George Lam about the diary. And his keenness to bring up Essenden's gambling debts was suspicious.

***

From Beach Street, Jorgensen and Suri walked the short distance to Tommy Essenden's place of work – the New George Town Shipping Company on Weld Quay. Its proprietors were British merchants, pillars of European society in Penang for over sixty years, and the doubtless reluctant employers of young Tommy, whose father, the chairman of the Peninsular Bank, was a long-standing friend.

The tall, three-storey building housing the New George Town Shipping Company was one of several whose classical facades adorned this stretch of the quayside. On the seaward side of the quay, all was a maelstrom of noise and urgent activity. Shirtless stevedores cursed loudly in a dozen languages, while they hauled sacks, bales and crates from the decks of tongkangs, wedged tightly alongside each other against the wharf side. While across the tramlines, pristine white building frontages, ornamented with columns, arches and balustrades gazed serenely down on the tumult below. Though behind those elaborate facades, the practicalities of a quayside godown were as evident as in the tin-sided sheds by Swettenham Pier.

In the New George Town Shipping Company's building, wide arches led from the quayside to double doors opening into a high-ceilinged storage area, where goods were stacked high in geometric rows. Sandwiched between it and the uppermost storage level, from where the aromas of sacks of spices permeated the entire building, was the business floor, accessed by a staircase from a narrow lobby.

Jorgensen, trailed by Suri, still ill at ease in the borrowed uniform, pushed through the front door and into the lobby's relative peace and cool.

"It's E&O business," he explained to the Eurasian woman at the small wooden reception desk, and as was often the case, the hotel's prestigious name opened doors. They were shown upstairs by an elaborately courteous Indian attendant and into a small wood-panelled anteroom with a view back across the quayside. A few moments later, Tommy Essenden breezed in.

Essenden was a dark-haired young man, with flashing dark eyes, high cheekbones, and full lips, which twitched into a cynical smile on catching sight of Jorgensen. Since returning from school in England several months earlier, Essenden had traded on those handsome features and an easy charm to earn great popularity among Penang's young social elite, though he knew from experience they had the opposite effect on Jorgensen.

"What's it about this time. My chit, I suppose?"

"Not this time Tommy," said Jorgensen. That was a task to look forward to on another day. When Arshak helped guests he pitied, planters afflicted by plummeting rubber prices, widows stranded in Penang waiting for their ship home, Jorgensen could only admire his boss's altruism. But when he pandered to men like Tommy Essenden, undeserving scions of wealthy families, it was harder to stomach.

"What then?" asked Essenden.

"I'm here for two reasons. You had another public row with Phyllis Smith the other night at the hotel."

"Pa went over this yesterday with the hotel manager."

"You're not listening Tommy. There are limits to what's acceptable at the E&O. Your father won't save you from a suspension if it happens again."

Essenden glared at Jorgensen, torn between indignant protestations over Jorgensen's nerve in speaking to him in this way and a desire to appear indifferent over the incident. In the end, vanity and a tendency to idleness won the day. "You've wasted your time," he drawled. "Phyllis has become rather tiresome of late. I shan't be bothering with her from now on."

"Okay," Jorgensen nodded. He did not believe a word of it, but Essenden's response would have to suffice for now. "Now about Tuesday night," he said. "You went on to a club after you left the E&O."

"What of it? It's no business of yours."

Jorgensen had not yet found an aspect of Tommy Essenden's character for which he had sympathy, and for this haughty response would have gladly marched him across Weld Quay and dumped him in the harbour. But Arshak Sarkies held accounts at old man Essenden's bank, so Jorgensen gritted his teeth and forced a patient expression.

"A guest of the E&O was robbed outside the club."

"That's awful luck."

"Don't you want to know who was robbed?"

"I rather suspect you're going to tell me."

The curl of Essenden's lip was designed to provoke, and indeed Jorgensen felt his pulse quicken.

"Arthur Cromford," he said, as equably as he could manage.

"That is bad luck. Poor Cromford."

"Now see here Tommy," said Jorgensen, the last flippant remark one too many to endure. He moved a step closer, causing Essenden to flinch. "Do I need to remind you I'm just a wild colonial?"

"You can't just march in here and throw your weight around, you know," said Essenden, emboldened by the belief that Jorgensen would not lay a hand on him in his place of work. "I'm not in the least bit intimidated by you."

"Cut out the braggadocio, Tommy, it doesn't suit you. I'm going to ask you some questions about the robbery. If you don't answer them, I'll have to let the police have a go. You see, Cromford's diary was stolen in that robbery – the same diary that you were reading passages from in Goldie's Bar the night before."

"Oh that," said Essenden. "I admit I was, but it was full of fanciful nonsense."

"It shows that you knew about the diary, and what was in it. The robbers were tipped off about its existence by a white man."

"It's not something I'd stoop to," said Essenden, with as much loftiness as he could muster.

"I'm relieved to hear it. You see, I got to thinking about why a white man would help these criminals. Their boss runs gambling houses in Chinatown, and I figured somebody saw this diary as an opportunity to settle their debts and raise some extra cash."

"You can't be suggesting I'm responsible."

"I'm told it's common knowledge you have gambling debts."

"Who doesn't?"

"I was told you owe a lot of money."

"Well, you were damn well misinformed. It's a piffling amount and I could settle any time I choose."

"What about your friends, the others who knew about the diary? McHugh and Chelmsall. Have either of them run up big gambling debts?"

"I don't see it's any business of yours. Besides, everybody gambles in Penang. Dickie and Ginger are no exception."

"There I'd disagree. You see, Cromford was a guest of the E&O and asked for my help. And it's clear to me it was someone who frequents the E&O who tipped off the robbers. That makes it my business."

"Then why aren't you questioning the fucking waiters?" Remembering the respect with which his father was always treated at the E&O, Essenden was beginning to enjoy antagonising his interrogator. "They hang on one's every word, loitering just over one's shoulder, and that night there were plenty who could have learnt all about the diary."

"It was a white man, Tommy. Now, one last question before I go. I guess you'll have heard of Frank Davies?"

"That's the fellow who got himself strangled, isn't it?"

"Did you know him?"

Jorgensen watched Essenden closely, hoping for a hint of discomfort. A nervous twitch, a guilty sidelong glance, but the only emotion he detected was a mild bafflement at the change of subject.

"It's impossible to escape the bloody fellow's name. Pops up in every conversation one has. I heard he was killed by some Arab."

"Did you know him before his death?"

"Hardly," Essenden snorted. "What would I have to do with a chap who lives among the natives?"

"He was an educated Englishman," said Jorgensen. "Down on his luck. Dickie Chelmsall knew him."

"Dickie?" Essenden's surprise seemed genuine enough. "Where on earth would Dickie stumble across a fellow like that?"

"A while back, before Davies's luck ran out."

Though he had posed the question, Essenden was singularly uninterested in Jorgensen's reply. "Look here," he said. "You've kept me long enough. I should be getting back to my desk."

"Go ahead," said Jorgensen dismissively. He watched as Essenden turned and left the room, leaving the door open in his wake, while he contemplated adding accomplished lying to the long list of Essenden's character failings. If Essenden was not telling the truth about gambling debts, then Jorgensen felt almost a grudging admiration for the ease with which the subject was so airily dismissed. On the other hand, if Essenden was being straight, then Jorgensen was no nearer discovering the identity of the person who had tipped off George Lam about the diary, and perhaps killed Frank Davies to protect their identity.

He turned to Suri, who virtually unnoticed by Essenden, for what interest was there for a man of his type in the behaviour of servants, had watched the whole exchange open-mouthed.

"It wasn't him, was it Suri?" Jorgensen asked.

"No sir, not him."

# Thirty-Four

At the porter's desk in the lobby of the E&O, Rama was waiting for Jorgensen's return.

"I have a message for you. From a woman. Kitchen staff say she was most distressed. I have it here." He lifted a hotel envelope from the porter's desk and handed it to Jorgensen. "It came without envelope. But better it is private."

Jorgensen slid the envelope open, extracted a single sheet of paper, and read the short, scribbled message.

*Mr Jorgensen,*

*Loddon did not come home last night. I am fearful he came to harm. Please help.*

*Zulla*

"When was the message left?"

"One hour ago only."

"Where is she now?"

"Staff tell her to wait by the kitchen gate."

Jorgensen left the hotel through the main gate, hurrying parallel with the hotel's boundary wall on Farquhar Street. Zulla was waiting at the kitchen gate, near a group of the hotel's gardeners who were crouched under the shade of the trees, enjoying a mid-morning break.

"Mr Jorgensen," she said, her voice cracking with relief at his appearance. "You have come to help."

"Come with me," he said. "We can talk inside."

He guided Zulla through the gate and away from the gardeners. Under the overhanging branches of trees planted against the boundary wall, he stepped off the path and turned to face her.

"Has this ever happened before?" he asked.

"Never. Loddon always comes back. I hoped he was with you."

"We didn't find him, though Ah Cheng was still looking."

"I worry he did something stupid."

"I'll take you back to Pulau Tikus in the hotel's car. You need to be at home in case he turns up today. On the way, you must tell me more."

"You will search for him?" she pleaded.

"I promise I will."

***

Superintendent Bob Cave greeted Jorgensen with a sour look. Through the open first-floor window behind Cave's desk came the sounds of Chowrasta Market on the other side of Penang Road: the calls of the traders, voices raised in disagreement, the rattle of wheels over cobbles.

"You've saved me a trip out to see you," Cave said.

Jorgensen raised a questioning eyebrow. "How so?"

"A complaint was received this morning about your harassment of a leading member of the community."

"Magnus Prescott," said Jorgensen.

"He telephoned. Rather irate, insisting you were reprimanded."

"What for?"

"Bothering his sister with some nonsense of yours. A young woman who is apparently quite ill and whose condition worsened after your interference. He claims you trespassed on their property last night after he'd warned you off."

"He's got a hell of an imagination."

"Do you deny it then?"

"I was invited there by Anne Prescott."

"I don't have time for games, Mac," Cave jabbed a finger in Jorgensen's direction. "You've pissed off the Prescotts and, much as I like you and respect your authority at the E&O, you simply cannot career around the island doing as you damn well please. A man was murdered yesterday, in case you'd forgotten, and this morning I need to prepare for the suspect's remand hearing, not waste time on clearing up after you."

"On that," said Jorgensen, who without waiting to be asked, slid a chair across the wooden floorboards to a position facing Cave's desk.

"Oh, help yourself," said Cave sarcastically as Jorgensen sat down. "Are you about to confess?"

"I'm here to report two missing people. An Englishman called Aubrey Loddon and a Chinese valet known as Ah Cheng."

"Is this Loddon the guest whose identity you were so shy about revealing? The one to whom Davies sent a letter?"

"Loddon isn't a guest. He's an ex-planter, living out at Pulau Tikus, who once worked as a plantation agent for Prescott's. Yesterday, I discovered that for several days this week, he was watching Frank Davies's lodgings."

"What did you say?" Cave felt his face flush at the conjunction of Prescott's and Frank Davies's names in the same sentence.

"Magnus Prescott employed Loddon to watch Frank Davies's lodgings to see if his sister Anne Prescott ever visited. To keep a record and report back to him."

Cave glared at Jorgensen across the desk. "Why the hell didn't you tell me this yesterday?"

"After Loddon admitted it all, I advised him to take his story to the police. I thought he would, but instead he's disappeared."

"Fucking hell, Mac. You've really overstepped the mark this time."

"His wife expected him back last night after he went into George Town. When he didn't return, she turned up in distress at the E&O this morning to ask for my help."

Cave rose abruptly from his chair and strode to the door to fling it open. "Batchelor," he yelled. "My office. And bring a notebook." Shaking his head, he returned to his chair and dropped irritably onto the seat, refusing to look Jorgensen in the eye.

"Major Jorgensen," said Batchelor, with a curl to his lip, as appeared at the door to Cave's office. He gave Cave a knowing look, as if Jorgensen's presence this morning was somehow a vindication of his own actions the day before.

"Take notes, Inspector," said Cave. "Jorgensen has information for us."

Batchelor pulled another chair across, placing it at the side of Cave's desk, so that he faced Jorgensen, then scribbled in a notebook while Jorgensen repeated what he had told Cave, going on to describe his meeting with Loddon in the Victoria Inn.

"This chap Loddon lives among the Malays?" Batchelor asked.

"The kampung at Pulau Tikus is a Eurasian settlement. Loddon's wife is Malay."

"And if I've understood your story correctly, you claim he was hired by Magnus Prescott to keep watch on Davies's lodgings?"

"He was seen doing so, and later admitted it."

"Was this admission made in the Victoria Inn?" Batchelor's increasingly smug expression was beginning to rile Jorgensen. "Was he drunk, Major? You'll pardon my stating the obvious, but have you considered that this chap Loddon's story doesn't ring particularly true? As just one example, if Prescott's saw fit to dismiss him, why on earth would Magnus Prescott trust him now?"

"Since he left the firm, he's carried out odd jobs for the Prescott family."

"That's what he claims, is it? Again, Major Jorgensen, you'll pardon my frankness, but it does appear you've swallowed every word of some desperate chap's imagination. Do you make a habit of listening to the fantasies of drunks and opium addicts?"

Superintendent Cave coughed awkwardly. He had noticed the tightening of Jorgensen's jaw. "That's rather strong, Inspector," he said. "Mr Jorgensen has proved a helpful witness in the past and he's no fool. Though I too am sceptical about this fellow Loddon's story, I propose we ask him for ourselves. If he's a possible witness, then we cannot afford to disregard him."

"Of course. If you say so, sir," Batchelor looked offended, either at the admonishment or at the suggestion Jorgensen's advice be followed.

"There's something else you should know," said Jorgensen. "Yesterday, Loddon was seen with a Chinese man called Kei Hin, who also visited Frank Davies at his lodgings. I'm sure you remember, Inspector, that I mentioned Davies owed three hundred dollars to a moneylender from Chinatown. This fellow Kei Hin is the moneylender's attack dog."

"If you're not involved in the death of Frank Davies – as you were at pains to make so clear yesterday, then how the devil do you know all this?" asked Batchelor tetchily.

"He's been carrying out a separate bloody investigation," Cave growled. "That's so, isn't it?"

"We can't permit that, sir, can we?" said Batchelor.

"You're right, Inspector, we can't. A murder case is not a stage for bloody amateurs."

"Now look here, Cave." Jorgensen's own anger spilled over. "I came in to report two missing people. One as a potential witness to Frank Davies's murder. Well, here's the description you'll need to find Aubrey Loddon – medium height with a thick neck and a big belly. Brown hair and prominent moustache: a walrus moustache I think you'd call it. He looks around sixty but is probably ten years or so younger. And last seen in the company of Kei Hin, a thug who operates out of Lam Copra Export Company of Rope Walk. I'll leave it to you officers of the Straits Settlements Police to decide whether to act on that information."

"I don't care for your tone, Major," said Batchelor.

Jorgensen opened his mouth as if about to respond to Batchelor's comment, but instead, clamped it shut again, rose from his chair, and headed for the door.

"I'm not joking, Mac," Cave called out after him. "We'll look out for this Loddon fellow, but do not poke your sharp nose in any further. And leave the Prescotts alone."

# Thirty-Five

Like Jorgensen, Ah Cheng too had woken before daylight. Prising his eyes open, then blinking to clear blurred vision, he gradually became aware that he was lying face down on rough wooden floorboards in a darkened room. He lay quietly for a minute, wincing at the throbbing pain at the back of his head that then ran down his spine. A cloying sweet odour, tinged with wood smoke, nagged at his nostrils.

One numbed arm was trapped beneath him. He dragged it free and hauled himself into a sitting position. There he stayed for several minutes, trying not to puke while the floor below him dipped and rose, as if he was tossing helplessly on a squally sea.

He traced the fingers of one hand over his face, flinching as they caught a swollen wound above his eye. Round to the back of his head, they met matted hair and the crustiness of hardened fluids. As he foraged, a fresh trickle of blood ran down his neck. He remembered now. It was a blow to the back of his head that first felled him in the alley. His fingers again traced over his face, to the raw tenderness above the eye. A stamp to the temple was the last thing he had seen coming.

Seated on the floor in the dark, he stretched his arms sideways, like an insect's antennae. Not encountering any obstacles, he tipped forward onto to his hands and knees, shuffle crawling the short distance towards the only visible source of light – a faint line at floor level. There, his outstretched arms felt the outline of a door and frame. He hoisted himself on to his feet, then, with his head swimming from the effort, leant in recovery against the door. With one arm bent against the panel for support, his fingers followed the door's perimeter, finding a keyhole but no handle. Crouching down again, he slipped the fingers of both hands under the crack below the door to pull it towards him. It moved the merest of fractions and then caught. The door was locked.

Still unsteady, with one hand against the walls to take his weight, he inched around the room, mapping the four corners. Little more than twenty short steps all the way – a small room, with no shuttered windows, no second doors. From the smell hanging in the air, which his recovering senses now recognised, he thought it must be an empty storage room for bags of copra. The lap completed, and back at the door, he pushed at the panel in its frame, banged it hard and shouted, in a voice initially croaky then stronger.

"Open the door," he cried. And banged hard again. "Open the door."

He stopped when he heard voices, then footsteps, and waited quietly for them to reach him.

"Shut your mouth," a voice snarled through the closed door.

"Let me out," said Ah Cheng.

"I said, shut your mouth."

"Let me speak to Kei Hin."

"No."

"Give me water then."

"You must shut your mouth. Or we will shut it for you."

"You will need four men like last time."

The footsteps receded, and Ah Cheng heard a door close behind them. He searched for the keyhole with his fingertips, then bent down to peer through it. A pinprick of light from the corridor outside, unimpeded by a key in the lock.

He went round the room again, feeling only rough-plastered walls. Dropping once more to his knees, he crawled backwards and forwards across the room, feeling for anything on the floor. Six feet across, ten feet long. Bare wooden floorboards, one or two prominent nail heads bent into the timber, with gaps no wider than a thumbnail between the timbers.

He sat with his back against the wall opposite the door. There was only one way out – through the door – and it was locked.

# Thirty-Six

Bailey, the manager of the Australia Hotel on Penang Road, was in his mid-forties. A little under medium height, wiry, with thinning dark hair turning to grey. To the surprise of whoever he was with, an otherwise unremarkable appearance was rendered memorable whenever he laughed, which was often, when he revealed tombstone teeth, seemingly two sizes too large for his face.

They were on prominent display when, from behind the front desk, he caught sight of Jorgensen advancing across the lobby.

"You're back again I see," he said, chuckling. "You had my clerk quaking in his boots yesterday. Must have been important." Beside him was Yang, the hotel's chief clerk, who glanced up briefly from the bills he was collating for departing guests. In contrast to Bailey, Yang's brow, under a pronounced widow's peak hairline, was creased in a perpetual frown.

"He didn't seem too worried," Jorgensen replied.

"That fellow will be manager here one day. You mark my words," said Bailey. "I guess you can't have got everything you were after, or you wouldn't have returned. So, how can I help the E&O? Are you chasing up old debtors?"

"Two men called in for a few minutes yesterday afternoon. A heavyset Englishman and a tough looking Chinese man. I'm trying to find out why they called. The clerks I spoke to last night claimed not to have seen them."

"Mr Bailey, sir," said Yang, bowing his head in apology for the interruption. "I saw these men."

"You did?" said Bailey.

"The Englishman was Mr Loddon," Yang said.

“Loddon?” said Bailey, eyebrows arching in surprise. “What was he doing here? I paid him his dues earlier in the week. You never mentioned this, Yang.”

“You know Loddon?” asked Jorgensen.

“Known him for years,” said Bailey. “In the old days he was a regular guest. Used to stay with us when he was visiting from the mainland. Though nowadays, all that’s beyond him.”

“You mentioned paying his dues. Was he working for you?”

“I’d hardly call it work. Once a month, he helps me out with the bookkeeping. I could handle it myself or have the clerks do it, as it’s only totting up outstanding bills owed to suppliers, but I guess I feel sorry for the old boy. I pay him in cash when he calls in.”

“And he called in recently? Which day was that?”

“Let me see,” Bailey rubbed his chin. “Wednesday it was. He was a touch too worse for the drink. Had to have words with him about it.” He turned to Yang. “I don’t understand why he called again yesterday.”

“Mr Loddon wanted the name of a guest,” said Yang. “He described him to me – a strong man with black hair. But many guests with black hair stay here. The man with Mr Loddon insisted I tell, but I cannot. Then, I sorry to say, he snatched the register and he and Mr Loddon looked at it. I protested but they ignored me.”

“Christ,” said Bailey. “Why didn’t you tell me about this before, Yang?”

“I apologise, Mr Bailey, but Mr Loddon is your friend,” said Yang.

“Not if he comes in here with people who behave like that, he isn’t. Does it make any sense to you, Jorgensen?”

“It might do.” Jorgensen withdrew from his pocket the sheet of Australia Hotel notepaper on which he had copied the names from the register the day before.

*Skine, Haigh, McAusland, Griffiths, Samini, Solly, Wentworth, Edmonds, Stubbock, McMaster, Driver, Vickerman, Jewell, Van Esten, Murphy, Corbett, Hilliard, Rorke, Chapman.*

"Can you tell me if any of these guests are dark-haired?" he asked.

"Are these our guests from last night? Let's have a look," said Bailey, taking the paper from Jorgensen's hands. "I don't know them all by sight, but Yang can help me. Can I write on your list?"

"Sure."

"I'll note down the hair colour of any I know so you can eliminate some of the names."

"Thanks."

"Are you going to tell me what's going on?"

Lost in thought for a moment, Jorgensen was slow to answer. "You don't have a Durrant listed here," he said. "Meant to arrive on Wednesday."

"No Mr Durrant here sir," Yang replied. "Nobody of that name."

"The fellow I'm thinking of left the E&O on Wednesday, telling me he was moving here. Somewhere he claimed to be well known. Was Durrant not a regular guest at the Australia Hotel?"

"I do not know him, sir," Yang replied, looking to Bailey for confirmation.

"Never heard of him either," Bailey volunteered.

"He fits the description Loddon gave you. Dark-haired, muscular. With his broken nose he has the look of an old boxer. Does that describe any of your guests?"

"Mr Solly, sir. You describe Mr Solly," said Yang.

Jorgensen looked down again at the register. Mr Garrett Solly, address given as Serangoon Road, Singapore. Arrived on Wednesday.

"Solly?" said Bailey. "I suppose he would fit the bill."

"A fellow Australian?" said Jorgensen.

"More's the pity," said Bailey. "He's far from a shining example to the rest of us. I remember there was a suspicion he'd had women in his room on a previous visit."

"That's the reason we threw him out of the E&O. He'd smuggled in a taxi dancer from the Strand, and she was still there at lunchtime."

"You might have warned us, Jorgensen."

"I wish I had. At the E&O he registered under the name of Durrant and verified it with a passport. I see on your register you did the same, so it looks like he's travelling with at least two passports, and one of them in a false name. Is he here now?"

Yang turned to the shelves behind him. "His key is here," he said. "He must be out."

"I'll need another favour, Bailey, so I'll tell you what I can. I've been searching for a dark-haired man in connection with another matter, and I believe now it's the same person Loddon was looking for. There's a good chance it could be Durrant. I'd like to bring in a young Tamil boy who got a good look at the man in question. He might recognise him among your guests."

"You're asking a lot."

"I'll see to it he looks presentable enough."

"What'll happen if your boy does recognise the man? Or the other way round. The Australia has a decent reputation these days. We can't afford a ruckus."

"We'll be discreet; we can put him somewhere where he won't be noticed. And if he identifies the man, I'll want to question him – that's all."

"What's he done, this bloke?"

"Maybe nothing at all. But he might have seen something."

# Thirty-Seven

When Jorgensen was dropped off back at the E&O, Vikat was shepherding a guest down the steps from the main doors and into a waiting rickshaw. Jorgensen waited until Vikat had snapped off a crisp salute of farewell, then caught the doorman's attention.

"Has Ah Cheng returned?" he asked when Vikat joined him at the top of the steps.

"No sign, Major Mac."

"No message?"

"No, sir. But inside is a policeman for you." He pointed towards the porter's desk just inside the lobby, then followed Jorgensen through the doors, keen to eavesdrop on the reason for the visit.

At the desk, the burly, bearded figure of Sergeant Singh was talking with Rama, but turned to face Jorgensen on hearing him approach.

"What brings you here, Sergeant?" Jorgensen asked.

"You sir. Superintendent Cave requests you come to the detective station."

"Couldn't he have telephoned? Sending two men seems a bit much."

"Two men, sir?"

"The constable in Superintendent Cave's car on Farquhar Street. I saw him as I came in."

"The Superintendent says it is important. Your driver may follow to take you back."

"So, I'm not under arrest?"

The sergeant's serious face broke into a sheepish smile. "Oh no, sir. If that were so, I would not ask so pleasantly."

"I'll check my messages at the desk, then I'll be with you."

The Sergeant bowed his head in acknowledgement and Jorgensen strode across the lobby to the reception desk, where the response was the same as Vikat's at the door. No messages from Ah Cheng.

"When he returns ask him to stay put, and I'll see him when I get back," Jorgensen told the clerk, then retraced his steps to rejoin Sergeant Singh.

"There's no need for my driver to follow," he said. "I can walk back down Penang Road."

"Better you ask him to come," Singh replied. "We go on from the detective station."

"Where to?"

"You will see, sir."

The two-car convoy set out from the E&O a few minutes later; Jorgensen joining Sergeant Singh and the Malay constable in Cave's long open-topped police Studebaker. Following close behind was Zamir, gripping the wheel of the hotel's blue Standard Tourer and mindful of Jorgensen's instructions not to lose touch.

At the detective station on Penang Road, the Sergeant explained to the constable on gate duty that Zamir could follow them in. A narrow track ran along the side of the building, from which both cars reversed under a canvas awning strung between trees. In the welcome shade it afforded, Jorgensen waited with the constable in the Studebaker, while Singh went in search of Cave.

"I'm gratified you came without a fuss, Mac," said Cave when he and Sergeant Singh appeared moments later. Cave climbing into the rear seat next to Jorgensen, Singh returning to the front passenger seat.

"You'd sent two men and a motor car. What else was I going to do?"

"Drive on, Constable," Cave commanded, and the Studebaker rumbled along the track and through the gate into Penang Road, followed once more by Zamir in the Standard.

"Your man wouldn't tell me where we're going," said Jorgensen. "I assume you will."

"To the mouth of the Prangin Canal," said Cave. "Inspector Batchelor awaits our arrival."

Jorgensen sat back in his seat. It was clear Cave was unwilling to reveal anything more. They turned east, running parallel with the mile long Prangin Canal: past the Anglo-Chinese school and the college, and past the Sia Boey market building.

As they reached the coast, where a sharp right-angled bend turned north onto Weld Quay, Cave ordered the driver to pull over. The Studebaker lurched up onto the dirt on the outside of the bend, braking to a halt amongst trees, closely followed by Zamir in the hotel's car. Behind them, a tram clanked round the corner, trailing wagons stacked with crates of tin ingots from the smelting works, heading for the godowns at Swettenham Pier and onward export.

"Tell your driver to stay in the car," Cave said to Jorgensen. "You and I are going for a short walk."

After speaking to Zamir, Jorgensen followed Cave and Sergeant Singh over the rough ground to the edge of the Prangin Canal – a canalised stream that once flowed from the old marshes on which much of George Town was built. Its original purpose was to give small boats access through the mud flats at low tide and on to wharves along its banks. Nowadays, it was used mainly by sampans tying up at the Sia Boey market, though it had a secondary role as an outflow for many of George Town's monsoon drains to escape to the sea. At low tide, as it was when Cave, Jorgensen and Singh reached the canal's edge, a stench of waste and sewage from the mud flats drifted in on the breeze.

It was towards the mud flats they headed. Turning seawards and initially walking along the canal's granite retaining wall, they passed a couple of zinc roofed shacks on their left before the narrow, muddy beach opened out in front of them. The canal's walls continued above the mud for another seventy yards to the low tidemark, where a cluster of small boats were beached.

Halfway across the mud flats, close to the raised canal wall, were three figures.

"Good," said Cave. "He's still there." He looked down at Jorgensen's cream linen trousers and polished shoes and grinned. "It shouldn't be too bad, the tide's been out for a couple of hours and the sun will have dried the top. It's sandy up against the wall."

"You lead, I'll follow," said Jorgensen, bending over to roll up both trouser legs and remove his shoes and socks, leaving them on the scrub at the fringe of the beach.

They picked their way across the crusting mud, where every few steps the surface cracked under their weight and slime oozed up between Jorgensen's toes. Away to their left, running up the eastern shore, was the length of Weld Quay: first, the low spread of the clan jetties, where hundreds of Chinese lived in huts suspended over the water in a tangle of rickety piers. Then a forest of tongkang masts and hulls beached on the mud at the wharf side. Finally, beyond them, were the superstructures of ships at the deep-water piers. The further out from the shore they walked, the more of the waterfront came into view, topped by the gleaming white tower of the FMS Railway Building halfway along the quayside.

As they neared the waiting group, Jorgensen saw they were gathered around a shape lodged against the retaining wall of the canal.

"Is that what I think it is?" Jorgensen asked Cave. He tried to tell himself it was unlikely, but the thought had taken hold that the bundle was a body, and he was being asked to identify Ah Cheng.

"I'm afraid it is," Cave replied. "From the description you gave, we think it might be the fellow you reported missing."

Alongside Inspector Batchelor, whose involuntary scowl at seeing Jorgensen approach was difficult to miss, were two Malay police constables. At their feet, a field stretcher lay unfurled on the mud, ready to transport the corpse back to dry land.

"We'll need to hurry, sir," said Batchelor to Cave. "The tide's turned and we'll be under water in less than an hour."

"Let's have a look, then," said Cave, moving towards the body, and beckoning Jorgensen to follow.

Now that they were closer, Jorgensen, to his relief, could see it was obviously not Ah Cheng. The body was that of a large man, with broad shoulders and a thicker waist, wearing a mud-matted shirt and trousers. His face was hidden from their view, as the body lay side on to the barnacled retaining wall, with one shoulder and part of a leg half-buried under sand, the other shoulder folded forward against the wall.

Jorgensen edged around the body's feet, supporting himself with an outstretched arm against the slimy retaining wall. He leant over as far as he could to peer at the man's half-hidden features.

"You'll have to move him," Jorgensen said. "I can't say for definite until I see all his face."

Cave barked orders at the two constables who, with some difficulty, heaved the bloated body onto its back and away from the wall, where it rolled awkwardly on the uneven ridges. The large head, despite the early rigor mortis, flopped backwards, exposing a creased, fleshy neck.

"It's Loddon, all right," said Jorgensen. The thick moustache, that an encrustation of mud and sand could not disguise, was unmistakeable. "He's wearing the same clothes I saw him in yesterday afternoon."

"That's two deaths of Englishmen in two days." Cave removed his cap and ran the fingers of one hand through his hair in helpless exasperation.

"And both deaths connected to Jorgensen," said Batchelor pointedly.

"Right, let's get the poor bastard shifted," said Cave. "And Jorgensen, we'll need to talk to you back at the detective station."

Jorgensen crouched down at the side of the body. "Look at Loddon's neck," he said. "As well as these purple blotches where his face lay on the mud, there are marks right here, round the throat. Difficult to see under the mud but look where they are."

Cave sighed and squatted beside Jorgensen.

"We haven't long, sir," said Batchelor. "It won't be easy getting the body back to the shore."

"One moment, Inspector, let me humour Mr Jorgensen."

"See here," said Jorgensen, pointing to Loddon's exposed neck. "Broken skin and bruising round the windpipe here and here. Look like strangulation marks to me."

"They could be anything," said Cave. "Who knows how long he was in the water? The fellow might have got caught up in mooring ropes or anchor chains further up the quay. There are dozens of boats nearby."

"Didn't you say Frank Davies was strangled?" Jorgensen asked.

Cave got to his feet, and, noting Batchelor was on the point of protesting, silenced him with a raised hand. "I did indeed."

"Was Davies strangled with a rope or a cord?"

"Really, sir, I can't see this is any business of Mr Jorgensen's," said a persistent Batchelor. "He was brought to identify the body, and nothing more."

Cave ignored the protest while he considered Jorgensen's question. "The Assistant Surgeon couldn't be sure, though he did suggest a thin rope might have been used. We found one at the suspect's home."

"You should ask the Assistant Surgeon to consider whether Loddon met his death the same way and by the same hand."

"Superintendent, sir," This time, the interruption came from Sergeant Singh. "The Inspector is correct. We must move the body soon."

Cave looked out to sea, where the tide line was beginning to creep towards them. "Very well. The ambulance should be here by now. You stay and supervise the move, Sergeant. The Inspector and I will accompany Mr Jorgensen back to Penang Road."

***

In Cave's first-floor office at the Penang Road detective station, Jorgensen was directed to the same seat he had occupied during his visit at seven that morning, once again facing the window overlooking Chowrasta Market. Though now, past midday, the window's jalousies were closed against the noon sun's glare, and the market was quietening.

Through the jalousie's slats, Jorgensen heard the crackling hum from overhead cables signalling the impending passing of a trolleybus. Its rackety clatter, when it arrived, mingled with the cries of rickshaw pullers touting for business, and, from inside the office, the buffeting whir of an electric fan.

"Tell me all you know about Aubrey Loddon," Batchelor had commanded, his peevish expression just one aspect of the ill-concealed antipathy he had shown Jorgensen since their return from the mouth of the Prangin Canal. For ten minutes Jorgensen had tried – a task made more difficult by Batchelor's sarcastic interruptions.

"Perhaps you can help me to understand, Major Jorgensen," said Batchelor. "How you are so knowledgeable about the two dead men. Isn't it quite a coincidence you spoke to both Davies and Loddon on the day of their deaths?"

Alongside the Inspector, Superintendent Cave leant back in impassive silence and ignored Jorgensen's eloquent glance in his direction.

"A hell of a coincidence," Jorgensen replied.

"Is that all it is?"

Jorgensen looked from Batchelor to Cave in turn, his gaze hovering on each of them for several seconds.

"Well?" said Batchelor. "I'm waiting for a reply."

"The fact you're both questioning me tells me one thing for certain," Jorgensen said. "You're no longer sure Bin Hakim is your man."

"How did you know about Bin Hakim?" asked Cave, breaking his silence, and leaning forward in his chair.

"The errand boy at Love Lane told me about the threats he made. But I guess you've developed some doubts about his guilt since then. Though let's get one thing clear. You'll get no help from me if you're going to treat me as a suspect."

"Until you explain yourself satisfactorily, how exactly should we treat you, Major?" asked Batchelor.

"With courtesy, for a start."

"Who the bloody hell do you think you're speaking to?" Batchelor retorted, his face reddening.

"Somebody who's wasting time. When are you going to let Loddon's wife know what's become of her husband?"

Batchelor leapt to his feet in fury, followed immediately by Cave who jumped up to place a restraining hand on the younger man's shoulder. "Hold steady, Inspector," he said.

"You're not going to let that remark stand are you, sir?" Batchelor asked, glaring at Jorgensen over the superintendent's shoulder. Cave eased Batchelor down onto his seat and, satisfied his anger had sufficiently abated, turned to face Jorgensen. "There's no call for that. The Inspector is merely doing his job."

"Come off it, Cave. He's needled me since we got here, while you've sat back and let him do it."

"It'd save a hell of a lot of time if you told us what you're mixed up in," said Cave, resuming his own seat. "What was your involvement with both men?"

"I told you yesterday why I called on Davies."

"I'm afraid I'm having trouble believing all the nonsense about a letter to an anonymous guest at the E&O. It just isn't going to wash."

"It's not relevant, Cave. As I told you yesterday, the guest in question left on Thursday morning. You should be looking elsewhere. I've tried to help you by telling you about the connections between Frank Davies and Aubrey Loddon. One of which is Magnus Prescott…"

"We've only your word for that," interrupted Batchelor.

"…and the other is Kei Hin."

"And you're a third," said Batchelor. "You spoke to both men shortly before their deaths, a coincidence that continues to demand an explanation."

"I've already explained why I spoke to Loddon, but you didn't listen. I understand why you don't like hearing about a connection between Frank Davies and Magnus Prescott. After all, old man Prescott is a pillar of the European community."

"It's your connection to the two dead men we're asking about," said Batchelor.

Jorgensen rose to his feet, his mind made up. "Loddon was tied up somehow with Kei Hin," he said. "They were together yesterday at the Australia Hotel, witnessed by two people. If you're not going to follow that lead, then I will."

"You're not leaving until we say so," said Batchelor.

"Who are those witnesses?" asked Cave.

"Yang, the clerk at the Australia Hotel, and Ah Cheng, a valet at the E&O," Jorgensen replied. "And I know that Kei Hin and his boss, George Lam, both threatened Frank Davies."

"George Lam?" asked Cave.

"He runs opium dens in Chinatown."

"I don't need you to tell me that," said Cave. "I know full well who George Lam is, and he's never caused any problems for us or the Chinese Protectorate."

Jorgensen shrugged. "I'm not surprised. He's a cool enough customer."

Cave leant forward and grasped his swagger stick from the desk where he had tossed it on arrival. "All right, Jorgensen. As much as it pains me to say it – you win. We'll go and see this Lam fellow."

"But Superintendent," said Batchelor in protest. "There's only the word of a pair of Chinese menials to go on."

"I realise that Inspector, but I'd prefer to prevent Mr Jorgensen coming to harm. Two dead Englishmen is enough for any week."

"Thanks," said Jorgensen. "But just to remind you – I'm Canadian."

# Thirty-Eight

Outside the detective station, where Cave's Studebaker was parked under the shade of the canvas awning, the superintendent beckoned Jorgensen to join him. "A quick chat before we set off would be in order," he said.

"Sure, as long as you're going to be civil." Jorgensen replied, and they moved a few yards beyond where the E&O's Standard Tourer was parked, to a spot where they found Zamir resting in the shade against the base of a tree.

"You go to the car, Zamir, and I'll join you in a moment," Jorgensen said. He and Cave waited while the driver trotted back to the Standard. Above their heads, a commotion of tree sparrows ricocheted between the branches in furious dispute.

"I'm serious about what I said upstairs, Mac," said Cave in a low voice. "It's time to come clean as to how you're mixed up in this. I need to know the identity of the guest at the E&O who received the letter from Davies."

"Are you admitting your mistake in arresting Bin Hakim?"

"Don't crow, Mac, though I confess we may have been a touch hasty. I'll admit that discovering Loddon's body has cast a new light on the situation, though that doesn't yet mean we'll release our man. Not until we're more confident Davies was killed by someone other than Bin Hakim. Is that good enough for you?"

"What I tell you has got to stay off the record. Batchelor can't know. There'd be a hell of a scandal if it got out. One the Resident Councillor, and even the governor, would prefer to keep quiet."

"Aren't you rather exaggerating?"

"Trust me on this, Cave. It goes back to important people in London."

Cave tapped his swagger stick against his calf several times, an unconscious but habitual act, while he considered Jorgensen's proposal. "Very well," he said. "I'll hear more."

"A guest was robbed on Tuesday night outside a brothel on Campbell Street. A pocketbook and a diary were stolen. Within the diary there's an incriminating passage about some bigwig in London. It fell into the wrong hands and an attempt was made to blackmail its owner – our guest."

"Am I permitted to ask the nature of the incriminating passage?"

"You can probably guess."

"Have you seen it?"

"I know who the nabob is, and I know I wouldn't want to be responsible for its publication in a Penang newspaper."

"Was Davies the blackmailer?"

Jorgensen shook his head. "The man behind it is George Lam. Davies owed Lam money and was pressured into writing the blackmail letter to pay off the debt."

Cave gave Jorgensen a shrewd look. "I'm beginning to see why you were so reticent. Would I be right in guessing that your mysterious guest decided to pay up, and you acted as intermediary?"

"At the time I didn't know who was behind it, but my instinct was they couldn't be trusted. And I was right. Lam is a dangerous double-crossing bastard and set an ambush, with the aim of both obtaining the money and keeping the diary."

"And you spoiled the party?"

"And got the diary back."

"I suppose it never occurred to you it should be a police matter?"

Jorgensen shrugged. "My hands were tied. The guest didn't wish to involve the police."

"If you recovered the diary, then how come you're still involved?"

"Because of Davies's death. I'd tracked Lam down through Davies, and I figured that Lam and his sidekick, Kei Hin, blamed him for not getting everything they wanted, and decided to take revenge. It seemed more plausible than Bin Hakim being the killer."

"So, you started up your own investigation? Despite my repeated warnings to keep your nose out of it."

"That's about the size of it."

"Do you still believe Lam was responsible?"

"I've had doubts once I learned about Magnus Prescott and Loddon's interest in Frank Davies. But now, knowing that Loddon was last seen with Kei Hin, it still seems the obvious conclusion."

"We'll see," said Cave. "While I'm grateful you're cooperating at last, I can't allow you to come along."

"I understand, Cave. But before you go there's one more thing," said Jorgensen. "I sent Ah Cheng to try and find Loddon last night, and I've not heard from him since."

"Who the hell is this Ah Cheng?"

"A valet who works at the E&O. He helped me retrieve the diary. With what happened to Loddon, I'm worried about him. You see, we didn't get away from Lam's gang without difficulty."

"Christ, Mac," said Cave. "What have you got yourself into? Are you concerned your man has come to harm?"

"They're a dangerous bunch. You and your men should take care."

"Thanks for the tip – and here's one in return. From now on, keep your nose well out of this case. Inspector Batchelor is convinced you're a liability and would be delighted to see you locked up, and there are times I find myself sharing his point of view. Do we understand each other?" Cave's tone was pleasant, but firm.

"Who's going to tell Loddon's wife that he's dead?" Jorgensen asked.

"Not you, Mac. That's police business."

# Thirty-Nine

It was the voices Ah Cheng heard first, muffled but growing louder, then the sound of a door opening and the approach of heavy footsteps. For hours he had sat on the floor of the locked room, listening first to the dawn call of birds, then the thrum of distant engines and faint metallic clangs. Sounds that indicated he was still in the city. Though he had heard no movement from above or below, and figured he must be in a single-storey annexe attached to a house.

He rose to his feet, putting an ear against the thick wood of the door. There were two sets of footsteps marching down the corridor outside. They stopped outside the door, and Ah Cheng heard the scrape of a key in the lock. Then suddenly, there was the sound of shouting from further away – from the direction the men at the door had come.

"I go to see what the trouble is," he heard one of the men say.

Ah Cheng strained to listen to the retreating footsteps, and to the raised voices from the far end of the corridor. Within seconds the footsteps returned, running this time. "Quick, come now," then both men retreated fast. Stilling his own breathing, Ah Cheng listened out for any sign of life from the other side of the door. Satisfied the coast was clear, he crouched down to the level of the keyhole and peered through it, exhaling in relief. In their hurry to leave, the men had left the key in place.

He took quick steps back across the darkened room, to the spot opposite the door where he had spent most of the last few hours sitting with his back against the wall. Running his fingers gently backwards and forwards across the floor, he found the sharp point he sought. Gently, he eased free a thickish splinter of wood, eight or so inches long. It had taken him a good couple of hours in the dark to work it loose from the ragged floorboard edge. A poor weapon, but good enough for a sharp stab into an unprotected eye, and then to take advantage of the scream, the blood, and the confusion it would create.

Holding the splinter with care, Ah Cheng returned to the door. Carefully placing it to one side, he removed his cotton shirt and smoothed it out on the floor, so that the hem at the waist lay tucked against the foot of the door. Then, taking gentle hold of the splinter, he used it to poke the shirt under the door, repeating the action along the length of its underside, a fraction of an inch at a time, until after several painstaking minutes, the cloth extended beyond the door, by two or three inches if he was lucky, less if it had rucked up.

All the while, he listened out for the men's returning footsteps, hearing instead more of the voices raised in disagreement from somewhere deep within the building. Six, seven, eight or more voices. He wondered what was happening but knew that he had to hurry.

Ah Cheng brought the splinter up to the keyhole, inserting its blunter end and feeling for resistance as it met the tip of the key. Holding the splinter with as many fingers as he could, to spread the load and lessen the risk of it snapping, he pushed gently against the key's tip. Softly, softly, he fed the splinter further into the keyhole, nudging the key with it, until, at last, all resistance vanished.

He drew back the splinter and put his eye to the keyhole. It was clear. With delicate fingertips he took hold of the shirt, feeling with a surge of relief the weight of the key on the material. Easing it towards him, taking care not to snag on the underside of the door, the bow end of a long black mortice key slowly slid into view.

Ah Cheng grabbed it, slipping it into the keyhole, a half-turn to the left, feeling the doorlatch click. He stood up and pulled the door open, his eyes flinching in the hallway's sudden glare. After a moment's pause on the threshold, he looked right, along a corridor towards a door left open. Through it, he saw a tiled floor, different from the wooden floorboards of the corridor, and heard the continuing commotion that had driven his captors away. He looked left, where a second door at the end of the corridor was just a few feet away. Grabbing his shirt from the floor, he reached the second door in three quick strides. A thumb latch opened the way into a large square room, dirt-floored, with corrugated tin sidings and a high pitched roof. Daylight leaking in through gaps in the eaves and holes in the tin revealed the outlines of irregular heaps of sacks and barrels stacked high on wooden pallets. On the far side, large wooden doors were pulled shut.

Behind him, he heard the rhythm of hard-soled shoes on tiles. At least two men were heading in his direction. He stepped into the storage room, pulling the door closed, and ran across to the double doors, finding them locked with iron hasps, and secured by a substantial padlock. He felt along the edges of the hasps. Some of the door slats to which they were attached were rotting and soft to the touch. Inserting his fingertips between one hasp and the door, he pulled, feeling the fastenings give way and allowing him a stronger grip. Raising a foot to brace himself against the door, he pulled harder, rewarded by the tear of splitting timbers. With one more heave, the hasp came away with a crack, and Ah Cheng fell to the ground.

"Hey, you!" a voice shouted from the doorway behind him. "Stop there. By order of the police."

Ah Cheng jumped to his feet and shouldered the door open, staggering through it into a small yard, from which a wide alley led between more buildings.

"Stop!" The policeman behind shouted again, but Ah Cheng ignored him and sprinted down the alley. At its end, he turned left with flailing arms and pumping legs into a sunlit street, narrowly missing an approaching bicycle laden with bursting panniers. He dodged between groups of women loading up hand carts and, within yards, found himself at the edge of Campbell Street Market, where hawkers were clearing up their food stalls.

Ducking behind one of the stalls, he turned to check and saw a Malay policeman at the entrance to the alley, looking around helplessly. Ah Cheng pushed quickly on, past the last of the food stalls and under the roof of the main market building, where he squatted low on his haunches behind a market trader's stone slab. While catching his breath, he heard a tutting sound close by. It came from an old Chinese woman, who shook her head at him as she scrubbed down an adjacent slab with a mop. A large bucket, half-full of dirty water, sat at her feet.

Ah Cheng raised his head above the slab and cast a look back but saw no sign of the policeman. He winked at the old woman, who met his eye with a disapproving scowl. Following the direction of her eyes he glanced down. The shirt gripped in his hand was bloodstained and dirty. He grinned sheepishly, rising slowly to his feet.

"Is there a tap, mother?" he asked.

She tutted loudly again and pointed towards a waist-high standpipe in the middle of the market hall, where a shirtless man was filling a pair of tin buckets. The trader stared wordlessly at Ah Cheng, then moved clear, leaving water gushing into the gulley below. Ah Cheng gingerly felt his face and neck and the dried blood matting his hair. Then, with a sharp intake of breath, he bent under the tap's flow, dousing his head, and rubbing himself clean, the wound at the back of his head stung sharply by the shock of cold water.

He shook the water clear, then thrust his shirt into the stream of water but the blood stains were too ingrained to rinse out. He wrung the cloth as dry as he could, then after a last backwards glance to check the coast was clear, walked bare chested out of the market hall onto Campbell Street, shirt held in one hand. Just another shirtless Chinese coolie wending his way through George Town's teeming streets.

# Forty

When Ah Cheng caught sight of his reflection in the windshield of the Standard Tourer parked in the stable yard, he soon realised why Abdul, Zamir and the two mechanics were staring at him. From above one eye, a lump the size of a rambutan fruit leaked a fresh track of blood that trickled down his cheek and onto his neck, there to join a separate rivulet from a bigger gash at the back of his head.

"Bring water," Abdul ordered the mechanics. Then, to Zamir, "Fetch Mr Mac straight away."

Zamir sprinted off, before stopping after a few yards to button up his tunic jacket, having remembered just in time that no emergency was excuse enough to enter the main hotel buildings improperly attired.

Abdul guided Ah Cheng to a stool in the workshop, then rummaged under the workbench for clean rags, which he handed to Ah Cheng. "You must wash your wounds," he said when the mechanics returned with a jug of water.

"I need to drink," said Ah Cheng.

"Yes, yes," said Abdul. "You must. I have tea." He turned to the mechanics. "You heard our friend. Tea – and be quick."

Jorgensen soon arrived, and immediately sent for the doctor, Eric Burtt, who, by chance was on the premises, dusting sandalwood powder onto the thighs of an unfortunate Swedish guest suffering from prickly heat: the consequence of inappropriate clothing and overexertion in the heat of the previous day.

Desperate as he was to fire off questions, Jorgensen suppressed his impatience until the doctor had finished tying off the white bandage that now sheathed Ah Cheng's head. They had moved upstairs to the sleeping quarters, where the hotel's drivers all shared a single dormitory. In the middle of the day the low-ceilinged room was suffocatingly stuffy, and Burtt wiped beads of sweat from his brow before stepping back to survey his handiwork.

"I recognise you now," he said to Ah Cheng. "You're the fellow who patched up Cromford's head last week."

Ah Cheng nodded. "Yes, doctor."

"You're Morley's valet, aren't you? Just what is going on here, Jorgensen?"

"I'll find out after Ah Cheng tells me what happened."

"Hmm," said Burtt, unimpressed by Jorgensen's evasion. "Have it your way. Your man needs plenty of rest and he should be up and about in a day or so." He chuckled to himself as he packed his instruments away in his bag. "That's the same advice I gave Cromford last week. Let's hope I'll be getting no more practice with head wounds at the E&O."

"I feel good, Doctor," said Ah Cheng. "Thank you."

Burtt wagged a finger at Ah Cheng. "You were knocked unconscious. So, don't take my advice lightly."

"Let's go somewhere else to talk," said Jorgensen to Ah Cheng as soon as Burtt left the room. "It's too hot in here, but first we need to get you a clean shirt."

The best Abdul could manage at short notice was a spare shirt from the tallest of the hotel's drivers. Then, Ah Cheng followed Jorgensen down the rickety staircase and along the circuitous route to Jorgensen's office that avoided the lobby and any guests who might question what a heavily bandaged Chinese man in an ill-fitting, half-buttoned shirt was doing in their midst. Jorgensen sent for more tea and settled Ah Cheng in the chair facing his desk.

Despite his long period of unconsciousness, there were precious few lapses in Ah Cheng's memory. He recounted seeing Loddon with Kei Hin in Rope Walk and then the attack in the alley.

"I do not understand why," Ah Cheng said. "But the police came to the house – and that is when I escaped. They were searching the building, I think. Lam's men heard them, ran into the house, and left the key in the door."

"I persuaded the police to go there," said Jorgensen. "You see, Loddon's body was washed up on the beach this morning, so I told them he was last seen with Kei Hin."

"Tuan Loddon is dead? But I saw him last night. Do you believe Lam and Kei Hin killed him?"

"It's possible. I still believe they killed Davies, in revenge for losing out on some of the blackmail proceeds, though I can't think what their motive is for killing Loddon."

"Maybe he saw them go to Davies's house?"

Jorgensen lit a cigarette while he thought about Ah Cheng's suggestion. "I don't think that's it. If Lam or Kei Hin thought he'd witnessed the killing, they'd have acted sooner to hush him up. Yet you saw Loddon go to the Australia Hotel with Kei Hin and he was with them again last night in Rope Walk. That makes me think they were working together. But on what, I wish I knew."

"It explains why they locked me away."

"That makes sense. To keep you out of the way so you didn't spoil their plans. The key to it all must be the Australia Hotel. When you followed Kei Hi and Loddon there, they were searching for a dark-haired white man. I found that out this morning."

"We will go to the Australia?" asked Ah Cheng.

"First, you must rest. As the doctor ordered."

***

"Telephone call for you, Mr Paul," Gopi said breathlessly. "From Inspector Batchelor."

Jorgensen turned to see the porter, who had pursued him up the main staircase to the first floor. He checked his watch. Just before three o'clock. He had been hoping for news of the police's visit to the Lam Copra Export Company for some time now, though he would have preferred it if Cave himself had telephoned – not Batchelor.

"Tell the operator I'll take it in my office," he said. His proposed call on Arshak Sarkies in his suite would have to wait.

"You took your time, Major," Batchelor said, when Jorgensen eventually picked up the earpiece from the telephone on his office desk. His tone was curt and the sneer in his pronunciation of Jorgensen's former military rank had returned. "I'm calling at the Superintendent's behest," he continued. "He's asked me to thank you for your cooperation."

"What did they have to say about Loddon?" Jorgensen asked.

"These are police matters," Batchelor replied. "I'm not at liberty to divulge anything."

"At least tell me if you arrested them."

"As I said, the Superintendent thanks you for your information and has made it clear that you should step away from any further involvement in the matter. If you persist in interfering, you'll be arrested for obstruction."

"Is that verbatim from Superintendent Cave, Inspector, or are you embellishing?" Jorgensen asked.

"The Superintendent's orders are clear enough. You're to stay out of our way," Batchelor said, his rising anger at Jorgensen's wisecrack palpable even over the crackling telephone line.

With a loud click, the line went dead. Batchelor had hung up.

Jorgensen replaced the receiver on the cradle and lit a cigarette. He had taken a chance in telling the superintendent about the blackmail letter, hoping for a more forthcoming response than the one just received from Inspector Batchelor. But there was no denying that he had once again been summarily warned off the case and reduced to guessing the outcome of the police's visit to Rope Walk. The most likely, he hoped, was that George Lam and Kei Hin had been taken in for questioning in the cells at the detective station. If that was the case, he could maybe understand Cave's reserve until a charge was brought. On the other hand, if no arrests were made, what reason could Cave have to cut him off so peremptorily? Whatever the reason – it was clear Cave was determined to keep him at arm's length from the case.

He stubbed the cigarette out in the ashtray. He had no intention of obeying Cave's directive. In the last hour or so, he had begun to feel he was finally making progress – that some of the tangled threads around the death of Davies, and now that of Loddon, were beginning to unravel.

In Jorgensen's mind – the most important of those threads was the identity of the dark-haired man who had called at Davies's lodgings prior to the murder. The conviction, rather than the possibility, that it was Joseph Durrant, had crept up on him, almost unnoticed, until the thought was lodged firmly in his head. Though at this stage, it was still no better than a hunch. While Durrant matched the description of the man Kei Hin and Loddon had attempted to track down, it was not a theory he could take to the police.

Proving that the caller was Durrant would require his identification by Suri. And there was the snag. How to secure that identification and keep Suri safe? Two men were dead. Both strangled, perhaps by the same deadly pair of hands.

Jorgensen swore under his breath, stopped short by the sudden realisation that his reasoning had gone one step further. He had begun to view Durrant as the killer. Remembering how Durrant's temper had flared at the E&O, there was little doubting either his short fuse or propensity to violence. And he was physically strong, easily strong enough to kill two men with his hands and to carry Loddon's body to the canal or the quayside.

Jorgensen could feel his heart beating faster. If he was right, then he needed to act quickly. If Durrant was the killer, identifying him as the dark-haired man who called at Love Lane was the priority.

# Forty-One

With an excited shine to his eyes, Dipi, the lift boy, knocked at Jorgensen's door.

"You sent for me, Mr Mac?"

"Another job for you," Jorgensen said. "We need to get hold of Suri again. Go and tell him to be ready. We will call for him in the motor car. And don't run in the hotel – we don't want to upset Rama."

Dipi grinned and ducked back through the door towards the lobby. Jorgensen picked up his hat, and, in the corridor, turned the other way, heading out onto the passageway that led to the stables. Inside the workshop he found the heavily bandaged Ah Cheng talking to Zamir.

"You're supposed to be resting," said Jorgensen.

"We go to the Australia Hotel now?" asked Ah Cheng brightly, pointedly ignoring Jorgensen's remark.

Jorgensen nodded. Ah Cheng seemed in good spirits and the prospect of tackling Durrant felt less intimidating with a little help at his side. "I think I know who Kei Hin and Loddon were searching for – a man called Durrant. Suri can tell us if it was him who called at Love Lane before the murder. But we need to find somewhere safe for him to watch without being spotted."

"From over the street. It is always busy by the *nasi kandar* restaurant."

Jorgensen thought for a moment. "Okay, we'll put you and Suri on the walkway opposite the hotel. And I'll wait in the car round the corner, from where we can keep an eye on you."

***

Across Penang Road from the Australia Hotel, Ah Cheng and Suri sat on the five-foot way, backs against the wall of a batik cloth merchant's shophouse. They squinted into the setting sun, their hands shielding their eyes as they watched the hotel's entrance. From the *nasi kandar* restaurant next door, the intense smells of fried onions, ginger and spices were already drawing a queue ready for its imminent opening.

They were soon joined by Zamir, shorn of his E&O driver's tunic, who crossed the busy intersection from the Australia Hotel, dodging the trolleybus turning the corner from Chulia Street.

"Clerk says he is still in his room," he said.

"We wait," Ah Cheng replied.

Zamir nodded and set off to where the Standard Tourer was parked twenty yards up Leith Road, one of five roads emanating from the intersection, and the one least visible from the bedroom windows of the Australia Hotel. There, Jorgensen waited under the cover of the five-foot way, for it was blisteringly hot inside the car.

Soon, the shadow line on Penang Road crept across the wide street onto the walkway, creeping up the wall of the batik merchant's house until it faded in a combination of the gathering gloom and the brightening glow of the newly lit streetlamps. As the stores around them closed for the day, crowds gathered outside the cinema on Penang Road and the queue doubled in length outside the now open *nasi kandar* restaurant.

Jorgensen was about to climb into the Standard Tourer to continue the wait when he saw Ah Cheng rushing towards him.

"Over there," said Ah Cheng, his outstretched finger pointing back towards the corner entrance to the Australia Hotel, where two figures were caught in the pale gleam of a streetlamp. "Kei Hin and one of his men," said Ah Cheng.

Jorgensen recognised the second man. The one they had nicknamed Straw Hat – the same man Ah Cheng saw with Loddon the night before. He was following half a pace behind the peacocking Kei Hin, who scanned the street from side to side as if he owned it. At the entrance to the hotel, the two men paused and swapped positions. Straw Hat leading the way into the lobby.

"What now?" Ah Cheng asked.

"Fetch Suri. Now it's dark, we'll stick together and move the car closer," Jorgensen replied.

Moments after Suri and Ah Cheng had joined Jorgensen in the Standard Tourer, Kei Hin and Straw Hat spilled back onto the walkway in front of the hotel. Kei Hin cursed viciously before turning to launch a savage kick at the front door. From the car, Jorgensen heard the impact, and then a second crack as the door bounced back. Kei Hin looked around with a wild glare and then stalked off down Penang Road, with Straw Hat following, a judicious yard behind.

"Keep your eyes peeled. Durrant might follow."

A further fifteen minutes elapsed before Jorgensen's prediction came true. From the hotel's front door, Durrant cast a slow look around him, taking in the restaurant opposite, the cars and rickshaws passing slowly by, until his eyes seemed to rest on the entrance to Leith Road.

With his chin thrust forward, and brawny shoulders rolling as he walked, Durrant crossed the junction and approached the Standard Tourer. Pausing at the driver's door, he bent down to glance in at Zamir, who fixed his gaze through the windscreen, fearful of catching his eye. About to move on to the rear window, Durrant stopped when Jorgensen opened the door and climbed out to meet him.

"Durrant, isn't it?" said Jorgensen.

"Well, would you believe it. The fucking undermanager from the E&O," Durrant replied mockingly. The two men stood less than a foot apart, their eyes locked, but with the car's open door between them. Jorgensen gripped its frame, with a leg braced against the door panel. If the Australian had come to fight, he did not want the door serving as a weapon.

On the other side of the car, Ah Cheng's bandaged head rose above the roof line, its stark white material briefly catching

Durrant's eye in the gloom, before his eyes bore once again into Jorgensen's.

"What are you doing here, undermanager?" he asked menacingly. "You're well away from the E&O."

"You're no longer a guest," said Jorgensen. "I don't much care where you're staying now."

"Are you sure about that? You've been parked here for hours."

"We're looking for the man who attacked my driver," said Jorgensen, indicating Ah Cheng with a nod of the head.

Durrant looked across the roof. "The Chinaman?" he said. "Why would you waste your fucking time on him?" He spat on the tarmac, and with one last baleful look at Jorgensen, turned on his heel and walked off towards Chulia Street.

Jorgensen watched him go, then bent to meet the eyes of Suri, sat next to Zamir on the front bench seat.

"It was him, sir," Suri said. "Straight away I knew him."

Jorgensen let out a low whistle. Though he had convinced himself Durrant was the man seen visiting Davies's lodging house before the murder, for it to be confirmed sent a shudder down his spine.

"We need to find out why Kei Hin and George Lam are so interested in him," he said to Ah Cheng. "Let's pay them another visit."

"Good," said Ah Cheng. "I am ready."

# Forty-Two

Later that evening, in the front office of Lam Copra Exports, the two clerks kept their heads down, fingers clicking on abacus beads, while trying to ignore the press of people around them.

Jorgensen, Ah Cheng and Abdul were standing just inside the entrance door. Facing them, from behind the clerk's desks, were Kei Hin, Straw Hat and two of Lam's bodyguards.

"You should pack these fellows off home," said Jorgensen, motioning towards the clerks. He stood with one hand inside his jacket, his fingers resting lightly on the butt of the pistol, and Kei Hin's frequent glances towards his chest indicated it was having the desired effect. Beside him, Ah Cheng and Abdul both held their favoured weapons at their sides: the wrench from Abdul's toolbox, and a jemmy, which Ah Cheng balanced calmly in the palm of his hand.

"That is for Mr Lam to decide," Kei Hin replied. "You come now to his office."

"We'll stay right here," said Jorgensen. "Out in the open where we can be seen." While he was sure the brothel barkers of Rope Walk and their single-minded customers would pay no attention to any fracas in the brightly lit office, it was reassuring to know that the Standard Tourer, with Zamir at the wheel, was just a few paces away. "I'm sure you don't want the police here again," he added. "We're not here to create trouble. We're just after some information."

Barrelling through the door behind Kei Hin, the squat figure of George Lam pushed past his bodyguards. Over the clerks' heads he surveyed his visitors with a mixture of suspicion and contempt.

"Mr Jorgensen, again," he said, chuckling as he glanced at the weapons in Ah Cheng and Abdul's hands, before switching his gaze to where Jorgensen's hand lay under his jacket.

"Leave now," he commanded the two clerks, who needed no second invitation – thrusting papers into a tray and scurrying out onto Rope Walk.

"Where is your friend Mr Michael Lim?" said Lam. "Are you not here under the protection of his father?"

"You made a promise not to harm Davies. Lim knows this."

"We broke no promises to Lim Yeok Sun," said Lam. "The murder of the *angmoh* was not our doing."

"Why should I believe you?"

"No profit in killing him," Lam opened his arms wide as if to draw Jorgensen's attention to the office and what it represented. "I am a businessman."

"Is that what you told the police?"

"It was most unfriendly of you to send them. Perhaps you are surprised to find me here?"

"It was lucky for you they didn't find Ah Cheng."

"You think the police would interfere in a dispute between Chinese?"

"They know Ah Cheng works for the E&O."

Lam shrugged. "They asked many questions, and they insisted on making a search. All because of you," he jabbed a stubby forefinger in Jorgensen's direction. "But they found no proof of your wild accusations."

"And no proof is your problem too."

"What do you mean?" Lam's eyes narrowed.

"Now that Loddon is dead, you don't have the proof you need for your next attempt at blackmail. But I guess you know that already."

"More accusations?" scoffed Lam, turning to Kei Hin as if to share his incredulity at Jorgensen's words.

"It's why you held Ah Cheng prisoner," said Jorgensen. Lam's unconvincing pretence had strengthened his conviction he was on the right track. "It was to buy time while you carried out your plan.

I'm sure you intended to release him once you'd got money from the Australian."

"I do not know any Australian."

"Solly is the name you know him by. Your man Kei Hin just returned from visiting him at the Australia Hotel – without the money you demanded. I guess Solly told you to get lost, and, with your witness dead you've run out of options."

Jorgensen watched the tightening of Lam's jaw muscles and the involuntary sideways glance towards Kei Hin. He had hit a nerve all right.

"I'm not interested in your failed attempt at blackmail," he said. "I won't be reporting it to the police. All I want from you – is to know everything that Loddon told you. Whatever he saw was enough to persuade you to blackmail Solly, and enough to get him killed."

"The old man's death was not our doing," said Lam.

"You're not blameless. Did Loddon believe you were going to cut him out of the takings? Something forced him into approaching Solly alone."

"What you say is no more than the barking of a dog in the night," said Lam. "It is late, and time for you to go, Mr Jorgensen."

"If you want to be rid of me, you'll need to tell me what Loddon saw. Otherwise, I'll take Ah Cheng to the detective station to make a statement about his abduction. With those wounds on his head, they'll be more inclined to believe him than you."

"How do I know you won't go to the police anyway?" Lam asked.

"No need," interjected Ah Cheng, surprising both Jorgensen and Lam. "I settle my own debts. When I am ready."

On hearing this, Kei Hin bristled, his eyes meeting Ah Cheng's in a challenging stare. "Is that so, cousin?"

"When I am ready," Ah Cheng repeated.

"There's your promise, Lam," said Jorgensen. "Now tell me what happened. Loddon came to you with what he knew. What was it he saw?"

Lam turned to his bodyguards. "Out!" he snapped. Straw Hat and his two burly companions obediently trooped through the door to the hallway behind, the sound of their heavy footsteps climbing the wooden staircase reverberating through the building, until drowned out by the continuing cries of the brothel barkers outside. Only Kei Hin, still seething at Ah Cheng's threat, remained at Lam's side.

"He saw what you suspect," Lam said to Jorgensen. "The *angmoh* Solly. At the house on Love Lane."

"When?"

"The night of the killing."

"And Loddon told you he recognised the man as a guest of the Australia Hotel?"

Lam made a dismissive gesture with his hand, as if Jorgensen's question was too obvious to bother answering. "Enough talk now," he said.

"Not quite," Jorgensen replied. With Loddon dead, there was still a shortage of evidence to take to the police. He needed more from Kei Hin. "What did Solly tell you?" he asked, addressing Lam's lieutenant directly.

"Why help you?" Kei Hin replied, his chin jutting forward in defiance.

"Help him understand," said Jorgensen to Lam.

"Tell the *angmoh*," said Lam. "Then we can be rid of him."

"He said the old man was dead and to tell my boss to forget the money."

"Some days the returns in business are less than we hope for," said Lam with an ingratiating smile. The phrase was a deliberate echo of his words to Michael when agreeing to accept the reduced payment for surrendering Cromford's diary.

"You don't care whether the killer is caught?" asked Jorgensen.

"If white men kill other white men, it is not my concern. One day they will all leave Penang."

Jorgensen shook his head in disgust. "You're a real piece of work."

Lam shrugged. "If you care so much, you will see him hang – but it will be without my help. Now, it is late. Kei Hin, see our visitors leave."

Kei Hin gestured towards the front door as Lam turned his back and left the office. "Goodbye, Mr hotel man," he said, with a mock bow. Then, turning to Ah Cheng, added, "I will see you again, cousin."

"It is a promise," Ah Cheng replied.

# Forty-Three

A message from Bailey at the Australia Hotel was awaiting Jorgensen on his return to the E&O. After reading it, he made straight across the lobby to the front desk, where he asked for the telephone.

"I think you spooked him, Jorgensen," said Bailey once the call was put through. "Your bloke checked out this evening."

"Do you know where he went? Another hotel maybe?"

"I sent the porter out to try and find out, but all I can tell you is Solly, or Durrant, or whatever the bloody hell his name is, got hold of a rickshaw and headed off down Chulia Street."

Eastwards, possibly towards the quayside. "Thanks Bailey."

As soon he hung up, Jorgensen lifted the earpiece again, "Put me through to Superintendent Cave at the detective station," he said to the operator.

Half a minute passed before her voice came back on the line. "The Superintendent has left for the day," she said. "But Inspector Batchelor is available."

Jorgensen cursed under his breath. Batchelor again. Even less likely than Cave to act on his information. "Thanks, please put me through."

"Inspector Batchelor here." The Lancashire vowels curiously absent over a telephone line. "What do you want, Major Jorgensen?"

"I've got new information on the Davies murder. Can I come and see you?"

"Didn't you understand my earlier warning to keep out of the case?"

"Do you want the information, or not?"

"Is there any point? Is it more reliable than the misleading nonsense you've already provided?"

Jorgensen gritted his teeth, while he pondered the wisdom of persisting. Without Cave at his side, Batchelor would delight in continuing his provocation, and Jorgensen was unsure his temper would stand it.

"There's a man you should interview about the murders of Frank Davies and Aubrey Loddon."

"I must admit, Major, your persistence is admirable. First it was Magnus Prescott who did it, then some Chinese gangsters, on whom we wasted considerable time and effort. Who is it this time?"

"I'm serious, Batchelor. Do you want to hear my information or not?"

"Let's get one thing straight, Major Jorgensen. I take people as I find them. You might be an old friend of the superintendent, but from what I've seen you're just a fucking nuisance."

"His name is Joseph Durrant," said Jorgensen, ignoring the insult. "Though he also uses the name Garrett Solly. He was seen calling at Frank Davies's lodgings on the day of his murder and was known to Aubrey Loddon. Loddon was looking for Durrant on the night he died."

"I've never heard of anybody called Durrant or Solly. Who is he?"

"An Australian who lives in Singapore, but, until this evening, was staying at the Australia Hotel."

"And you claim he was seen calling at Davies's lodgings?"

"By the errand boy. He saw Durrant go up to Davies's room."

"All right, Major," said Batchelor. "If you come to the detective station in the morning to give a description, I'll be prepared to look for this fellow. Though you'll have some explaining to do to the superintendent. He isn't going to be pleased you're still interfering in the case."

"It's more urgent than that," said Jorgensen. "Durrant just checked out of the Australia Hotel. He knows he's under suspicion. I think he's heading for the quayside to get away."

"What exactly do you expect from me, Major? I've done you the courtesy of listening. But, other than the word of an uneducated boy, you've not provided any evidence that would merit calling out the entire on-duty force on a manhunt. Come to the detective station tomorrow morning and we'll take it from there. Now good night."

# Forty-Four

For much of his childhood, Ah Cheng rarely strayed from the quayside and its crowded, narrow lanes. It was here, that as a young boy, he had stumbled, alone and frightened, down the gangway of a ship from Fujian province – one of hundreds of immigrants crammed into every available space on board. And here where he was taken in by the old couple who lived on Lim jetty. Their single room shack on the main boardwalk was the first place he remembered as home. He had no memory left of China, of his father and mother, or of the long voyage, during which, the old couple once told him, his mother had died of fever.

As a boy he was a typical 'water rat', the insult hurled at children from the clan jetties by those whose homes were on dry land and who looked down on their less fortunate brethren, even if they were from the same clan. Though the insult, however, was seldom hurled more than once at Ah Cheng, if its caller wished to avoid an immediate and painful retribution.

But being a water rat was a life that Ah Cheng relished. Every morning, the second thing he saw, after waking and emerging through the shack's low doorway, was the bright azure of the sea beyond the far end of the boardwalk. The sea across which one day he dreamed of sailing to new and hopeful lands. The old man helped crew a tongkang, sometimes smuggling Ah Cheng aboard. Out in the channel he saw the steamers close-up. It was the sight and smell of these ships, bound for Hong Kong, Shanghai, Yokohama, Batavia, Galle and Calcutta, that first kindled his desire to travel to these exotic sounding destinations.

As a water rat he learnt the feel and smell of every single inch of the quayside. Every timber-shored wall, every weed-festooned pile supporting its piers. The hawk and spit of every boatman and which ones to avoid at all costs. Knowledge that helped him survive the later deaths of the old couple and then enabled him to prove his worth within the Lim clan.

Though he hoped that water rat life was now in the past, it was recent enough for his tread to be sure on the quayside and for his eyes, ears, and nose to tell him exactly where he was in the darkness.

His search started at the railway pier and moved north up Weld Quay, looking out for the few tongkangs and sampans still active after dark: some on legitimate business, authorised by the harbourmaster's office – ferrying crew members to their vessels in the channel, officers who had dined onshore, or crew whose pay packets were spent in the pubs and brothels. Others slipped out of the harbour without lights, to collect illicit cargoes absent from a ship's manifest. These boatmen were members of smugglers' rings, evading duty on alcohol and opium and, in some cases, carrying terrified young women to resupply George Town's brothels.

Halfway up the quayside, at the entrance to Church Street Ghaut Pier, a Chinese nightwatchman sat on a low stool under a light high in the overhanging tin roof. Cigarette in mouth, he glanced up suspiciously as Ah Cheng approached, struck by the sight of his wide-brimmed straw hat. In the nightwatchman's eyes, it was a hat more suited to daylight, to protect against the sun's burning rays.

"I come from the E&O, cousin," said Ah Cheng, pulling the card case given to him by Jorgensen from his pocket, then handing a card to the still seated nightwatchman. "My boss. Mr Jorgensen from the E&O."

The nightwatchman peered at the card. Though he could not read English, he had no trouble in recognising the hotel's distinctive palm tree and sunset design.

"Why you wear the hat?" he asked.

Ah Cheng removed it to expose the bandage swathing his head.

"Knocked my head."

"Tssk," the nightwatchman sucked his teeth noisily and stubbed out his cigarette on the ground, unmoved by the sight of Ah Cheng's injuries.

"Sampans go out to steamers from here, yes?" Ah Cheng asked.

"Many."

"Boss wants to know about any *angmoh*s that came through here tonight."

"Boss give you dollars?"

"Cents only."

"Tssk." Another disapproving suck of the teeth. "Cannot remember for cents only."

"You try cousin. Big man with black hair. Passenger on a steamer, not crewman."

"How many cents?"

"Twenty."

Twenty cents, the price of dim sum and soup for breakfast. With a toss of his head, the nightwatchman indicated the pier behind him. "Right side," he said. "One boatman waiting for passengers to come."

"Thanks cousin." Ah Cheng handed over the promised twenty cents and walked past the nightwatchman's stool onto the pier.

From above, Church Street Ghaut Pier resembled an elongated T, with a kink to the left of the upright just before it reached the cross of the T. A corrugated tin roof, supported by steel columns, ran seawards from the shore entrance, joining a similar structure which covered half of the cross section, where the water was deeper and suitable for the larger vessels tied up alongside. There, two tall engine sheds provided the power to hoist and lower gangways, along which automobiles and bullock carts boarded the ferry across the channel to Butterworth on the mainland.

Church Street Ghaut Pier served almost every type of vessel found in Penang Harbour. As well as the ferry, there were the small steamers moored against the cross-section. Then, on each long side of the pier – the boats that brought in cargoes from the larger steamers anchored in the channel. Single-masted tongkangs were tied up against its northern side, while a second, lower deck made the southern side a favoured boarding point for the smaller oar-powered sampans. Every few yards, short flights of wooden steps led to the waterline. In daylight, at the foot of these thirty or so flights, dozens of sampans jostled for position to unload.

Ah Cheng walked onto the darkened pier, steering towards that right edge, where moonlight illuminated the nearest steps, dropping eight feet into gently lapping water. He walked on slowly, passing a dozen more flights before he spotted the lone sampan. In it, hunched down on a plank across its centre, sat the boatman, who on hearing Ah Cheng's footsteps on the deck above, glanced up in expectation.

"Hello uncle," Ah Cheng called down.

"Cannot take one only," the boatman shouted up. "Must be more."

"Uncle, I am not a passenger for you. I come for information."

Ah Cheng descended the flight until he drew level with the vessel's bow. It was typical of the sampans used as water taxis: wooden-hulled and flat-bottomed with a sharply raised bow and stern.

"I see you are Tay clan," Ah Cheng said, indicating the striking eye shapes painted either side of the pointed bow to ward off evil spirits.

"I got the licence," said the boatman, distrustful of this strange night visitor. Up close, Ah Cheng saw that he was a thin, stooping figure.

"I see it," said Ah Cheng. The plaque showing the boatman's licence number was bolted to the sampan's hull, just below Ah Cheng's feet. "I come from the E&O Hotel," he added. "In search of a guest. The nightwatchman said you took him out tonight – a white man, tall and strong with dark hair and a broken nose."

The boatman shrugged his bony shoulders. "Many *angmoh* tonight."

"This one a passenger only. Not crew."

"Cannot remember."

"Ah. Maybe some coins help you remember?"

The boatman shrugged again.

"Uncle, I am good friend of Lim Wooi Gee," Ah Cheng tapped the licence plaque with the toe of his shoe. "He approve this, eh?"

"Look like a boxer? The *angmoh*?"

"That's him," said Ah Cheng. "Like a boxer. Which ship did you take him to?"

"How much you give him?" the boatman said, tossing his chin in the direction of the nightwatchman at the pier's entrance.

"Twenty cents."

"Same same."

Ah Cheng fished in his pocket for two ten-cent coins and held them up in the moonlight for the boatman to see.

"*Singkep*," the boatman rose to a crouch so he could stretch a wiry arm across the gunwale to take the coins.

"Do you go again tonight to *Singkep*?" asked Ah Cheng.

The boatman shook his head. "All aboard now."

"Thank you, uncle."

The boatman grunted in reply and busied himself dropping the coins into a small purse. Ah Cheng climbed back up the steps and walked briskly back along the pier to the quayside.

# Forty-Five

The Lim jetty was one of the original clan jetties, the first rickety piers of which were erected by the five chief Hokkien clans in the early nineteenth century. Since then, the jetties continued to grow, until they resembled small floating villages, whose ramshackle houses, wooden-framed and roofed with corrugated tin sheeting, were propped up on stilts over the tidal mudbanks. Short stubby boardwalk alleys forked at angles from the main jetty, like straggling mangrove roots.

The jetties' inhabitants had changed little over the last century. Still largely the boatmen whose tongkangs ferried cargo from the ships moored in the channel to the quayside or fishermen with smaller sampans tied up alongside their shacks.

It was on the Lim jetty where Ah Cheng had lived as a young child with the old couple who took pity on him. And he remembered every timber of it, from the shrine at the entrance to the temple at its seaward end.

He waited next to the shrine for Jorgensen to arrive. To his right, further up the quayside, the illuminated clockface on the tower of the railway building was showing a quarter to ten. Half an hour earlier, he had persuaded a porter there to let him ring the E&O. At that time, Jorgensen had not yet returned, but the desk clerk promised to pass on his message as soon as he saw him.

From the shelter of the shrine, a young boy and girl, no older than eight or nine, about Ah Cheng's age when his guardians died, watched his every movement. He had shooed them away several times, but they soon crept back to hide behind the red-painted columns that supported the ornate carved roof.

He turned to them now and spoke. "You know Wooi Gee?"

The children's heads popped up from below a low timber wall to nod in unison, their wide eyes reflecting the moonlight.

"Go tell him to get ready. The *angmoh* will be here soon."

They scampered away onto the planks of the main boardwalk. Moments later, and no doubt to the children's disappointment at missing the event, for it was the promise of a rare visit onto the jetty of a white man that had drawn their initial attention, a dark-green Morris Bullnose, with Zamir at the wheel, bumped onto the scrubby patch of ground at the jetty's entrance.

Jorgensen leapt out of the passenger seat and hurried over to where Ah Cheng waited.

"Which ship did he go to?" Jorgensen asked.

Ah Cheng jerked a thumb in the direction of the channel that separated Penang from the mainland. "Out to the *SS Singkep*."

"I know it," said Jorgensen. The *Singkep* was a cargo steamer of the Dutch KPM line. Six and half thousand tonnes with twin masts and well decks. He had sailed on a similar ship in the KPM fleet and remembered running across her in Singapore on a few occasions. Her skipper at the time was Andersen, a Dane with a short temper and a reputation as a heavy drinker.

"A sampan boatman told me," Ah Cheng explained. "He took crewmen and officers out to their ships."

"Can you trust what you were told?"

Ah Cheng grinned. "I threatened him with Wooi Gee from the Harbourmaster's Office. Wooi Gee works in the Chinese section. Responsible for licences, so the boatman must show respect."

Jorgensen nodded in appreciation, although whether this was as a mark of Ah Cheng's cunning or because of the useful people he somehow knew, he was unsure.

"When does the *Singkep* sail?" he asked.

"At sunrise."

"Christ," instinctively Jorgensen glanced at his wristwatch. "He's going to get away before we can do anything about it."

"Maybe not," said Ah Cheng. "There's a sampan ready to take us out there."

"It's after the harbour curfew."

"Wooi Gee will not be caught," said Ah Cheng.

"Your friend, Wooi Gee," said Jorgensen. "So, he's a smuggler as well as a government official. How much does he want?"

"No money. But he will not wait long. I took him away from family."

Jorgensen considered Ah Cheng's suggestion. Inspector Batchelor had made it plain the police would not act until the morning. If Durrant's escape was to be prevented, then there was no alternative. "Okay," he said. "But first I'll send a message to the hotel."

He pulled a small notebook from inside his jacket and took a few steps closer to the shrine, where lanterns hanging from the roof cast a weak light over the adjacent bare ground. On a fresh page, he scribbled a short message, before tearing the sheet free, folding it once, then walking back to the Morris, where he leant through the window and handed it to Zamir.

"Do you know where Mr Michael lives?" he asked.

Zamir nodded. "I have driven him to his home."

"Good. Take him this message and then come straight back here and wait for me to return."

"Right away, Mr Paul," said Zamir.

The Morris manoeuvred backwards and forwards over the rough patch of ground, before rumbling away back up Weld Quay.

"Let's go see Wooi Gee," said Jorgensen to Ah Cheng.

# Forty-Six

It was only the second time Jorgensen had set foot on a clan jetty. The first, a year earlier, was on the neighbouring Chew jetty, a sprawling affair twice the width of the Lim jetty. He had gone at the invitation of a member of the Khoo Kongsi to drink tea and witness a ceremony at the small temple perched at the jetty's outer extremities.

All the clan jetties had similar temples at their seaward limits – dedicated to gods protecting them against the perils of the water. He had seen the Lim jetty temple several times, looking down from the deck of the railway ferry as it pulled in at the pier.

Jorgensen followed Ah Cheng over the uneven planks of the main boardwalk, their way lit by red and yellow lanterns decorating dwellings adjoining both sides. As they walked, curious faces turned towards them through open doors; from families squatting on woven rattan rugs, and tucking into bowls of soup and rice, to toothless old men and women, sat on low stools just inside their shacks, who spent their evenings watching passers-by.

Soon, the houses flanking one side of the boardwalk gave way to mooring posts to which low sampans were tied. When the outermost end of the jetty came into view, Jorgensen saw the small temple building framed against the night sky. Opposite it, beyond the low tide mark, several larger tongkangs were moored.

"Here Mr Mac," Ah Cheng stopped level with the last house on their right, short of the first of the tongkangs. "Here is Wooi Gee."

A man stepped out to join them on the boardwalk. A full foot shorter than Ah Cheng, Wooi Gee was bald on top with a ring of dark hair wrapping around the back and sides of his head. Sturdy, fat-calved legs protruded from a pair of dark shorts, matched by thick forearms carrying a lantern, the light from which illuminated a face puckered in an irritated frown.

"How do you intend to get on board?" queried Wooi Gee, lifting the lantern to examine Jorgensen. "Clear sky tonight," he said. "The watch may see our approach."

"I'm no pirate," said Jorgensen. "I'll hail when we're close. Is Andersen still the skipper?"

"You know him?"

"I doubt he'll remember me. Where's she sailing in the morning?"

"Belawan, then on to Singapore," said Wooi Gee. "Regular voyage."

Jorgensen remembered that Durrant had provided addresses in Singapore when checking in at both the E&O and the Australia Hotel. It pointed to that as his destination, rather than the port of Belawan in Sumatra, or Medan, the city that it served.

"Come," said Wooi Gee, leading the way further along the jetty.

A dozen small sampans bobbed gently on the incoming tide. A few were masted and loaded with coiled-up fishing nets. Others, including the one Wooi Gee climbed down into, had a numbered plaque fastened to the outside of its hull, denoting that it was licensed to carry passengers.

Jorgensen and Ah Cheng clambered in and sat on a cross board serving as a rudimentary seat. Wooi Gee unhitched the mooring rope and pushed past them to the stern to take hold of the single long oar. Stood between the two forks of the raised stern, he manoeuvred the sampan clear of the jetty and, pulling hard on the oar, steered out past the end of the railway pier and into the channel.

"Is this your sampan?" Jorgensen asked.

"Borrowed," replied Wooi Gee, his eyes fixed ahead, over the prow. Jorgensen twisted on the cross-plank to follow the same view. Faint moonlight, set to vanish behind Penang Hill by midnight, lit a wispy, silvery surface around the sampan, while, further out in the channel, pinpricks of light against the dark mass of the mainland hills were the only means of distinguishing the moored ships.

It was soon clear to Jorgensen that Wooi Gee was no ordinary clerk from the Harbourmaster's office. His brawny forearms pulled on the long oar with ease, fast leaving the lights of the quayside behind and skimming the sampan over placid inshore waters into the gentlest of swells, where Jorgensen savoured the breeze that cooled his face and neck.

"Thanks for your help," said Jorgensen.

"I do it for Ah Cheng," Wooi Gee replied, staring above their heads out into the channel.

No other words were spoken for ten minutes until Wooi Gee said softly. "Quiet now."

Jorgensen turned to see the raised stern of a steamer ahead, a few hundred yards to their right. The ship's bow pointed south, head into the incoming high-water current. A bright white light hung from the stern, a higher one from its bow, with duller deck lights strung between. From their low position on the water, Jorgensen could not make out the outline of the ship's bridge.

Faint voices and the odd metallic clang from the steamer's decks carried on the breeze as with steady strokes, Wooi Gee slipped the sampan past its stern.

"The *Kuching*," he said, when they were clear. "Tin from Port Swettenham. Unloading tomorrow."

The ship now lay behind Wooi Gee's right shoulder, and, as they pulled away from it, the outline of its funnel and superstructure was framed against the pale moonlit sky behind.

"Between the lines now," said Wooi Gee, as he continued his seemingly effortless sculling, pulling harder on one side to steer them parallel with the distant shores. They were navigating between two rows of anchored ships, going against the gentle tidal current.

Jorgensen turned again to look forward. Up ahead on the left he picked out the lights of a second vessel. Then minutes later, two more vessels in the line came into view. A third on the left, a much larger steamer on the right.

"Up ahead to port, the *Singkep*," Wooi Gee announced after several more minutes.

As they closed, and the deck lights came into focus, Jorgensen found himself picturing the *Singkep's* lines. Most ships in the KPM fleet were built in Holland, and shared similarities in design, so though Jorgensen had never boarded the *Singkep*, the traces of its lights were familiar enough. The raised forecastle, the goalposts fore and aft, and their booms, used to haul its cargoes to and from the holds, as well as the bridge superstructure, the black and white striped funnel of the KPM line and the aft deckhouse.

When they were about a hundred feet away, Wooi Gee dragged his oar in the water, and they drifted in line with the anchored steamer. Jorgensen rose to his feet on the bare bottom planks of the sampan. On the decks of the *Singkep* – all was quiet.

"Ahoy!" he yelled. "Ahoy the *Singkep*!"

His voice carried across the calm waters and echoed against the steel of the *Singkep*'s hull. He waited a beat then called out twice more, before hearing the distant clang of a closing door, and then indistinct voices in conversation.

"Ahoy!" a voice called. "Who's there?" The accent was Dutch, the high-pitched voice that of a youngish man. The third mate, on anchor watch, Jorgensen calculated, if he remembered the rota correctly.

"Jorgensen from the E&O," he shouted back. "With papers for a passenger."

"Come alongside!" came the response. "We will throw the pilot ladder down."

Wooi Gee steered the sampan towards the *Singkep*. A searchlight trained from the deck above briefly shone on them, before illuminating the side of the hull where the rope ladder dropped to the water's surface.

When the sampan was alongside, Wooi Gee reached out to grab the ladder sides. Above their heads, a different, deeper, and gruffer voice called down.

"What's your business?"

Jorgensen looked up to see the heads and shoulders of two figures leant over the ship's rail.

"Carrying papers for a passenger," he replied. "Is that Captain Andersen?"

"Who are you?"

"Jorgensen from the E&O."

"From the E&O? It is long after nightfall, Mr Jorgensen. Why are these papers so important? Who are they for?"

"Allow me to board and I will tell you," Jorgensen shouted up. "I must respect privacy."

"Very well. For the famous E&O." Andersen turned to yell to the crew member manning the searchlight. "Keep the light steady on the ladder."

Jorgensen grabbed hold of the side ropes and quickly scaled the wooden rungs. Every few feet, a wide spreader plank, extending over a foot each side of the ladder, took the place of a rung, holding the ladder tight against the hull and preventing it from twisting.

At the head, Jorgensen swung his legs over the bulwark rail and landed on the main deck, his nose immediately picking up the familiar smells of a tramp steamer. Coal smoke, freshly applied grease and, particular to the *Singkep,* the unmistakeable scent of Sumatran pepper – a residue from the ship's last cargo unloaded in Penang.

"Not your first time on a pilot ladder," observed Andersen.

The captain stood next to the junior officer, their backs to the main deckhouse wall behind them. Shadows from sparse lights hid half of Andersen's face, but there was no mistaking the disgruntled look with which he surveyed Jorgensen. A short barrel-chested man dressed in rumpled shorts and a greasy cotton short-sleeve shirt; apparently roused from his cabin at short notice and not troubling to hide his displeasure.

"I was second mate on the *Hebe,*" Jorgensen replied.

"So, you were under van Feggelen? That explains why you imagine you can board at this hour." He moved closer to

Jorgensen to study his face. "I don't believe I ever met you. Jorgensen, you say. You are not Danish though?"

"Canadian, Captain."

"Shame. It is always a pleasure to meet a fellow Dane. So, Mr Jorgensen of the E&O, for whom are the papers?"

"Mr Durrant, and I need to place them in his hands."

Andersen turned to the young officer who had maintained his silent place by his captain's side.

"Mr Leemhuis, do we have a passenger on board by the name of Durrant?"

Leemhuis, as youthful looking as his voice had sounded, and clad in clean shirt and shorts, appropriate for the officer of the watch in port, almost stood to attention as he replied.

"No, Captain."

"Also uses the name Solly," said Jorgensen. "He boarded earlier tonight."

"Mr Jorgensen," said Andersen. "What am I to make of you carrying documents for a man whose name you don't remember?"

Jorgensen hoped that any signs of hesitation on his face would be hidden from Andersen by the gloomy light. If he failed to say the right thing, the old bastard would take great delight in sending him back to shore, famous E&O or not.

"I called him Durrant because that's the name he used at the E&O." Now he had to gamble. "I carry papers from Magnus Prescott, for Mr Solly."

"From Prescott," there was a noticeable thawing in Andersen's tone. "Why didn't you explain so the first time?"

"Where can I find Mr Solly?"

"Mr Leemhuis will show you the way. I presume you carried passengers on the *Hebe*?"

"We did."

"Then you'll know what to expect. Our other passengers will board tomorrow at daylight, so Mr Solly is alone on the passenger deck." Andersen turned to leave. "As your unexpected arrival brought me onto deck, I will take a tour of the ship. I hope that you are gone by the time I return to the deckhouse. Goodnight Mr Jorgensen."

Andersen marched off towards the stern without looking back, leaving Jorgensen with the junior officer.

"Which cabin is he in?" Jorgensen asked.

"Number Four," Leemhuis replied.

There were two deckhouses on the *Singkep,* the larger one, four decks high, topped by the bridge, sat forward of the central funnel. If, as Jorgensen expected, the vessel was similar in layout to others in the KPM fleet, the passenger cabins and saloon, housing ten or twelve people at the most, would be found on the two decks immediately below the bridge, with doors opening onto a short promenade deck wrapped around the deckhouse. If a passenger wanted to stroll along the length and breadth of a ship at will, then a tramp steamer was not the way to travel.

Leemhuis showed the way to a nearby weathertight door, and, once inside the deckhouse, led Jorgensen up an adjacent staircase. At the next level, he opened another door onto a narrow, covered deck. Here, the doors and portholes of the passenger cabins were to their left, while to their right the outer structure extended only to waist height, the expanse above the handrail exposed to the elements. Jorgensen peered over the rail to the top of the pilot ladder below but, because of the angle of the bulwark, could not see the waterline or Wooi Gee's sampan.

"I'll find it from here," he said to Leemhuis, tapping him on the shoulder to halt his progress. "It's on the port side, isn't it?"

Uncertainty was writ large across Leemhuis's unlined face, but Jorgensen pushed past him before he had a chance to respond.

"I'll see you back at the pilot ladder," Jorgensen said, turning the corner out of Leemhuis's sight. There, he paused, briefly leaning on the rail while he gathered his thoughts. Dreaming up a story to get on board was one thing but how he would confront Durrant face to face was another. The forrard section of the *Singkep* lay in front of him – two cargo holds, both sealed and tied down for the short voyage ahead to Sumatra. The goalposts between the holds loomed above him, their raised cargo booms like the legs of some giant spider astride the deck. No crew members were visible, all presumably below decks, with most no doubt already asleep.

Off to his right were the lights of Penang harbour and at their extreme, the stubby harbour lighthouse, atop its latticed wooden frame at the edge of old Fort Cornwallis. Beyond that, the darkness of the Andaman Sea. To his left, shone the fainter lights of the Butterworth jetties on the mainland.

Durrant's cabin was just around the next corner, facing the mainland. He felt for the reassuring heft of the pistol under his armpit, forgetting for a moment he had left it behind. Boarding the *Singkep* under a false pretext was a risk, but to do so armed could be considered an act of piracy. He took a deep breath, there was little time to waste, and pushed off the rail, heading for the next corner on the promenade deck.

He was halfway round it when a fist, swinging from the darkness, clubbed him square in the side of the head, sending him staggering towards the bulwark rail. A second vicious chopping blow on the top of his head brought him to his knees, and he saw the furious, dark features of Durrant closing in. He raised an arm, part parrying the next punch, but it landed with enough force that his head bounced off the wooden deck. Before he could react, a knee pressed into his back. Durrant was on top of him. Then, he felt the scrape of a thin rope across his forehead, down over his eyes, his nose. Panicking, Jorgensen, stretched up a hand, jamming it under the cord just as it reached his neck.

Jorgensen felt the cord tightening, cutting into his hand as Durrant's knee pressed harder into his back. His other arm flailed wildly and ineffectually as Durrant heaved on the cord, lifting Jorgensen's shoulder, and twisting his body to one side. Jorgensen kicked out with his feet and found an upright bulwark rail. With a bent knee he braced hard against it. Durrant's knee lost its purchase against his spine and the men two rolled so that Jorgensen lay face up, Durrant beneath him, with Jorgensen's trapped hand still struggling to stop the cord from tightening around his throat.

He rammed his free elbow into Durrant's ribs, once, twice, three times, while his other hand pulled frantically against the cord, desperate to free it from his neck. But Durrant, with guttural groans, tightened his hold further. Jorgensen's vision blurred, the underside of the deck above floating in and out of focus. He gasped for breath and, with one last lung-busting effort forced his elbow once more into Durrant's body, finding his solar plexus. His own body twisted a fraction, and with the same arm he reached down, thrusting his hand under Durrant's trouser belt, grasping for the softness of his testicles. Jorgensen grabbed hold, squeezing with all the might he had left.

Durrant's stifled cries of pain were inches from his ear. Jorgensen squeezed hard again, at last feeling the pressure of the cord loosen. With a fierce heave from his trapped hand, he dragged the cord clear of his neck and over his head. He staggered to his feet and Durrant rose to meet him in the narrow walkway. Jorgensen lunged forward, and with legs pumping like pistons, charged Durrant, shoving him backwards into one of the steel pillars supporting the deck above.

Jorgensen ducked a punch, arcing in a wide hook, and planted a right deep into the pit of Durrant's stomach, following it with the left and then a knee into the crotch. This time, it was Durrant who slumped to his knees. Jorgensen stepped back and brought both fists together down onto the Australian's bowed head, collapsing him to the deck.

Hands on his knees, and fighting for breath, Jorgensen bent over Durrant's prostrate form. He had knocked him clean out. He listened out for the sound of footsteps up ladders or rushing around the promenade deck, but to his surprise, none came. Somehow the fight had escaped the crew's attention.

Jorgensen looked around. Durrant lay diagonally across the promenade deck. The corner where Durrant had staged the ambush was behind him. Jorgensen turned and found the cord, dropped where Durrant had risen to his feet. He picked it up and returned to Durrant's body. Roughly turning him onto his front, he used the cord to tie Durrant's hands behind his back. Then he flipped him over again and dragged him by the feet backwards and around the corner.

A cabin door lay open, and Jorgensen dragged Durrant through it, stepping back over his body to close the door. He flicked the light switch and turned to survey the austere interior. A double bunk bed took up one side, while a washbasin and small cupboard stood against the end wall below a shelved mirror – out of which, the reflection of his own bruised and bloody face stared back. The shelf was empty. He stepped over Durrant and bent to pull open the cupboard drawers and shelves. They too were empty.

Durrant's case sat on the top bunk. Jorgensen pulled it to the edge of the thin mattress, away from the shaped side guards and opened the clasps. A shaving kit, a hairbrush and a passport lay on top of a few items of carelessly packed clothing. Jorgensen rummaged through the contents, tossing the items onto the mattress one by one. He lifted the mattress and felt underneath it all the way back to the cabin wall, then bent to repeat the search under the lower bunk. At the far end his fingers touched on the ridged edge of a flat rectangular package, about an inch thick. He slid it clear and into the light. Below his feet he heard Durrant stirring.

The package was a waxed canvas document pouch, tied shut with coarse ribbon. Jorgensen loosened the knot, opened the flap, and tilted it towards the wall light so he could see inside. The short edges of five stacks of dollar banknotes, neatly squared away, met his eyes. He pulled a couple of the stacks free and thumbed through them. Ten-dollar notes and ten bundles in all, each wrapped with a numbered money band from the Peninsular Bank. By his quick estimate – ten thousand Straits Dollars in total.

Jorgensen breathed a sigh of relief. The money in the document pouch changed everything. Until now, with no definite connection between Durrant and Frank Davies, there was no obvious motive for murder. But if he killed Davies for money, that had to be evidence enough to bring the police out to the

*Singkep*. Now all he needed to do was persuade Captain Andersen to call them.

"Time to see the captain," he said to Durrant, whose eyes blinked slowly as he returned to consciousness.

"Fuck you," the Australian growled, looking up at Jorgensen with fury in his eyes.

Jorgensen stepped around behind Durrant's head. He reached under his armpits and hauled him to his feet. Then, with one hand gripping the cord tied around Durrant's wrists, shoved him to the side of the cabin, banging Durrant's head on the top bunk so he could slide past to open the door.

"I'll fucking kill you, you bastard," said Durrant.

"You tried and failed. Now shut up or I'll drag you there unconscious."

Jorgensen hauled Durrant out onto the promenade deck. "Round we go," he said, pushing Durrant ahead of him.

Halfway round the deck, overlooking the forward cargo holds, Jorgensen heard approaching footsteps. He stopped, and Captain Andersen and Leemhuis, the junior officer, appeared from round the next corner.

"I've been attacked," Durrant was first to speak. Spitting out the words before Jorgensen had a chance to react.

"What the hell is going on here?" Andersen demanded.

"This man is wanted for murder," said Jorgensen, raising his voice over Durrant's continued protestations.

"That's a fucking lie," Durrant snarled. "He came to steal my money. He's a thief."

"I'm bringing him to you, Captain Andersen, so you can signal the harbourmaster," said Jorgensen. "Get him to send for Superintendent Cave. Your passenger killed two people and you're still in Straits Settlements waters."

"How dare you tell me what to do," Andersen spat. "This is my ship and you lied to me when you boarded."

"I'm sorry," said Jorgensen. "But I had to see if it was the same man."

"Can't you see, the bastard's tied me up," Durrant protested, half-turning to show the ship's officers the cord lashed around his wrists.

"He tried to strangle me with that same cord," said Jorgensen. He shoved Durrant out of his way, and approached Andersen, close enough that he could smell the gin on the captain's breath. "Look at these marks," he said, pulling the collar of his shirt down. "The same as Superintendent Cave found on the bodies of the two men Durrant murdered."

"I cannot see a damn thing in this light, Mr Jorgensen," said Andersen hotly, after the briefest of glances. "Nevertheless, I must take your accusation seriously." He turned to the junior officer. "Mr Leemhuis, fetch the first mate and a seaman. I will remain with Mr Jorgensen and our passenger until your return."

# Forty-Seven

It was past two in the morning when Jorgensen first heard the distant grumble of the harbourmaster's motor launch.

Durrant was locked in his cabin, wrists still tied. A Javan seaman, roused from his sleep on account of his brawny physique, stood guard on the promenade deck outside. On the same promenade deck level, Jorgensen leant on the rail, looking west towards the Fort Cornwallis lighthouse, until he picked out the lights of the approaching launch.

Above him in the deckhouse block, a furious Captain Andersen waited on the bridge. Though forced to act by Jorgensen's account, he was unprepared to forgive him for the subterfuge with which he had boarded the *Singkep*. As soon as Durrant had been locked in his cabin by the first mate, the young officer Leemhuis, and the seaman summoned to assist them, Andersen had stalked off without a further word.

Wooi Gee and Ah Cheng had long departed in the sampan from the foot of the pilot ladder. They needed no second invitation to disappear into the darkness once they heard a harbour master official and the police were on their way.

Jorgensen made his way down to the head of the pilot ladder when the launch came alongside and was waiting there when Captain Andersen appeared. No words were exchanged, and together with Leemhuis, they stood in frosty silence, apart from Andersen's shouted instruction to the deck hand manning the searchlight.

The harbourmaster official, McGill, a middle-aged Eurasian, was first to puff his way up the pilot ladder and greet the captain.

Next over the rail was Superintendent Cave. He cast a questioning sideways glance at Jorgensen, whose head was wrapped in a bandage applied by the first mate, before joining

McGill and Andersen. The captain guided them a few feet away, where they spoke in lowered voices. Though Jorgensen could not hear the conversation, the drift of it from Andersen's angry tones was clear enough.

After the group separated, with Andersen returning to the bridge, Cave approached Jorgensen, shaking his head.

"You'd better tell me what the hell you've been playing at, Jorgensen," he said. "Captain Andersen wants to throw the book at you."

Jorgensen called over Leemhuis, who was standing attentively close by. "Superintendent Cave wants to speak to me in private. Can we use one of the cabins?"

Leemhuis nodded, leading them up to a cabin on the starboard side of the deckhouse. Inside, it was identical to the one in which Durrant was temporarily imprisoned.

"Spit it out, then," said Cave, as he closed the door to the promenade deck behind him. "And it'd better be convincing." He sat down on the bottom bunk alongside Jorgensen and flinched when he caught sight of the livid red welts on Jorgensen's neck.

"Looks familiar, doesn't it," said Jorgensen, seeing the direction of Cave's stare, and bringing the tips of his fingers up to gently trace the marks. "Durrant almost strangled me too."

"Christ, Mac," said Cave. "What were you doing out here?"

"Catching the bastard before he got away." Jorgensen said. "Batchelor wasn't interested so I took it upon myself."

"The Inspector assured me you had no evidence on which he could act."

Jorgensen let out a derisive laugh. "I told Batchelor that Durrant was seen at Davies's place before the murder, and that he was known to Loddon, but he put off taking any action until the morning. Said what I had wasn't evidence enough." He pulled his shirt collar down to better reveal the fresh wounds on his neck. "How about these for evidence, eh?"

"You were damn lucky to survive," said Cave.

"Luck had nothing to do with it. It was desperation."

"They look bloody nasty. A doctor should see them."

"Get the police surgeon to examine me in the morning. My guess is he'll confirm the marks are almost identical to those found on Davies and Loddon's necks."

Cave leant in closer. "You could be right. Where's the rope?"

"It was a cord, and right now it's tying Durrant's wrists behind his back."

"I hope you're joking. That's not going to help us in compiling evidence."

"There was nothing else at hand."

Cave shook his head, his lips pursed. "You've made this difficult for us, Jorgensen."

"Aren't you forgetting that without my intervention he'd have been out of reach in Sumatra by tomorrow night?"

"Did he admit the killings?"

"He was on me before I knew he was there. And afterwards claimed I attempted to rob him."

"Rob him of what?"

"The ten thousand Straits dollars that were hidden under a bunk in his cabin."

"Ten thousand?" exclaimed Cave in disbelief.

"He killed Davies for that money, Cave. And then Loddon because he knew too much."

"Where is the money now?"

"All in a document case the captain locked in his safe. There's nothing to show who it came from except that the money wraps are from the Peninsular Bank. But whoever it was, they hired Durrant to kill Davies."

"I accept it's a line to pursue when we take him ashore for questioning," said Cave.

"Ask him if the money came from Magnus Prescott," Jorgensen said.

"You're obsessed with Magnus Prescott," said Cave dismissively. "Not liking a fellow isn't grounds to repeatedly accuse him of complicity in murder. If you recall, that's what I said to Inspector Batchelor in your defence."

"Sooner or later, you'll come round to my way of thinking," said Jorgensen. "Though I doubt you'll get much help from Durrant. Watch him carefully, Cave. He's dangerous."

"There's a sergeant and two constables in the launch. We'll have no trouble with him. You'll have to come back with us. We'll need a full statement of what happened here, and your injuries need fixing."

"What about Andersen? Does he want me charged?"

"The *Singkep* is due to sail at dawn. If Captain Andersen doesn't want to be held up for another twenty-four hours. I'm sure I can smooth it over." Cave rose from the bunk, then stopped halfway to the cabin door. "By the way, how did you get out here? McGill from the harbourmaster's office was keen to know. Apparently, they're trying to crack down on illicit night-time movements."

"I hired a sampan."

"You'll be asked from whom. I see the boatman didn't hang around for you."

Jorgensen shrugged. "Why would he?"

# Forty-Eight

After making a brief formal statement at the detective station, Jorgensen was taken by police motor car to the General Hospital, out by the racecourse, where a night duty nurse re-dressed the cut above his eye and applied fresh bandaging. Less than two hours later, when he woke in his own bed with a throbbing pain in his head, he almost wished he had asked her for morphine.

He washed and shaved from a jug of water and splashed his face, sourly noting his battered reflection in the shaving mirror. He dressed, experimenting with a turned-up shirt collar, which only partly hid the ligature marks on his neck. As for his head, a panama hat refused to sit properly over the bandage, and he tossed it onto the sideboard. There was no hiding that injury.

It was still dark when Jorgensen took the short walk along Penang Road to Chowrasta Market. There, in the brightly lit main hall, he found a stall selling lengths of silk cloth, draped in a kaleidoscope of vivid colours over the front counter and a rail at the back. He pointed to the soberest and plainest pattern available. For a few cents extra, the trader fetched a seamstress, who quickly fashioned the cloth into a rectangular red and blue facsimile of an Ascot tie. Jorgensen had seen them worn at the Penang Club and the Swimming Club and, in front of a scratched mirror, he did his best to copy the style, tying it as loose as possible so it spilled over the open neckline of his shirt and hid the wounds on his neck.

From the market, he walked north up Penang Road to the E&O, entering through the kitchen gates and finding his way to the managers' offices via the side passageways.

Broomes' jaw dropped in astonishment when he saw Jorgensen at the door of his office, though whether it was at the sight of his bandaged head, or the vivid cravat was not immediately clear.

"What the devil..." he spluttered.

"It's not as bad as it looks, though there's another injury under here," said Jorgensen touching his tie.

Broomes stared at him, lost for words, his face a picture of genuine concern for Jorgensen's wellbeing.

"I was almost a victim of the man who killed Frank Davies," said Jorgensen, deciding that the time was long overdue for Broomes to be told about the investigation, at least in part. "But the police have him now."

"My God." Broomes face was ashen. "How did it happen?"

"Arshak asked me to look into Davies's death and I guess I got a little too close."

"What is the injury on your neck?" Broomes asked tentatively, as if dreading the answer.

"Some nasty looking welts," said Jorgensen. "But don't worry, I'll keep them hidden."

"Is it sensible for you to be here?" asked Broomes. "Shouldn't you be resting up?"

"I feel fine," said Jorgensen, though his throbbing head belied his words. "I was at the hospital last night and I'm seeing the police surgeon at eight for another examination."

"If you're sure," Broomes said dubiously. Then, a sudden thought occurred to him. "Did you say that it was Arshak who asked you to look into the poor chap's death?"

Jorgensen nodded.

"Is that because the hotel is connected in any way? Was one of our guests involved? You must tell me that at least, Jorgensen."

"I can't say any more, Broomes, I'm sorry. The police have sworn me to secrecy. I should go and see Arshak now, even though I can't tell him much either."

"You've missed him, I'm afraid. He went to visit Robinson at his home and then he'll be going on to church."

"How's Robinson doing?"

"It was a bad bout, but he's over the worst of it at last, I'm told; his wife rang last night to say he can see visitors. I'm hoping to call later after I attend the morning service at St George's."

"I'm glad to hear it."

"Are you finally finished with this business now, Jorgensen? God knows we could do with you back on normal duties – though not until you've got rid of that ghastly bandage."

"Not yet."

In the anteroom, Jorgensen saw that Michael had returned to his desk.

"You've been in the wars again, Mr Paul," said the secretary. "And now with that bandage you are a twin brother to Ah Cheng."

Jorgensen reached up to gingerly touch the dressing. "I guess it looks that way."

"Though that is a very dashing cravat, Mr Paul, if I may say so," added Michael with a smile. "Were you aware the Prince of Wales favours such a tie? I have seen photographs in the English magazines."

Jorgensen grinned. "I'm not sure Broomes liked it. He's asked me to keep away from the patrons."

"Last night, Ah Cheng told me you were safe. I did not realise you had been hurt."

"I didn't tell him. Where did you see him?"

"At the Lim jetty. After I received your message from Zamir, I went straight there."

"I didn't expect you to do that."

"I could not return to sleep, so why not? Once Ah Cheng returned and I knew you were safe, I was able to return home. So, you caught the man who killed Frank Davies? Congratulations, Mr Paul."

"It's a little premature for that. If he doesn't confess, we'll never know who paid him to do it."

"You believe he was a hired killer? Was he connected with George Lam?"

Jorgensen nodded. "He had a pile of cash in his baggage. But I've promised the police I'll say nothing more to anybody until they've interrogated him – and that includes Broomes and Arshak."

"I understand your meaning, Mr Paul. You may rely on me."

With an hour to pass until the appointed time for Cave to collect him from the hotel, Jorgensen wandered through to Goldie's Bar. It was deserted, as expected at that early hour of the morning, apart from behind the counter, where Goldie was counting stock.

"Mr Mac," he said, frowning with concern at Jorgensen's appearance. "Looks painful."

"It is."

"Drop of medicine?" Goldie asked, lifting a bottle of Scotch.

Jorgensen considered the offer for a moment longer than he should have done, but was saved by a voice at his shoulder, that of Gopi.

"A car has come for you, sir."

# Forty-Nine

At the General Hospital, Cave and Jorgensen were ushered into the office of the doctor who also acted as surgeon for the Straits Settlements Police – Nigel Thurmacott, an Englishman in his late forties, with a flinty sense of humour.

"Good god, man," he said on seeing Jorgensen's bandaged head. "In that turban I almost mistook you for Sergeant Singh. We'll see if we can kit you out in something a little less conspicuous before you leave."

"Do you have the cord?" Cave asked. The cord, untied from Durrant's wrists before they disembarked the *Singkep*, had been left at the hospital overnight.

"Are you aware of the time, Cave?" Thurmacott replied. "It's eight-thirty, in case you weren't sure, a mere two hours on from when you rang to disturb my breakfast."

"I appreciate that, but it's the reason I've brought Jorgensen along."

"Of course, I've got the bloody cord. It hasn't left my side all morning. I suppose you want to know my preliminary conclusion? And I stress the word preliminary."

Cave nodded. "It would be a great help."

"Both deaths were a result of strangulation. To be confirmed in the post-mortem report, of course, but you can take it from me that's the cause of death in both cases. Not drowning, like your Inspector tried to suggest for our most recent victim."

"With the same cord?"

"Let me finish my damn sentence," Thurmacott grumbled. He pulled open a drawer in his desk and took out a series of photographs. "Luckily for you, I had these taken yesterday." He spread the photographs on the desk for Cave and Jorgensen to look over. There were eight in total, four each of the ligature marks on the necks of Frank Davies and Aubrey Loddon, all taken from slightly different angles.

"Back in England I could no doubt draw on greater expertise on the subject," Thurmacott continued. "But I'm afraid that here in Penang, you'll have to rely on my opinion alone. Which is, that both men were strangled using the same instrument. You can see the clear similarities in ligature wound width and depth. It doesn't show up so well in these photographs, but I can tell you that on close re-examination of the bodies this morning, there are also similarities in the nature of the tears to the flesh."

Cave opened his mouth, ready to repeat his earlier question about the cord, then thought better of it when he saw Thurmacott's sharp glance in his direction.

"I re-examined both bodies again this morning," Thurmacott repeated. "With the cord at hand. I held it close to the wounds, and, in my opinion, it's probable that it, or the same thickness and type of cord, was used to strangle them."

"What about the blood on the cord?" Cave asked. "Would that help to confirm it?"

"I see you've been keeping up with the latest scientific advances on blood types. If we were in London, then it might do, but let me remind you that we're thousands of miles away. There are no facilities here to make such an analysis."

Thurmacott turned to Jorgensen. "Let's have a look at your wounds then, Jorgensen."

Jorgensen untied the makeshift cravat and undid a couple more shirt buttons, while Thurmacott returned to his desk drawer to retrieve a magnifying glass.

"Take a seat here," Thurmacott ordered, pointing to a chair in front of his desk, then leant in close to Jorgensen's neck to examine the still raw wounds, muttering softly to himself as he did so.

"I was attacked with the cord you now have," Jorgensen said.

"Yes, yes, I know that," said Thurmacott. "The wounds are a little different on you."

"I managed to jam my hand under the cord."

"That might explain it. They're nowhere near as deep."

Thurmacott pulled away from Jorgensen, then used the magnifying glass to study the photographs on his desk, before returning to a final examination of Jorgensen's neck.

"It's a close match," he said eventually.

"Is it the same cord used to strangle the two murder victims?" Cave asked.

"I can testify that there's a high probability it's the same cord, but I cannot be certain."

"That's something, I suppose," said Cave.

"And with Mr Jorgensen here, you have a witness who survived an attack."

"I want the bastard tried for murder, not attempted murder," said Cave.

"I appreciate that, Superintendent Cave, but if its certainty you're after, I cannot provide it. Now, let's get a nurse to tend to Mr Jorgensen's dressings."

***

Under the cluster of tall trees providing shade to the hospital entrance, Cave waved his baton to attract the attention of his driver, parked fifty yards away down the side of the Padang Polo Field, the huge area of greensward that was home to the Penang Polo Club. Across to their left, glimpsed through the trees of its grounds, were the white walls and red-tiled roofs of the Residency buildings, the home and offices of the British Resident Councillor.

"What do you think, Cave? Is that enough evidence to charge him?" Jorgensen asked.

Cave grimaced. "The examination? It doesn't harm our case, I'll grant you, but it may not be enough on its own."

"You should know that on the night of Davies's murder, Durrant was staying at the Australia Hotel, using the name Garrett Solly."

"That's the name he used to board the *Singkep* as a passenger."

"I asked the Australia's manager, Bailey, about Durrant's movements that night. He wasn't on duty – but said he'd check with their night porter."

"I'll send Inspector Batchelor to question him."

"Have you got anything out of Durrant yet?"

Cave snorted. "We had to patch him up too. You gave him a pretty bad beating, Jorgensen. And since then, all he's prepared to say is that you attempted to steal his money. He's a tough customer."

"If he doesn't talk, you won't reach whoever paid him for killing Davies."

"If anybody did. That's still only conjecture on your part."

"Come on, Cave. You know it stacks up. Why else would a man like Durrant have all that cash on him?"

"We'll break him down eventually. Until then, as I told you last night, I want to keep his arrest quiet. Can I give you a lift back to the E&O?"

Beside them, the superintendent's car glided to a halt.

"Tell Durrant you know it's Magnus Prescott," said Jorgensen. "That might rattle him."

Cave who had stretched forward in the act of opening the rear door of the car, paused, and glared at Jorgensen.

"I'll do no such bloody thing," he said, in indignation. He flung the door open and climbed in. "You coming?" he snapped. Jorgensen nodded and followed him into the back of the car.

After instructing the driver to head for the E&O, Cave turned to face his fellow passenger. "Look old man," he said, in more emollient tones. "You did us a damn good service by tracking down Durrant and I'm grateful you ignored my warnings to keep clear. But now we have him in custody, try becoming reacquainted with the normal order of things – where the police investigate crimes and members of the public wait to read about them in the Straits Echo."

Jorgensen sat back in the seat, while the driver made a U-turn in the street and sped away down Race Course Road, past the sweeping end curve of the racetrack on their left. He had no intention of abandoning his own investigation, not until he had found who paid Durrant to kill Frank Davies. Casting a sidelong glance at Cave, he saw that the superintendent was watching him as if he too understood that fact but would never openly acknowledge it.

# Fifty

Every Sunday evening, the E&O hosted an orchestral concert – another weekly ritual for many of Penang's European residents, which took place on the seafront lawn under the Angsana trees.

Under the supervision of the assistant head boy, Ah Ming, a small army of waiters and porters carried chairs from the storeroom to the lawn, arranging them in rows, and placing low occasional tables at strategic points to hold refreshments. Once dusk fell, and the audience was in place, the sixteen-man hotel orchestra would begin to play, headed by their Irish conductor and pianist, F. O'Neill-Shaw, and featuring three exiled Russians and a Pole among their otherwise Chinese and Malay membership. With their backs to the sea, and under strings of light bulbs suspended in the branches above, they would breeze through a familiar repertoire – closed every week by a stirring rendition of God Save the King, to signal the usual exodus to the dining room.

With the weather set fair and no storm expected for that evening, many of the eager concertgoers were gathering at the hotel in advance. After a patrol of the grounds, Jorgensen, now able to wear his panama hat over a slimmed-down head dressing, had placed himself in a chair to one side of the lobby to watch their arrivals. His primary interest was in the members of the young crowd who were in the bar with Cromford on the night he dropped the diary; still certain that it was one of them who had alerted George Lam to the diary's existence and lacking any better ideas to make progress in the case.

As it was a Sunday, he did not expect to see them all. For the younger, healthier members of the European community, a Sunday was a time for sport. Golf at the racecourse, horse-riding in the spice groves, rugby or cricket on the Padang. And for many, a long afternoon at the Penang Swimming Club, which nestled in a beautiful cove five miles west of George Town. Either crowded around the new seawater pool formed by a retaining wall among the rocks or stood three-deep at the bar in the old wooden clubhouse higher up the cliff.

In ones and twos and small family groups, the concertgoers alighted from motor cars in the gateway's long shadows. Once inside the E&O, they dispersed to the lounge, the bar, or the lobby according to their habit or arrangements made with friends. Meeting for pre-concert drinks was as big a draw as the concert itself. A handful of the audience members drifted out to the seawall to catch the very last of the sun's rays.

Tommy Essenden, together with his mother and father, passed by Jorgensen as they strolled through the lobby, but affected not to notice him. Shortly afterwards, Phyllis Smith followed, trailing her parents while her eyes roved from side to side, searching for someone.

Then, around ten minutes before the concert began, as the discordant sounds of tuning violins and cellos drifted in from the lawn, the Prescott family entered the lobby. Lawrence and Mary swept past Jorgensen, in much the same manner as the Essendens, but Magnus stopped to face him with an accusing look.

"I'd expected your apology, by now," he said witheringly. "I told your manager, Robinson, or whatever the man's name is, to speak to you. I expect a fulsome apology and nothing less."

"Mr Robinson is ill, but Mr Broomes told me of your call."

"Broomes. That's it. I warned him about your intolerable conduct. So, let's have it. Let's hear your grovelling apology." At his side, his wife Gwendoline cast apprehensive glances towards the lobby's other occupants, fearful of an embarrassing scene.

"I don't see any reason for me to apologise," said Jorgensen, rising to his feet.

"Don't try to be clever, Jorgensen. You harassed my sister with a phone call, then, after I warned you off, I discovered you trespassed onto the family property."

"Miss Prescott invited me to visit. That's not trespass. Which is what I told Superintendent Cave. I guess you complained to the police too."

"You'd do well to watch your tone and remember where you are."

"That's a good point," said Jorgensen, making a show of looking around him. "Let's continue the conversation where there's a little more privacy. You see, I want to ask you about Frank Davies."

Prescott's mouth tightened, but he forced a thin smile from it. "Should I know the name?"

"I think you recognised it well enough. Frank Davies: the man found dead on Wednesday night in Love Lane."

"I read the newspapers."

"I'll give you another name. Aubrey Loddon: the man you employed to watch Frank Davies's lodgings."

"What have you been saying to my sister?" Prescott hissed. "If you've been filling her head with this nonsense, I'll make you pay for it."

"I know why you were having Frank Davies watched, and so does your sister. What I don't know is what you did next."

"What the devil do you mean by that?" Prescott's voice grew louder as his anger heightened. Gwendoline pulled at his arm, conscious that though most of the concertgoers had by now made their way through to the lawn, there were still one or two in earshot.

"Magnus, we'll be late," she pleaded.

As if suddenly aware of his surroundings, Magnus noticed the watching faces. "Come," he said, taking Gwendoline by the arm and marching off towards the lounge and its doors through to the lawn.

Jorgensen followed them as the orchestra slipped softly into their opening number, 'Fountains', a perennial favourite with its audience. On the verandah, he found Broomes at the rear of the makeshift auditorium. He tapped him on the shoulder and grinned at the assistant manager's raised eyebrows, for it was a matter of record that Jorgensen never voluntarily attended the Sunday orchestral concerts.

The programme was a mix of well-known excerpts from classical works and a handful of popular songs played by the orchestra at the E&O's twice-weekly balls. For the Sunday concert, the audience generally watched in respectful silence. These performances, and those of guest orchestras from visiting ocean liners, serving as tangible links to their old lives in Europe.

After thirty minutes, when the lugubrious O'Neill-Shaw lowered his baton to announce a fifteen-minute interval, the audience rose as one, scurrying this way and that, like fallen leaves caught in an eddy, before settling into smaller groups.

From the raised viewpoint of the verandah, Jorgensen watched Tommy Essenden make his way over towards Phyllis Smith, the two of them gravitating to the sea wall. Determined to seize this chance, he stepped onto the stone path and worked his way through the scattered audience until he was alongside them. Beyond the wall, gentle waves lapped against the rocks, and other groups chattered away nearby.

Phyllis Smith's dark hair peeked under a woven straw hat, and she wore a green drop waisted dress, which made her seem taller, with a thin shawl to protect her arms and shoulders from mosquitoes.

"Are we not allowed on the seawall?" she asked, her dainty features growing sullen on catching sight of Jorgensen. "Have you come to warn us about our behaviour again? It's becoming rather a bore."

"Good evening, Miss Smith, and Mr Essenden."

"I didn't see you at church this morning, Mr Jorgensen," said Essenden sniffily.

"I'm afraid I never go." With the interval period fast running out, Jorgensen chose to dispense with any notions of subtlety. "I need to ask Miss Smith some questions. You can stay or leave, Tommy, it's up to you."

"How dare you address us in that way," said Phyllis indignantly. "We are your guests."

"You're right, of course. If it's inconvenient, I'll call on you at home tomorrow night."

Phyllis looked askance at Jorgensen's suggestion, the risk that her public rows with Essenden might come to her father's attention at the forefront of her mind. "Is that absolutely necessary?"

"It relates to a theft – so I'm obliged to follow up."

"Oh, very well. If you're going to cause a fuss one way or another, then you might as well go ahead now."

Beside her, Essenden yawned, and cast idle glances towards his own parents.

"Sure Miss Smith. Now, last Monday night you and Mr Essenden were reading Arthur Cromford's diary. I'm checking on who else might have seen it."

"How on earth do you know about that?"

"You see, the diary was subsequently stolen and I'm trying to find out who else knew of its existence."

"Are you accusing me of stealing it?" Phyllis Smith's eyes blazed in anger.

"I know who stole it. But I don't know how they learned of its existence. Did any of the friends who were with you on Monday night get to read the diary, or was it just you and Mr Essenden?"

"I'm afraid I'll disappoint you then, for I really cannot recall. Now if you'll excuse me, I'm sure I can see Mama gesticulating at me." She turned to Essenden. "I'm sorry, Tommy. I must go."

Without a backward glance, Phyllis Smith hurried away to join her parents. Essenden opened his mouth, as if on the point of chastising Jorgensen, but instead, he too, turned on his heel to rejoin his own family.

Jorgensen watched them go. The musicians had returned to their positions and the plucks and scrapes of their retuning were drawing the audience back to their seats. Instead of taking his place again on the lounge verandah, Jorgensen walked off in the other direction, away from the concert, towards the western end of the E&O's long seafront. He felt uneasy, worrying whether the rush of excitement from capturing Durrant the previous night had led him to go too far. That in confronting both Magnus Prescott and Phyllis Smith in the grounds of the E&O, he was betraying Arshak Sarkies' trust and putting the hotel's reputation for discretion at risk.

# Fifty-One

On the Monday morning, after several hours spent on routine tasks while he wondered if Cave would pass on any news from Durrant's interrogation, or for some other inspiration to strike him, Jorgensen was summoned by a porter to the front desk. There, he found Richard Hong ready to present him with a letter.

"From Alor Star," Hong said. "Postmarked Saturday."

"Thanks." Jorgensen took the envelope and read the address: Mr Jorgensen, Undermanager, care of the E&O, all written in a flowing hand with several decorative flourishes. He returned to his small office, where he ran a finger under the flap of the envelope, then pulled out two small sheets of handwritten letter paper bearing the crest of the British Adviser to the State of Kedah. The writer's signature was that of Hilton Morley.

> *My Dear Jorgensen,*
>
> *I write this from the rather splendid verandah overlooking our hosts' garden, where the Malayan peninsula's limited colour palate is at last leavened by splashes of colour. The endless green hues of the countryside viewed through railway carriage windows on our journey proved less fascinating than I had imagined beforehand, though its monotony did provide me an opportunity to reflect. Our host did his utmost to engage our attention by pointing out the remarkable variety in the scenery, changing as it did from plantations of rubber to those of oil of palm, and stretches of untamed jungle. I confess the differences between them were hard to discern.*
>
> *You will be amused to learn that two of our fellow travellers to Alor Star speak of you with great affection, though a degree of cynicism on my part asserts that they do so purely because they were made aware of our acquaintance. I refer to Mr and Mrs Rowland Burgon. A perplexing couple, who were at first an entertaining diversion from the*

*lengthy topographical descriptions of our host. The fascinating nature of their quest – to locate the missing brother of Mrs Burgon deep in the jungle beyond Kuala Nerang was positively Conradian in its scope. An enterprise that, they were at pains to impress upon us, engendered valuable assistance from you. Were Arthur and I not bound by the obligation to honour our hosts' invitation, then the romantic notion of trekking up-country, with its boundless possibilities, may have tempted us to accompany the Burgons further on their adventure.*

*Imagine then, if you will, our bafflement on discovering they are not wholly serious in their endeavours. Despite regaling us with picaresque tales of both the missing brother's history and their own travails in pursuing him, they have not yet gone on to Kuala Nerang. Instead, they remain in Alor Star, lunching and dining at the club, having engaged a local agent to travel on in their place. We hear that the roads at this time of year, though mere tracks through the jungle, are far from impassable, yet the prospect of temporary discomfort for Mrs Winifred Burgon appears to outweigh her passionately proclaimed desire for a sibling reunion.*

*I do not complain, for the mystery tickles my writer's natural curiosity, though for your part I hope you will henceforth regard them with a greater circumspection. Both Arthur and I are profoundly grateful for your recent assistance and feel that to 'give you the lowdown' is the least we can do.*

*In terms of our return, it is likely to be much sooner than originally anticipated. Perhaps as soon as this week. The conversation of the Hills grows drearier by the hour.*

*Your friend, Hilton Morley*

With a frown, Jorgensen began to re-read the letter. In the tumult of the last two days, he had almost forgotten about the Burgons and their search. But, unless his memory was playing tricks, he was sure Winifred Burgon had said that the disappeared man was a partner in her husband's firm of solicitors; not that he was her brother. She had sounded plausible enough when relating her story, though Jorgensen remembered suspecting that her and her husband's motives for the search were more to do with money than any real concern for the missing man.

As for their choosing not to complete the last leg of their journey, that made little sense. Morley was right in what he said about the road to Kuala Nerang. Jorgensen remembered his own visit to the area, two years previously. Though a long and uncomfortable journey by motor vehicle, winding through the jungle on dusty uneven tracks, it was far from hazardous out of monsoon season. As the Burgons had already travelled halfway across the globe on their search, it was puzzling that they would baulk at the last minor obstacle.

He lit another cigarette, to help in remembering their last conversation, and blew smoke rings into the air, where they were whisked away by the whirring blades of the ceiling fan.

He had spoken to the Burgons in the lobby, where they awaited their transport to the railway building, and were, as Morley stated in his letter, seemingly elated at the prospect of finally finding the missing man. Leslie Worrilow, that was his name. Jorgensen remembered now. Then, he remembered Rowland Burgon's mention of a photograph of Worrilow – to be sent to the E&O by their solicitor in Penang.

A knock on the door interrupted his thoughts. It was Gopi.

"Please to see Mr Broomes," the porter said. "Most important."

When isn't it? Jorgensen thought, but obediently followed Gopi to the lobby before taking the corridor to the managers' offices.

Michael was at his desk in the anteroom and to Jorgensen's surprise on entering, had changed from the dark lounge suit worn earlier, into a cream-coloured linen jacket and trousers.

He glanced up from his desk and noted Jorgensen's appraising look. "For lunch at the Chinese Recreation Club," he explained.

"What's the occasion?"

"The monthly tennis club lunch."

"I didn't realise you played."

"I was once semi-finalist in the men's doubles championship. Though my brother and I were soundly beaten by Khoo Hooi Hye and his partner."

"I don't play tennis, but I do read the newspapers, and him I know. I guess he always wins."

"Except at the All England Championships."

"What does Broomes want?" asked Jorgensen with a gesture towards the assistant manager's office door.

"There's a visitor for you," said Michael. "Miss Prescott."

"In with Broomes?"

"Mr Broomes is overseeing some modifications to the library, but he invited Miss Prescott to wait in his office."

At the door, Jorgensen paused before entering, his hand on the handle. "Anything I should know?" he asked Michael.

"She wishes to keep her visit secret from her family."

"Right," Jorgensen nodded and pushed open the door. Anne Prescott was sitting in the chair opposite Broomes' desk. She twisted round to face Jorgensen, then frowned as she noticed the dressing on Jorgensen's forehead.

"What happened?" she asked.

"It's nothing." He pulled a chair up to the corner of the desk, close to Anne. "Is everything all right, Miss Prescott?" he asked.

"My father and brother don't know I'm here. I'd rather you didn't tell them."

"There's no reason for me to."

Her smile was grateful rather than nervous. To Jorgensen she seemed more poised than on the night after Davies's death.

"It's for Frank, that I'm here," she said. "I cared for him, perhaps more as a sister than before, but he needed somebody."

"He was lucky to have you," said Jorgensen.

"If only that were true. I can't help thinking that I let him down."

"I doubt that."

"I've come to tell you about Magnus," she said, her tone firm, her chin jutting forward as if in defiance of invisible shackles that, by speaking now, she was shaking off. "I overheard him talking with Papa, and I thought you should know about the money."

"What money?"

"Magnus withdrew thousands of Straits Dollars from the bank last week. You see, my room is above the dining room where they were breakfasting and as I was sitting out on the verandah, I heard him arguing with Papa about it."

"What exactly did you hear?" Jorgensen asked.

"I didn't catch every word – only bits and pieces. Papa was furious with Magnus, calling him reckless. Saying it was Magnus's responsibility to set it right."

Jorgensen recalled the afternoon at the Peninsular Bank when he picked up the ransom payment for Cromford's diary, and inwardly cursed himself for not making the connection before now. Bell, the junior bank official, had remarked that his transaction was the second large cash withdrawal that day. And when he saw Magnus Prescott leaving the manager's office, sheepish at coming across Jorgensen, it was evident who had made the first.

"Who was the money meant for?" he asked.

Anne hesitated before answering, "Payment for the murder of Frank."

"They said that?"

"No," she shook her head. "They were careful not to. But I'm positive it's the case. Magnus once told me I'd be sorry if I saw Frank again, and it'd be my fault if Frank suffered. I assumed then that he and Papa were threatening to blacken Frank's name again, that they'd connive to prevent him working as a letter writer. Not that they'd kill him."

Anne gazed steadily at Jorgensen before continuing. "And then, after you told me Magnus had arranged to have Frank watched, I remembered Magnus's disappearance after dinner last Thursday. It was the night that Frank was killed. I lay awake for hours going over and over it in my mind."

"Tell me more."

"It was two hours before Magnus came back to Hamstead to collect Gwendoline," Anne said. "Papa must have been in on it too. He told Gwendoline to stop making such a fuss, saying Magnus had to make an urgent business call. At the time I'd thought it related to Choo Fat Yee."

"Choo Fat Yee?" said Jorgensen in surprise. "What's he got to do with it?"

"Papa and Magnus are negotiating a new shipping contract with Mr Choo for his Sumatran tobacco plantations. At the curry tiffin lunch last week, he was the family's guest, and the conversation came round to fundraising for a new children's ward at the Chinese Methodist Hospital. Papa took the hint and promised a substantial donation."

"There you are – the cash was the donation for the hospital."

Anne shook her head. "I'd thought so too at first, before remembering that for something of that nature Papa would insist on a bank draft. He is always very meticulous about any philanthropic gestures."

Jorgensen thought for a moment. "There could be a simpler explanation," he said. "To get things done in business out here, there's often a secondary payment associated with the contract. Cash to a fixer, or even direct to Choo. It's just the way of the world."

"I suppose you think I'm deluded." Anne looked searchingly into Jorgensen's eyes. "I haven't imagined all this, you know. Papa and Magnus are glad Frank is dead. I can see it in the way they act."

"That doesn't mean they were behind it."

"That's what I've been trying to tell myself, but in my heart, I know it's not true. You see, though Frank wasn't strong, I also know that Magnus is a coward. The money was to pay somebody else to do it. It must be that Loddon man you told me about – though I can't believe it of him."

"I'm afraid Loddon is dead," said Jorgensen.

Anne's eyes opened wide in disbelief. "Another death?"

"His body was washed up on the mudflats by the harbour."

"My God." She held a trembling hand over her mouth. "Was he killed too?"

"The police believe so."

Jorgensen wanted to tell her about the arrest of Durrant. It fitted with her belief that Magnus was ultimately responsible, but he knew it would be premature. Without more definite proof, he must stick to his agreement with Cave to keep Durrant's arrest as secret as possible.

"Let's suppose you might be right," he said. "Were any names mentioned by your father or brother?"

"No," she replied. "That's why I thought it must be Mr Loddon."

"You should take this information to the police," said Jorgensen.

"I can't do that. They'll think I'm a silly little girl overcome with grief. And besides, didn't they arrest one of Frank's clients?"

"Superintendent Cave is a decent man. I'm sure he'd listen to you."

"I wish that were true. My father is considered too important for the police to believe accusations against him. You'll help me though, won't you, Mr Jorgensen? If it wasn't Mr Loddon, then it must be somebody else. Will you help find out who?"

"I'll do what I can Miss Prescott, but you must consider that the most likely explanation is the money went to Choo Fat Yee, as you first thought."

"I know," she sighed. "But thank you for listening to me."

"If I'm going to help, then there's something I must ask."

"What is it?" An uneasy expression clouded her face.

"Did Frank tell you why I first visited him?"

"I know he was in some kind of trouble, and you promised to help."

"Because he owed money, he was forced into writing a letter, a blackmail letter to one of the guests at the E&O. I traced it back to him. Did he ever tell you about it?"

"You must be mistaken, Mr Jorgensen. Frank would never get involved in anything like that."

"He admitted it, Miss Prescott. But I kept the police away because our guest wanted the matter settled without fuss."

"I just can't believe it of him. Poor Frank. To have been dragged down to something so sordid."

"Are you sure he never mentioned any of this to you? Who else was in on the scheme? It could be connected to his death."

"I'm sorry Mr Jorgensen. I suppose he was too ashamed to tell me," Anne shot Jorgensen a sudden fierce look. "If you think that's why he was killed, does that mean you don't believe me?"

"I must keep an open mind. But let me reassure you – that includes considering your brother as a suspect."

"What will you do next?"

"Get you home first."

Anne shook her head emphatically. "I couldn't bear going back there tonight. Can I stay at the E&O?"

"Your family will wonder where you are."

"I'll agree to send them a message, but I'm not going back."

"All right. Wait here," said Jorgensen. "And I'll fix it up."

***

To Jorgensen's relief, Michael had not yet departed for lunch, and was still in the anteroom.

On the point of asking the secretary to make the arrangements for Anne Prescott's stay, Jorgensen was stopped short by a picture that suddenly appeared in his mind – the view of a tennis court laid out next to the lawn that he had seen from Choo Fat Yee's mansion.

"Is Choo Fat Yee a member of the tennis club?" he asked Michael.

"He is a committee member. Why do you ask?"

"Will he be at the lunch today?"

"Perhaps." Michael gave Jorgensen a shrewd look. "You wish me to do something for you," he said. "Is it related to Miss Prescott?"

"To a business arrangement between Choo, and Lawrence and Magnus Prescott."

"Mr Choo may be a friend of my father, but friendship and business are two quite distinct spheres. It is not advisable to mix the two."

"Isn't your brother married to Choo's niece? Doesn't that blur the distinction a little?"

Michael inclined his head in acknowledgment of Jorgensen's point. "What is it you wish to know?"

"It's difficult to explain, but it relates to the death of Frank Davies."

"How is Mr Choo connected?"

"I'll explain what I can. I need to find out what happened to a large sum of cash that Magnus Prescott withdrew from the Peninsular Bank." Jorgensen paused, uncertain over his next choice of words. "It's possible Choo might know something of it. You see, Prescotts are after an export contract from Choo's new tobacco plantation in Sumatra. And I heard they agreed to make a large donation towards Choo's charity – the new children's ward at the Chinese Methodist Hospital. So far, so normal. I want to know whether the cash Prescott withdrew constituted an additional under the counter payment to further smooth the way."

"Should I put this question about a bribe to Mr Choo before or after the loyal toast to the King?"

"It's not an easy question to ask," Jorgensen conceded.

"Especially for a youngest son with little standing and to a man of such honourable reputation."

"It's a long shot," said Jorgensen. "But it could be important. And if there was a bribe – that's the end of it as far as I'm concerned. It'd mean the money withdrawn by Prescott wasn't the source of the pile of cash I found on the *Singkep*."

"You ask a great deal of me, Mr Paul," said Michael. "Though I believe that your clever understanding of family honour encourages you. When we went to see George Lam, we acted as representatives of my father, and your warning not to harm Frank

Davies was also, therefore, in my father's name. Do you now hope that when I explain the connection, my father will agree to help?"

"I'll be in your father's debt."

"I believe you already are, Mr Paul."

# Fifty-Two

Back in his office, Jorgensen did not think too long and hard before picking up the telephone receiver. Though Cave had warned him to leave matters to the police, he knew it was important that Anne Prescott's story should be heard.

"Hello Margaret," he said to the operator. "Superintendent Cave at the detective station, please."

"What is it this time, Jorgensen?" said Cave, when his voice finally came on the other end of the line.

"Anne Prescott came into the hotel today, to escape her family," Jorgensen replied. "She had something to say. And you should know about it."

"About what?"

"Magnus Prescott withdrew a large sum of cash from the bank last week. And it's her belief the money was used to pay Davies's killer."

"Christ Mac, not Prescott again. Won't you let that drop?"

"It's not me making the accusation, Cave – it's his sister. She was warned by her brother that Davies would come to harm if she continued seeing him. Then recently, she overheard a row between Magnus Prescott and his father, in which they discussed this cash withdrawal. Lawrence Prescott was furious about Magnus's recklessness and told him it was his responsibility to put it right."

"Did she hear any mention of Davies's or Durrant's names during this row?"

"No."

"Well then. The row could be over anything."

"The money wraps around the stacks of banknotes were from the Peninsular Bank. I know Magnus Prescott withdrew a large cash sum from the Peninsular Bank last week – I was there, and I saw him."

"Why didn't you mention this before?"

"You'd have told me I was obsessed with Magnus Prescott, and it was irrelevant."

"I'd have probably been right."

"Come on Cave. You've got to take this seriously."

"Her own brother, though? Why would he do it?"

"Anne was close to Davies a few years back. The family objected and Lawrence Prescott packed her off to England then saw to it that Davies's career at his law office was ruined. In her mind, arranging for Davies to be murdered is just one further step along the same path for her father and brother."

"I hope you didn't encourage her along that path. Have you considered the likelihood that she's been knocked sideways by a close friend's death and is allowing her imagination to run away with her?"

"She's grieving, that's true – but she wasn't incoherent. She acknowledged the money could have gone elsewhere – to pay a bribe, and I'm checking that out."

"A bribe. Who the hell to?"

"Doesn't matter, Cave. If it was a bribe, then it didn't go to Davies's killer."

"You make my life a living hell at times, Jorgensen. I suppose I'm going to have to question Anne Prescott to see if she backs up what you're saying."

"She's taken a room here at the E&O. But don't you think that by waiting to question Anne, you're only delaying what you should be doing?"

"Go on," there was a menace in Cave's tone. There to warn Jorgensen not to overstep the mark.

"Forget it's me laying this out for a moment," said Jorgensen. "And look at the facts. Both Loddon and Davies are dead – strangled by Durrant. The only person other than Durrant to connect Loddon and Davies is Magnus Prescott. He paid Loddon to watch Davies's lodgings. And now we have his sister convinced

Magnus paid somebody else to kill Davies. Shouldn't you be questioning him?"

"You know how things work in Penang, Jorgensen. If you think I'm going to lay waste to my career by confronting the Prescotts at their place of work or their home based on your guesswork, then you're naïve at best."

"They'll come to the E&O tonight," said Jorgensen. "As soon as they find out that's where Anne has run to. If you're not going to tackle them, then I will."

"Don't be such a self-regarding idiot," Cave said, his voice rising in anger. "It's about time…" but Jorgensen hung the earpiece back on its cradle before the sentence was completed.

# Fifty-Three

Jorgensen walked up to Anne Prescott's room, to tell her that he had asked Superintendent Cave to visit. Descending the main stairs afterwards, he prayed that he would not be proved wrong. Pressing Cave too hard on the telephone call had been rash. It was important the police heard Anne's story and he had put that at risk.

He thought about patrolling the grounds, but the feeling of restlessness that had consumed him ever since he learned of Frank Davies's death was too strong. The need to act – to make something happen, had not been wholly checked by the capture of Durrant, and there were other unanswered matters to attend to.

Ten minutes later, he and Zamir left the E&O in the Standard Tourer to head for Bishop Street. It was as good a place as any to begin his search. Though the offices of solicitors were concentrated around Beach Street and its side streets, the pre-eminent firms all practised out of Bishop Street. Three firms in the space of five buildings, all with views from their first-floor windows of the Whiteaway Laidlaw department store across the street.

At the premises of McDonald and Lightfoot, a male secretary showed him into the sumptuous office of Richard Lightfoot, the senior partner. Hanging in the air, the smell of cigar smoke mingled with recently polished wood.

"Jorgensen, what brings you here?" Lightfoot's voice boomed with the confidence borne of his many positions of authority in Penang. Captain of the golf club, trustee of the history museum, officer at the Town Club. "I don't believe I've ever seen you outside of the E&O." In his mid-forties, Lightfoot, the eldest son of one of the firm's founders, rushed forward to shake his visitor's hand.

"I'm not entirely sure I've come to the right place," Jorgensen said. "Are Mr Rowland Burgon and Mrs Winifred Burgon clients of yours? They tell me they engaged a solicitor in their search for a Mr Leslie Worrilow."

"Straight down to business, I see," Lightfoot remarked, a little disconcerted by Jorgensen's directness, and the opportunity therefore missed to pour out a scotch and soda. "I wouldn't go so far as to call them clients, but we did agree to make enquiries on their behalf."

Jorgensen puffed out his cheeks in relief. Starting with the E&O's solicitor had paid off. "Do you have a copy of the photograph of Mr Worrilow that they left with you?" he asked.

"At one point, certainly we did. I remember seeing it. I'd have to check whether it's still in our possession."

"The Burgons asked me to view it in case I happened to recognise him. Would it be possible to check straightaway?"

A small hand bell sat on the corner of Lightfoot's desk. He picked it up and rang it twice, vigorously, to bring his male assistant hurrying back.

"Ask Perryman to join us," said Lightfoot to the assistant when he reappeared at the door. "And tell him to bring the Burgon file."

The assistant nodded and departed as quickly as he had entered, returning within a minute with an English colleague, who was carrying a card-backed document folder.

"This is Jorgensen, from the E&O," Lightfoot indicated to Perryman, a plumpish man whose ruddy face showed a delighted curiosity over the presence of a manager from the E&O. Producing the requested file with a flourish, he placed it on Lightfoot's desk.

"Is the photograph inside?" Lightfoot asked.

Perryman opened the file on the desktop. Its contents were slim. Three sheets of handwritten notes and below them a single photograph.

"May I?" said Jorgensen, picking it up.

It was a formal portrait, taken at a photographic studio, with a hanging plain cloth as its background. Its subject, a young man, with dark hair oiled into submission either side of a severe parting, was trussed uneasily in a suit, tie, and waistcoat. Trusting eyes gazed at the camera above smooth unlined cheeks, while his delicate, almost feminine, mouth seemed poised on the brink of speaking.

"Did the Burgons say what their relationship was to Mr Worrilow?" Jorgensen asked Lightfoot.

"A former partner in Mr Burgon's firm I believe," Lightfoot replied, surprised that Jorgensen was unaware of that fact.

"That's what they told me, but they've told others that he is Mrs Burgon's brother."

"How odd," Lightfoot's brow furrowed in confusion.

Jorgensen studied the photograph again, noticing the name of the studio, in Oxford, in the bottom corner alongside the date, October 1919.

"Is this a university portrait?" he asked Lightfoot, handing him the photograph.

"So they told me. He read law at Oxford after the war."

That might make him perhaps twenty-six or twenty-seven now. Jorgensen's heart skipped a beat and he wanted to shout out in triumph.

It was as a clerk at a law firm that Frank Davies began work in Penang. And though he had appeared considerably older, ravaged as he was by drink and opium, Jorgensen's instinct was that Davies was no more than in his mid-twenties when he died.

He took the photograph back from Lightfoot, then stared hard at it, growing more certain with each second that passed. It was the same man. His eyes, his nose and his lips were undeniably those of the same man.

He replaced it on the desk, glancing up to see Lightfoot eyeing him shrewdly.

"I see you recognise him," Lightfoot said.

"I'm afraid so," Jorgensen replied. "I must ask you to telephone the detective station on Penang Road and ask for Superintendent Cave or Inspector Batchelor. They'll need to see this photograph urgently." The police surgeon, Thurmacott, would need to inspect it too. As well as those who had known Davies when he was alive. "I believe it's of a man I knew as Frank Davies."

"That name sounds familiar. Who is he?"

"The man found dead last week in Love Lane."

"Good God," Lightfoot turned to Perryman. "Do as Jorgensen asks, and telephone the police." As soon as Perryman left the office, barely subsuming the excitement he felt at this unexpected departure from the humdrum, Lightfoot picked up the photograph. "The poor fellow was murdered, wasn't he? At least that's what the jungle drums are saying."

"It's what the police believe."

"Christ, who's going to tell his family?"

"They're up in Kedah state. But I imagine you knew that?"

Lightfoot shook his head. "I've not seen them for several days. I'm afraid we had nothing to share with them – until now."

"I'd understood they went on a tip-off from their solicitor."

"Not us, old boy, not us."

# Fifty-Four

"Mr Paul, Mr Paul!"

As Jorgensen strode through the lobby on his return to the E&O, he saw Richard Hong, the chief desk clerk, waving to him from the reception desk.

"Mr Morley and Mr Cromford return this afternoon, Mr Paul," said Hong once Jorgensen reached the desk. "The gentlemen sent a telegram to confirm their arrival time and to request a car from the railway building at three-thirty."

Jorgensen guessed Hilton Morley's tolerance of the charms of Mrs Hill was exhausted even sooner than his letter hinted. He checked his watch. Half an hour to go.

"I'll meet them there," he said, thinking of the opportunity to question both men about the Burgons' odd behaviour in Alor Star. "Is their suite ready?"

"At Mr Morley's request it was kept free for their return."

"Good."

"Mr and Mrs Burgon will return on the same train," Hong added.

"What?" Jorgensen was unsure if he had heard the chief clerk correctly.

"Mr and Mrs Burgon," Hong repeated. "Their telegram was sent from the Alor Star Club, and they return on the same train."

That soon. Jorgensen had to think fast, and Cave needed to be told. "I see. Which room are the Burgons taking?"

"They requested the same room as last week, but we could not accommodate them. A French gentleman occupies the room now. I hope they will not mind." Hong's smile indicated that a complaint was nevertheless expected. "Sixteen is their new room, also on the first floor of the old wing. Porters and housekeeping will move their luggage in from storage in time for their arrival."

"Did they ask for it to be unpacked?" asked Jorgensen, the thought flashing through his mind of rifling through their belongings before they arrived.

"No, Mr Paul. Should we?"

Jorgensen shook his head, "Best not."

***

The rains came again in the middle of the afternoon. Towering dark clouds rolled over the ridges of Penang Hill and down the eastward slopes, chasing away startling blue skies and plunging George Town into premature twilight.

Standing on the quayside at the landward end of the Railway Jetty, Jorgensen listened to the approaching storm. Great rolls of thunder were building from deep within the slate-grey stacks, crashing to a roaring crescendo as the first flashes of lightning hit the coconut groves behind the town.

He turned to gaze eastwards across the channel, where a still cloudless blue sky reflected off calm waters, through which the railway ferry ploughed towards them. By the time it reached the jetty the storm would be overhead. Five minutes at the most.

As the storm closed, the tall brilliant white tower of the Malayan Railway Building stood in stark contrast to the black shroud behind it. Jorgensen sprinted across Weld Quay, dodging the plodding bullock carts as the first heavy droplets bounced off his hat and shoulders. Within seconds, the quayside was awash. Behind him, the crews of the tongkangs dived beneath unfurled sailcloth, while on the quay stevedores ran for cover wherever they could find it. Rickshaw pullers hoisted their canvas hoods over the high passenger seats, climbing under them for shelter, while passengers scattered from a tram that clanged to a halt outside the railway building.

A mournful hoot from the channel, barely audible above the incessant hammering of the rain, announced the ferry's impending arrival.

Stood amid the crowd jamming the colonnaded walkway that wrapped around two sides of the railway building, Jorgensen stepped to one side of the doors, giving way to an oncoming army of Malay porters, dressed in black felt *songkots*, olive green tunics and trousers, and hoisting identical black umbrellas. He watched them hurry out, splashing across the quayside on their mission to greet the ferry's first-class passengers.

The rain continued in torrents. Water surged down storm drains along China Street Ghaut, through the conduits running under Weld Quay, before gushing from outlets on the seaward side, causing the tongkangs tied up nearby to pitch and roll in the sudden swell. Through the murk Jorgensen watched the outline of the ferry as it closed to the jetty.

He stayed under the colonnade until the first of the returning railway porters emerged from under the jetty's roof, their umbrellas angled against the rain to protect the passengers they accompanied. Then, pushing through the crowd around the door, he entered the cavernous main hall of the railway building. Inside, clusters of porters decked out in the uniforms of the different George Town hotels, waited alongside junior officials from government offices and groups of relatives, all set to greet the arrivals from the ferry. Jorgensen moved to join the two porters from the E&O, one of whom was David, just as the first of the ferry's passengers began to stream through the doors.

Amid the cries of greeting, mingling with loud exclamations and laughter over the fierceness of the storm, Jorgensen hailed the approaching pair of Hilton Morley and Arthur Cromford. David rushed over to take possession of their bags from the railway porter.

"Ah, Jorgensen. Good to see you." said Morley, shaking beads of water from the sleeves of his jacket.

"Welcome back to Penang, gentlemen," Jorgensen replied.

"I must say, I'm glad to be back," said Morley. "To my surprise, I rather missed the feeling of jeopardy we experienced here."

After tipping the railway porter, Cromford returned to their side. "Though we could have done without the company of those fucking awful people who latched on to us on the journey up. One couldn't avoid them at the club in Alor Star, and then devil take it they were on the train back with us."

"Be a little more discreet, Arthur," said Morley. "They'll be here soon."

"Is it them you're here for, Jorgensen. The Burgons?" asked Cromford. "They were full of tales about how resourceful you are. I don't suppose those talents would run to making them disappear?"

At that moment, Rowland and Winifred Burgon entered the hall, accompanied by a railway porter. "I'll see what I can do," Jorgensen said to Cromford. "Now, if you'll excuse me."

At first, the Burgons failed to notice him, preoccupied as they were with checking all their pieces of luggage were intact but then Rowland Burgon glanced up in surprise.

"It's Jorgensen, isn't it?" he asked.

"Good afternoon, Mr Burgon," said Jorgensen, then bowing his head to Winifred Burgon, who appeared even more surprised than her husband. "And Mrs Burgon."

"Oh hello, Mr Jorgensen," Winifred replied. "Do you have news for us? Have you found Leslie?"

Jorgensen beckoned over the second E&O porter. "Samy here will take care of your bags. I wanted a quick word with you both."

"Can't it wait until we're back at the hotel?" said Burgon. "We're rather fatigued after that journey." His words tailed off as he noticed the approach of a tall sandy-haired man wearing a blue peaked cap, khaki uniform tunic, and khaki shorts.

"This is Superintendent Cave of the Straits Settlements Police," said Jorgensen. "It's him who needs to speak with you."

"You must be Mr Rowland and Mrs Winifred Burgon." Cave said. Behind him, a Malay constable, wearing the police sash and black *songkot* hat, kept a respectful distance.

Burgon looked from Cave to Jorgensen in confusion as Winifred took a step closer to her husband. "What the hell's going on?" he asked Jorgensen.

"I need to speak to you both in private," said Cave. "It's a sensitive matter."

"What's happening, Rowland?" asked Winifred, linking her arm with her husband's, an anxious look on her face.

"Don't worry about your bags," said Jorgensen. "They'll be taken to the hotel."

"This way please. And Jorgensen, would you come along too." Cave led the way across the waiting hall, past the door to the ticket office and through a separate door into the administration offices. Burgon and Winifred followed, trailed in their turn by the constable.

Before Jorgensen too followed the procession, he heard Cromford calling his name. He stopped to see him in pursuit, pushing through the crowds in the hall, followed at a more dignified pace by Morley. Cromford's eyes were bright with mischief. "Good God, Jorgensen, what excitement have we missed? What do the police want with the Burgons?"

"I can't say," Jorgensen replied.

"What is it you cannot say?" Morley asked, arriving in time for Jorgensen's response.

"He's being tight-lipped about the police's interest in the Burgons," Cromford explained.

"Mr Jorgensen is taciturn at the best of times. Are you surprised to see them back here so soon, Mr Jorgensen?"

"Weren't they due to go somewhere up country?" Jorgensen asked. There was a chance Morley and Cromford could add some useful information.

"I was never convinced they had any such intention," said Morley. "The notion that the roads often become impassable rather seemed to put them off."

"So, they decided to return with you?"

"They received a telegram, which they insisted on showing to all and sundry at the Alor Star Club, though it was hard to sympathise as they seemed to care so little themselves. It seems that their agent misled them – and the lady's brother wasn't after all to be found in the jungle."

"To our misfortune," added Cromford. "There's something rather enervating about their company, isn't that right Hilton?"

"When compared to the mysterious Jorgensen here, I'd agree. What is it you cannot tell us? Are the Burgons opium smugglers, or agents of the Bolsheviks?"

"Are you quite sure that the man they were searching for was Mrs Burgon's brother?" Jorgensen asked.

"So they told us," Morley replied. "Was it not the truth?"

"They told me something different."

"Now I think of it, Arthur heard them mention the woman's brother, and they seemed rather upset that he'd done so. At the time we put it down to their taking offence at being overheard."

"Excuse me, I'm expected," said Jorgensen, and with a brief nod of farewell headed for the door to the administration offices, while behind him, Morley and Cromford exchanged bemused looks.

Jorgensen entered a short corridor serving several offices, where he found the constable standing guard outside the open door to the stationmaster's office. Inside, Cave was motioning the Burgons into two rattan chairs, placed in front of a dark teak desk, behind which he took the stationmaster's chair. Through an open window to the rear the rain drummed heavily on a tin roofed outbuilding.

Jorgensen leant against the wall next to the door, which was pulled shut by the constable outside.

"Superintendent, why have you dragged us in here?" asked Rowland Burgon.

Cave lifted a rigid card-backed envelope off the desktop and from it pulled out a photograph. "Is this Mr Leslie Worrilow?"

"Where did you get that?" Rowland Burgon asked.

"From McDonald and Lightfoot, a solicitor's firm you engaged."

"Yes, that's Leslie," said Winifred. "It's a very old picture, but all that we had."

"What is your relationship to Mr Worrilow?" Cave asked.

Rowland and Winifred exchanged glances, before Winifred answered. "He is my younger brother."

As she replied, Rowland was looking over to where Jorgensen was standing, as if expecting a reaction, but Jorgensen remained impassive.

"Then I'm very sorry," said Cave. "I have bad news. Your brother was found dead on Thursday night, here in George Town."

Winifred's right hand flew to her mouth. "Oh, God."

Burgon reached out to comfort her and she grasped his hand tightly.

"I'm afraid that we have reason to believe he was killed," said Cave.

"It can't be," Winifred wailed. "It can't possibly be." She collapsed in sobs, burying her face in her hands, her shoulders heaving.

Burgon moved his hand to her shoulder and held it there consolingly. "Are you sure it's him, Superintendent?" he asked.

"We will need you to formally identify the body, but we believe so, Mr Burgon. And I'm truly sorry for your loss."

"Knowing for how many months we searched, it's beyond cruel to learn he was here in Penang without us finding him." Rowland said, shaking his head in sorrow. "What can you tell us about him? What did he do?"

"In Penang, he was known as Frank Davies. It was Jorgensen here, who informed us of his original identity."

Burgon looked towards Jorgensen. "Thank you," he said.

"Frank Davies," Winifred repeated, dabbing her tear-streaked cheeks with a lace handkerchief, and pronouncing the words as if they were part of a foreign language. "Why would he take such an ordinary name?" she asked.

"Davies," Rowland too repeated the name as if it was somehow alien. "People were talking about that name in the club in Alor Star. It was in the newspapers."

"He worked as a letter writer," said Cave. "Helping non-English speakers. You should know that he wasn't a wealthy man. I believe he'd had a difficult time."

"Poor Leslie," Winifred murmured, her brother's name barely audible as she became overcome by sobs.

Rowland rose from his seat to stoop over Winifred, hugging her shoulders. "You mustn't distress yourself, Winnie my dear." He turned to Cave. "I think it's best if we return to the hotel now," he said. "My wife is quite overcome and must rest."

"I quite understand," said Cave. "I will arrange the formal identification of Mr Leslie Worrilow's body for this evening. Say, six o'clock, and we will send an officer to collect either you or Mrs Burgon."

"We'll both attend, of course," said Burgon, squeezing Winifred's hand as he spoke. Then he placed a hand under her elbow to gently guide her to her feet. "Let's get to the hotel."

"The constable here will escort you," said Cave.

"Thank you, Superintendent."

"The assistant manager, Mr Broomes, is waiting for you at the hotel. He'll ensure you can go straight to your room," Jorgensen added.

He and Cave watched the Burgons leave, then returned together to the main railway hall.

"That's twice in two days I've had to inform people of a family member's death," said Cave.

"I thought that the husband took it all pretty coolly," said Jorgensen. "That line, about how many months they'd been searching for Davies, sounded practised to me."

"What are you suggesting?"

"I can't get past the strangeness of their behaviour. They told both me and Lightfoot that it was a business partner they were searching for. Not Mrs Burgon's brother. Why on earth would they do that? And then there's the coincidence of him turning up dead the same week."

"For Christ's sake, Jorgensen. You saw how grief-stricken she was."

"I think she could be a fine actress."

"At times you're even more cynical than I am, Jorgensen. I don't know how to read you after you've spent the last two days trying to convince me that Magnus Prescott was involved in Frank Davies's death. Do you no longer believe that?"

"Anne certainly does."

"As you've told me. I suppose I should take you back to the E&O so that I can question her."

"She's expecting you. What I am certain of, is that Durrant killed Davies because somebody paid him to do it."

"I'm less convinced, I'm afraid. This notion of a hired killer still seems far-fetched. I came across one many years ago, but that was a killing among the Chinese gangs in Singapore. The victims here are two down-at-heel Englishmen and I'm sure the truth will be far more prosaic. When we finally get to it. For the moment – Durrant still isn't telling us anything."

"Try telling him the Burgons have admitted everything."

"You already suggested that ruse, but about Magnus Prescott. I think we can devise our own stratagems without your help – but thanks all the same."

# Fifty-Four

The Penang General Post Office was an imposing stone building in a prominent position overlooking Weld Quay, where it formed a corner of the horseshoe shaped complex of government buildings between Beach Street and the quayside.

Stepping into its echoing hall, where marble clad columns rose high to an ornate plaster ceiling, an Englishman could be forgiven for thinking he was instead entering the Central Post Office in London. Spanning one side of the hall, the long teak-topped service counter, clad with yet more marble set in intricate and colourful patterns, was an uncanny imitation of its London inspiration, right down to the polished brass grilles behind which the clerks stood. Though the row of ceiling fans oscillating crankily above, and the deafening cracks of tropical thunder through its open windows, soon reminded that same Englishman that he was unlikely to glimpse St. Paul's Cathedral through its main doors.

At the threshold of those doors, Ah Cheng paused, dripping wet from the tail end of the storm. He caught the beady-eyed scrutiny of a gaunt Sikh doorkeeper, whose attention had initially been drawn to the sodden white bandages covering Ah Cheng's head. But on catching sight of the E&O waistcoat, the doorkeeper gave a stiff nod, as if to confirm Ah Cheng's authorisation to enter.

It was Ah Cheng's first time inside a building that he had passed a hundred times before, and as he walked through the hall towards his destination – the telegraph office at the far end of the counter, he savoured the novelty of his surroundings. Ahead of him, Indian porters in shorts and Malay porters in sarongs dragged parcel sacks, fresh off the railway ferry, across the tiled floor from a side door opening onto Weld Quay. Through it, Ah Cheng glimpsed the bullock cart that had transported the load the short distance along the quayside, and its driver struggling with the heavy tarpaulin that protected his cargo.

He passed customers, mainly European or Chinese, conversing in hushed tones with the clerks behind the brass grilles, though at one station there was a queue of Malay messengers clutching the day's outgoing post from banks and insurance houses.

When he reached the large sign denoting the section of the counter belonging to the telegraph office, Ah Cheng approached the first grille, speaking through the opening to a dapper Eurasian man with a pencil moustache and oiled hair.

"From the E&O for Mr Robless," he said.

"I am Robless," the man replied.

"I come from Mr Jorgensen. He seeks your help." Ah Cheng pushed one of Jorgensen's cards through the aperture.

"Ah, from Mr Jorgensen" said Robless, nodding knowingly. He glanced quickly left and right before leaning closer to the grille. "I will come out to you," he added. "Wait by the table over there."

Ah Cheng turned to see a large wooden desk in the centre of the hall, where a florid faced white man fanned himself with a solar topee while hunched over a telegram notepad.

"Best not to be overheard," said Robless once he had slipped out from a door at the end of the hall and guided Ah Cheng beyond the desk and out of earshot. "What does Mr Jorgensen wish from me?" he asked.

Ah Cheng handed Robless a scrap of paper on which two names were written. "Guests of the E&O," he said. "Went up to Alor Star on Thursday." He pointed to another line on the paper. "To the Alor Star Club. Mr Jorgensen wants to know if they were sent a telegram from here."

Robless frowned. His expressive face switching in an instant from a dimpled smile to an uneasy introspection. "Mr Jorgensen asks a lot," he said.

"He says to tell you it is important." Ah Cheng tried to remember the tack Jorgensen had suggested he take. "Mr Sarkies asks for this."

"Mr Sarkies," said Robless. "Will he know I helped?"

Ah Cheng nodded vigorously. "Mr Jorgensen will tell him."

Robless's cheeks flushed at the prospect of being in Arshak Sarkies' good books. "A telegram to the Alor Star Club," he said with more enthusiasm, looking again at the scrap of paper. "For Mr Rowland Burgon or Mrs Winifred Burgon."

"Or to the hotel in Alor Star," said Ah Cheng.

"I see what I can find," said Robless. "But we close soon, so it must be tomorrow. Shall I telephone Mr Jorgensen when I have information?"

"I will return tomorrow morning."

# Fifty-Five

At eight o'clock that evening, Jorgensen was joined in his small office by Superintendent Cave, who cast an amused glance around the cramped room.

"I'd always assumed Sarkies thought well of you," he said.

"I try never to be in here," Jorgensen replied. "So it suits me just fine. How was Miss Prescott?"

Cave placed his swagger stick and cap on Jorgensen's desk and accepted the offer of a cigarette. "She confirmed what she'd told you this morning," he said. "Though she didn't sound as sure of her story as you made out."

"Which part?"

"Her brother's responsibility for Davies's death. When I pressed her, it's the threats he made that initially convinced her. Now, perhaps with time to reflect on it, she's less certain."

"There's the money."

"You told me yourself it might be a bribe – though you wouldn't say to whom."

"So, you're not going to question Magnus? Even knowing that he set Loddon up to spy on Davies?"

"I didn't say that. Though with Loddon dead, I'm left with only your word to go on that he was spying for Magnus. I'll question him – but I'll have to tread carefully, and before you say it – yes, it is because the Prescotts have friends in high places."

Jorgensen sighed in exasperation at Cave's caution. "What about the Burgons?" he asked. "Did you question them after they identified the body?"

Cave's mouth tightened, the look he gave Jorgensen containing more than a hint of exasperation. "In the circumstances of Davies's death, I was able to ask a few questions about why, after so many years, they had travelled out East in search of him. The only reason I'm sharing any of this with you is because you've got a bee in your bonnet and won't stop until one of us has got to the bottom of it. However much it pisses me off."

"I apologise," said Jorgensen, not quite through gritted teeth, but recognising the importance of staying on the right side of Cave. Not just for the sake of the E&O, but to solve this case. "I know you want to get to the truth," he added.

"Very astute of you." In irritation, Cave stubbed out his cigarette in the ashtray on Jorgensen's desk. "They told me that Davies abandoned his studies at Oxford and was sent to Australia to take up a position in an uncle's mining venture. But instead, he disembarked in Singapore and in consequence, his father disowned him and struck him from the will. Though it was still the old boy's dying wish that his son should be found."

"That's a little difficult to swallow, don't you think?"

"I asked how they intended to explain his disinheritance when they found him. In reply, Rowland Burgon said they were under no illusions about the awkwardness of the situation."

"They must have brought a copy of the will. Otherwise, why would Davies believe them?"

"Apparently not. As he wasn't a beneficiary, it wasn't deemed necessary."

"I'd like to see that will. I figure that at the very least the Burgons wouldn't benefit from it unless they found Davies. It's a more credible explanation for them being here than respecting a dying father's wish. Have you considered the other explanation?"

"That Davies was a beneficiary and Winifred Burgon stood to inherit the entire estate if he was no longer alive? Of course I bloody have. I wasn't born yesterday. Not that I believe they arranged his death. When I saw them this evening, she was as grief-stricken as this afternoon. But even if I was suspicious, the problem I face is that the will sits in a solicitor's office in England. I'd have to write to Scotland Yard to gain sight of it, and by the time I receive a response, the Burgons will be long gone. And, again, before you say it, I have considered the fact of their being a day's travel away in Alor Star when Davies was murdered might be more than an unhappy coincidence."

"You're left with Durrant then."

"And we still can't get a word out of him. Do you know, I think he's enjoying the interrogation. It's almost as if he's taking part in some ghoulish parlour game."

A knock on the door was followed by David's entrance. "Mr Paul, sir, please come to the lobby."

"What's up?"

"The Mr Prescotts are here – to see Mr Sarkies."

***

"Good evening, Mr Prescott," said Jorgensen.

With ill-concealed scowls on their faces, Lawrence and Magnus Prescott turned to see who had addressed them. "Where the hell is my daughter?" said Lawrence Prescott, the fury in his voice sufficient to pause the conversations of the nearby handful of patrons on the lobby's comfortable sofas.

"Let me take you to Mr Sarkies' office," Jorgensen replied.

"He'd better damn well resolve this." Lawrence Prescott was respected throughout George Town as a man who valued the preservation of his dignity. But in his righteous anger that evening, he was oblivious to the puzzled stares he attracted as he and Magnus stalked after Jorgensen across the lobby to the grand staircase.

On reaching Sarkies' office on the first floor, Jorgensen held the door open for the Prescotts to enter, following them in, but leaving the door ajar behind him.

Through the open windows behind Sarkies' desk, the light bulbs suspended in the branches of the Angsana trees rippled in the gentle sea breeze, while a quiet buzz of conversation drifted up from patrons on the lawn.

"There's nobody here," said Lawrence Prescott, standing alongside Magnus in the middle of the room. "Where's Sarkies?"

"He travelled to Singapore today, on one of his routine visits to the Raffles Hotel," Jorgensen replied, as behind him, Superintendent Cave followed through the open door, clutching his cap and swagger stick in his right hand.

"Has something happened to Anne?" Prescott asked, a momentary flicker of fear in his eyes on catching sight of Cave.

"She's quite safe, Mr Prescott," Jorgensen replied, moving to close the door. "But I'm afraid she doesn't wish to see you."

"Well, I wish to see her," said Prescott. "Cave," he added, turning to the superintendent. "You will oblige by seeing that I'm not obstructed in doing so. The girl is unwell and needs to return home tonight – to her mother's care. I must insist upon it."

"It's not quite so straightforward, if you don't mind my saying," said Cave in a placatory tone. "I spoke to her this evening. And she made it quite clear that, for the moment, she wishes to remain at the hotel."

"Her wishes have damn all to do with it," Prescott spluttered. "She's my daughter and will obey my commands."

"Miss Anne has reached the age of majority and cannot be compelled to return if it is against her wishes," said Cave. "I think it would be best if you left her here at the E&O, where she is in good hands, until such time as she is prepared to change her mind."

Out of the corner of his eye, Jorgensen cast an admiring glance at Cave, though wondering at his seemingly sudden change of heart. No longer was he kowtowing to the Prescotts. Taken aback by Cave's response, Lawrence Prescott stared at him in amazement.

"Why were you speaking to Anne this evening?" asked Magnus accusingly, stepping into the breach created by his father's silence. "She's not well, not of her right mind."

"Since Frank Davies was killed, I guess," said Jorgensen.

"I won't have that man mentioned in my presence," the elder Prescott thundered, fixing Jorgensen with a furious glare.

"Then I'm sorry to disappoint you, Mr Prescott," said Cave. "But it was to speak of Frank Davies that Miss Anne asked to see me."

"You heard what my father said," said Magnus Prescott. "He won't permit it. And I must insist you oblige him."

"What the devil do you mean by that?" Lawrence Prescott demanded of Cave. "What possible reason could she have for seeing you?"

"She alleged that Mr Magnus made threats against Davies."

"She's not been well," said Lawrence dismissively. "I hope you took account of that. At times the poor girl suffers from a rather fevered imagination."

"I do understand," said Cave, stroking his moustache in a thoughtful manner. "She was undeniably upset about the two deaths. She hadn't heard about the second one – that of Aubrey Loddon."

"Aubrey Loddon? What's he to do with Anne?" said Lawrence Prescott.

"The body of Mr Aubrey Loddon was found on the mudflats below the clan jetties. He'd been killed by the same means as Frank Davies."

Neither Lawrence nor Magnus Prescott spoke. The older man's expression was unreadable, while Magnus cast an involuntary glance in Jorgensen's direction.

Cave waited in silence for several seconds, allowing the news to sink in, before continuing. "You knew Loddon, I take it, Mr Prescott. When did you last see him?"

"Months ago, perhaps a year or longer. Loddon is a former employee, you know, though it's been many years since he last worked for the firm."

"And you, Mr Magnus?" asked Cave, turning to the son.

Magnus affected to think hard about his answer. "Quite recently, I suppose. Loddon does odd jobs for us from time to time. Trivial matters usually – but he's grateful for the work."

"And with which trivial matter was he engaged on your behalf last week? It wasn't by any chance to watch over the house of Frank Davies?"

Magnus's laugh was bitter. "If you're suggesting I had anything to do with Davies's death, then you're all at sea."

"It's an insulting suggestion," Lawrence Prescott growled, summoning all the authority he believed his high status on the island commanded.

"I make no such suggestion, Mr Prescott," Cave replied with an impressive equanimity. "Though I expect you understand why I must make these difficult enquiries. It is a murder I'm investigating."

"I'm perfectly aware of that fact, Superintendent Cave. And, that you arrested the killer two days ago."

"The suspect was released," said Cave. "Perhaps it's not yet common knowledge."

"If you had the wrong man, then why the devil aren't you chasing after the right one, instead of bothering respectable citizens with such impertinent questions? The Resident Councillor shall hear of this harassment, of that you can be certain."

"I expect the Resident Councillor will be gratified the murder is being fully investigated, Mr Prescott." Cave's composure in the face of Prescott's bluster showed no sign of cracking. "I shan't keep you much longer, gentlemen, I assure you, but there is a further matter Mr Magnus could help with before you leave. What can you tell me about Joseph Durrant?"

"Don't know the fellow, who is he?" Magnus replied.

"An Australian who also uses the name Garrett Solly."

"Sorry, Cave. Never heard of him."

"That's a relief. You see, we've arrested Joseph Durrant for the murders of Frank Davies and Aubrey Loddon."

Once again, Cave paused for several moments, this time to watch for the reactions on the faces of Lawrence and Magnus Prescott. "When Durrant was arrested," he continued, having seen no tell-tale twitches or unbidden reddening of their cheeks. "A document case holding ten thousand Straits dollars was found in his possession. The bundles of banknotes – and there were dozens of them – were held by Peninsular Bank money wraps."

Lawrence Prescott cleared his throat. "I'm most terribly sorry for Loddon, he was once a fine planter, but I don't see what this has to do with us."

This time it was Jorgensen who replied. "Magnus withdrew a large sum of cash from the Peninsular Bank last week. I saw him there on Wednesday."

"It would help us to know the purpose of that withdrawal," said Cave.

"Confidential business matters are none of your concern," said Lawrence Prescott haughtily.

"In the ordinary way, I'd agree with you Mr Prescott, but a murder investigation isn't the ordinary way. It would help to know the money in Durrant's possession didn't come from Mr Magnus."

"This discussion has gone on long enough," said Lawrence Prescott. "We came with the intention of collecting Anne and have instead found ourselves subject to one gross insinuation after another. I refuse to tolerate it any longer."

He turned and strode to the door, followed by Magnus who gave one last contemptuous look around the room before slamming the door behind him.

Cave puffed out his cheeks and exhaled deeply. "I've rather enjoyed this posting in Penang, Jorgensen," he said. "Though I've got an uneasy feeling it's about to end in tears. My tears, as I'm packed off to some frozen outpost in the Hindu Kush."

"They were both rattled on hearing that Loddon was killed," said Jorgensen. "They hadn't realised. You could be on the right path."

"I'm on the path you set me on." Cave said resignedly. "Though it's my fucking fault I followed it. If you're wrong, that old leech will finish my career – and he'll hurt the E&O too. I don't know why I listened to you. Only an hour ago you were trying to convince me Rowland and Winifred Burgon were behind Davies's killing."

"You've got something more solid now," said Jorgensen. "Knowing the money came from Magnus Prescott."

"We don't know that for certain, Jorgensen. It could have gone on that bribe you mentioned." Cave picked up his hat and stick from Sarkies' desk and rose to his feet. "I'm off to get some shut eye. Thanks to your escapades over the weekend, I've had bugger all. Why don't you try the same?"

# Fifty-Six

Early the following morning, Jorgensen pushed open the door to the anteroom between the managers' offices at the E&O. As he had hoped, Michael was already at his desk.

"Good morning, Mr Paul," Michael said. "Mr Broomes is in his office."

"It's you I've come to see. How was your lunch yesterday?"

"Amusing, thank you."

"I can tell you've got something to tell me," Jorgensen said, noticing the quiet smile of satisfaction spreading across Michael's face.

"You are now in greater debt to my father than ever," Michael said. "The matter was difficult to raise. My father had to exercise enormous delicacy so as not to offend Mr Choo."

"Did your father attend the lunch?"

"He did not. However, he did prepare the ground for me to call on Mr Choo yesterday evening. And from that conversation, I can tell you that Mr Choo was thrilled to receive a cash donation for the new children's hospital ward from Mr Magnus Prescott."

"A donation for the hospital? Not a bribe then."

"A cash donation of ten thousand dollars. Matching an earlier donation made by bank draft from Mr Lawrence Prescott."

Jorgensen nodded thoughtfully. It looked as if Anne Prescott was mistaken. The money Prescott withdrew from the Peninsular Bank had been heading to Choo Fat Yee all along. Call it a bribe or a donation to a worthy cause – it made no difference. It was not the source of the money under the bunk in Durrant's cabin.

"Did Choo receive the money in person?" he asked.

"A nephew received it on his behalf."

"Was it Magnus Prescott who paid it?"

"It was."

"Tell your father I'm grateful for his help," Jorgensen said. "And assure him, and Mr Choo, this information will go no further."

"Mr Choo understood your interest in this matter lay elsewhere, though he emphasises he has nothing to hide. The hospital's books will show all is above board."

Jorgensen smiled, hoping Choo would not bear a grudge at the loss of a useful back-door kitty of ten thousand dollars.

"Mr Choo thought you should also know about the delay in making the donation," Michael added.

"Delay?"

"It was expected by Thursday last week, but not received until Monday. Until it arrived, he was greatly perturbed."

"I guess there's a protocol to everything," said Jorgensen.

Michael inclined his head in acknowledgement of Jorgensen's sardonic remark. "Shall I show you through to Mr Broomes?" he asked.

Jorgensen shook his head. "Tell him I'll be around later."

Leaving the anteroom behind him, Jorgensen paused in the corridor outside to mull over Michael's news, and how much it undermined any case against Magnus Prescott. Cave would be deeply unhappy on hearing it – that much was certain, given how he had stuck his neck out last night.

He checked his watch. Seven-thirty. Leaving the corridor, he crossed the lobby floor to the dining room doors, where he caught the attention of Hindenburg.

"A table, Mr Mac?" asked Hindenburg, beaming both at Jorgensen's unexpected appearance, and the mistaken conviction that he was finally winning him round to a regular breakfast in the dining room.

"Is Miss Prescott here?" Jorgensen asked.

"Breakfast was taken to her room."

With a grunt of thanks, Jorgensen headed for the grand staircase, bounding up two steps at a time. Though when he reached the door to Anne Prescott's room, he hesitated. She was still ignorant about Frank Davies's real identity and deserved to be told the truth. But with that truth would come the Burgons. For now, he decided, it was prudent to wait. He knocked twice.

"Come in." Anne Prescott's voice rang clear. "I haven't finished yet," she added as she heard the door open.

When she saw it was Jorgensen standing in the entrance, she giggled in embarrassment. "I'm terribly sorry. I'd thought you must be a waiter come to collect the breakfast things."

She was sat at a small table, over a half-eaten plate of toast and eggs next to a coffee pot, cup, and a bowl of sliced fruits.

"Didn't you feel like eating in the dining room?" he asked.

"Not yet," Anne gave an apologetic smile. "I hope I'm not being too much of a nuisance, but I couldn't bear the thought of people recognising me and wondering why I was there on my own."

"I'll come back when you're ready."

She pushed the plate away. "No need, I've had enough for now. I suppose my father came for me yesterday?"

"He did."

"Thank you for not surrendering to him. I imagine he made demands."

"He was forceful," Jorgensen said, then added. "Do you mind if I sit with you? There's something I need to ask."

"Is there?" Her brow puckered in worry, and she watched as Jorgensen pulled a second rattan chair over to the table.

"Superintendent Cave questioned your father and brother yesterday evening, based on what you told us. Are you still confident that you remembered everything correctly?"

Anne's eyes strayed to the open shutters of the jalousie, and the glimpses of the sea beyond. Under the growing cloud cover, it was a less startling blue than normal.

"I've had another sleepless night going over and over it in my head. But despite what you suggested about my mistaking the purpose of the money Magnus withdrew, I'm more certain than ever."

"The trouble is, Miss Prescott, I was right in what I suggested. It's been confirmed to me that Magnus did pay a bribe to Choo Fat Yee."

To Jorgensen's surprise, Anne took this news calmly.

"I'm glad you came to see me this morning Mr Jorgensen," she said. "You see I've been kicking myself for forgetting to tell you and Mr Cave everything I heard when Papa and Magnus argued. It dawned on me during the night that I'd missed something important out."

"Go on," Jorgensen said.

"What I heard was that Magnus was to go back to the bank to make another large withdrawal. It was part of his setting things right that Papa insisted upon. I'm sorry I didn't make that clear before now. Could it be that the second withdrawal was the money that was given to Mr Choo, not the first one?"

"You're sure of this?" Jorgensen asked. He had to be certain it was not a ploy to keep Magnus under suspicion by inventing another story. "Which day was it you heard them arguing?"

"Two days ago. On Sunday."

"Do you know if Magnus did as he was asked?"

"I don't, not for certain," Anne replied, disconcerted by the sudden urgency in Jorgensen's voice. "He didn't come to the house again that night or before I fled here. Does it help that I've remembered?"

Jorgensen stood up. "It does. I'll inform Superintendent Cave immediately, then I'll look in on you again later."

"I'm grateful for your help, Mr Jorgensen. I hope you appreciate that."

# Fifty-Seven

Damn bloody Jorgensen. Damn him to hell.

Inspector Batchelor slammed the passenger door of the Studebaker shut, startling the driver alongside him as the car shook at its impact.

Damn bloody Jorgensen to hell.

Batchelor had telephoned Superintendent Cave from the manager's office at the Peninsular Bank. Greig was the pompous manager's name, a man who not content with offering up timewasting objections to a legitimate police request for information, then insisted on hanging around near the telephone as Batchelor spoke to his superior.

"Magnus Prescott made two cash withdrawals," he had informed Cave. "Each of ten thousand Straits Dollars. One on Wednesday, and a second on Monday."

"Jorgensen was right, then," Cave had replied. And then, to pour salt onto the wound. "I did suggest you were being overly dismissive of our friend. He's a pain in the arse, I'll grant you, but at times, he can be a great help."

Damn bloody Jorgensen to hell.

"What are you waiting for?" Batchelor yelled at the driver.

"Where to, sir?" the driver replied diffidently.

It was a good question. Batchelor had little desire for an immediate return to the detective station in case Jorgensen was there with Cave and crowing at his triumph.

Then he remembered the envelope on the back seat, with the old photograph of Frank Davies inside. He had used it the previous day, to gain the confirmation from the police surgeon that Leslie Worrilow had become Frank Davies. And then yesterday evening, Mrs Burgon herself formally identified the body. Bloody Jorgensen had been right about that too.

The hotel manager had been a step ahead throughout and it infuriated Batchelor. It was not simply jealousy. It was a matter of standing up for the reputation of the police service and the sanctity of its procedures. The principle that an amateur should not be allowed to interfere in police business when he had no right to do so.

In Batchelor's eyes, Jorgensen had struck lucky with his guess about Magnus Prescott, but could so easily have been wrong. Damn the man to hell.

In disgust, the inspector turned to his driver. "Penang Road," he barked.

The driver started the engine and crunched the gearbox into first gear, pulling slowly out behind a passing rickshaw.

"No, wait," said Batchelor suddenly. "Take me to Chulia Street – to the Victoria Inn."

# Fifty-Eight

After telephoning Cave with the news about Magnus Prescott's second withdrawal of ten thousand pounds, Jorgensen prowled the grounds and accommodation of the E&O with only half his mind on the job. The other half was occupied trawling through the events of the past few days. He knew he was still missing a piece of the puzzle. A small moment, a comment, a look, which would help him figure out who paid Durrant for Davies's killing. He was certain that Durrant was a hired killer. That he worked for Magnus Prescott made the most sense, but the Burgons could not be discounted. Though proving it either way seemed to be beyond the reach of either him or the police. Even knowing that Prescott had made a second unexplained cash withdrawal was not evidence enough for a conviction. The banknotes in Durrant's cabin were old and mixed, untraceable back to Prescott.

Finding himself on the seafront lawn, he leant against one of the cannons and lit a cigarette. He tried to focus on the confrontation with Lawrence and Magnus Prescott in Sarkies' office, hoping for a sudden insight, but instead his mind kept drifting to his earlier discussion with Cave about the Burgons. What was it that he could not put his finger on? The unhappy coincidence, as Cave referred to it, that when Davies was killed, the Burgons were allegedly searching for him over a day's travel away – up country in Kedah state. Ever since Morley had cast doubt on the seriousness of their search in his letter, suspicions about their motive for the trip had nagged away at him.

He remembered the Burgons' hints that the news about a sighting had come from a lawyer, but Jorgensen had heard Lightfoot's denial that it emanated from his office. Though Rowland Burgon had visited more than one solicitor's firm, and

Winifred had mentioned there was more than one photograph in existence.

Jorgensen walked to the sea wall and flicked his cigarette stub into the waves that lapped below. Finding out if the tip-off about Kuala Nerang was genuine might help solve the puzzle. His mind made up, he set off for the main doors to find a rickshaw.

***

After a fruitless hour at the solicitors' firms on Bishop Street, Jorgensen then headed round the corner, onto Beach Street, where his first port of call was the offices of Thomas and Gawthorn, solicitors, on the second floor of the Logan Buildings.

From behind the desk in his private office, Christopher Gawthorn, grandson of the founding partner, rose to greet his visitor with a handshake.

"You must work with Broomes," he said. "Capital old fellow, though it's best not to tell him so. Chooses to hide his light under a bushel, does Broomes. He's joining us for lunch at the Town Club later. A fortnightly affair, you understand."

From this breathless introduction, Jorgensen deduced that Gawthorn was a member of the Penang Chamber of Commerce, for that was where he knew Broomes had been invited.

"Yes, I do."

"Do take a seat," said Gawthorn, a fair-haired man in his thirties with a cherubic and perennially cheerful face. "How can I help the E&O?" The last words said with an emphasis designed to demonstrate the esteem in which he held the establishment.

"Are you acting for two of our guests – Mr and Mrs Rowland Burgon?" Jorgensen asked, conscious that none of his earlier calls had gone beyond this point.

"Why yes. Though not exclusively. Mr Burgon gave us to understand he was also seeking the assistance of at least one other firm in Penang."

"Assistance in finding Mr Leslie Worrilow, I assume. They also asked for my help, saying a photograph of the gentleman would be sent to me at the E&O Hotel. As I've not yet received it, I'm out chasing it down."

"They made no mention of this, but perhaps you're unaware that he might have been found. It was one of our chaps that was lucky enough to uncover his whereabouts," Gawthorn said with pride. "Mr Worrilow was identified as a planter working up in Kedah."

"I'm a little confused," said Jorgensen. "That turned out to be a false trail. The Burgons returned empty-handed yesterday afternoon."

"Oh, good heavens," said Gawthorn. "I had no idea. How embarrassing that I should not be aware."

"I'm told that the Burgons received a telegram from their agent, informing them of the mistake. Was that not sent from your firm?"

"I… I... I'm not sure," Gawthorn's embarrassment manifested as an awkward stutter, while his baby-faced cheeks turned pink. "This is terribly awkward," he said. "I should have known if we sent such a message."

"The E&O would appreciate your help in getting to the bottom of this. Can you tell me who in your firm first heard about Mr Worrilow being in Kedah state?"

"It was Soares. He's a senior clerk, a very reliable man who we often use for such matters."

"And where did he get the information?"

"From a visiting agent, I understand. A chap who knows planters the length and breadth of the peninsular, so Soares told me."

"Do you know his name?"

"I'm afraid not. But Soares will."

Soares was a wiry, dark-haired man, with a large nose and sunken cheeks. Summoned to Gawthorn's office, he eyed Jorgensen nervously, a discomfort that only increased on hearing from where Jorgensen came and why he was there.

"I can only apologise," he said, on hearing about the mistake. "I should have known better."

"Who gave you the information?" Jorgensen asked.

At this question, the corners of Soares' mouth turned down in misery. "I should have known better," he repeated. "It was a man called Loddon, and he had been drinking."

"Aubrey Loddon?" asked Jorgensen sharply. "From Pulau Tikus?"

"Yes," Soares nodded sorrowfully, making the sign of the cross on his chest.

"That's the name of the man found dead on the beach," Gawthorn exclaimed. "It was in the Straits Times this morning."

"When did you speak to Loddon?" Jorgensen asked Soares. His mind was racing, desperate to make sense of what he was hearing.

"It was last Wednesday, in the afternoon – at the Victoria Inn on Chulia Street. I showed him the photograph and he studied it for some time, as if he knew the face but could not immediately place it. He was the first person I met who had shown any recognition of the man in the photograph."

Jorgensen ran through in his mind what Loddon had told him. By Wednesday, he had been watching the lodging house on Love Lane for at least a day. He must have realised it was a photograph of Davies, yet deliberately fed Soares false information.

"Did you agree to meet Loddon in the Victoria Inn?" he asked Soares, a new suspicion forming in his mind.

Soares shook his head. "We met by accident. I was making enquiries in the Victoria Inn and happened to see Mr Loddon. He was one of two white men in the place, so I approached him."

"It was my idea to send Soares into the Victoria Inn," Gawthorn interjected. "There, and other inns."

"Did the Burgons suggest you try pubs and bars?" Jorgensen asked the solicitor.

A puzzled look came over Gawthorn's expressive face. "Yes. They said a similar approach had proved useful in Singapore and Kuala Lumpur. How did you know?"

"I'll explain in a moment," Jorgensen replied. "But first I have one last question for Mr Soares. Did you know Loddon beforehand?"

"Yes, sir. I have relatives in the kampung at Pulau Tikus and have met him there – though he is not a close friend. I did know that he was once a visiting agent for Prescott's. That is why I believed his story."

Jorgensen took a deep breath. "I'm going to tell you some news that must remain between us, and us alone. Leslie Worrilow changed his name to Frank Davies. He too was found dead in this last week – here in Penang." He saw the shock on Gawthorn's face as the name registered. "Before I leave here, I'll ring for Superintendent Cave at the police detective station. They are investigating the cause of Davies's death and will want to question you. You must tell them everything you know."

"Good God," said Gawthorn.

"And importantly, if the Burgons happen to contact you, you must say nothing of my visit."

# Fifty-Nine

Outside the E&O's main doors, Vikat hurried down the steps to greet Jorgensen as he alighted from a rickshaw. "Major Mac, sir," he said, firing off a salute. "Many staffs are waiting for you."

"Why? What's up?"

"Please to see Mr Michael, sir. He will explain."

Jorgensen was halfway across the lobby when he was met by Michael, with Rama, the head porter, at his shoulder.

"Mr Paul," said Michael. "Mr and Mrs Burgon checked out half-an-hour ago. With all their luggage."

"Where did they go?"

"To the railway building by motor car. They are to take the railway ferry, then the train from Butterworth to Kuala Lumpur. David and Ah Cheng accompanied them."

"Ah Cheng? Why?"

"He asked to go," Michael replied. "There is an important matter he wishes to tell you about the Burgons. You must go straight to the railway building to speak to him."

Jorgensen looked up at the lobby clock. The afternoon train down to Taiping, Ipoh and Kuala Lumpur was not due until mid-afternoon. There was no need for the Burgons to leave the E&O this early. Then he remembered the train going north to Alor Star. It left earlier, and the railway ferry would soon be carrying passengers across the channel for that connection. The Burgons would know the timings as it was only a few days since they made the same journey. Jorgensen was certain of it now. The Burgons wanted to get off the island as soon as they could. They had no intention of organising the funeral of Winifred Burgon's brother. They were cutting and running.

"Right," he said. "Ask Abdul to prepare a motor car."

"It is already done," Michael replied.

"First, I need to check something." Jorgensen walked to the front desk, where Richard Hong, the chief desk clerk, was on duty with one of his subordinates.

"Mr Paul," he said brightly, on seeing Jorgensen. "You come to ask about Mr and Mrs Burgon?"

"Yes. Were there any messages waiting for them when they returned yesterday?" Jorgensen asked.

Hong frowned. The question was not what he had expected. He exchanged words with the junior clerk and turned back to Jorgensen. "No messages, Mr Paul."

"Let me ask you a different question. Do you remember when Mr Durrant checked out of the hotel? This was last Wednesday."

"Oh yes, certainly. You ejected him."

"That's the man. Well, did he leave any messages for anybody – perhaps for Mr and Mrs Burgon?"

Hong turned round, facing the wall behind the desk, where polished wooden pigeon-holes, each with a small brass plate indicating the room number, reached three quarters of the way to the ceiling. He half-lifted an arm, as if trying to trigger the memory of a movement, before turning back to face Jorgensen. "Yes, Mr Paul. He left a message for Mr and Mrs Burgon. It was given to them that afternoon."

Jorgensen turned to Michael. "Telephone Superintendent Cave and tell him where I'm going."

***

In the main hall of the railway building, the stirring of railway porters, in their olive-green tunics and black *songkot*s, began to worry Ah Cheng. They were congregating close to the main corner doors, a sure sign that the ferry was approaching the jetty. Soon, those same porters would dash across Weld Quay to greet the ferry's passengers – and Ah Cheng would have run out of time.

Inside the hall, the passengers for the ferry's return journey to the mainland waited in pairs or small groups, some resting on high-backed wooden benches, others standing in conversational clusters. Close at hand to all of them were piles of luggage attended by a mix of railway and hotel porters in their various uniforms.

Among them was David, immaculate in his E&O hall porter's uniform, and Ah Cheng, less so in a shirt borrowed from the hotel's chef and a too tight porter's waistcoat. In the centre of the hall, they stood guard over a trolley loaded with the trunk and suitcases of Rowland and Winifred Burgon, who sat side by side on an adjacent bench.

Ah Cheng risked a look up at the main hall clock. Almost half an hour had passed since they arrived. He tapped David on the shoulder and nodded towards the side door to signal his intentions.

"Where's that man going?" said Rowland Burgon sharply to David, as he saw Ah Cheng moving away.

"To see if the ferry is here, sir."

Satisfied with the explanation, Burgon settled back on the bench and took his own furtive glance up at the clock. To him, the clock's hands seemed stuck fast at five to the hour.

There were two side doors leading from the railway hall to Church Street Ghaut, and Ah Cheng took the nearest, exiting onto the colonnaded walkway. The E&O's Standard Tourer was parked thirty yards away, waiting for new guests due to arrive on the ferry, and he waved to its driver, but it was a glimpse of the hotel's Morris Bullnose that he was hoping for – the vehicle standing by at the stables for Jorgensen's return.

He retraced his steps, and on re-entering the hall, glanced up once more at the clock, whose hands, in contrast to Rowland Burgon's perception, seemed to Ah Cheng to be flying round the dial.

"Any sign of the ferry, porter?" Burgon asked as Ah Cheng returned to his station by the luggage.

"Not yet, sir." And not for some time, Ah Cheng silently prayed.

His hopes were dashed within a few minutes, when the plaintive horn of the railway ferry sounded from the channel, and over by the main entrance, a hubbub arose among the porters.

Burgon heard it too and rose to his feet to survey the swell of movement in the hall. "At last," he said. He bent to place a hand under Winifred's arm. "Come, dear. Time for us to leave."

David's eyes met those of Ah Cheng, who shook his head. Neither made any move towards the trunk and suitcases. For a few moments, with a complacent smile spreading across his face, Burgon was oblivious to their immobility while he patted down his pockets in a last-minute check for tickets and pocketbook, then smoothed out some creases in his jacket and trousers.

Winifred's preparations took a little longer, but it was she who first noticed their porters' lack of urgency. "Come along," she chided them.

"We must first wait for disembarking passengers," David said, receiving a sidelong glance of approval from Ah Cheng. "You will not wish to stand in the heat."

Winifred tutted in irritation but contented herself with fussing over the hem of her jacket and imagining a view of Penang's retreating shoreline from the ferry's stern.

As surreptitiously as he could, Ah Cheng scanned all the doors: the side doors to China Street Ghaut, and the main entrance on the corner, but to no avail. There was still no sign of Jorgensen.

Five more minutes passed, interminably for Rowland and Winifred Burgon, but in the blink of an eye for Ah Cheng, before the procession of railway porters returned from the jetty with their charges and pushing trolleys bearing their luggage.

"Porter, let's waste no more time," said Burgon.

Both Ah Cheng and David pretended not to hear the command, making no effort to shift the trolley, and in exasperation, Burgon looked to his wife for help.

"You two, take the luggage now," she ordered, wagging an admonishing finger at them.

"No need to go so early, mem," said Ah Cheng. "Not all the passengers have disembarked yet."

"I ordered you to take the luggage," Winifred repeated icily. "If we choose to go the jetty now, we will."

Still, Ah Cheng and David did not move.

"This is intolerable," she said, her voice rising in both pitch and volume. "I demand you follow my instructions." She glared fiercely at them both, forcing David, trained to never maintain eye contact with Europeans, to look down at his feet, whereas Ah Cheng merely returned her look with an impassive gaze of his own. "We'll see about this," she hissed, and leaving her husband behind, marched over to where a railway porter stood alone.

"Help me with my luggage," she demanded, gesturing towards the small trolley, stacked high with trunks and suitcases, next to where Rowland remained.

The porter, a young Malay, slim and narrow shouldered, bowed his head in acknowledgment of the instruction, and began to follow Winifred. Halfway to the trolley he was blocked from progressing further by Ah Cheng, who had slipped past Winifred.

"From E&O," Ah Cheng said, and then in Malay. "You leave this mad *mat saleh* to us. She is an E&O guest. Our responsibility." His tone allowed no room for dissent, and the porter wavered, caught between a European and the E&O.

"Go now," said Ah Cheng, and the porter backed away, cowed by the reputation of the E&O's name but equally anxious to avoid the growing fury of the white woman.

"Get back here," Winifred shouted after him, before directing her anger at Ah Cheng. "What the devil were you saying to him?"

Though the crowd of travellers around them was thinning by the minute, there were still one or two startled by the raised voice in their midst. It was not the fact of a woman shouting at a porter that grabbed their attention, more that it seemed to be having little effect. Among those nearby who could not help but overhear was the deputy stationmaster, Simpkin. Having supervised the exodus of porters to greet the railway ferry, he was returning to the ticket office when he noticed the commotion and diverted towards it.

"Is there some difficulty, madam?" he asked Winifred.

She turned and saw with some relief that the questioner was English. Or at least he spoke like an Englishman, though his leathery, nut-brown complexion was quite unlike most of the Englishmen that Winifred had encountered, apart from one or two of the planters at the Alor Star Club.

Simpkin, whose spindly frame was outfitted in a uniform tunic, which may once have fitted but now hung in melancholy folds, raised an eyebrow at the presence of porters from the E&O. Problems with porters were commonplace enough, but not with those from the E&O. Though the tall fellow with the bandage around his head was not one he had seen before.

"This man is preventing my husband and I from boarding the ferry," said Winifred, pointing at Ah Cheng, and straining to appear composed. "Rowland, if you please, the tickets," she gestured to her husband, who fished them from his jacket pocket. "See here, we have tickets for Kuala Lumpur," she said, thrusting them under Simpkin's nose. "But these insolent porters refuse to carry the bags. I do hope you'll be able to intervene."

"We'll soon resolve the situation, madam," Simpkin turned to Ah Cheng, speaking in the firm but gentle tone that generally commanded respect in the railway building. "Take this lady's luggage to the jetty. And hurry."

Ah Cheng looked around the hall before responding. Still no sign of Jorgensen, and the Burgons were about to slip away. "Cannot," he said, and tilted his chin in defiance.

Astounded by the response, Simpkin was initially lost for words. It was not what he expected from the E&O nor had ever previously experienced.

"Get another porter to carry the bags," said Winifred. "You won't make this fellow see sense."

Simpkin clapped his hands to summon more porters. "Of course, madam." Two porters, including the one who moments before had backed away under Ah Cheng's persuasion, made their way over to what was now the last untouched stack of luggage in the waiting hall.

Then, to Ah Cheng's relief, an idea occurred, fully formed, as if from nowhere. He took Jorgensen's card from his pocket and presented it to Simpkin. "Please, boss. These guests owe money to the E&O and try to leave without paying. They cannot board the ferry until they speak with Mr Jorgensen – he will be here soon."

He watched Simpkin expectantly, hoping above all else that Jorgensen would soon arrive to back him up.

As for Simpkin, he was more than familiar with Jorgensen. As a deputy stationmaster at the railway building, it was essential to know who was who on the island. And in his eyes, the importance of managers from the E&O Hotel, the Runnymede, or the International, matched that of any officials from the government offices or the municipal council. He stared at the card in puzzlement until Winifred's indignant protest caused him to look up.

"Please pay no attention to this nonsense," she said waspishly. "We settled our bills in full before leaving. I cannot profess to understand what this native's game is, but he must not be permitted to delay us a moment longer."

As Simpkin struggled to decide on a course of action, he grimaced at a series of unpleasant twinges from deep inside his stomach. A more than familiar sensation whenever faced with a difficult situation. On the one hand, his duty was to ensure passengers were not delayed, and these two held valid tickets. But on the other hand, there was the E&O to consider.

It was then that Simpkin remembered he had seen Winifred before. Hearing Jorgensen's name had triggered the memory. To confirm his recollection, he glanced across to where Rowland Burgon stood. Yes – he was right. They were indeed the couple he saw yesterday accompanying the police to the stationmaster's office, followed by Jorgensen.

He glanced down again at Jorgensen's card and then met Winifred's frosty look with a hesitant smile.

"Well?" she said.

# Sixty

Hurrying in to the railway building by a side-door from China Street Ghaut, Jorgensen saw that the main hall was emptying fast. Porters were escorting newly arrived passengers to waiting cars and rickshaws, while almost all departing passengers had already boarded the ferry. But, by some miracle, the Burgons remained. Over by the far wall, next to the ticket office, he saw them with Simpkin, the deputy stationmaster, and Ah Cheng.

Jorgensen strode across the tiled floor, his footsteps echoing in the high-ceilinged hall. He passed David and two confused looking railway porters.

Ah Cheng saw Jorgensen approaching before the others and he stepped forward to intercept him. "Mr Burgon did not pay all the bill," he said quickly. The look in his eye imploring Jorgensen to follow his lead. "I try to explain."

The reactions to Jorgensen's arrival from the Burgons and Simpkin were markedly different. A flushed hostility from the Burgons and a look of relief from Simpkin, who was hopeful that the predicament in which he found himself would soon be resolved.

"I told Mrs Burgon they must go back to the E&O," Ah Cheng continued.

"You were right to do so," said Jorgensen, hoping he had understood Ah Cheng's hints well enough. "I'm sorry, Mrs Burgon. There's a discrepancy with your bill."

"Nothing was said when we checked out," she replied tartly.

"An error on our part. If you could return to the hotel, we'll clear it up."

"Send the bill on and my husband will settle it before we leave Singapore. It's hardly likely to be a significant enough sum to merit delaying our departure."

"Too great an amount for that, I'm afraid," replied Jorgensen. "There's an outstanding sum owed for the days your suite was kept in your name."

Winifred turned to her husband, as if urging him into action. He blinked twice behind his round-framed spectacles. "You're quite mistaken," he said. "Not once did we request the room be held." Fortified by an encouraging look from Winifred, he puffed his chest out. "Now, we've a ferry and a train to catch. I'm sorry Mr Jorgensen, but irrespective of whether it suits your hotel. I must insist you stand aside."

"I can't do that, Mr Burgon," said Jorgensen.

"How dare you," Burgon blustered. "My wife is distraught with grief, and yet here you are on some pettifogging errand." He turned to Simpkin, who had surreptitiously signalled to the two railway porters to hold their positions. "Kindly arrange for our bags to be taken to the ferry," he commanded.

Jorgensen felt a sheet of paper pressed into his hand and looked down to see it came from Ah Cheng.

"From Robless at the post office," Ah Cheng said.

"What should I do, Mr Jorgensen?" said Simpkin, looking helplessly from Jorgensen to Burgon and back again.

"One moment," said Jorgensen, unfolding the sheet of paper.

"Telegrams sent to Mr Burgon – and reply," explained Ah Cheng. "Copied out by Mr Robless from the Post Office. I went back this morning."

Jorgensen turned to the expectant Simpkin. "Please telephone for Superintendent Cave from the Straits Settlements Police detective station. Tell him to come here as soon as he can. Mr and Mrs Burgon and I will wait for him. And your porters are to leave the luggage to the E&O's men."

***

"We're not too late, sir. The ferry is still at the jetty."

Outside the railway building, on Church Street Ghaut, close to the corner with Weld Quay, Batchelor had run from his motor car to the open window of the Studebaker carrying Superintendent Cave.

"Do I have your permission to hold the vessel?" he asked.

Cave nodded. "You'd better get a move on."

Batchelor saluted, and, summoning his driver to accompany him, set off at a brisk pace across the quayside towards the railway jetty.

With the end of his swagger stick, Cave tapped the shoulder of his sergeant in the front seat. "Sergeant Singh, you'd better come with me." He climbed out of the car, hopped over the storm drain under the colonnade, and entered the waiting hall of the railway building.

Inside, the hall was virtually deserted. Of Rowland and Winifred Burgon, there was no sign. Nor of Jorgensen.

"Keep an eye on things in here," Cave said to Singh. "I'll find the stationmaster."

He strode towards the ticket office, cursing under his breath. Where the hell was Jorgensen? That secretary from the E&O was insistent Jorgensen had gone to the railway building to intercept the Burgons. Had he missed them?

"Superintendent!" The call came from behind him, where Simpkin, the deputy stationmaster, was advancing towards him from the main entrance.

"Thank you for coming. I was waiting for you at the corner," Simpkin said. He paused to regain his breath from the sudden rush to catch up with Cave and the stresses of the past half an hour. "Though I didn't expect you so soon. Mr Jorgensen is in the stationmaster's office." Trailing Simpkin was Ah Cheng, to Cave's eyes an unknown but unusually tall young Chinese man, sporting a grubby bandage around his head and wearing an E&O uniform waistcoat that clearly belonged to someone half a foot shorter.

"What do you mean, you were expecting me?" Cave replied.

"I rang the detective station at Mr Jorgensen's request. He wanted you here as soon as possible."

"Is anyone with Jorgensen?" Cave asked. "A man and a woman, maybe?"

It was the Chinese man who stepped forward to answer "Mr and Mrs Burgon," he said. "And Mr Jorgensen has information for you."

"Who the hell are you?" Cave asked brusquely.

"I am Ah Cheng, sir."

Cave beckoned Sergeant Singh closer. "Get Inspector Batchelor back here to join me in the stationmaster's office. There's no need to hold the ferry. And be quick about it."

Singh hurried off, and Cave looked Ah Cheng up and down. "I've never seen you at the E&O, but I'm sure I know you."

"Maybe you saw me with Mr Jorgensen."

"Hmm," Cave grunted. "That's not it."

"Shall I show you the way, Superintendent?" asked Simpkin. He held an arm out as if to direct Cave.

"I know where it is."

"Yes, of course. How stupid of me. You were there only yesterday."

Before Simpkin had finished his sentence, Cave was already halfway to the door leading to the railway building's offices, where he soon found the stationmaster's room. Inside, Rowland and Winifred Burgon were in the same seats they had occupied the day before, while facing them from the seat behind the desk, was Jorgensen.

"Cave," said Jorgensen, in surprise. "You were quick."

"Do you mind if I take your seat, Jorgensen? I've a few questions to put to Mr and Mrs Burgon."

As he eased round the desk to replace Jorgensen in the stationmaster's chair, he appraised the Burgons. There was a marked change in their demeanour from the day before. Gone was the emotional display of grief from Winifred. Instead, she coolly studied the backs of her hands while Rowland Burgon returned Cave's look with an impassive demeanour.

"I'm pleased you're here," said Rowland Burgon once Cave was seated, while Jorgensen moved away, to rest his backside on a cabinet against the side wall. "Mr Jorgensen invented a rather absurd pretext to prevent us boarding the ferry, so now that you're with us, I hope we'll soon overcome any misunderstanding." He spoke in elaborately measured tones, like a seasoned barrister prefacing a summing up with a few well-chosen remarks.

"There are a few things to clear up first," said Cave.

"I suppose you're wondering why we haven't remained for Leslie's funeral. The fact of the matter is it would be too hard on Winifred to do so. To have come so far, so near to finding her brother, and for it to end in this way has been deeply distressing. Isn't that right, my dear?" Rowland reached out to give Winifred's hand a reassuring squeeze.

"I'm afraid Rowland is correct," Winifred said, her voice more composed than the previous evening. "I couldn't go through with it. I realise it seems cowardly, but there it is."

"Of course, we shall make all necessary arrangements for a decent Christian burial for Leslie," said Rowland.

"I'm sure you will," said Cave. "Though that's not what I want to ask you about. Do you remember when we spoke yesterday, we touched on the photograph of the late Mr Leslie Worrilow? The one you brought with you?"

Rowland nodded, though he looked puzzled at the question.

"The copy we showed you was obtained from McDonald and Lightfoot," said Cave. "And a second copy remains in the possession of Presgrave and Matthews – another solicitor you engaged in your search."

"You hardly expect us to worry about old photographs, Superintendent. We have pictures of Leslie back in England, and we care little what happens to any copies left behind in Penang."

"That's not why I raised it. You see, we discovered today that a man visited several bars and pubs in George Town asking about Leslie Worrilow. He was carrying an identical photograph to help with his enquiries. Though not as well cared for. The landlord at the Red Lion Inn told Inspector Batchelor the picture in question was dog-eared, as if it had been in and out of pockets a hundred times. Can you help me by explaining where this man obtained the photograph?"

Cave glanced up at Jorgensen, who nodded in acknowledgement. So that was how Cave had turned up so quickly, he realised. It was Batchelor unearthing new information that had independently led Cave to come in pursuit of the Burgons.

"I should imagine he was a solicitors' agent," said Burgon. "I didn't dictate how or where they should conduct their search."

"It was a different photograph, Mr Burgon," said Cave. "Dog-eared, according to the landlord of the Red Lion Inn. Not the pristine copies held by McDonald and Lightfoot, and Presgrave Matthews."

"I didn't keep track of all the copies," said Burgon, retaining his unruffled tone. "It's been a long and arduous search over many weeks, as I'm sure you recall me saying yesterday."

Cave pushed his fingertips together, as if in prayer. "It was an Australian man who made the enquiries at the Red Lion Inn," he said. "His description matched that of a man called Joseph Durrant. Do you recognise the name?"

"I'm afraid I dealt solely with the partners."

"How about Garrett Solly?"

"Again, I can't help you."

"Nobody at McDonald and Lightfoot or at Presgrave Matthews has any record of a Joseph Durrant or a Garrett Solly. Those were the firms you engaged?"

"Yes, by all accounts they are highly reputable, though I did speak to one or two of their rivals."

"So, I understand," said Cave. "And so did Inspector Batchelor. None of the solicitors' firms in George Town employs anyone called Durrant or Solly."

"I don't understand what you expect from us, Superintendent," said Burgon. "We're ignorant of both names, as I have been at pains to explain."

"You're insistent that you don't know Joseph Durrant?"

"I am positive, Superintendent. I cannot conceive as to how anybody of that name became involved in our affairs."

There was a knock on the door and Inspector Batchelor entered. In the pause to the questioning brought about by his appearance and ignoring the look of irritation that passed across Batchelor's face upon seeing him, Jorgensen pulled a folded sheet of paper from his pocket. It was the one Ah Cheng had given him in the waiting hall. "I've got something here I'd like to ask Mr Burgon about," he said to Cave. "It's the text of a telegram sent from the General Post Office to Mr Burgon while he was staying in Alor Star."

Cave shot Jorgensen a quizzical glance. The questioning had not been going as smoothly as he had hoped. That Durrant had been in possession of a copy of Leslie Worrilow's photograph was failing to dislodge Burgon from his complacency.

"Go ahead, Jorgensen," he said.

"I must lodge a protest," said Rowland Burgon. "Does Mr Jorgensen have any right to interrogate us? He's not a policeman."

"He has my permission. And that's good enough. Carry on, Jorgensen."

"It was sent on Saturday. '*REGRET WORRILOW NOT IN KUALA NERANG STOP CASE OF MISTAKEN IDENTITY G*'. Who is G, Mr Burgon?"

"I can't recollect his exact name, but it's from the solicitors' man who informed us Leslie was in Kedah."

"It was the firm of Thomas and Gawthorn who gave you that tip-off, I believe."

"Yes."

"The partner you dealt with is Christopher Gawthorn. However, he did not send this telegram, and nor did anybody from his office. It was sent from the General Post Office on the quayside by a man matching the description of Joseph Durrant. How do you explain that?"

"There's nothing to explain," said Burgon. "I've repeated several times that I do not know of anybody called Durrant, and frankly I'm growing tired of this whole charade."

"The charade was your trip to Alor Star," said Jorgensen. By now, he had worked his way round to be stood alongside Cave, facing Rowland and Winifred Burgon across the stationmaster's desk. "You arranged for the tip-off to be given to Thomas and Gawthorn. It was cleverly done. You suggested to Gawthorn that they try showing the photograph in pubs and bars, such as the Victoria Inn, knowing that you had primed a man with the false information that Leslie Worrilow had been seen in Kuala Nerang. That's why, when you reached Alor Star, you remained in comfort at the club until your confederate, Durrant, signalled it was safe to return."

"This is all quite preposterous," Burgon protested.

"You came to Malaya, because, unless you discovered what had become of Leslie, Mrs Burgon stood to inherit less than the entire estate. But finding him dead meant that she would inherit it all." Jorgensen knew the accusation was nothing more than a guess, but it was the explanation that made the most sense.

Burgon turned to Cave in appeal. "Superintendent, you cannot permit him to continue in this vein."

"As far as I'm concerned, he's doing fine," Cave replied. "Carry on Jorgensen."

"And to make sure that Leslie Worrilow's body was correctly identified, you roped me in. You planned that I should have a copy of Leslie Worrilow's photograph, and you hoped I'd make the connection that I did."

"That's not why we asked for your help, Mr Jorgensen." This time it was Winifred who protested. "How can you accuse us of such a deed?"

"You found Durrant when you reached Singapore," Jorgensen continued. "And you sent him on ahead of you to Penang. That's why he stayed at the E&O when he first arrived – so he'd be easy to contact."

"As Rowland has said, we know nothing of this man Durrant."

"What was the message he left for you at the E&O on the day he left? The clerks remember handing it to you, Mrs Burgon."

By this time, even Batchelor was allowing the trace of a smile to appear on his face. Cave was leaning forward, the better to read the expressions on the faces of both Rowland and Winifred.

Jorgensen held up the sheet of paper again. "You replied to the telegram straightaway. *WILL RETURN THIS WEEK*."

Rowland Burgon's face retained the look of injured dignity he had adopted since Jorgensen began his questioning. Alongside him, however, Winifred turned to her husband, the first traces of fear in her eyes.

"The message was sent to Joseph Durrant, Care of the General Post Office, George Town, Penang."

Behind his rounded spectacles, Burgon blinked rapidly. Winifred could not bear to look at her husband and turned away in silence. Whether in disgust, reproach or disappointment, Jorgensen could not quite tell.

"Thank you, Jorgensen," said Cave. He turned to the Burgons. "Joseph Durrant was arrested for the murder of Frank Davies, who we now know to be your brother, Mrs Burgon – the former Leslie Worrilow."

"We have nothing further to add, Superintendent." Burgon's whole body seemed to have frozen stiff. His hands rested immobile on his lap. The rapid blinking had subsided, and he now stared sightlessly straight ahead.

"You came to Malaya with the intention of murdering Leslie Worrilow – if he wasn't dead already," said Jorgensen. "In Singapore you unearthed someone willing to do the killing. Only you chose badly. You chose someone, Joseph Durrant, who was reckless."

"Do you still have nothing to say, Mr Burgon?" Cave asked.

"Nothing."

"How about you Mrs Burgon?" Cave asked.

Winifred turned her head to face Cave with a faint smile of superiority.

"Other than this is all a farrago of nonsense, nothing," she said, as calmly as if asked her opinion on the weather.

"Let me see those telegrams, Jorgensen," said Cave.

Jorgensen handed him the sheet of paper. "They're copied verbatim from the records. Your men will be able to check they're genuine."

Cave read the messages through twice then held out the sheet for Batchelor to do the same.

He rose to his feet. He was sure that Jorgensen was guessing about the contents of the will but that could be checked. A telegram to Scotland Yard in London would set the wheels in motion, and now he had enough evidence of conspiracy to murder to hold both Rowland and Winifred Burgon in Penang for as long as it took to receive a reply. As he glanced across the desk, his eyes met those of the husband and wife, both gazing implacably back at him.

"Inspector Batchelor will take you to the detective station for further questioning," he said.

Batchelor pulled open the office door. "Sergeant Singh, bring your men in here."

# Sixty-One

After the Burgons were led away from the stationmaster's office, Cave and Jorgensen were left alone. "I'm hoping you'll tie up these loose ends for me," the superintendent said, returning to the stationmaster's chair, and motioning Jorgensen to take a seat opposite. "It's time to turn your theories into cold, hard witness statements."

"Where do you want to start?" Jorgensen replied.

"The only place to start, much as it pains me to admit it, Mac, is that we wouldn't have caught the Burgons or Durrant without your persistence."

Jorgensen shrugged. "From the little I saw of him – I liked Davies."

"He had a rum enough deal, the poor bastard. Is that why you kept at it? Because you felt sorry for him?"

"I owed him," Jorgensen replied. "Back when I thought George Lam or Kei Hin killed him in revenge for their failed blackmail plot, I was convinced it was my fault, that I'd let him down, and knew I had to set it right."

"Whatever the reason, I'm relieved that I listened to you," said Cave. "Now, to these loose ends. The telegraph office. Who was your source?" He picked up the sheet of paper, on which were written the telegrams sent to and from the Burgons in Alor Star.

"Robless was the man who helped, but go easy, I don't want him to lose his job for helping me out. He's probably broken a rule or two."

"Of course," said Cave, pocketing the sheet. "I'll go through the right channels and pretend you didn't get there first."

"It was Ah Cheng – not me."

"Who?"

"The fellow outside, with Simpkin."

"I've seen him before, you know. And am sure it wasn't in the most propitious circumstances, though I'm damned if I can remember exactly where and when."

"Don't try too hard. He's been invaluable over the last few days."

"Have it your way but keep an eye on him. Now, to the Victoria Inn. Who was the fellow dispensing the false tip-offs?"

"It was Loddon."

Halfway through drawing his cigarette case from his tunic pocket, Cave froze in astonishment, leaving the silver case held in suspension above the desk. "Loddon," he repeated blankly, then remembering the cigarettes, placed the case softly on the desk, but did not open it or offer one to Jorgensen. "Was he working with the Burgons?" he asked. "Was he killed because he knew too much?"

"Loddon was no fool, though he wasn't any good at staying hidden," said Jorgensen. "Ah Cheng spotted him watching Davies's lodgings on Love Lane, and I guess Durrant noticed him just as easily. Durrant must have followed him to the Victoria Inn, or somewhere similar, then pressured him to reveal why he was watching the house. Once Durrant learned that Loddon used to be a visiting agent to rubber plantations, he realised he was perfect for the fake tip-off. It wouldn't have cost the Burgons too much, Loddon was always desperate for money."

"Killing Loddon for that small part in the deception seems unnecessary," said Cave.

"I don't believe that was the reason he was killed. I think Loddon got greedy. His wife told me that he had grand plans to buy a motor car, to reclaim part of what he once had in life. After Davies was killed, Loddon calculated that Durrant was paid for doing it and saw the opportunity to get a share of the money. But he was too terrified of Durrant to challenge him directly. Instead, he approached Kei Hin and George Lam to do the dirty work for him. He'd witnessed Kei Hin visiting Davies and guessed he was a gangster. Maybe Loddon followed Kei Hin back to Rope Walk and decided to risk making the proposal. His timing was good, because Lam and Kei Hin had lost out on money from the attempted blackmail of Arthur Cromford."

"If Loddon conspired with Lam and Kei Hin to blackmail Durrant, then why not the Burgons too?"

"My guess is that Durrant never told him who he was working for," Jorgensen replied.

"When we arrested Durrant on the *Singkep,* the case was chock full of money. No sign of anything missing."

"That's because when Lam's gang tried to put the squeeze on, it didn't work. Then the next day, Kei Hin tried again. I saw him leave the Australia Hotel in a blind fury. With Loddon dead, he had no leverage. Lam admitted as much later."

"Your theory is that Durrant killed Loddon to avoid paying up?"

"And to dispose of a witness. I think Loddon took one chance too many. He tried again to blackmail Durrant, but this time on his own, without the protection of Lam's gang. Durrant killed him and dumped the body in the Prangin Canal, from where it washed out onto the mudflats."

Cave shook his head in quiet despair. "If all that's true, it shows what a ruthless murdering bastard we have on our hands."

"You've got him now, though. And the people behind it."

"Thank God," said Cave. "I'd better get hold of the Resident Councillor. He'll want to hear about today's work. Thanks again, Mac."

Cave rose and extended a hand, which Jorgensen stepped forward to shake. As he did so, Cave chuckled. "It's a bloody good job I didn't listen to everything you said though, isn't it? Otherwise, I'd have arrested Magnus Prescott as well." At the door, he paused for one final word. "Don't give Batchelor too much of a hard time over your witness statement, there's a good fellow. He did his bit too. And he was right about Prescott – you were obsessed." With a farewell wave of his swagger stick, Cave slipped away before Jorgensen could respond.

Smiling ruefully, Jorgensen followed Cave out into the railway hall, where Ah Cheng and David were waiting alongside Simpkin, the deputy stationmaster.

"I saw the police leading that couple away," Simpkin asked Jorgensen eagerly. "What have they done?"

"I can't say anything for the moment, other than you did the right thing, Simpkin. And to say thank you, I'll invite you to join me at the curry tiffin lunch next week. By then, I'll probably know more."

"The curry tiffin lunch at the E&O," Simpkin repeated, as if he could scarcely believe his good fortune. He had attended before, though not for a couple of years. "Thank you, Mr Jorgensen, I'd be glad to join you."

"Now about those bags," said Jorgensen, pointing to the Burgons' abandoned luggage. "David here will arrange to store them at the E&O." The opportunity to rifle through them, before the same idea occurred to Cave or Batchelor, was too great a temptation to resist this time around.

# Sixty-Two

After two long hours at the detective station going over his evidence, Jorgensen found himself back at the E&O, pondering the dilemma in which he found himself caught. He owed it to Anne Prescott to tell her that the police had arrested Frank Davies's killer. And beyond that, to finally tell her what he had learned of Davies's prior life as Leslie Worrilow. But he could not bring himself to do it. Not yet. Not while the nagging question of Magnus Prescott's behaviour was unresolved.

It was the bag of money on the *Singkep* that most played on Jorgensen's mind. Unless Choo Fat Yee was lying, he had received only one cash payment of ten thousand Straits Dollars from Magnus. That left the second withdrawal from the Peninsular Bank unaccounted for – matching the sum found in Durrant's cabin. And then there was Anne Prescott's own belief that her brother was capable of ordering Davies's death.

But how to square his unresolved suspicions about Magnus with the fact that the Burgons had been arrested for conspiracy to murder? And that he was the person most responsible for providing the police with their evidence? It made no sense to continue to investigate. No sense at all.

He lit a cigarette, but impatiently stubbed it out in the ashtray. If the money in Durrant's cabin did come from Prescott – then he had to prove it – or not. He had to settle the question.

The banknotes were untraceable, the Peninsular Bank money-wraps were unnumbered, and could not therefore be linked to a specific transaction, and there was no witness to any meeting between Prescott and Durrant. Jorgensen pictured the waxed canvas document pouch holding the money that he had found under the mattress in Durrant's cabin. It was a khaki-coloured military style bag, new and unmarked, but it was not the tan leather document case which Jorgensen had seen Prescott carrying from the Peninsular Bank.

He checked his watch. Almost five o'clock. At this stage he doubted that news of the Burgons' arrest would have spread far. By tomorrow, the Prescott family may have heard the news. The beginnings of an idea were forming in Jorgensen's mind. It was a long shot. Worse than that – it was a reckless long shot.

He dragged the telephone stand across his desk and lifted the receiver. "Hello Margaret," he said, when the operator came on the line. "Get me Mr Magnus Prescott at Merrydown."

Magnus Prescott's houseboy answered the call and went scuttling away after Jorgensen suggested he had Anne Prescott on the line for Mr Magnus.

"Anne," said Magnus belligerently, when he picked up the receiver. "What the fuck are you playing at?"

"It's Jorgensen here. I have a message for you from Anne."

"I don't wish to hear from you, Jorgensen. Put Anne on the line immediately."

"She refuses to speak to you. But she does have a message."

"I don't…" Magnus began, then checked himself. "You'd better tell me."

"After Superintendent Cave spoke to her this afternoon, she asked me to see her. The message is – Durrant has begun to confess, and she knows what you did. She wants you to give yourself up, to spare the rest of the family."

At the other end of the line there was silence. Jorgensen could hear the ticking of his wristwatch. Then an abrupt click as the line went dead.

***

The nightwatchman, perched on his stool at the entrance to the Church Street Ghaut Pier, looked Ah Cheng up and down.

"No hat today, huh?" he said. "But head still hurt?"

Ah Cheng's fingertips were drawn to the bandage, grubbier than a few nights earlier, that was wrapped around his head.

"Better today, cousin. You want a cigarette?" He proffered an opened pack to the nightwatchman. "Take two or three. Long night ahead."

Happy to oblige, the nightwatchman fumbled three cigarettes free from the pack and placed them in his own pocket.

"One for now too," said Ah Cheng, offering the pack again.

Once the nightwatchman had lit up, he gave Ah Cheng a knowing look. "Is true you from E&O, or not?" he asked.

"From E&O. No lie."

"You porter? Kitchen boy?"

"Boss is a manager. I help him out on some jobs."

The nightwatchman nodded sagely, as if he had known all along. "Did not find the *angmoh*, huh?" he asked.

"We found him. Now boss is looking for a different *angmoh*. I will wait here with you."

"Twenty cent again?" The nightwatchman's expression was hopeful.

"Ten cent. Thirty if you see him first. Dark hair. Act important – like a *datuk*. But he is the weak son of a *datuk* only. You see him?"

"See too many *angmoh* just like that," the nightwatchman replied, spitting on the decking between his legs. "But nobody tonight."

His stool was positioned below the overhang of the tin roof that spanned the entrance to the pier. From it, he commanded a view of Weld Quay in both directions, and straight ahead up Church Street Ghaut, leading up to Beach Street. Ah Cheng moved forward to sit on the timber decking close to him, his back leaning against one of the steel pillars that supported the roof.

The two men sat in silence, their eyes roving up and down the preternatural hush of the quayside, from the tower of the railway building on their left, to the flickering deck lights of the great passenger steamer moored at Swettenham Pier to their right. Every so often, a lone rickshaw puller padded past, and both Ah Cheng and the nightwatchman leant forward to try and catch a glimpse of the passenger.

A motor car, roaring down Church Street Ghaut, bathed them in its headlights. But it turned left, towards the goods sheds opposite Swettenham Pier, before disappearing round the far corner of the government buildings.

The nightwatchman stood. "I go to make rounds."

"You only nightwatchman one?" Ah Cheng asked.

"Another one already up at pier end. Small office there." The nightwatchman pointed to the collection of buildings at the seaward end of the pier.

"Telephone there?"

The nightwatchman nodded, and leaving Ah Cheng behind, began a slow walk up the length of the pier.

He returned around five minutes later, resuming his place on the stool, and lit up another of Ah Cheng's cigarettes.

"Thirty cent?" he said.

"If you see him first."

"*Angmoh* coming now," the nightwatchman said, pointing to his left. There, on the far side of the quay, a white man was hurrying towards them, passing the railway building and carrying what looked to Ah Cheng like a black Gladstone bag in one hand.

"How many boatmen here?" Ah Cheng asked the nightwatchman.

"One only," the nightwatchman replied. "Same uncle you saw before."

Ah Cheng stood up as the white man crossed the tramlines running the length of the quayside and arrived at the pier's entrance. It was Magnus Prescott all right. Ah Cheng recognised him from both Jorgensen's description and an earlier occasion – when he had served drinks to Prescott and his father at *Towkay* Choo's mansion.

"Where are the water taxis?" Prescott demanded. He was panting and beads of sweat trickled down his forehead from his matted fringe.

"I will speak to him," Ah Cheng told the nightwatchman in rapid Hokkien. "You go to the telephone and ring Tuan Jorgensen at E&O hotel. This is the man my boss looks for."

The nightwatchman rose slowly from his stool.

"Go quick," Ah Cheng urged.

"Stop jabbering away to each other and answer my fucking question," barked Prescott, incensed at being ignored. "Where are the water taxis?"

"So sorry, Tuan," said Ah Cheng in English. He stepped forward to take Prescott's bag from his hand. "This way, please."

Before leading Prescott further onto the pier, Ah Cheng turned to glare at the still static nightwatchman. "Go now," he hissed, in Hokkien.

"Which ship, Tuan?" he said in English to Prescott, as he took a few funereal steps towards the sampan moorings on the southern side of the pier.

"The *Sembilan*. Look, can't you hurry up?"

Ah Cheng halted, turning to face Prescott. "Sorry, Tuan. Boatman will not take one only. He will wait for more passengers."

"You leave that to me," Prescott snapped. "Just take me to him."

Ah Cheng set off again, leading Prescott towards the far end of the pier and the last of the many sets of steps down to the water's edge. He had taken no more than a few sluggish paces when a voice shouted out his name from the entrance to the pier. He turned to see a squat figure bustling across the decking.

"Ah, Wooi Gee," he said as soon as the figure was close enough to be recognised.

"I followed from the Railway Pier," Wooi Gee said in Hokkien, careful not to look at Prescott as he spoke. "Is it him?"

"It is," Ah Cheng answered, also in Hokkien. "I sent the nightwatchman to telephone for Mr Jorgensen. Can you check on him, then ring the detective station?"

"Where did he go?"

"Will you fucking people stop wasting time," Prescott snapped, unable to contain his impatience at this further delay.

Ah Cheng turned to him with an ingratiating smile. "One minute, sir," he said, and then in Hokkien to Wooi Gee. "Office at end of the pier. Mr Jorgensen at the E&O, then ring the police."

Though Prescott spoke Malay, and a little Cantonese, he had not troubled to follow much of the irritating Chinese chatter that was hampering his progress. Until perhaps because hearing from Jorgensen was fresh in his mind, he picked up on the man's name and in the same sentence, what sounded to him like the E&O.

"What's that you said?" he demanded of Ah Cheng. "You mentioned Jorgensen of the E&O."

Ah Cheng feigned a look of bafflement, "E&O Hotel, Tuan?" he said. "You wish to go to E&O?"

Wooi Gee was already yards away on his way to the nightwatchmen.

"You mentioned Jorgensen's name. I heard you." Prescott moved to grab his bag out of Ah Cheng's hands. "Give me that!" he yelled. But Ah Cheng swung it out of his reach.

"Give me that, you bastard!" Prescott lunged forward again but was met by a firm hand off in the chest from Ah Cheng, which dumped the Englishman on his backside. "You'll fucking pay for this," Prescott shouted, flecks of spittle flying from his mouth. He staggered to his feet and glared at Ah Cheng, but then, as if realising for the first time the physical mismatch between the two, turned suddenly and started to run back towards the quayside. Ah Cheng dropped the bag, sprinting in pursuit, and enveloped Prescott in a bear hug yards from the entrance. The two men reeled and swayed in a drunken waltz before Ah Cheng dropped to his knees, bringing Prescott crashing to the ground.

"You stay here, Mr Prescott," he said, as he twisted Prescott's right arm behind his back, bringing an end to the struggle.

"How dare you do this to me," Prescott wailed.

"Police will be here soon," said Ah Cheng. "Now you stay quiet."

Ah Cheng rose to his feet, bringing Prescott upright with him. Pushing him ahead while keeping a tight grip on his arm, Ah Cheng marched him away from the entrance deeper onto the pier, away from the risk of a passing harbour official or a policeman seeing him manhandling a white man. Far safer to keep out of sight until Jorgensen or a policeman from the detective station arrived.

Their progress was stuttering, as Prescott made several attempts to wriggle free. Each of them ending in Ah Cheng tightening his grip, until eventually Prescott submitted, and allowed himself to be guided.

The nightwatchman, now accompanied by an equally apprehensive colleague, drawn from his post to witness the unfolding confrontation, stopped dead in fright on seeing Ah Cheng's hold on Prescott.

"What are you doing?" the terror in the first nightwatchman's voice was unmistakeable. "Police are coming. You will be punished. We will all be punished."

"This man is trying to escape the police," Ah Cheng said. "Did you speak to Tuan Jorgensen?"

The second nightwatchman, whose own tone betrayed even greater dread than the first, stammered a reply. "He comes soon." Though neither watchman had personally laid a hand on the *angmoh* they suspected it would count for little in their favour once the police arrived.

Their nervousness unsettled Ah Cheng and he loosened his grip on Prescott's arm. "Do not run, Tuan," he said in English. "Mr Jorgensen will soon arrive."

The pier end nightwatchman was sent to fetch a stool, on which a now subdued Prescott sat and from where he looked around furtively, listening out for the approach of anybody who could help him escape.

Wooi Gee reappeared, and with an enigmatic smile, surveyed the scene. "I will wait at the entrance for Jorgensen."

Five minutes elapsed, a nerve-rackingly long five minutes for the two nightwatchmen, before a motor car pulled up on the quayside. Silhouetted in its headlights, three figures walked onto the pier, one sweeping the beam of a torch across the decking.

"Over here," Ah Cheng called out.

The beam swung in Ah Cheng's direction, coming closer as three sets of footsteps clattered across the pier's wooden boarding, before blinding him in its light.

"Police," said the man holding the torch. "What is happening here?"

"This fucking Chinaman assaulted me, I want him arrested," shouted Prescott, rising from his stool.

The torch, held by the leading policeman, Sergeant Singh, lingered on Prescott for a moment while the two other policemen, Inspector Batchelor, and a Malay constable, approached the group.

"Mr Prescott," said Batchelor. He tapped the tip of his stick to the brim of his cap. A reflex salute as befitted a prominent European citizen. "What are you doing here?"

"I was making my way out to one of our vessels to deliver some important documents when this chap jumped me," Prescott replied, his confidence flooding back on recognising Batchelor. "He pushed me to the floor and then damn near broke my arm. I've got the bruising to prove it."

"Did he now?" Batchelor looked Ah Cheng up and down, pausing in his assessment to study the bruising on Ah Cheng's face and the bandage around his head.

"It is not true, Inspector," protested Ah Cheng.

"Keep quiet," Batchelor snapped back. "You'll talk only when I tell you to." He turned to Sergeant Singh. "Take all their names. You first," he added, pointing the silver-topped end of his swagger stick at Ah Cheng.

"I am Ah Cheng, sir."

"Your real name. Don't pull any funny tricks with me. You're no more an Ah Cheng than I am."

"I work for Mr Jorgensen at the E&O."

"What did you say?" Batchelor's heart sank as he remembered why the name Ah Cheng had sounded familiar. He had heard it from Jorgensen's lips as the witness who saw Loddon on the night before his death.

"Yes, sir," repeated Ah Cheng. "I work for Mr Jorgensen."

The repetition of Jorgensen's name was too much for Batchelor to tolerate. "I don't care who you fucking well work for," he barked. "You don't assault an Englishman and get away with it. Sergeant, arrest this man."

Sergeant Singh signalled to the constable to join him, and moved towards Ah Cheng, whose eyes darted left and right, muscles tensed, poised to run, until over the sergeant's shoulder he saw with relief that a second car had pulled up at the pier entrance. In the hope it was Jorgensen, he relaxed and allowed the sergeant to take hold of his arm.

"Thank you, Batchelor," said Prescott. "I'll fetch my bag if I may."

"Batchelor, wait!" The echo of Jorgensen's voice reverberated among the wooden rafters and tin sheets of the roof above their heads. He had heard Batchelor's voice the moment he climbed out of the Morris Bullnose. "Don't let Prescott go," he shouted.

Though Batchelor could not immediately place the voice, his worst fears were confirmed once he turned round to see Jorgensen was only a few yards away.

"What the hell are you doing here?" he said.

"Prescott's making a run for it because Cave wants to question him in the morning," Jorgensen said. Noticing Batchelor's eyes narrow, he added. "I spoke to him a few minutes ago. And I sent Ah Cheng here because this is how Durrant tried to escape. Other men are positioned along the quayside in case Prescott tried elsewhere."

Prescott, who had watched Batchelor closely while Jorgensen spoke, must have seen something in a change of the inspector's expression, for he suddenly made another break for freedom, dashing clear towards the edge of the pier. But he had reckoned without Wooi Gee, who had followed Jorgensen in from the entrance, and perhaps sensing Prescott's intentions had placed himself between the group and the water taxi. He caught Prescott in a bear hug, in almost the same way that Ah Cheng had done earlier, stopping him in his tracks.

"You, man!" shouted Batchelor at Wooi Gee. "Let him go." Then to Jorgensen. "There's no need for your private army of Chinamen, Jorgensen, Mr Prescott will return with me to the detective station to sort this matter out."

"As you say, Inspector," said Jorgensen.

"Sergeant, take Mr Prescott to the car," Batchelor ordered, and Singh left Ah Cheng's side and moved to relieve Wooi Gee of the man whose arm he still gripped.

"Constable, take the Chinaman in too," Batchelor added.

The constable looked from Ah Cheng to Wooi Gee in confusion.

"This one," Batchelor snapped, pointing at Ah Cheng.

"He was acting on my orders," Jorgensen protested. "Why are you arresting him?"

"A charge of assault was made, Mr Jorgensen. Your little gang isn't above the law."

# Sixty-Three

Ah Cheng spent what was left of Tuesday night in a humid, stinking cell on the ground floor of the Penang Road detective station. For a bed, there was a bare wooden bench, and for company, a man in a bloodstained shirt who muttered incomprehensibly throughout the night.

At daybreak, a bowl of noodles for breakfast was slid into his cell, then another airless hour passed, until, without a word of explanation, a Malay constable unlocked the cell door, shoved his cellmate against the cell wall and ushered Ah Cheng upstairs and into a room furnished with a scuffed wooden table and a handful of stools.

A clock on the wall told him it was eight-thirty.

"Sit there," said the constable, pointing at one of the stools. Ah Cheng obeyed and the constable stood guard by the door.

After several minutes, during which the constable's eyes remained locked on the far wall, the door opened, and Inspector Batchelor entered the room.

He stared disdainfully down at Ah Cheng. "I know who you are. When we brought you in last night, I was sure I'd seen you before, and this morning I remembered. You were arrested after a gang fight. You and several other nasty pieces of work." He snorted in derision. "Nothing more than a gangster – that's all you are. Jorgensen knows how to pick them all right."

"I was released," said Ah Cheng. "The fight was nothing to do with me."

"You were let go, but it doesn't mean you were innocent," Batchelor took Ah Cheng by the shoulders and twisted him on the stool, so that he was forced to face the inspector who stood intimidatingly above him. "You don't fool me," Batchelor continued, "I know what you really are – and I'll be watching you, ready for the first time you take a false step."

Ah Cheng looked away, down at the wooden floorboards at his feet, feeling Batchelor's hot breath on the top of his head, willing himself not to be provoked. Much as he wanted to return Batchelor's challenging glare, his previous experience with the police warned him otherwise.

"Do you hear me, Ah Cheng, if that is your real name?"

"Yes, sir," Ah Cheng replied.

"Good. As long as we understand each other." Batchelor turned on his heel and moved towards the door. "Let him go," he said to the constable.

Within a few minutes, Ah Cheng was outside on Penang Road, blinking furiously in the bright morning glare. At a brisk pace, he set off on foot for the E&O, struck, after a few yards, by the sudden realisation that he was thinking of the place as his home.

***

Half an hour later, Jorgensen stood in the corridor at the doorway of Inspector Batchelor's office, and watched as Lawrence Prescott, accompanied by the Prescott family's solicitor, and escorted by Sergeant Singh, entered Superintendent Cave's office.

"Now see here, Cave…" Prescott began to bluster, but the rest of the sentence was lost to Jorgensen, as Sergeant Singh pulled the door shut behind him.

Jorgensen lit a cigarette and listened to the sound of raised voices through the closed door, dominated by the increasingly agitated tones of Lawrence Prescott. Though the voices were muffled, Jorgensen could easily imagine how the argument was proceeding, knowing as he did what Cave's intentions were. And soon enough, as he expected, the door burst open and Lawrence Prescott strode through it and down the corridor, pausing only to cast a baleful glance at Jorgensen as he passed.

The solicitor, a stooped figure in a white linen suit that hung limply from his rounded shoulders, hastened after Prescott, calling out in a thin, reedy voice for his client to stop. Behind him, Sergeant Singh proceeded at a more measured pace, exchanging a complicit grin with Jorgensen, before he, like the others, pushed through the door at the end of the corridor that led to the staircase.

Jorgensen sauntered down the now quiet corridor to Cave's office, knocking on the door and walking in. From behind the desk, Cave gave him a rueful smile.

"I guess he wasn't pleased," said Jorgensen.

"He blew his top," Cave replied. "It wouldn't surprise me if he didn't go straight to the Resident Councillor's office to complain."

"It's not too late to change your mind," Jorgensen said.

"That's rich, coming from you," Cave snorted in derision. "I've lost count of the number of times you've changed your mind on this case. And every time you dream up a new theory, I end up looking an even bigger idiot than I did before."

"That's what I mean. If you're unsure, then let Magnus go. Don't risk your career."

"And ignore the information you brought in," Cave shook his head. "No. That's not the duty of a police detective, as I understand it. Now that I'm committed, I intend to take the damn plunge."

"What about Prescott's solicitor? Have you banished him from the interview as well?"

"Thankfully, yes. There are many disadvantages to policing in Malaya, but having to adhere to protocols expected in London, is not one of them."

A knock on the door signalled the return of Sergeant Singh to the office, this time in the company of Magnus Prescott, whose face showed the strain of the sleepless hours spent in a cell on the ground floor. Guided to a chair placed in front of Cave's desk, he cast a bitter glance at Jorgensen, who was standing against a side wall.

"Jorgensen is here on my authority, Mr Prescott," said Cave. "He has new information that I wish to put to you."

Magnus gave a sullen nod.

"Let's return to the matter we didn't resolve the other day," Cave continued. "The money withdrawn by you last week from the Peninsular Bank and witnessed by Jorgensen here. Was that intended for Joseph Durrant?"

"It was not," Magnus said, straightening his posture, as if willing himself to show some fight. "As I've said before, I don't know of any man by that name."

"Who then, was the intended recipient?"

"On this point, I must repeat my father's words. It relates to a confidential business matter."

"That won't wash, Magnus. A murder investigation trumps your company's business arrangements."

"Maybe I can help," Jorgensen moved to the side of Cave's desk. "It was intended as a payment to Mr Choo Fat Yee. A generous donation of ten thousand dollars towards the new children's ward at the Chinese Methodist Hospital. Mr Choo confirmed it yesterday."

"Is that correct, Magnus?" Cave asked.

"Yes." For the first time that morning, there was a ray of hope in Magnus's eyes.

"When did you pass the ten thousand dollars over to Choo?" Cave asked.

"On Monday."

"According to Choo, that was four days later than agreed," said Jorgensen. "You'd withdrawn the money from the Peninsular Bank on the Wednesday. Why didn't you hand it over on the Thursday, as arranged?"

"It wasn't convenient."

"That's not the reason at all, is it Magnus? You couldn't pay it on Thursday because you'd already handed the whole sum to Joseph Durrant, as payment for the murder of Frank Davies."

"The money was for Choo Fat Yee," Magnus said. "I paid it on Monday, as I've already admitted. I don't know this Durrant man you keep banging on about." He turned to Cave in an appeal to save him from Jorgensen's accusations.

"It wasn't the same batch of dollar notes though, was it?" said Cave. "On Monday you made a second withdrawal of ten thousand dollars. Inspector Batchelor has already confirmed this with the Peninsular Bank. That's the money you gave to Mr Choo, and that's why there was a delay to his receiving it."

"That's not the case," said Prescott.

"We know it's the case. Your sister heard you and your father discussing it on Sunday."

"She's lying. She's not been herself since…"

"Since you had her good friend killed," Jorgensen interjected.

Prescott's eyes were fixed on Cave, as if by doing so he could refuse to acknowledge Jorgensen's presence, or any truth in his words.

"The trouble is," said Cave. "It's difficult to believe your story that the first batch of ten thousand Straits Dollars was for a separate business matter. As you won't tell us on what it was spent, claiming business confidentiality, then we can reasonably conclude that it constituted the money found on Durrant when we arrested him."

"That's not the case," Prescott repeated.

"By that, I assume you mean we can't prove it."

"If you've been told otherwise, then you've been lied to."

"You're referring to Durrant's confession, I take it," said Cave, with a sidelong glance at Jorgensen.

"For a while, I couldn't understand why you had Davies killed," said Jorgensen to Magnus. "Anne told me how much you hated him, but it never seemed reason enough. Too much of a risk for a coward like you."

"You're mistaken," said Magnus. "All right, I'll admit I didn't like Davies. But why would I want him killed?"

"Because in the end, it was too easy," said Jorgensen. "You allowed Durrant to persuade you there'd be no risk or effort on your part. He'd heard from Loddon about your worries over the family's reputation. How you'd tried to force Davies to leave Penang by making his life a misery. How obsessed you were about the harm he could still cause the family through Anne. Durrant suggested a simple solution. And as chance would have it, you had the money at your disposal: ten thousand dollars ready to hand over to Choo. Instead, you handed over the money to Durrant on Thursday night and by the time you woke in your bed at home the next morning, Davies was dead."

"That's not true," Magnus protested. "None of it is true."

"The bag puzzled me," said Jorgensen. "When I saw you at the Peninsular Bank you were carrying a smart new leather document case. But the bag I found in Durrant's cabin was a cheaper affair – a canvas document pouch, though also new and unmarked."

Magnus Prescott glared at Jorgensen. A glare full of loathing.

"For a while I admired your cunning, in swapping the cash over from one bag to another," Jorgensen continued. "But you weren't cunning at all. In fact, you were just stupid. As I found out when I visited Lock & Co on Beach Street this morning. Anne told me you have an account at the store, as well as one at Pritchard & Co and Whiteaway Laidlaw. You know what I'm referring to, don't you, Magnus?"

Magnus's shoulders sagged, as if the fight had gone out of him, and he hung his head low, his chin buried in his chest.

"Last week you bought two bags from Lock & Co. On Wednesday, you bought a tan leather document case – the one I saw you with at the Peninsular Bank. Then you went back and bought a cheaper waxed canvas document pouch – the one we found in Durrant's cabin. And the dumbest part of it, or maybe the most arrogant part – was that you charged both items to your account."

"You've got a choice now, Magnus," said Cave. "You'll hang for murder over this, unless you can show you were somehow forced into it by Durrant. Do you understand?"

"It wasn't my doing," Magnus said, so softly that Cave had to lean closer to hear him. "It was Davies's family who wanted him dead. Durrant told me it could all be blamed on Davies's family."

"What do you know of Davies's family?"

"Only that they were searching for him in connection with an inheritance and hoping to find that he'd died."

"What's the name of this family?"

"Burgon. There's two of them, a husband and wife. They were at the E&O, but Durrant had set things up, so they were elsewhere when Davies was killed. He said it made them look guilty."

"So, you agreed to pay?"

"He said he'd make it look as if the Burgons were responsible."

"I hope you're telling me the truth, Magnus. It's your only chance of avoiding the rope."

"I am. I swear it."

# Sixty-Four

*Two Months Later*

It was a Thursday evening at the E&O Hotel. Night had fallen. In the peaceful lobby, Jorgensen was sitting in a chair facing the main doors, a copy of the Straits Echo in his lap. The loudest sounds he could hear were the steady whir of the electric ceiling fans and the ping of the bell from the lift. Dinner was underway in the sparsely filled dining room, and, on the chairs and sofas dotted around there were fewer than half a dozen people engaged in murmured conversation.

At the entrance, Vikat, the head doorman, was ushering in Superintendent Bob Cave. Jorgensen gave him a wave, and Cave removed his cap and wandered over.

"Have you seen this?" Jorgensen passed Cave the newspaper, pointing to an article towards the bottom of the front page.

*PENANG EXECUTION*
*DOUBLE MURDERER PAYS EXTREME PENALTY*

*Joseph Francis Durrant, the Love Lane double murderer, who was sentenced to be hanged at the last Penang Assizes, was executed at 7:30 this morning at the Penang gaol.*

*There present besides N.D. Cavill, Superintendent of Prisons and Mr Higham (the Coroner) were Dr Seeveritnam and the executioner, Warder Davenport, who had arrived from Singapore the previous day.*

*At 9 am. an inquest was held by the coroner who returned the usual verdict of death by judicial hanging.*

*Durrant was convicted of the murders of Leslie Worrilow and Aubrey Loddon in George Town. The trial was before Mr Justice*

*Whittley, and a special jury who unanimously found the accused guilty.*

*The co-accused, Magnus Lawrence Beamish Prescott, also convicted of murder, remains in Penang gaol, awaiting the outcome of an appeal granted by the Penang High Court against the penalty of death.*

Cave took the chair next to Jorgensen and read the article in silence.

"A grisly business," he said, with a sorrowful shake of the head, as he dropped the paper back onto a nearby table next to his cap and stick.

"Were you there?"

"Christ, no. Watching a man put to death is not for me. I've seen enough killing to last me a lifetime."

"It won't happen to Magnus Prescott," said Jorgensen. "Sentence commuted to life imprisonment would be my best guess – thanks to his father's membership of the Town Club, the Turf Club and the Golf Club."

"There are times, Jorgensen, when I wonder at your cynicism. And besides, Lawrence Prescott is no longer a member of any of those clubs."

"Nor welcome in the E&O. A modern day pariah, and deservedly so. He was fortunate not to have been charged alongside Magnus."

"He's not the only one," Cave replied, offering Jorgensen a cigarette from his case, before lighting it, and his own.

"I suppose you had no choice," said Jorgensen. "Once Durrant decided to spare the Burgons. I still can't understand why he did it."

"So, you're still convinced they were as guilty as Magnus Prescott?"

Jorgensen shrugged. "I don't know for sure. Though they had more of a motive than Magnus Prescott. Winifred stood to inherit a greater share of their father's estate with her brother dead. And why else did they hire Durrant in Singapore, if not to track down and kill Frank Davies?"

"Just to help track him down, according to Durrant's confession."

"Do you believe that? A thug like Durrant?"

It was Cave's turn to shrug. "We'll never really know. As soon as Durrant was confronted with Magnus's confession, he decided to take Magnus down with him. Which left the Burgons in the clear. After that, there was no chance of the Attorney General prosecuting them for the same crime as Durrant and Magnus Prescott. The risk that none of the prosecutions would succeed was too great. Too great a risk for his reputation."

"Now who's being cynical?"

Cave grinned. "Though, if I'm honest, I was relieved too. I was never entirely convinced of the Burgons' guilt. Winifred's reaction, when she first heard of her brother's death, was heartfelt, in my judgement. It was only afterwards, when they realised the killer was Durrant, that they began to lie – to protect themselves." He rose to his feet. "I'd best get on to my dinner appointment."

"Anybody I know?"

"As if you didn't already know."

"You know what I think?" said Jorgensen, following Cave to his feet.

"About my dinner appointment?"

"About why Durrant didn't incriminate the Burgons. He did a deal with them somehow, probably through a solicitor. He was married, wasn't he?"

Cave nodded. "I'm not sure it was legal, but yes. He had a wife in Singapore."

"It wouldn't surprise me if she's come into some money."

"Time to move on, Mac," Cave replied. He bent to retrieve his cap and stick from the low table, as at that moment, Broomes approached, his own hat in hand.

"Good evening, Superintendent," he said. "I apologise for interrupting."

"Good evening, Mr Broomes. I'll leave Jorgensen to you. I'm running late." With a last nod to Jorgensen, he slipped away, leaving Broomes standing irresolute before his undermanager. The issue Broomes had intended to raise could not help but seem impossibly trivial by comparison with the matters he had just overheard.

"You probably wanted to see me about the jockeys," Jorgensen suggested helpfully. "I'll speak to the promoter tomorrow. He's in Ipoh for the weekend meeting there."

"I'd be grateful if you could. The rowdiness on their last visit was quite unacceptable."

"Sure."

Broomes hesitated. There was another matter on his mind, that he could not quite bring himself to raise. "Good. Very good," he said, then as if an afterthought. "Did you see Morley off?"

Jorgensen nodded. "This morning at Swettenham Pier. And Cromford too."

"Did our esteemed guest have much to say?"

"Nothing unexpected. A few compliments to the hotel, that kind of thing."

"No mention of his work?"

"The stories he's been writing, do you mean?"

It was common knowledge among the E&O's staff that over the past two weeks Hilton Morley had become almost a recluse, hard at work at his desk, taking meals in his room and only leaving the suite for a few brief pre-dawn strolls along the sea wall.

"Yes, exactly," said Broomes testily, anxious to get to the point. "Did he say what they're about?" Speculation was rife that the subject of Morley's latest stories were the two recent murders in George Town.

"I didn't get round to asking him."

"But he's been talking to you. You must have some idea."

In truth, apart from unavoidable encounters on Morley's early morning strolls, Jorgensen had steered as clear as he could manage of both the author and his secretary. Morley's fascination with the murders of Frank Davies and Aubrey Loddon had grown from the occasional casual question to actively seeking out people with any tenuous connection to either the victims or the perpetrators in Penang Prison.

Though as Jorgensen could not help but note, any notion of a visit to the kampung beyond Pulau Tikus to speak to Loddon's wife, or to the house in Love Lane to meet Davies's fellow lodgers never seemed to occur to the author. Instead, all his enquiries were conducted either within the walls of the E&O Hotel – where, every day, he devoured all the local newspapers – or at the homes of its wealthier patrons who were suitably honoured to invite him and Cromford to dinner.

On the handful of occasions when Jorgensen could not escape Morley's questions, he feigned an ignorance of all but the most well-known events. An evasion he knew Morley saw clean through. Eventually, the author gave up pressing the point. Perhaps he had enough to go on from information gleaned elsewhere, because his energies were soon diverted to the writing desk in his suite.

"I'm afraid I've no idea what's in the stories, Broomes," Jorgensen said. "We'll have to wait until publication – like everybody else."

"I do hope he shows the E&O in a good light. And that he doesn't blame us for that unfortunate robbery."

"He could have moved to the Runnymede but chose not to. I don't think he bears a grudge."

"I hope you're right, Jorgensen. Now, this business over the jockeys. Don't let me down."

"Goodnight, Broomes."

"Goodnight." Broomes turned on his heel to head for the door but stopped suddenly to once again face Jorgensen. "I've just remembered. Arshak asked me to tell you that he's bought a motor car for your use."

"I see." It was news to Jorgensen.

"Does that mean that your Ah Cheng fellow has now learned to drive?"

"I guess so." He knew that Ah Cheng had spent several days in Abdul's company.

"You know that I don't approve of Arshak taking him on. Especially after Inspector Batchelor's warnings."

"I'd pay those no attention. I think Inspector Batchelor was a little confused over identities."

"If you say so." Distractedly humming a refrain he had heard the pianist play earlier that day, Broomes left the lobby through the front doors, pausing briefly to acknowledge Vikat's salute with a tip of his hat.

Jorgensen wandered through to Goldie's Bar at the back of the hotel. All the verandah doors were open, and he could feel the faintest hint of the evening breeze off the sea, carrying with it a peal of laughter from the lawns outside.

"Mr Mac, hello, hello," said Goldie, unleashing a broad grin on seeing his new customer. "Lemon or orange today?"

"Lemon. Who's out on the lawn?" he asked.

"They've been no trouble, Mr Mac. I expect no more quarrels."

"It's that crowd, is it? Is Miss Anne with them?"

Goldie placed Jorgensen's drink on the bar top. The ice cubes clinked gently against the rim. "There already."

"Thanks." Jorgensen picked up the glass and walked through the open doors onto the verandah.

Beyond the Angsana trees, festooned with twinkling lights, a small group were gathered on the sea wall in a hum of bright chatter.

Jorgensen strolled across the lawn towards them. As he drew closer, he could make out the group's members. Tommy Essenden's hand rested lightly in the small of Phyllis Smith's back. Now and then, she glanced at his face and smiled at something he said. With them were Gordon McHugh, Dickie Chelmsall and Anne Prescott.

Seeing Essenden, so at home on the E&O's lawn, so cocksure of his right to be there, caused Jorgensen to briefly check his progress. It was two weeks since Essenden had idly boasted to friends that it was him who had tipped off George Lam about Cromford's diary. Two weeks in which Jorgensen had been forced to hold his natural instincts in check. Though he had accepted that the blackmail of Arthur Cromford did not lead directly to Frank Davies's death, it rankled that the greed of one of the E&O's patrons had so nearly tarnished the hotel's reputation.

Though Arshak Sarkies had made it plain that there was to be no immediate retribution – no punishment for Essenden. It was a matter of business. While negotiations were underway for additional loans with the Peninsular Bank to pay for the hotel's new east wing, it was too great a risk to make an enemy of Albert Essenden, the bank's chairman, and Tommy's father.

Jorgensen took a deep breath, bringing the first stirrings of anger back under control. Thankfully, Anne Prescott saw him approaching, and detached herself from her companions, meeting him a few yards up the path.

"You got my message," Jorgensen said.

"I'm glad you sent it," she replied.

"When do you leave?"

"On Monday. I should imagine Phyllis will be glad to be rid of my disapproving looks every time she sees Tommy. She really does deserve better than that cad."

"It was good of her family to put you up," Jorgensen raised his glass. "Well, here's bon voyage."

"Thank you for everything you've done for Frank."

"I wish I'd done more when he was alive."

"You ensured justice was done."

Anne took a sip of her gin pahit. The brittleness behind the brave outward façade was impossible not to notice. A pretence of coping that she had adopted for the sake of others, particularly the Smith family, at whose house she had stayed for the last six weeks since leaving the E&O.

"There are times when I think the Burgons deserved it too," she said, with a grim smile. "They never cared for Frank for one single moment. To them, his murder was nothing more than a happy accident. I hope they rot in hell."

Jorgensen reflected on the truth of Anne's brutal observation, knowing that he could never share with her his own reservations about their level of culpability.

"So, you won't visit his old home?" Jorgensen asked.

Anne shook her head vehemently. "Not while the Burgons are there. Though I'd like to see Frank's old school. He often spoke fondly of the place; I think he was happy there."

"Where will you stay in England?" Jorgensen asked.

"It's all arranged. I'll stay in the nurses' rooms at Guy's Hospital. It's what I'd have done one day anyway. Returning to Penang was only ever meant to be temporary."

"I guess the island holds too many bad memories."

"It would be beyond awful if I stayed. George Town is such a small place, and I don't believe that people's morbid curiosity will ever fully die down. I carry the Prescott name, and with it I carry the disgrace of Magnus's actions."

"Now, now, Jorgensen," Tommy Essenden had appeared at their side, a mocking sneer on his face. "It simply won't do. I don't wish to chide, but Anne is our guest for this evening, and everybody has resolved that we should have a good time. Two minutes in your company, and already the poor darling looks gloomier. Come, Anne. We need you to settle an argument about Ginger's dancing."

"I'll rejoin you all in a moment," Anne said to Essenden. "I promise."

Essenden retreated, the curled lip still in place, while with a sad half-smile, Anne Prescott looked up at Jorgensen. "I'd better go. I think we've said all that we can."

"Before you do," Jorgensen removed from his pocket the piece of folded card that held a lock of Anne's hair, and a small leather jewellery case that held an engagement ring. "I found these in Frank's room."

Anne studied the two objects in the broad palm of Jorgensen's hand. "I know what they are," she said. "I hope you won't be disappointed if I don't take them. I have Frank's letters, and they're enough for me to remember him by."

Jorgensen replaced both items in his jacket pocket. Anne was right. There was not much more to be said.

"Will you remember him, Mr Jorgensen?" she asked.

Jorgensen nodded. He had plans to commemorate Frank Davies by using the five thousand dollars in the hotel safe that he had held back from George Lam and never repaid to Hilton Morley. It was enough to set up a letter-writer's office in Davies's name, pay a salary to its occupant and for Suri to be employed as an assistant. One day in the future, when the office was up and running, he would write to Anne Prescott to tell her about it.

"I will," he said.

"Goodbye." Anne turned away and rejoined her companions on the sea wall, just as Essenden broke away from them to again approach Jorgensen.

"What is it, Tommy?" Jorgensen said.

"You rather looked as if you had something to say to me." Essenden was tilting his head backwards, all the better to look down his nose at Jorgensen.

"I know it was you," Jorgensen said. The words were out of his mouth before he could stop them. "You told George Lam about Cromford's diary."

"Oh Jorgensen, you are a hoot. There's always something you're quick to accuse me of. And the most entertaining aspect is that you're powerless to do anything about it."

Jorgensen shook his head, as if in regret. He could already picture the look of reproach on Arshak's face.

"Almost right, Tommy," he said, and stepping forward punched Essenden on the jaw with a short-arm jab. Just enough to knock him off his feet onto the manicured lawn, damp with an evening dew that quickly darkened Essenden's jacket and trousers.

With a grin towards the astonished group on the sea wall, he stood over Essenden's prostrate form.

"And pay your damn chits on time."

Printed in Great Britain
by Amazon

48324945R10229